The Dwellers

Alyssa Cassese

To Tina,

Hope you enjoy it! Can't wait to read 'Harry Hid It'!

Cover design by Kaitlyn Gamboa

Copyright © 2015 by Alyssa Cassese
All rights reserved. No part of this book may be reproduced, scanned, or distributed in any printed or electronic form without permission.
First Edition: June 2015
Printed in the United States of America
ISBN: 978-1-63-318748-1

To Mum, Dad, and Stephen, for dealing with my outrageous obsessions for all these years
From movies to books to television,
Maybe this "writing" obsession can be beneficial for all of us
I don't say it enough, but I love you all so much

To all my friends across the streets, states, oceans, and continents, thank you for never giving up on me and this story
Endless nights being distracted by twitter, hours of complaining and procrastinating, and a few short years later, it's done
I don't know how I got so lucky to have met all of you

And finally to Misha, I wouldn't be alive today doing what I love if it wasn't for you
Thank you for inspiring me when nothing else did and thank you for everything you've done and continue to do for me
I knew I'd never be able to accurately encapsulate how much you mean to me in a letter, so instead I wrote a book
This one's for you

Prologue

Frosting tasted better than he remembered. He had almost forgotten the taste of cake.

Emma had quietly shrunk into his cell and handed him a small lopsided cake with a messily scribbled "Happy Birthday" on top. Ashton was incredibly grateful for the sweet gesture and attempted a small smile while reaching for Emma's hand. But she instantly pulled away, with wide, terrified eyes, and mumbled a "you're welcome" as she ran from the small space.

The gesture made Ashton's stomach drop as he lowered his head. He wondered if there would ever be anyone in the penitentiary that wouldn't avoid him like the plague. He scooped the cake into his mouth quietly. Subsequently, he threw the plate in the small bin in the corner of his cell.

All in all, he could spend the day feeling sorry for himself, or he could put his plan into action.

***

Simon was someone he really never wanted to associate with.

He walked with a prominent swing in his step, despite being holed up in the penitentiary for over six years now. His hazel eyes, usually red-rimmed from lack of sleep, followed you like the eyes in a painting. His hair was an unruly blond, which stuck up in different directions around his head. He was short but built like a house, which usually caused people to steer clear of him.

Most people feared Simon, but Ashton was past the point of fearing anyone. He did not steer clear of Simon, but he definitely did not attempt to initiate any sort of communication. Ashton did not know much about him, aside from what he had heard about him from others.

On any other day, in any other circumstance, there would have been absolutely no reason for Ashton to walk over to Simon during their short outdoor recreation period. But Simon was known for stealing, and that was what Ashton needed.

Simon never stole anything large, or anything someone would end up missing. Despite the fact that Simon was in prison for drugs, not larceny, he was quite a criminal when it came to taking things that he didn't own. The stealing had started with utensils, such as forks and knives, and then had escalated into things like wallets, small radios, and recreation equipment.

The stealing, though, was the easy part. Convincing Simon to get something for you was a lot harder, especially if you weren't in his circle of prison brutes locked up for heroin. But Ashton had cigarettes and secrets and enough of them to make the penitentiary "currency" worth something.

Simon didn't stare as Ashton walked over to the huddle, but did not look away. When Ashton coughed, some people in the circle took a step backward, intimidated by him, but Simon stepped forward, ready to listen.

"Hello, Blue Eyes," he said with a smirk. "What can I do for ya?"

"Blue Eyes" was a nickname he had acquired after being at the prison for a few years. Most of the time, the inmates avoided him because of his story, but his eyes seemed to draw people in, just like they always had when he was young. The nickname was started by the first psychotherapist they had allowed in to see him, who had said, "So Blue Eyes, what're you in for?"

From there, most of the guards, doctors, and other inmates hadn't even bothered to learn his name. "Blue Eyes" was enough identification when he went outside to the rec area, and the name wasn't exactly offensive, compared to the nicknames other inmates had gotten over the years.

"I need something, but I don't know how to get it," Ashton began, not timidly, but in a monotone voice, showing as much respect as he could to avoid getting his ass kicked.

Ashton swore that if Simon knew how to smile, he would have been smiling right then, but soon the expression was off his face, and he was stone cold once again. He motioned for the men circled around him to leave, with a wave of his hand, and motioned for Ashton to come closer.

"What do you need?" he asked quietly, once they were out of earshot.

Ashton wrung his hands together, wondering if what he needed was too big of a favor to ask from Simon, considering that Simon could probably rip his own face off if he tried hard enough. He coughed and looked up at Simon, who was considerably taller than him. "I need a camera, like a . . . um a video one."

Simon looked at him long and hard for a few seconds before rubbing his hands together. "What can you get me in return?"

Ashton reached into his back pocket, pulling out a packet of Marlboros. He pushed the box into Simon's hands and said, "And a lot more where that came from."

Simon smirked, honest to God, *smirked* and handed the pack of cigarettes back to Ashton. "You got balls, kid." He eyeballed Ashton up and down. He leaned in a bit closer, as though he was interested in the offer.

"But a camera is quite the steal, buddy. They don't got many around here aside from the security ones, and I'll have to hotwire those. It's a big job, and a few packs of cigs ain't gonna—"

"I've got more than a few packs of cigs."

Simon huffed and pulled the box of cigarettes toward him again. "You drive a hard bargain, but I'll do it, kid—as long as you promise not to ask me for anything again."

"Trust me—I won't need anything else after this."

***

It was set to go down at four o'clock in the morning. Simon was dressed in a stolen guard's outfit and stood idly outside the security room. He took one more look around him before quickly and professionally picking the lock on the door. He quickly let himself in. Ashton sat in his cell watching Simon through the camera that Simon had hacked on his (extremely illegal) GPS phone.

Simon looked around the small security room, taking it in. He looked at the wall of small television sets and surveyed the entirety of the penitentiary. Considering the time of morning, no one was awake except for the guards that slowly paced up and down the halls, yawning occasionally and sipping hot cups of coffee. Simon studied every angle that the prison could be watched from, and his eyes were drawn to the television in the bottom right corner of the display. The screen showed a wall of small television sets and one man in a blue suit. Simon smirked and raised his hand, waving slightly and watching as the man in the picture did the same.

Simon turned around slowly, surveying the corners of the ceiling for a lens or blinking light. He finally spotted the red light in the corner closest to the door and raised his arms in victory.

Finally, with his hands around the camera that Ashton was watching, Simon pulled the cords around toward the lens and smirked once into the camera before tugging harshly. The picture in front of Ashton's face turned to black, and he put the GPS device on his bed, silently hoping that Simon didn't get caught with the big mess of cables that would be trailing behind him.

Simon arrived in front of his cell a half an hour later, panting quietly, claiming that he had seen a guard and had run for his life

The Dwellers

with the camera tucked under his shirt.

"You owe me big time for this, Blue Eyes," Simon said, exasperated.

"My name is Ashton," Ashton responded, with a little more confidence. Then he pulled the cords haphazardly through the cell bars.

"Yeah, yeah whatever, Squirt," Simon said, pushing the camera and lens through the bar with a slow exhale. "I'm ready for my friggin' payment."

Ashton held the camera in his hands and smiled. After a small victorious laugh, he reached behind the small cot and grabbed the tall stack of cigarette boxes he had piled up.

"There should be at least 27 packs," Ashton said quietly, dropping the large pile into Simon's outstretched arms.

Simon stared down at the riches that he practically held in his arms, and his jaw dropped a bit. Ashton expected him to turn around and leave, but he turned toward the cell bars once more.

"You know, I don't need this many packs of menthols, kid. I appreciate you tryin' to pay me back and all, but this looks like all the packs you got."

"There's more where that came from, and I don't even smoke. Take them, and thank you for helping me."

Ashton turned away from the bars and toward the camera. He didn't want to create any sort of friendship, especially not with Simon and especially not tonight. Simon took in a short breath and turned to walk away. He took a few steps before he turned his head back again and said, "Y'know, you're all right Blue Eyes. Even if you're bat-shit crazy like everyone says."

That's all it took for Ashton to turn around and pick up the camera once more.

***

Crimson.

He had never liked the color. He always thought it was too dark and eerie. Now, the blood stained his hands, though washed away years ago. He got up from his place on the floor again, running his fingers through his hair, the black dye close to fading out completely, as his hair was slowly turning blond again.

He went over to the sink in the corner of his small cell and washed his hands for the 17th time that day. It had become a habit over the years, washing his small calloused hands constantly, even though Ashton knew they would never be clean—no matter how many times he washed them.

With shaky hands, he reached down to the floor, picking up the stolen camera and positioning it carefully on the cot. He sat down in front of it, pushed the green button, and pulled the covers up around the base to muffle the noise it made.

He then walked toward the sink where he had washed his hands only minutes previously. He bent down under the sink to access the flimsy piece of cardboard loosely stapled to the wall and pulled on the loosest corner. The cardboard came off easily and quietly, uncovering a small secret hole holding numerous cigarette packages and a silver dagger.

He placed his hand hesitantly on the silver dagger and debated for a few seconds before grabbing it and sitting down on the floor in front of the camera. He placed the knife down next to him, still keeping it firmly in his grip.

He slowly positioned the lens so that it was angled at his face as he sat down again on the floor. He coughed slowly, phantom blood lingering in his throat, as he tapped the record button with his finger and stared into the camera's lens, opening his mouth to speak.

"My name is Ashton Dweller. And this is my story."

1

The house was a beautiful little thing. It wasn't big—not at all—but it was quaint, comforting, and it felt like *home*. Sandra looked up at the house, smiled softly to herself, and absentmindedly patted her bulging stomach lightly as her husband walked around her and squeezed her shoulders tightly.

"What are you thinking about?" he said softly, chuckling in her ear.

"The house next door," she replied, laughing. "It doesn't exactly fit in."

The tall black house was monstrous and stood out on the small block, which was mostly filled with small, lightly painted houses. The black house was not exactly threatening. It had flowers in the window boxes and bright drapes over the large windows, but it stood tall and menacing over the small street. Having the house and its inhabitants living next door was a bit disconcerting, but that was another worry for another time. Right now, she was content right where she was.

She walked into the house once more, carrying as many boxes as she could. The weight of some of the boxes was too much for a pregnant woman, but Sandra lugged all of them into the front room of the house before collapsing against the soft ottoman. Her husband walked around the chair and placed a hand on his wife's head.

"You're going to hurt yourself if you keep lifting all of these boxes," he said softly.

"Mason, I swear, if you pull another 'you're pregnant so you can't help' lecture, I'm going to end you," she huffed, turning her head.

He laughed softly, kissing the side of her temple and reaching for a large box that was placed down near the fireplace. "I'm going to take this upstairs," he said, his voice cracking as he grasped the large box from the bottom. "Yell if you need anything."

Sandra let out a small sigh once again, disappointed that *pregnant* basically meant the same as *disabled*, at least in her husband's eyes. She stood slowly off the ottoman and walked around the small table as quietly as she could. She reached down slowly to put her hands around the bottom of a purple box, when she discovered that her husband basically had the hearing abilities of an owl.

"Sandra Mitchell, if you don't get your hands off of that box-"

"All right, all right! If you don't want me to help you unpack, I'll just go meet the neighbors without you!" she yelled up the stairs.

That had Mason sprinting down the staircase, practically smashing into the wall after the bottom step and panting like a dog. "You are *not* going to meet the people in the Monster House without me."

"The *Monster House*?"

"Yes it's the Monster House—named it myself," he replied with a smirk and a glint in his gray eyes.

Sandra rolled her eyes, wrapped an arm around Mason's middle, and smiled up at him.

"Ready to go meet the neighbors?"

***

Mason discovered the need to give the house a new nickname when he saw who answered the door.

The girl couldn't have been more than seven years old, with huge blue eyes peeking out from behind her long blond hair, which covered part of her face. She said, "What can I do for you,

The Dwellers

mister?" in a small voice that was sweet as honey. She blinked her eyes rapidly and smiled, missing teeth and all.

The intense staring did not last long, however, because a woman soon appeared in the doorway. She was a *very pregnant woman*, with cookie batter on her face and piercing blue eyes that matched the young girl's.

"Beth, I told you not to open the door for strangers."

"I'm sorry, Momma," she replied, grabbing onto her mother's leg.

The woman was a bit older than her, Sandra realized, but her wrinkles weren't prominent, more like crinkles by her eyes because she smiled too often. Her wide blue eyes, as well as the cookie batter plastered on the side of her face, made her look like a curious child, but her blond bun with small streaks of gray proved otherwise. She was definitely *not* who Sandra would've imagined living here. The woman smiled widely at the strange couple in the doorway before shooing her daughter back into the kitchen and motioning for Sandra and Mason to come inside.

"You must be the new neighbors," she said excitedly, clapping her hands together as they sat on the couch, the woman using a rag to wipe the batter off her face.

Sandra smiled curtly, motioning to herself and then her husband. "Yes, I'm Sandra, and this is my husband Mason." They both held an outstretched hand to the woman.

She shook each of their hands once and looked up at them once again. "I'm Madeline Dweller, and my husband's name is Nathan, but he's at work currently . . ." She smiled as she finished the sentence: "leaving me home with the Crazies."

"The Crazies" turned out to be the exact reason Madeline's face was covered in chocolate chips and the reason why the kitchen looked like a bomb had hit it. "The Crazies" also turned out to be four energetic, blond, wide-eyed children making cookies in a way-too-small space.

"Crazies, come in here, so you can meet the neighbors," Madeline called, not moving from her place on the couch.

The four children cocked their heads curiously. The tallest brother picked up the smallest and carried him over to their mother. The two others, Beth and another boy, followed closely behind. They stood next to each other in a line as their mother introduced them.

"This is Lucas and Chase," Madeline said, motioning toward the tallest boy holding the squirming toddler. "Lucas is 10, and Chase is 4."

Lucas was taller than an average 10-year-old, with a pointed face and a long torso and blue eyes that matched his mother's. He stood tall with a proud look on his face. Chase was a chubby toddler. He had blond hair matted to his forehead with what looked like egg yolk, and he was licking batter off of his thumb. However, he did not have blue eyes, but brown ones that were wide and questioning. Lucas extended a hand to Sandra and Mason, repositioning Chase on his arm so that he could get a better hold on his bottom.

"Hello," he said after shaking both of their hands. He promptly turned back around toward the kitchen and placed Chase on the ground with a soft thud, where the toddler resumed his previous act of cleaning his hands of batter with his mouth.

The other boy, introduced as Thomas, was nine. He was brown-eyed like Chase. Unlike Chase, however, Thomas was lean and lanky, and his eyes held not curiosity, but a mischievous glint. He also wore a coy smile. A "hi" was all Sandra and Mason got before the boy had turned on his heel, running back into the kitchen after his older brother.

The girl, Beth, was introduced once again, nodding and smiling, her bottom two teeth missing. The six-year-old energetically

The Dwellers

shook the hands of the two adults before giggling "hello again" and skipping into the kitchen.

Sandra laughed fondly, turning back to Madeline. "Four of them," she breathed in amazement, "and another on the way."

Madeline laughed loudly, putting a hand on her chest and looking from Mason to Sandra. "Well, I'm a teacher. I deal with tons of kids on a regular basis, so my own are a little easier to handle. I'm guessing that's your first," she smiled, gesturing to Sandra's stomach.

Sandra and Mason shared a look before smiling at their neighbor and nodding. Madeline opened her mouth to speak again just as the door opened with a bang, the wood swinging against the hinges. A tall man stepped inside the house, shrugging his coat off of his shoulders.

He said, "People just do *not* know how to drive anymore . . ." His voice trailed off as he walked into the living room to take a seat on the couch.

The man was not incredibly handsome, but not unattractive, Sandra noted. His curious brown eyes peeked out from behind his sandy blond hair, which hung over his forehead in messy bangs. He had a pointed chin that looked a bit like Lucas's and a button nose similar to Chase's. The man was most definitely the father of the "Crazies," acting just as hyped up and energetic as them as he took a seat across from the couple and next to his wife.

"Are these the new neighbors?" he said quickly—before his bottom hit the seat. "I wanted to say hello this morning, but I was off to work in a rush."

Mason was hit with the realization that he recognized the Dweller's last name. Nathan Dweller was the Iowa state representative for the second congressional district. The man didn't appear on television and in the news as often as the other three senators did, but he was the one who had caught Mason's attention the most, mainly because he seemed goodhearted.

That discovery led to a conversation filled with questions, such as "What do you do?" and "Who do you work with?" The conversation evolved into politics and heated opinions. But the two men got along remarkably well for people that had only known each other for a half an hour or so. However, their voices were soon booming with angry rants, and Sandra and Madeline decided that it was time to start a separate conversation somewhere else—the two pregnant women wanted nothing more than a little peace.

They moved their conversation to the back porch, Sandra mainly asking Madeline questions about childbirth and how badly she was feeling; Madeline answering patiently and helpfully, giving Sandra as many tips as she could muster. Madeline spoke enthusiastically about the process, being generous and thorough, maybe at times a little *too* thorough, but Sandra quickly decided that she liked the woman a lot, and felt a friendship growing between the two of them.

Sandra told Madeline of her fears and of the horribly taken sonogram that showed a picture of what *seemed* like a girl, which was what Sandra was hoping for.

"You can never trust the flimsy sonograms," Madeline shrugged, patting Sandra on the shoulder. "Before Nathan and I could afford the more detailed ones, they told me Thomas was going to be a Tammy."

That caused fits of laughter to erupt from the porch, enough for the two men to come outside from the living room just to make sure everyone was okay.

***

"You know, your kids are adorable," Sandra said after a bit of silence following the fits of laughter over Madeline's pregnancy stories.

The Dwellers

"Yes, adorable," Madeline agreed before adding, "and pains in the ass after they passed the age of three—constant whining isn't very cute anymore."

Sandra laughed, in an understanding way, thinking of her numerous nieces and nephews ranging from the ages of five to twelve who were pesky, rowdy little things. But nevertheless, she urged Madeline on, wanting to hear more about her children, more than what she had already found out. While the four kids continued making a sloppy batch of cookies, Sandra smiled and said, "They can't be so bad."

Madeline looked at her hard in the eyes, trying to be angry, but failing miserably—Sandra's smile was an evil little thing. She was about to learn how much trouble four little kids could really cause.

***

Three bedtime tuck-ins, twelve bottles of water, two political arguments, and five fits of laughter later, Sandra and Mason wholeheartedly decided that they liked their neighbors very much.

Mason and Nathan had talked for hours before they realized how long their conversation had been running. The two men laughed loudly, turning to the clock and groaning. The digital clock blinked teasingly, *9:43 pm* flashing across the black surface.

Madeline was in the middle of a story about Chase, when Mason stepped outside on to the porch, telling Sandra that he had to get to bed if he wanted to be on time to work the following day.

Sandra knew that it would be best if they left then. They had a lot of preparing to do, still not having all of the things they needed to care for the new baby. But she didn't want to leave as well; she wanted to hear more stories about Madeline's children, although she soon realized that she'd soon get to know them much better. They *did* live right next door.

She stood up to leave, thanking Madeline for having them and patting her shoulder lightly. Madeline walked them to the door, while Nathan walked to the back hallway, Sandra assumed, to make sure the kids were asleep. Just as the couple was about to walk out the door, Madeline paused and waved Sandra over to ask one more question.

"I was going to ask you before, but it kind of slipped my mind. How many months are you?"

Sandra stood confused for a few seconds before realizing that Madeline was referring to her pregnancy. She smiled softly and rested a hand on her stomach. "Six, going on seven months," she breathed. "What about you?"

"I'm due next month," Madeline laughed, while Sandra stood open-mouthed before practically shoving the woman back inside, out of the still-blaring heat of August.

"You're absolutely crazy to still be out here asking questions," Sandra huffed in fond frustration.

"I could say the same thing to you, young lady," Madeline shot back.

Sandra threw one last wave over her shoulder and smiled before turning around again and walking back toward the house, with her fingers intertwined with Mason's.

Yes, she was definitely going to like it here.

***

Sandra and Mason adapted to the town very quickly, the people in the community being helpful and sweet. Although everyone was sweet to the Mitchells, they spent most of their time with Madeline and Nathan Dweller and their children, the two families growing incredibly close.

The summer passed by too quickly, full of barbeques and

block parties, and ended abruptly with a significant drop in temperature and cold gusts of autumn wind. The neighbors quickly took a liking to the Mitchells, giving them tips and recommendations about the town, telling them about the best restaurants and shops.

Madeline's baby was born on the 15th of September in a hospital that was 20 minutes from the town square. He was a puny little thing, with a few thin locks of white hair on his head and wide blue eyes to match his mother's. He was brought home two days after his birth, only to be fawned over by not only the Mitchells, but by most of the town. Madeline and Nathan named the boy Ashton because they joked of the quiet baby being stone-faced, like a tree.

Ashton Dweller was a quiet little thing, small and curious. He spent most of his time sleeping but seemed to enjoy himself most when he was squished between Sandra and Madeline on a couch in one of their houses. Sandra would absentmindedly run a hand through the infant's thin, blond hair while speaking excitedly about how her approaching due date and how she was planning on naming her daughter Cayla.

The baby was born on the 21st of December, and "Cayla" turned out to not be a Cayla, but a Cayden, proving Sandra's assumption about the inaccurate sonogram. Cayden was slightly taller and wider than Ashton, with darker, thicker hair and hazel eyes. He was louder than Ashton, more vocal with his crying and blabbering than the older infant who stayed remotely quiet.

Though the two boys were polar opposites, they seemed to enjoy spending time together. Ashton watched and smiled as Cayden blabbered on about nothing, and Cayden was seemingly content with sitting in complete silence when Ashton was asleep or in a bad mood.

Cayden started speaking real words instead of blabber much

quicker than Ashton, despite being about three months younger. Though Cayden was speaking and babbling at eight months old, he was speaking longer sentences at about one and a half, developing quicker than the age suggested by the parenting websites that Sandra and Mason had visited.

When Cayden and Ashton turned two, there was an addition to the group of children living on the right side of Woodland Drive. Ashton's younger sister Alana was born just as Cayden turned two, only a year before Cayden was given a younger sister of his own. Cayden's sister Alexandra was smaller than Alana, but only by a bit, and the Dwellers and Mitchells could see the two girls becoming as close as their boys were, despite being a year apart. Soon, Alana and Alexandra were chatterboxes as well, constantly gurgling and trying to form coherent syllables to communicate.

Ashton was another story. The absence of loud wailing at infancy was something that Madeline saw as a blessing. But as Cayden's speech continued to develop, Ashton stayed quiet as could be. Although Cayden didn't seem to mind that his best friend didn't babble and wail as he did, the parents were concerned about a speech or hearing disability.

The one thing that stopped Madeline and Nathan from getting help right away was the fact that as Ashton grew, he didn't speak much to his siblings and parents, but his vocabulary improved and grew as he did. The only times the Dwellers heard him talking, miraculously, was when he was around Cayden, who never let anyone get a word in edgewise.

Although the couples were neighbors and great friends, that wasn't what caused Ashton and Cayden to become so close. The boys took it upon themselves to start talking and babbling, making up games, and rolling around as early as a year old. By the time they were off to elementary school, the two were inseparable. And even though Ashton was all wide-eyed stares to his family, he would chat quietly with Cayden while clutching one strap of his backpack and walking into the unfamiliar school building.

***

Numerous therapists, pathologists, associations, and one year of elementary school later, Ashton was diagnosed with selective mutism.

The therapists gave Madeline and Nathan a list of causes of selective mutism to try to figure out where the root of the problem was. A common cause of selective mutism was an actual speech or hearing problem, which was the first cause the Dwellers looked into, making a conference with Ashton's kindergarten teacher.

Ashton's teacher, a tall, bubbly woman with freckles splashed over her dark face, seemed extremely excited to meet Ashton's parents. She also had Cayden in her class and spoke fondly of the friendship between the two boys. She did, however, mention the quietness subtly, but brushed it off as shyness or nerves about starting school.

"You really don't think it's a hearing problem?" Madeline asked.

She played with her hands as she looked back to Mrs. Robertson and waited for a response. The woman looked at her quizzically and let out a small laugh.

"Not if his grades are any indication of it. He's at the top of my class. If he had a speech, hearing, or learning disability, I don't think he would be doing as well as he is."

Madeline and Nathan bid Mrs. Robertson good-bye with a small smile and headed to the school psychologist who had met with Ashton at his parents' request. Besides the usual shyness and murmuring, the psychologist, a short, smiley man with round spectacles, told the Dwellers that there was no indication of any kind of self-esteem problems or other issues that were linked to selective mutism.

Despite what the doctors had told the Dwellers, Ashton's mutism was pushed to the back of everyone's minds, especially when the third Mitchell child was born five years after Cayden: a premature boy named Noah. Noah became the main concern of the two couples, as the baby was fighting for his life in an incubator. His chances of survival were low. And though the families were occupied with Noah for over a month, they were still oblivious to one thing, the secret that had been brewing since long before Noah was born: the cause of Ashton's mutism and the danger that came along with it.

***

Ashton's secret wasn't exactly hard to hide, but it *was* something that could be revealed accidentally if he wasn't careful.

It started when he was too young to understand the way people followed his orders. As a two- or three-year-old child, he assumed that all children requested things such as diaper changes or milk through thought, with adults around them instantly dropping everything to get it for them. But as Ashton grew, he realized that children giving commands telepathically was not common in the slightest. He tried hard to push any commanding thoughts out of his head and eventually tried to stop talking and thinking completely. At only four years old, the young boy was terrified about what could possibly come of his newfound skill, and he did everything in his power to prevent it from evolving. Eventually, he ceased all commanding thoughts that came through his brain and decided for himself that the power was gone.

The first time that Ashton realized he could control people with a vocal command was a complete accident. Regardless of the fact that Mrs. Robertson knew about Ashton's muteness, she would frequently ask him questions to try to get him to talk. Ashton was becoming a bit annoyed with the constant questions and pestering, so he decided to take matters into his own hands.

The class was discussing the planets and the seasons, with the children perking up and excitedly rambling about how much they loved swimming in the summer or talking about how many of them had birthdays in the winter.

"How about you Ashton?" Mrs. Robertson's voice echoed across the classroom. "What's your favorite season?"

Dread pooled in the pit of Ashton's stomach, for this was the fifth question he'd answered today, and it wasn't even time for lunch yet. Cayden gave him a half smile from across the classroom, making him feel a little braver, although his voice still wavered as he answered the question.

"Um . . . spring," he answered, almost uncertainly. He grew a bit braver and added quietly, "Stop asking me questions."

The look that flew across Mrs. Robertson's face in a split second was almost terrifying, her eyes flashing, with almost all the color leaving them before the look was gone. Her regular warm facial expression returned quickly. Ashton sat in his seat, wringing his hands together, terrified over what he had witnessed. He looked around at the other students, but none of them had seemed to notice. Maybe he had just imagined it.

But then days, weeks, and months went by, and Mrs. Robertson pretended that Ashton didn't exist. At first, Ashton thought they were playing some kind of game, and he really didn't mind not being called on. But after the first month passed, he realized the impact his command had had on his teacher. He sat for a little longer in his seat, fiddling with his hands once again before he said in a quiet voice to his teacher, "Ask me questions."

The flash happened again, the color draining from Mrs. Robertson's eyes in a millisecond before returning to normal as if nothing had happened. Yet, this time, Cayden turned to Ashton in his seat and said in a quieter-than-usual voice, "Did you see that?"

***

Despite the setbacks, such as discovering he could control people's minds with a thought or command, Ashton's school life went remarkably well. His grades were always in the high 90s, and his teachers only had positive comments as he and Cayden made their way through elementary school.

Teachers would mention the shyness every year, asking Madeline and Nathan questions about selective mutism. With six children, including Ashton, the Dwellers tried the best they could, but by the time Ashton was in fifth grade, his selective mutism had been downgraded to shyness. Madeline and Nathan would back up their claim by talking about how Ashton was just "antisocial" and "talked all the time to Cayden."

Their claims were partially true, of course. Cayden was basically the only one person Ashton talked to about everything, except about the secret powers. The two were inseparable, just like they had been as infants, and when it came time for middle school, nothing changed. The part of the Dweller's claims that weren't accurate however, was the fact that Ashton was "antisocial" in any way and the fact that his mutism was long gone.

Ashton's mutism stayed with him for most of his elementary school years, as he talked to no one except Cayden, and he tried to keep his powers hidden for as long as he possibly could. Soon, he realized, giving commands through thought became a hassle, and he came to the conclusion that keeping his powers dormant was the only way to stop them. There was no reason for the powers to be active because Ashton didn't have any friends besides Cayden, and he never intended to use the powers on him. *Ever.*

Besides the effects of the powers, Ashton found other things regarding them disconcerting. The powers did not work on his family. He couldn't make his siblings pick up his laundry, no matter if he gave them a verbal or subconscious command. It didn't work on his parents either, explaining why he couldn't communicate what he wanted as a baby to them. Ashton tried to push those doubtful thoughts to the back of his mind.

Soon enough, life was hectic again for the Mitchells and Dwellers, and Woodland Drive became a street full of parties and "congratulations!" yelled across front porches. Lucas Dweller, just a 10-year-old boy making cookies when Sandra had first met him, was graduating from Saint Ambrose University and heading off to become a business education teacher at only 22. The little 10-year-old had grown significantly and was taller than both Madeline and Sandra. He waved his diploma in the air as he walked off the stage in his purple gown.

Thomas Dweller, the genius, was now 21, and boy did he take advantage of that. Despite getting into quite a bit of trouble on his 21st birthday (going streaking through Eastern Davenport), he was whizzing through Kaplan University, going for his master's in psychology. Although the growth spurt in his 20s hadn't made him as tall as Lucas, his shoulders had become broader and the mischievous glint in his eye had only gotten deeper, his Cheshire cat smile only growing.

Beth Dweller, not the energetic six-year-old anymore, but a high school senior, graduated as the salutatorian of her class with a "basically male model boyfriend," as Chase would tease. She had big dreams of moving to California but also felt obligated to stay home and hang out with her brothers and sisters. She claimed, "Lucas is egotistical, and Thomas will end up corrupting them." No one willingly admitted it, but everyone secretly knew she was right.

Chase Dweller grew up following in Thomas' footsteps to everyone's dismay. He had become a total prankster whose ultimate goal was to defy every principal or rule that was set either at home or in school. He felt that turning 16 was a huge milestone, and he deserved to be treated like a king. However, Madeline and Nathan or the Iowa Police Department shot down most of his ideas for sweet 16 parties, so graduations were the main focus of the summer block parties. That verdict left Chase sulking at most of the summer barbeques, only hanging around tiny Noah Mitchell and ranting that the seven-year-old was "the only one who understood him."

Ashton and Cayden's graduation from elementary school would have been a bigger party if it weren't for all the parties for their older siblings. To their parents' surprise, the two boys didn't mind not having a large party; they were content with a small barbeque featuring only the Mitchells and Dwellers where the boys could sit in Ashton's tree house and read or make up games. The boys were also fine with Alana and Alexandra climbing up the rope ladder and asking to join their games, both too taken with their little sisters to be able to say no.

By the end of the night of the boys' graduation party, Ashton and Cayden were curled up in a large comforter in the corner of the tree house, assuring their parents that it was still warm enough to sleep outside, even though August was coming to an end. Their parents laughed before bidding each other good-bye and parting ways to their respective houses for the night.

"Only three more weeks till middle school, Ash—can you believe it?" Cayden asked incredulously, obviously excited.

Ashton smiled at the nickname, Cayden being the only one to ever call him that. Cayden thought it suited him better, but Ashton knew the name had stuck from when they were younger, and Cay-

The Dwellers

den had trouble pronouncing the "sht."

Then Cayden's words sunk in and Ashton froze, thinking about a new school and more people: new teachers that didn't know him and more people he would have to hide himself from. The powers had gotten easier and easier to control over the years, but there was always a constant fear in the back of his mind that they would become too hard to control and that he would end up accidentally controlling a teacher or another student. Cayden must have felt Ashton tense up because he ran a hand through his friend's hair and laughed softly.

"You're gonna be fine; you're a genius," he laughed, pulling his friend closer.

"Cayden, are we always going to be best friends?"

Cayden stared at Ashton long and hard after that question before laughing and laughing for 10 minutes, trying to keep his voice down and failing, his laugh echoing through the wooden house.

"Of course, you idiot," Cayden said after calming down a bit.

"Forever?"

"Yes, forever."

Forever, however, is a very dangerous word.

2

The snow was cold and wet and disgusting, and Ashton hated it.

Walking home from school in the snow was definitely 10 times worse than the snow itself, in Ashton's opinion, and even Cayden's excited chattering was gnawing away at his nerves. All he could think about was the Geometry midterm and his European History paper and the stupid bits of frozen water that dripped down his collar onto his back, as he tilted his head down to read from the book he clutched in his hands. The cold February wind bit into his face.

Of course, the snow never bothered Cayden. Nothing bothered Cayden, and Ashton was envious. No, Cayden had the audacity to stick out his tongue and laugh, trying to catch the flakes on his tongue. He had the ability to merely smile brightly and pull the flaps of his red hat down to cover his ears from the chill. He had stopped to make snow angels at least four times on the walk home, his eyes crinkling at the corners while he laughed at the drops covering his face and falling into his eyes.

"Hey, are you okay?" Cayden asked halfway through the journey, realizing that Ashton had his fingers clenched into balls at his sides and that he was chewing at his lip anxiously.

"Yeah—yeah, I'm okay," Ashton said, turning quickly and trying to shoot a small smile. He failed, as his lips quirked downwards.

Cayden knocked Ashton's shoulder playfully with his own shoulder and tried to grab the book out of Ashton's hand while mumbling something like, "It's dangerous to read while you walk." He finally got a firm grip on the spine and tugged it out of Ashton's hands, closing it and shoving it into his jacket. Ashton huffed in annoyance, shoving his hands into his pockets and glaring at his friend's jacket.

They were quiet for a few minutes before Cayden, with a smirk on his lips, took the book out of his jacket and handed it back to Ashton and gave him another playful shoulder bump.

"Come over," Cayden said with another breathy laugh. "My mom took Noah to karate, and we can go build a fort." Hope glistened in Cayden's eyes as he pulled the red hat off his head and slid it onto his friend's. "You need a break from the books, man."

Ashton sighed fondly, walking a few more steps and stepping in front of their two houses. He looked from Cayden's house to his own, wishing desperately that they could hang out at least for that night. "My parents are going away for the weekend," he sighed dejectedly. "I have to watch Alana and make sure she doesn't burn the house down trying to make cookies."

Cayden laughed softly, knowing how much of a handful the girl was, despite only being two years younger than them. Yet, he also knew that Ashton seemed stressed and needed some time to rest and clear his mind. "Y'know, she's 12," he started. "She can't take care of herself?"

"When my parents are at work or away, I'm the only one left to take care of her. It's not a big job, though. She doesn't give me too much trouble, because when Mom and Dad aren't home, I'm the only one who really looks after her," Ashton said, looking crestfallen.

"It's not like you don't have four older siblings or anything," Cayden mumbled sarcastically. "Do they even do anything?"

Ashton seemed surprised, but not offended by the accusation about his older brothers and sister. He shrugged and said simply, "Lucas got a new job in Philadelphia. Thomas had to beg, but Lucas is taking him with him when he moves out next week. Apparently there's a great practice just outside where Lucas is living, and Thomas might be able to get a job there. They've been packing for days."

"Beth? Chase?"

"Beth is paranoid about her boyfriend breaking up with her, and Chase is a senior now. All he does is drink and party," Ashton said shrugging again.

Cayden huffed and crossed his arms. "Well that doesn't seem fair at all. You have brothers and sisters in their 20s to look after Alana. You're only 15!" He didn't know why he was so pissed exactly; how his friend spent his weekends was none of his concern, but Ashton was stressed and flustered and it just wasn't *fair*. But when Ashton didn't want to talk, which was usually, Cayden wasn't going to push him.

Ashton gave him a soft smile and pulled his friend's hat off his own head, returning it. "I'll be fine, I promise. I'll see you tomorrow?"

Cayden returned the smile, grabbing his hat from Ashton's hands. "Sure, Ash," he breathed, the cold starting to get to him. "I mean, as long as your sister doesn't burn your house down making cookies, I see no reason why—"

Ashton cut him off with a snowball to the face.

***

The house was warm when Ashton stepped in the doorway, the radiator's reverberating heat wrapping around him like a blanket. He took off his coat and set his bag down by the stairs before walking into the kitchen to get something to eat.

Alana was sitting at the kitchen table, with a pen in her mouth, staring down at the sixth-grade algebra homework like it was the bane of her existence. She groaned and bit into the bagel that was sitting beside her, pushing the notebook away from her with her free hand. Ashton grabbed his own bagel from the bowl in the middle of the island and walked over to where his sister was sitting.

Alana looked up when her brother walked beside her, giving him a small smile. Ashton raised an eyebrow at her, gesturing his hand toward her forgotten math notebook. Alana rolled her eyes and sighed.

"It's too hard, Ashton," she whined. "I don't understand half of what we're learning, and my algebra teacher talks super quick and won't slow down when we ask questions—something about 'preparing us for college' or something dumb like that."

Ashton smiled at his sister's air quotes as she imitated her teacher and pulled the math notebook closer to himself. He opened up to the page Alana had just been on, staring down at the graphed inequalities and wrinkling his nose in disgust. Alana laughed, "I'm guessing you didn't like these either."

Ashton gave a sympathetic shake of his head as he grabbed Alana's pen and motioned for her to watch while he worked on a problem. He divided the graph with a dashed line, gesturing to the slope of the problem, and watched his sister intently to make sure she was confident with what he was explaining. Finally, he shaded in the respectable side of the graph and watched as Alana's eyes widened in understanding. She clapped her hands together and smiled as she sat next to Ashton on the chair and started working on the next problem. Ashton watched her as she worked, checking her progress as she went until she was done with the problem. Ashton checked it over and smiled, putting his hand up for a high five. Alana reciprocated and smiled a silent thank you.

Ashton and his sister had fallen into that rapport over the years. While his parents were always desperate to get him to talk to them and his older siblings used his muteness to their advantage,

Alana had always just accepted the fact that Ashton didn't like to talk. She was never exactly quiet when talking to him; she liked to rant on and on to him about the girls in her grade and how horrible her teachers were and *oh God, Ashton, you don't even understand how gross the boys are.* And even though she got on his nerves frequently and was a huge troublemaker, Ashton felt closest to her.

Ashton left the kitchen with his bagel and walked toward the stairs to put his bag away, when the ceiling shook. He heard Alana groan from the kitchen, and he looked upwards and glared at the ceiling, as though Chase would get the message.

Five years ago, when Chase was 13, he discovered a metal rod that stuck out from the side of the Dweller home. The metal rod was about four feet off of the ground and a few inches in thickness. Chase, a tall, lean teenager at the time, became fascinated with the rod and, being the reckless kid that he was, decided to test his hypothesis that the rod could hold his weight. Miraculously, the rod held its place as Chase stepped onto it and was strong enough for Chase to bounce a bit while he was standing on it. Giving a little jump off the metal rod made it incredibly easy to get onto the roof of the Dweller home, which was exactly what Chase had in mind. Since then, Chase's favorite activity had been "Roof Hopping," his own dangerous game in which he climbed the metal rod onto the Dweller roof and climbed, swung, and pulled himself onto neighboring roofs. This would continue until one of the neighbors caught him or until he broke a bone, which happened pretty frequently.

Five years later, 18-year-old Chase still hopped roofs like it was an Olympic sport, rattling the house on its hinges and making the ceiling shake. Ashton turned back toward the kitchen to where Alana was also glaring up at the ceiling. The rattling continued as Lucas' voice, mumbling a string of profanities, came from the top of the stairs. He ran down the stairs and headed out the front door. Alana's glare fell off her lips, and a smile emerged as she turned to smirk at her brother. She nodded at Ashton, mouthing "three—two—one—"

"Chase Dweller, you better be down from the roof in 10 seconds or so help me *God*—"

***

Madeline and Nathan arrived home from work at 6:30 and 7:00 p.m., respectively. Madeline greeted Chase, Ashton, and Alana with a hug before running up the stairs to get the last of her bags packed. Nathan did the same when he returned home, immediately loosening his tie and ripping his suit jacket off like it was on fire. He jogged up the stairs to finish getting his amenities together for the weekend trip.

Chase's index finger on his left hand was purple when he returned from roof hopping. Lucas was behind him, holding his shoulder and scolding him like a parent would scold their second grader. The look on Chase's face was somewhere between amusement and pain as he cradled his seemingly broken finger in his right hand. Lucas returned upstairs with a huff after getting Chase situated on a recliner, putting a hand on Ashton's shoulder and stating blankly, "Do not let him get up."

Fifteen minutes later, Madeline and Nathan had all of their bags packed and lined up near the front door, where Lucas and Thomas had begun loading them into their Acura, and Madeline was setting the ground rules.

"Beth, try not to blow up the cell phone bill."
"Chase, absolutely *no* damn roof hopping—no exceptions."
"Ashton, look out for Alana, please. And Alana, try not to give

him too much trouble."

Lucas and Thomas did not have "rules" they were supposed to follow; however, they *were* supposed to enforce the rules, no matter what. Whether that meant confiscating Beth's phone or literally dragging Chase off the Mitchell roof, the two eldest were in charge in every sense of the phrase.

Madeline and Nathan hugged their children good-bye, reminding them all to be good one last time before closing the door and laughing. "See you in a few days, Crazies!"

After Madeline and Nathan had left, Thomas and Lucas returned upstairs to finish packing, while Beth sat next to Chase on the sofa, making sure he didn't get up to go roof hopping again. His index finger was starting to look pretty painful, and Ashton handed him an ice pack silently as Chase smiled in gratitude.

The rest of the night progressed slowly. Ashton made significant improvements to his European history paper, while Alana sat quietly beside him, graphing inequalities. The hour passed by in a welcome silence, broken only by the scratching of pencils and the occasional question. Ashton and Alana retreated to the living room a little while later to watch television, while the weatherman on the news strictly advised everyone to stay indoors and set up blizzard precautions.

Fifteen minutes later, all that could be heard from outside were whirlwinds whipping up snow in heaps and splattering them across the house's windows. Blizzards were common in Iowa, and Lucas returned downstairs only once to check on Ashton and Alana before returning upstairs to finish the last of his packing.

Alana was curled into her brother's chest, trying to focus on the television but jerking slightly every time there was a particularly loud roar of thunder. She had always hated storms—thunder, lightning, rain, or snow, it didn't matter. Loud noises had always made Ashton uneasy, but he enjoyed storms and felt oddly calmed by the sound of the wind outside. Chase was fast asleep, the ice pack still resting on his finger. He was a particularly heavy sleeper, and his subconscious paid no mind to the sounds outside.

As the minutes progressed, the storm outside only grew stronger, and by the time nine o'clock rolled around, the power went out. The television shut off abruptly, and the lights in the kitchen flickered and then died. Thomas came down the stairs after that to check on the youngest siblings again, and Chase finally woke up.

Alana was slightly trembling in the darkness, and Ashton pulled her a bit closer while Thomas picked up the landline.

"No dial tone," he announced after listening into it for a few seconds. He sighed and walked back to the foot of the staircase. "Lucas, I think we should give up on packing for the night and stay down here."

Lucas walked down the stairs a few minutes later, a disgruntled Beth on his arm. She rolled her eyes when Lucas finally let her go at the bottom, waving off his concerned looks and slurring out, "Luke, I'm not drunk."

While it was a blatant lie, Beth was *clearly* tipsy; Lucas let her go, as she stumbled her way over to the couch. He then walked into the kitchen to grab a water bottle from the fridge and shoved it into his sister's hands.

"You've gotta sober up, Elizabeth," he said, smirking.

"Don't *ever* call me Elizabeth," Beth growled, grabbing the collar of Lucas' shirt, causing him to laugh and push her away.

The Dwellers settled down in the living room, each finding their comfortable spots. Lucas sat on the couch next to Beth, while Thomas opted for the chair next to Chase's, who had fallen asleep again after the initial surprise of the power outage. Alana and Ashton were still sharing a chair, Alana hiding her face under the blankets to try to block out the thunder.

The wind and snow pounding on the window only increased in intensity as time went by, and most of the Dweller children slowly fell asleep.

They were awakened by the sharp ringing of a telephone at one o'clock in the morning. At first, Ashton thought he was dreaming; the landline hadn't had a dial tone the last time they had checked it, and all the power in the house was supposed to be out. But looking over at Lucas, the phone clutched tightly in his hands, Ashton knew he was awake.

He shook Alana awake from where she slept next to him and gestured for her to keep quiet, while Lucas spoke quietly into the phone. He looked pale and sickly, as he whispered into the phone like a terrified child, and Ashton could only wonder who was on the other end.

Soon, the other Dwellers were roused from their sleep by Lucas's voice, as it got louder as he spoke to the person on the phone. There were tears in Lucas's eyes now, and he was silently whispering "no" into the speaker. Thomas moved closer to his brother and laid a hand on his shoulder, trying to make eye contact and figure out what was going on.

When Lucas finally hung up the phone, he put his head in his hands, trembling slightly. When Beth asked quietly if the power was back on, Lucas only nodded slowly without picking his head up. "Who was on the phone, Lucas?" Thomas asked after a few moments.

"The police," Lucas said, shakily.

"Why would the police call here?" Thomas looked at Chase as he spoke, and Chase's eyes widened in fear.

"I haven't done anything!" Chase squeaked when the eyes of his siblings fell onto him. "I swear!"

"It wasn't about Chase," Lucas said, trying to regain his composure and calm down the accusations. He chewed on his lip and sighed shakily before saying, "They called because Mom and Dad are dead."

The effect was instantaneous. Beth's mouth dropped open, and Thomas whipped his head around from where he had been glaring at Chase. Tears welled in Alana's eyes, and Ashton felt paralyzed. A resounding "what?" echoed through the room.

"What the hell are you talking about?" Thomas said, his voice sounding panicky.

"The police called to tell us that Mom and Dad were hit by a drunk driver on Tanglewood a few hours ago."

The minute Lucas's words sank in, loud voices erupted again, only drowned out by the sound of crying. Thomas tried to calm the siblings to no avail, while Lucas was still trying to explain what had happened.

"I'll tell you the whole story if you all just *calm down*," Lucas repeated, trying to keep his voice calm but authoritative and loud. The chatter died down, as the siblings were anxious to know what had happened to their parents.

Lucas took a deep breath and ran a hand over his face. "Tanglewood is that long strip of road running from Davenport all the way to the other cities in Iowa. It has only one lane on each side, and Mom and Dad were driving down it when the blizzard hit. There was some . . . idiot driving drunk in the other direction, and he just swerved out of his lane and—"

Lucas didn't have to continue for the siblings to understand what had happened. He proceeded quietly after that. "The police couldn't get in touch with us after the power went out, and they couldn't even get to the crash site until a half hour after it happened. They said that Dad died on impact and Mom a minute later because of blood loss. When they finally got to the scene, there was nothing they could do."

Lucas was crying by the time he finally stopped talking, wringing his hands together and trying to calm his breathing, while his siblings dealt with the news in their own ways.

Chase stood up suddenly and walked out of the living room, practically running up the stairs, and slammed the door to his bedroom the minute he walked inside. He was never a person who was particularly fond of feelings or showing his emotions, but when he did, they were extreme.

Thomas was usually the one to follow him after an outburst, but Thomas merely sat on the chair opposite Lucas with a blank expression on his face, completely unreadable. He looked completely petrified, like he would tip over with a gust of wind. Lucas couldn't bring himself to move either.

Alana was sitting up now, crying into her hands. Beth, her face also streaked with tears, walked over to the chair that Alana and Ashton were sitting on and pulled Alana close to her chest. They both cried together, even though Beth was mostly trying to console her younger sister.

Ashton finally sat up from the chair, and with the movement, he felt like his head might explode. There were too many feelings at once: too many stimuli. One wrong move, one tear, one word, and he knew he could lose control of the *power*. He felt closed in and completely free at the same time, desperately clawing at one of his palms to keep it together. The wind and snow still pounded on the window, and it was too loud—everything was too *loud*. All of his senses were on high alert, and he was keenly aware of every tear that fell from his sisters' cheeks and every small movement that Lucas's body made.

He stood up from the chair, and his head swam again, making his vision blurry. Lucas and Thomas stared at him, confusion etched into their features, and Ashton did the only thing he knew how to do: run.

Ashton ran toward the front door and threw it open, running out into the blizzard without a second thought. After he took his fifth step, he knew it was ridiculous that he had not put on a coat, but he pushed through the freezing air nevertheless. He could hear Lucas screaming from the front steps to come back inside. "Ashton, you're going to freeze to death!" he screamed, followed by, "It's too cold, Ash. Please come back!" He tried to run off the steps to chase Ashton, but Thomas held him back, pushing him back inside.

Thomas closed the door after he had successfully gotten Lucas back inside and blocked the door from his path when his older brother tried to open it again. "Lucas," Thomas said, grabbing his brother by the wrists and trying to calm him down.

"What are you doing, Thomas?" Lucas fought, panicking again. "We're just going to let him freeze to death out there because he wants to?"

"Lucas, you idiot," Thomas sighed. "Do you think he's going to just stand out there? You know him, I know him. You know where he's going. Where does he always go when he's overwhelmed?"

Lucas breathed a sigh of relief that sounded a lot like "Cayden." Thomas clapped a hand on his brother's shoulder and led him back into the living room, where Alana was curled up next to Beth, still crying silently.

Outside, the frostbite was fierce, tearing like knives at Ashton's skin and bones. The quickest way to get next door would be to walk across their lawns, but said lawns were covered in thick heaps of snow. Ashton tried to run, but he fell more than once, landing in a freezing pile of snow that soaked his pant legs right through to his skin. When he finally got to the door of the Mitchell home, his teeth were chattering, and he could swear that his fingers were purple. He knocked on the door with a shaky hand and waited for an answer.

When the door swung open, Ashton all but collapsed onto the person who opened the door. His legs didn't feel like they could work anymore, and whether that was the cold or the grief or the power running through his veins, he couldn't tell.

He didn't know exactly whom he had fallen onto until he was being pulled by the collar into the house and the door was being shut behind him. "Whoa, there," Cayden's voice soothed as Ashton trembled violently. "Why the hell were you out in this weather—are you crazy?" Cayden led him over to the couch, mostly dragging him, and pushed him down, begging his legs to give way. The minute his friend was seated on the couch, Cayden wrapped a blanket around him, trying to force the shaking to stop. When it was clear that a blanket wouldn't be enough to stop the shaking, Cayden sat on the couch next to Ashton and pulled him closer, rubbing a hand up and down his arm to try and create heat.

When there was suddenly water on his shoulder, Cayden assumed Ashton's hair was dripping with melted snow, but he was proved wrong when he felt sobs wracking Ashton's body and felt his friend clinging to him for dear life.

"Ash, what happened—what's wrong?" Cayden asked, pulling Ashton's head off of his shoulder and forcing him to make eye contact.

"My parents got in an accident," Ashton choked out, tears still running down his cheeks. "My dad died on impact, my mom lost too much blood, and Alana was crying and Lucas wasn't moving and—"

Cayden didn't need to hear any more before he was pulling Ashton back down into their previous position, letting Ashton cry onto his shoulder and cling to him. Cayden had no idea what it was like to lose a parent, but Madeline and Nathan were like his family. He let out a few of his own tears, but blinked them back quickly, knowing that it was Ashton who needed to grieve, not him.

Ashton cried and trembled until he passed out. Cayden promptly passed out next to him, the two of them tangled together on the couch in a jumble of blankets and tears.

***

Ashton was awakened by a soft voice rousing him from sleep, and when he opened his eyes, he saw Sandra kneeling in front of him and Mason and Alex standing behind her expectantly.

He tried to open his eyes. The first time he tried, it physically hurt, as if there were large bruises covering each of his eyes. They were swollen shut, from crying. Ashton remembered as the events of the previous night came back and hit him like whiplash.

His eyes welled up with tears again before he could even stop them, and he launched himself into Sandra's arms the minute he saw her sit back on her heels. She wrapped her arms around him and rubbed his back, trying to stop him from crying again.

"Listen Ashton, I know you don't like talking, okay? We all know. But something's wrong now, and I need you to tell me what it is. Please, talk to me."

"My parents are dead," was the first thing that came out of Ashton's mouth before anything else. Sandra pulled away and looked at him with confusion before staring at him.

"What happened, Ashton?"

Ashton tried to catch his breath, taking long slow breaths and trying to force the tears to stop. He wiped his eyes and stared at Sandra, wondering where to begin. "The snowstorm last night," he said, still trying to compose himself. "My parents were going on a trip across the state . . . to . . . to Cedar Rapids . . . or Iowa City . . . or one of those big cities."

Sandra grabbed his hand and looked at him sincerely. "Did

they go by car?"

"Yeah," Ashton said, his voice cracking a bit again. "Yeah, they went by car. And last night, apparently, even before the snow started coming down hard, they were closing off the major roadways out of Davenport, so they took Tanglewood as an alternate route—and . . . you know how skinny the lanes are."

Sandra nodded and squeezed his hand tighter. "What happened then, and how did you find out any of this?"

"We got a call at like two o'clock in the morning; Lucas picked it up and told us that it was the police department and that they had found Mom and Dad's car with the whole front wrecked. When they were driving down Tanglewood, there was another guy coming in the opposite direction, a drunken guy. He, um, he swerved out of his lane and smashed into my parents' car. There weren't any survivors. Lucas told us. And everyone in my house was crying, and I couldn't . . . couldn't stay there and listen to it. So, I . . . I went to the only place I knew I could go."

Sandra and Mason shared a look before tears were flowing again, this time not out of Ashton's eyes. Alex hugged her knees up to her chest and quietly cried into her hands. Cayden dropped off the couch and walked over to Ashton on the floor, initiating the hug this time. Ashton hugged him and let his friend cry on his shoulder, reversing their roles from the previous night. Sandra and Mason were clinging to each other like their lives depended on it, both crying silent tears onto each other.

Ashton knew he was grieving harder than Sandra and Mason were, but he wondered how it felt to lose a best friend. He hugged Cayden a little tighter.

***

Sandra called the Dweller house a little while later after everyone had mostly composed themselves to let Lucas know that Ashton had come to their house the previous night and was, as she put it, "as fine as a child who had just lost his parents could be."

Noah woke up a few hours later while Ashton was still over, asking why everyone looked like they had been crying. Sandra and Mason took him to the living room to explain to him what had happened while Ashton, Cayden, and Alex ate breakfast silently in the kitchen.

Lucas arrived a little while later, apologizing for Ashton's antics, but only getting three words out before Sandra was squeezing him into a bone-crushing hug. He relaxed then, letting Sandra tear up on his shoulder a little bit. He only allowed himself to be hugged for a few moments before he was apologizing again and asking Sandra if Ashton had told her the entire story. Sandra nodded and moved out of earshot of the kitchen to ask a few more questions.

"What are you going to do now?" she said.

"I'm working on postponing all of our flights for next week. Thomas and I were supposed to be flying out of here on Wednesday for work, but we're working on funeral arrangements now." Lucas kept his hands in his pockets and didn't make much eye contact, mostly staring at the floor.

"You're too young to be making funeral arrangements," Sandra mumbled, grabbing his hand. "Let Mason and I help you with the arrangements. You have enough to worry about with your siblings."

Lucas pulled his hand out of Sandra's grasp and put it up to protest, but she slapped it away. "Whatever you're about to say, don't say it," she said. "Ashton and Alana can stay here with Cayden and Mason while I go with you to work out the general details. You can't do this alone." She grabbed his shoulder and squeezed, almost begging him to comply. He sighed and nodded, finally, after a few moments of intense staring.

Lucas left the Mitchell home with Sandra a little later, but Ashton spent the day with Cayden, Alex, and Noah. No one was in the mood to play any games, or laugh, or even speak. A somber silence fell over Cayden's room, where the four of them were—five when Alana was dropped off a few hours later.

As the older Dweller siblings worked on funeral arrangements and how to alert the town on the death of a senator, the two youngest sat quiet and helpless, while Mason and Cayden tried to get them to smile.

By the time night fell and Sandra had returned home, her face was pale, and the fake smile plastered on her face was transparent. Alana sat at the table next to Ashton, where the children were eating dinner. Mason stood up from the table to hug her, and Ashton couldn't tear his eyes away.

Under the table, Alana squeezed his hand, and when he looked up, her eyes were filled with unshed tears again. "I'm scared," she whispered, "about what's going to happen now."

Ashton squeezed her hand back. *Me too.*

3

Ashton tugged at the collar of the dress shirt and stared down at his shoes. He looked over at Alana, draped in black and drowning in her dress. Ashton knew his sister. She was strong, independent, and determined. She didn't scare easily, she didn't let anyone push her around, and she *definitely* didn't cry. But standing in the huge black dress, with her hands clasped together in front, she looked so *small* that it almost made Ashton cry.

He sent her a reassuring smile and walked over to her slowly, wrapping her up in a hug. She rested her chin on her brother's shoulder for a moment before whispering in his ear, "Ashton, I don't think this is going to end well."

He pulled away and squinted in confusion at his sister. Alana sighed dejectedly and looked at him in earnest.

"Do you really think that Lucas and Thomas are going to be able to take care of us? Neither of them have stable jobs right now, and they may not be able to get custody," she said.

"It's gonna be okay," Ashton mumbled, trying to smile at her. Deep down, he knew everything was *far* from okay, but he needed to make sure Alana was ready for the day and everything that was going to come afterward. He knew that their parents' funeral was only the start of everything that would come with the death of their parents, and he knew that he needed to prepare Alana for the future.

The funeral service was difficult to sit through. Beth walked out at one point to compose herself during Lucas' eulogy. The church pews were filled with Madeline and Nathan's families, but with people from the government to a larger extent. Countless numbers of men and woman from city hall filled the last few rows of the pews, many already dressed in their work clothes. Ashton recognized some of them and knew that many of them had truly cared for his father, but most of them looked uninterested.

Ashton tried to sit through the service without letting the power wash over him. There were many times during the funeral when he had wanted to just command the priest to say something else. The priest focused on how much Madeline and Nathan had meant to the community, speaking of their occupations through the entire service. It made Ashton's skin crawl to listen to the priest babble on about the fact that Nathan Dweller had been a senator and to barely mention the fact that he had also been a father.

The people from the government in the pews behind Ashton barely spared the orphans a second glace when the service was over, walking out of the church quickly and hopping into their cars. Ashton gave most of them dirty looks, wiping the tears from his eyes and keeping Alana pressed up against his side while he climbed into the backseat of Lucas's car.

The cemetery service and burial were just as heartbreaking as the funeral service, and Ashton desperately wanted to go home and sleep for the rest of his life. He didn't think he had any tears left in his body, and the government officials breathing down his neck did nothing to lift his spirits.

After the ceremonies, Lucas had organized a large dinner at a restaurant to accommodate the large number of people who had attended the funeral. As much as Ashton wanted to return home, he knew that his older siblings needed him to sit through one more thing, so he sat quietly and ate in silence.

Halfway through the dinner, the three eldest Dwellers moved to the corner of the restaurant, and a few minutes later, their voices had considerably increased in volume. Chase tried to intervene once but was sent back to his seat with a stern look from Lucas that would leave anyone shaking in their boots. When Ashton and

Alana tried to question Chase about it, he ignored them in favor of his dinner.

When dinner was over, the eldest Dwellers were still conspiring in a corner, and Ashton's curiosity got the best of him. He stood up from the table, excused himself, and walked discreetly over to the bathrooms, conveniently placed near the corner of the restaurant.

Ashton heard Lucas' voice first, as he slipped behind a potted plant to listen in on their conversation and try to decipher their facial expressions.

"There's always Damon," Lucas said, while Thomas looked as if he was going over options in his mind. Beth looked at them in amazement, her expression quickly turning from exasperated to angry.

"No way in hell I'm letting you do that. We're not just dropping them off somewhere and letting some uncle—who we haven't seen in years—take care of them." Beth looked furious, slapping her eldest brother on the arm and shaking her head.

Lucas looked at her sadly. "Do you think that Thomas and I will actually be able to raise them right? Chase will be in college next year, and you're in between jobs now. They're two teenagers who need more than what we can offer. They need a stable home, and the person looking out for them needs to have a stable income."

"Don't lie to me," Beth snarled. "The only reason you're hesitant to take them in is because you're desperate for that job in Philly. And Thomas wants to work in that stupid psych practice so bad, he's willing to ditch Davenport for Philly too! The two of you give me a headache!"

Ashton heard Beth's last sentence and stepped out from behind the plant. He walked closer to his siblings with a confused expression on his face, as he tried to figure out why they were arguing at a time when they finally had a chance to relax.

"What's going on?" Ashton whispered.

The three eldest Dwellers whipped their heads around quickly and stared at their youngest brother, trying to hide their angry expressions. "You remember Uncle Damon, right?" Thomas asked hesitantly, his eyes pleading with Ashton to agree.

Ashton thought hard, but no image of an "Uncle Damon" came to his mind. "Who's he?" he asked.

Beth put her hands on her hips and scoffed. "You see," she quipped. "He has no idea who Damon is. Neither does Alana, I'll bet."

Ashton's head was spinning, and he desperately wanted to know what was going on. "Why'd you even ask me that?" he asked Thomas quietly. "What are you all doing back here, anyway?"

Beth sighed and looked to Lucas for an answer, but Lucas looked hesitant to comply. He shoved his hands into the pockets of his dress pants and tried staring at the ground, but soon Ashton's gaze broke him.

"You and Alana are teenagers," he explained. "Thomas and I . . . we just can't take care of you the way an adult can. I called our Uncle Damon, who lives in California. In Mom and Dad's will, it says that he's the one who gets custody of any child under 18 in the event of their deaths—if we can't take on the burden."

The only thing Ashton could think to blurt out was, "California?"

"He used to live in Iowa," Thomas explained. "He moved to California when you were four, which is probably why you don't remember him. He's a custodian and security guard at a school, so he has a stable income and a nice home. He offered to take you and Alana in if Lucas and I couldn't handle it."

"So what happens now?" Ashton said, voice trembling.

"The paperwork is filled out—has been for days. We can get

you and Alana on a plane soon, so you're not forced back into school right away. You can have a slow transition back in."

Ashton couldn't believe what he was hearing. Moving meant giving up everything he had fought to keep stable in his life: his family, his school, and his relationships with his sister and Cayden. He couldn't just let Lucas send them away.

"I should get a say in this," Ashton all but whispered, tugging on Lucas' sleeve.

Lucas looked at him sympathetically before his facial expression changed to something resembling anger. "No, Ash, you don't get a say. You're 14. And since when have you ever wanted a *say* in anything."

Ashton recoiled; his brother had never used his muteness as an insult before. He turned on his heel, grabbed Alana's arm, and walked toward a group of particularly mean politicians. Ashton knew that they couldn't care less about his mother and father and were only here for the good publicity. The thought made Ashton's stomach churn unpleasantly, and his eyes watered as he continued to drag Alana through the sea of people, who didn't really *know* his parents and never would. He could hear Lucas calling after him and begging him to stop running, but with every yell, Ashton picked up the pace.

When they finally reached the exit, Ashton pushed the door open, and the cool air hit him in the face. He sat on the curb outside of the restaurant, tears running down his cheeks as Alana sat down next to him, curious as to what was wrong.

"We're leaving," Ashton whispered to her. "We're getting shipped off to California to live with some uncle and never coming back."

Alana looked confused, and soon she just looked upset. "I told you they wouldn't be able to take care of us," she said, her eyes welling up with tears as she put her head in her hands.

A few seconds later, Lucas and Thomas joined them on the curb in front of the restaurant, trying to calm them down, but the pair just shook them off.

"It's the only thing we can do," Thomas said, softly. "You'll have a good life there."

"You could at least *try*," Alana cried, refusing to look up at them, "instead of just handing us over to some uncle we've never met."

Lucas sighed. "But you *have* met him before. You just don't remember it. You were too young. He's the one who's supposed to get custody of you two in Mom and Dad's will if we can't take care of you. Don't you trust their judgment?"

Ashton glared daggers at his eldest brother. He was being condescending and trying to invalidate their feelings, as usual. It was all a ploy to use their dead parents as scapegoats. Ashton wanted to be sick again.

"This isn't about them," Ashton growled, trying to pluck up as much courage as he could muster to raise his voice. "This is about us—and you."

Lucas's eyes widened, as hearing Ashton speak above a whisper and without stuttering was rare. "Thomas and I can't take care of you and Alana, Ashton," he said. "I'm sorry, but that's the way it is."

With nothing more than that, Lucas stood up from the curb and beckoned for Thomas to follow him back inside the restaurant, leaving Alana and Ashton alone again. Ashton felt as if he didn't have any tears left. Alana looked at him expectantly, as she always did. She waited in vain for an explanation of what had just happened. It occurred to Ashton that even if he had the confidence and power to speak and explain to Alana what was happening, he wouldn't even know how to begin.

The Dwellers

***

Packing up his room was more difficult than he thought it would be. When they had left the restaurant on the day of the funeral, Ashton had assumed that he would have a few weeks or months to say his good-byes to the people he loved in Davenport and to pack up everything he needed for Uncle Damon's house. However, the minute they had arrived home from the restaurant, with Ashton and Alana sill refusing to acknowledge Lucas, Beth had sat the two of them down with watery eyes and told them that they were scheduled to leave in three days.

Ashton looked around his bedroom and sighed, staring at the pictures taped to his wall. Cayden was lying on his bed, not saying much of anything as he watched Ashton take his clothes out of his dressers and pack them into large boxes.

"And you don't have any say in this? At all?" Cayden finally said, quietly. Ashton had been avoiding Cayden ever since he had gotten the news about what was happening. Cayden had found out from Lucas a few hours previously, and while he had originally barged into Ashton's room furious at his friend for not telling him, one look at Ashton's face caused his argument to die on his lips. He had simply looked dejected, falling onto Ashton's bed and watching wordlessly as his friend packed away mostly everything in his room.

Ashton turned his head to Cayden after he asked the question and shook his head solemnly before turning back toward the moving boxes. He didn't want to talk about how he had no say over the fact that he was packing up his stuff right then and probably never coming back. He didn't want to talk about how he had no say over the fact that he and Alana were moving to live with an uncle that neither of them remembered ever meeting. He didn't want to talk about how he had no say over the fact that he was probably never going to see Cayden again. He just didn't want to talk.

Not like he was the biggest talker anyway.

Cayden understood and kept his mouth shut, watching as Ashton packed away almost everything from his desks and his drawers. After the boxes were taken away by Beth and wrapped up with masking tape, Ashton joined Cayden on his bed, putting his arms under his head and staring up at the ceiling.

"California has really nice weather," Cayden said quietly, trying to make conversation. "You'll never have to deal with blizzards ever again or crazy fall windstorms—just a lot of sun."

Ashton looked at Cayden and attempted a smile, but it turned into a grimace as he realized that a blizzard was what had gotten him into this situation in the first place. If he never had to see snow ever again, he wouldn't complain.

"Beth told me that your uncle lives in Lawndale. Apparently, the weather over there is amazing. Plus, it's in LA County, which means you'll be like super close to Hollywood. Maybe you'll get to meet some celebrities."

Ashton knew that Cayden was just trying to make him feel better and to be able to see the positives in moving away from Davenport, but the more Cayden talked, the sicker he felt. Cayden realized that after a little bit and stopped talking entirely again. They sat in an uncomfortable silence as Cayden stared at Ashton's empty room.

When Lucas called up the stairs to Cayden to tell him that Sandra wanted him home, Ashton sat up and Cayden hugged him again before he left, telling him that Sandra had said they would be meeting the Dwellers at the airport the following day. Ashton waved goodbye as Cayden left and then returned to his bedroom silently. Beth sent Lucas and Thomas upstairs every few hours to check on Ashton, but after the third check-in, Ashton locked his

The Dwellers

door.

If they cared so much about his well being, they wouldn't be sending him away.

***

Lucas, Thomas, Beth, and Chase packed Ashton and Alana's bags into the trunk of Lucas's car the following morning, as Ashton and Alana hopped into the backseat. The car ride to the airport was so silent that Ashton wanted to scream. Alana wouldn't look up from her lap, and Thomas had to calm Lucas down every few minutes when he got too aggressive on the gas pedal.

They arrived at the airport only a few minutes after Sandra, Mason, Alex, and Noah. No one said much of anything, as Ashton and Alana were led through security and the baggage check, Lucas showing the airline representatives his ID at every checkpoint. A group of small red-haired children bounced excitedly next to Alana, some clutching blankets and babbling about their trip to who knows where. The TSA officers smiled at the red-haired children, but their faces fell when they saw Ashton and Alana's somber expressions. The officers gave a questioning look to Lucas, who shrugged and urged his siblings along.

If the Dwellers were quiet, the Mitchells were quieter. Not one person said a word except for the occasional "sorry," when a bag was rolled over someone's foot accidentally. Cayden's face was blank and unreadable, while Alex and Noah were visibly upset, holding each other's hands tightly with watery eyes.

The checkpoints passed too quickly, and after going through security for the last time, the two families sat quietly on stiff blue chairs waiting for Ashton and Alana's flight to be called.

When flight 528 was called and people began to board, Ashton's stomach sank lower. Alana ran into Sandra's arms, and Ashton could tell that her eyes were glassy, but she didn't let any tears fall as she picked Alana up and spun her around.

"We'll see each other again," she promised, when she finally put Alana down.

The two families lasted about three minutes before almost everyone was crying. Alex and Noah, the smallest two, were sitting on their parents laps and sobbing, even though they didn't completely understand why Ashton and Alana were leaving.

Ashton stayed as far away as he could, biting his tongue until he tasted blood to stop himself from becoming overwhelmed. The last thing he needed was to control someone in a crowded airport. He hugged everyone solemnly and let Sandra hold on for a little longer, as she pressed a kiss to his forehead. When he pulled away, she was crying, and he had to turn away quickly to keep from crying himself.

Cayden was last, and Ashton partly wanted to just skip him altogether, hop on the plane, and not look back. But Cayden already looked defeated, slumped in his seat, trying to avoid everyone. Ashton plopped into the seat next to his best friend and turned to look at him sadly, resting his cheek on his hand. With all of his courage, he tried to be nonchalant and spoke in a voice that was louder than a whisper.

"I have a cell phone, y'know," he said.

Cayden turned to stare at him, his face half sad and half confused.

"I promise I'll call you. Something. I'll keep in touch as best as I can—"

Ashton didn't get to finish his sentence before Cayden was launching himself into his friend's arms and burying his face into Ashton's shoulder. It didn't register that Cayden was crying until Ashton felt him shaking.

"Don't leave; you can't leave," he cried, tightening his hands in the back of Ashton's jacket.

Ashton had promised himself that he wouldn't cry and that he would stay strong for Alana to make sure she was always looked after. But he dropped his bag on the ground and hugged him back, cursing himself when he felt hot tears streaming down his own cheeks.

"I wish I didn't have to," Ashton whispered, letting Cayden cry into his shoulder.

The two of them had always been as close as they could possibly be, but at the same time, they had never been the overly touchy-feely sort of friends. Ashton felt that he and Cayden had cried on each other more in the past month than they had in the entire duration of their friendship.

And maybe Ashton had more feelings for Cayden than he was willing to admit to himself, but if he was ever going to move on from Davenport, as Lucas had said, he needed to cut his ties.

And maybe this was what Cayden needed. As the intensity of Ashton's emotions increased, so did the nature of the *power*. It felt more powerful than it had ever been, like the death of his parents had caused his brain to short-circuit, throwing the power into overdrive. Ashton had made himself a promise when he was young to never use his power on his best friend, and maybe he had to get away from Cayden in order to keep that promise.

Despite the maybes swimming through Ashton's mind, he found it almost impossible to pull away from Cayden, who still had his arms wrapped tightly around Ashton's waist, rooting him to the spot. Lucas had to physically separate them by the time Ashton and Alana needed to board the flight, and Cayden looked like a wreck.

Sandra held Cayden close to her chest as Ashton and Alana boarded. Ashton waved back at the Mitchells sadly. He had to turn away when Cayden waved back. Ashton looked straight in front of him and grabbed Alana's hand to steady himself. She squeezed back and only turned back once to glare at Lucas before pulling her brother along.

Sitting down in his seat on the plane, Ashton curled his fingernails into the leather of the seat and prayed to whoever was listening. Alana wrapped her fingers around his wrist, trying to calm him, even though her heart was pulsing at the same rate. She didn't know if Ashton was angry or nervous or afraid of flying, but she steadied him with her hand when the plane took off.

Maybe the plane would crash, Ashton thought. Maybe his uncle would be nice and welcoming and he'd spend time with them. Maybe he'd make a friend, someone who understood him like Cayden did. But who knew?

Now, Ashton's life was just a jumbled cluster of *maybes*.

***

Uncle Damon was not nice.

Uncle Damon was a surly man with a poorly shaved goatee. He had an ex-wife and a drinking problem.

Uncle Damon was not nice when he was drunk.

The first year at Damon's house in California was nothing less than hell on earth. Ashton's mutism was not Damon's favorite thing in the world, and he was pretty convinced that he would be able to beat it out of him.

That didn't work. But he kept trying.

When Damon tried to go after Alana, Ashton would intervene, Alana would get angry, and Damon would go out to a bar. He'd come home from the bar drunker and angrier. He'd try to go after Alana again, Ashton would intervene, and the cycle would repeat itself.

The Dwellers

The year passed in a blur of bruises and bloody wounds, and eventually Damon decided to ignore Ashton and Alana altogether, only getting angry at them when the house wasn't clean or when there wasn't enough liquor in the cabinet to keep him satisfied. He was paranoid about the siblings having contact with the outside world, so he would confiscate Ashton's phone the minute he walked in the door from school. Halfway through the first year at Damon's house, he took Ashton's phone and never returned it. Ashton was too scared to call Cayden anyway, so maybe it was for the best.

Ashton ignored the constant questions from teachers at his new school. They constantly asked him whether or not he was okay and where his bruises kept coming from. He lied about getting into fights when he got called down to the guidance counselor. When the counselor remarked that he "didn't look like the kind of kid that got into fights," he shrugged and walked out of the office without waiting to be dismissed.

Alana liked to go out. Ashton had a hard time figuring out *where* exactly she disappeared to, but she'd always come back before Damon got home from the bar. Her pupils would be dilated sometimes, and she frequently seemed to have a hard time walking in a straight line when she walked through the door, but it wasn't any of Ashton's business. As long as she was safe at home and back before Damon could throw a hissy fit, Ashton didn't care.

Another year passed in the same painstaking way, and then another. Every year that passed without a word from their siblings made Ashton more and more furious. At 17, Ashton was a mute and passive-aggressive outcast, and Alana would come home every night at three o'clock in the morning, a few minutes before Damon would begrudgingly stumble through the door, completely wasted.

A few weeks into Ashton's junior year, Alana flipped Ashton's life upside down in a matter of days. And it all started with a boy. How pathetic is that?

***

Ashton lightly touched his throbbing cheekbone while he brought the ice pack to his lip. This was going to be an agonizingly long Saturday.

Alana woke up at half passed noon, mumbling about breakfast as she headed to the cupboards. Ashton could tell that she was nursing a hangover, but the minute he was able to catch her eyes, she just smiled.

Alana had become all too used to the negative effects of alcohol, maybe a little *too* acquainted with them, being only 15. She wouldn't stop drinking though; Ashton knew that. Alcohol was her coping mechanism. When she was out with her group of (pathetic excuses for) friends, she could get drunk and smile and pretend that everything was okay.

At first, Ashton would quietly remind her to go slow and not to have too much. But soon, he had given up completely. In his mind, if she had found something to dull the pain of the punches, God bless her.

Alana chewed on a granola bar, bringing her eyes back to Ashton's and smiling at him again. She squinted then, as if her brother was blurry, and then opened her eyes like she was seeing him for the first time. "What the hell happened to your face?" she said, rushing over and cradling his cheek in her hand, as if he were a child.

"Damon woke up pissed because the kitchen wasn't clean. He freaked and stormed out as usual. It's no big deal," he tried, pushing her away.

"What the hell do you mean 'no big deal'? He punched you in

the face, correct?" Alana ran her thumb across his cheek and grabbed his hand in hers.

He hated when she got like that: motherly and protective. He was the older brother, and it was *his* job to make sure *Alana* was okay, not the other way around. As much as Ashton tried to protest, Alana would baby him constantly. She would tend to his wounds whenever Damon would beat him too badly, and she was always making sure he had something to eat, even when their uncle forgot to go shopping.

"I'm *fine*, Alana. I promise," Ashton said quietly, pushing her hand away and replacing the ice pack onto the bruise.

"You're *not* fine," she said, harshly. "I swear to God that I'm going to kill him. I'm gonna *kill* him."

Ashton took his sister's hand in his and looked at her sincerely. "Alana, I am going to be *fine*. Stop worrying about me so much, okay? It's my job to look after you, not the other way around."

"Will you stop with that crap? You know that's not true," she said. "We need to look out for *each other* if we're going to survive the next three years."

She became quiet after that, and the elephant in the room began stomping on the floor. It was no secret to Alana that Ashton was free to leave Damon's hellhole after he turned 18; she wasn't naïve. But the idea of Ashton abandoning her after he came of age made her sick to her stomach, so she just ignored it altogether.

"You're right," Ashton agreed, trying to sound sincere. "But I look after you before you look after me. You don't have to worry about me."

"That's bull," Alana scoffed, finishing her granola bar and throwing the wrapper away. "You're slowly becoming less mute, you get beat every single day by Damon, and you never leave the damn house. Do you have any friends—at all?"

Ashton swallowed and contemplated the question. Alana was

wrong. He *had* to have friends. There was the girl who always asked to borrow his pencils in Chemistry and the loud boy who had helped him cook a soufflé one time during Home Economics. And of course there was the boy in the bathroom, Jake, who sat on the windowsill and offered a blunt to Ashton every time he walked in during eighth period. They were his friends.

"I have friends," Ashton replied defensively, though his words didn't sound convincing.

Instead of laughing as Ashton thought she would, Alana just looked pitiful, which was worse.

"Listen, I know you're not the biggest fan of the drinking I do or the friends that I hang out with, but I'll make you a deal," she said, smiling.

Ashton raised his eyebrows cautiously. He never really knew what to expect when Alana made deals. But he nodded his head to let her know that he was listening.

"If you come out tomorrow night with me and my friends and actually party the night away for once in your life, I'll clean Damon's room every day for two weeks."

Ashton's eyes widened in surprise. He and Alana had switched on and off cleaning Damon's room since they had arrived there—or at least since Damon had thrown his first fit about his room not being spotless. The room looked disgusting every day and smelled even worse. Ashton would give his firstborn to never have to step foot in the room ever again. If Alana was offering to clean it every day, it was an offer Ashton couldn't possibly turn down.

"Just one party?" he clarified.

"Only one," Alana assured. "You come to *one* party with me and stay the whole night, and we've got a deal."

Ashton held out his hand for Alana to shake, and she reciprocated with a laugh and a firm grip. "There's just one condition though," she mumbled, pulling her hand away.

Ashton groaned.

"Calm yourself," Alana giggled. "The only condition is that you let me doll you up when we go to the party tomorrow night. Y'know? Make you look all spiffy."

Ashton rolled his eyes but nodded and whispered, "fine."

***

The first thing Ashton realized about his sister Sunday night was that she was very energetic when she was drunk.

Ashton had never actually *seen* Alana drunk. The first night she had come home with alcohol in her system, Ashton had smelled it from three rooms away and ushered her quickly into her bedroom before Damon could smell her.

But now she was a fireball, dancing around the club with nameless guys and sipping out of a small flask once in a while. She looked old enough to flash a fake ID at the bouncer as Ashton had; however, she didn't look old enough to order a drink at the bar. She was happily buzzed when she returned to Ashton a half an hour later, approaching him where he was hidden in the corner of the club, drinking a water bottle.

"What are you doing?" she screamed into his ear, the bass of the music too loud to be heard over. "You're supposed to be dancing and drinking and having fun, not hiding! C'mon, there's someone I want you to meet." She grabbed Ashton's hand and pulled him up from the chair he was sitting on, tugging him toward the long black couch that was pressed up against one of the walls of the club. She approached the closest table, waving to a boy who was typing away on his phone. When she called his name, James, he looked up and waved back.

"Who's your friend, Alana?" James's voice broke Ashton away from his thoughts. He smiled at her before repeating his previous question. Alana smiled at him and stood up from the couch again, pulling Ashton over to where James was sitting.

"This is my big brother Ashton," she said, gesturing to Ashton, who was standing awkwardly in front of the couch.

"He's cute," James said to Alana, although he said it so loudly that Ashton was sure everyone in the nightclub could hear him. Ashton could feel his ears burning, and he pulled Alana's arm, signaling her that he was ready to leave. She latched onto his arm and kept him in place.

Alana nodded and smiled. "Isn't he? I just wish he would socialize more with my friends and go out or *do* something—or maybe just try *talking* to someone."

Ashton narrowed his eyes at his sister angrily, trying to pull away from her iron grip. She held on to him though, forcing him to stay put in front of her and James.

"So, he doesn't talk much?"

Ashton glared at the boy with distaste. There was something *off* about him. He didn't look much older than Ashton himself; sure he was taller, leaner, but he couldn't have been older than 18.

"He's been mute since he was a little kid," Alana explained. "We still don't know why. He's practically a genius—talking just isn't his thing. He barely talks to me unless he's defending himself or telling me off." She pulled Ashton's arm forcefully so he would fall next to her on the couch.

Ashton sat quietly next to Alana, listening to the bass thump in his ears and wringing his hands together anxiously. He desperately wanted to get out of the club, and keeping commanding thoughts at bay was becoming more difficult by the minute.

The boy turned to Ashton and smirked. When he spoke, his voice was gentle and almost condescending. "Talking's not your thing?"

Ashton kept his glare firm, raising his voice louder than he usually did. "I can talk if I want to. However, you don't seem like the most educated person to have a conversation with."

Alana stared open-mouthed at her brother and watched as James barked out a laugh, his cigarette almost falling from his lips. There was no malice or anger behind the laugh; he sounded genuinely surprised to hear Ashton speak.

"I'm definitely not the most educated person to have a conversation with," James laughed. "That's no question. But I am a pretty fun person to party with, and the last time I checked, you're in a nightclub."

"I don't like parties or nightclubs," Ashton said bluntly, crossing his arms and leaning back against the black couch. "Alana forced me to come to this one."

"Who doesn't like parties?" James asked incredulously.

"Me," Ashton snapped.

The boy smirked at that and took another drink, while Alana rolled her eyes at her brother and stood up from the couch.

"You two spend some quality time getting to know each other," she instructed. "I'm gonna go find something to drink." She disappeared quickly after that, moving her way effortlessly through the sea of people and leaving Ashton and James alone on the couch together.

"You should dye your hair," James said, running his hand through Ashton's blond strands.

Ashton pulled away from the touch and slunk back into his seat. James laughed, not offended by Ashton's rejection in the slightest. "Black would be a really nice color on you," he continued, not bothering to wait for a reply. "It would fit, since you're all mysterious and quiet and sulky."

Ashton glared. "I'm not sulky."

"You're sulking right now."

Ashton rolled his eyes and turned away from the boy, almost

begging him to go away and find someone else to annoy. He tried to keep his cool, however, and merely kept his back turned, not uttering another word.

James didn't stop though. "Plus, I think black hair would look really good on you. It would bring out those pretty blue eyes of yours."

Ashton blushed and mentally cursed himself for doing so. Why was he *blushing*? James was not exactly the best person to get a compliment from, considering Ashton had seen him making out with four different people within the last two hours. But even though he was annoying and didn't understand the concepts of boundaries or personal space, he wasn't mean or judgmental, and he definitely wasn't unattractive.

"You ever try acid?"

Ashton whipped around so quickly that he felt the blush drain out of his cheeks. "What the hell? No!" he answered. James nodded, processing this new bit of information.

"Mary Jane?"

Ashton caught his breath and squinted in confusion until he understood. James was asking him about teenager things that normal teenagers in Lawndale did on the weekends. Considering that Ashton had never done anything remotely rebellious in his life, he hoped his goody-two-shoes image was enough to send James running for the hills. He shook his head to the question about marijuana. There was no point in lying.

"Ever smoke a cigarette?" he said, pointing to the one currently in his hand.

Ashton shook his head again, watching James's eyes widen in surprise. He tapped a finger to his chin, leaning back and taking a drag.

"Ever drank alcohol?"

"No."

James laughed loudly in disbelief. "Holy crap," he breathed. "You've had to have done *something*. This is the most boring game of 'never have I ever' that I've ever played."

Ashton shrugged, which was an invitation for James to walk away now that he knew that Ashton was not someone he was going to be able to smoke a blunt with. His powers were hard enough to control when he was sober and clean. If he were to add being drunk or high into the mess that was his life, he definitely wouldn't be able to stop himself from mentally manipulating people. But James didn't move from his place, and he contemplated more things to ask Ashton about.

"Okay, fine," he sighed. "Have you ever kissed anyone?"

When Ashton shook his head again, the cigarette practically fell out of James's mouth. "How have you never kissed anyone?" he asked in astonishment. "That should be, like, illegal."

Ashton crossed his arms again and debated turning his back to James once again, but the boy's hand on his arm forced him to stay put.

"Seriously, what kind of teenager are you?"

Ashton rolled his eyes and stood up from the black couch to pull up the hem of his t-shirt.

"Whoa," James said, wiggling his eyebrows and winking. "Keep your clothes on; we haven't even passed first base yet."

Ashton was 100% sure if he rolled his eyes any more, they would roll right back into his brain.

Pointing to the purplish bruise that covered half his ribcage, Ashton said, "This is why I haven't done any of the stuff you just mentioned. If *this* happens when I don't clean the kitchen properly, imagine what would happen to me if I were to come home drunk, stoned, or with black hair."

James instantly snapped his mouth shut and stared in horror at the bruise covering most of Ashton's chest. His pale skin made the bruise look even purpler, and in the flashy lights of the nightclub, Ashton realized his chest must have genuinely looked terrible. He pulled down his shirt, cheeks flushing, as he said quietly, "Now you see why I don't rebel."

"Alana rebelled," James said.

"But she has someone there to look after her."

"And someone to take the punches."

Ashton glared at James again, the same distaste in his eyes that he had when he had first met the boy that evening. An uncomfortable silence fell over both of them until Ashton decided to take a leap of faith and break the silence.

"She's just a kid," he sighed. "I'm just a kid. You're just a kid too."

James tilted his head in confusion and laughed, stomping his short cigarette out on the ground and reaching into his pocket to light another one. "Do I look like a kid to you?" he asked—it sounded more like a mumble, as the cigarette was hanging out of the corner of James's mouth.

"There's no way that you're much older than me," Ashton said. "And you're not legal yet, because you used a fake ID to get in here just like I did."

James sighed again. "How old are you?"

"I just turned 17."

James went quiet at that, but Ashton continued to pester him about his age.

"C'mon, how old are you?" he asked until he was frustrated. James sat still the whole time, puffing on his cigarette and trying to look mature, even though Ashton could see right through him.

"Tell me how old you are," Ashton said finally and slapped a hand over his mouth a second later.

It happened so quickly that Ashton wanted to be sick. The color drained from James's eyes, and his smiling expression all but melted off of his face. He answered, "I am 17 years old" in a monotone voice, and when the color returned to his eyes, he could see Ashton still gaping like a fish.

James acted like nothing had happened, and to Ashton's knowledge, people he controlled weren't even under the impression that they were being controlled. James still had a smug smirk on his face and had barely reacted to the meddling inside his mind. He pushed his beer away, laughed, and said, "I'm 90% sure I've had too many of these."

Ashton tried for a smile, but it went sour, and he tried to close his eyes and count to 10. It had been ages since the last time he'd accidentally controlled someone, and it always had him feeling dirty and *wrong*. It was like a relapse to him—like his power was an addiction that he was recovering from. He clamped his mouth shut and stared at his hands in his lap; he hoped James would take the hint and leave.

"Hey, don't get all quiet on me now. I'm pretty sure you've talked to me more in the last hour than you have to anyone all year."

James had a point, but Ashton needed to get out of the nightclub fast before he did something else that he regretted. Accidentally controlling people was one thing, but allowing himself to let Alana and James get him drunk or high was another story.

"That's true," Ashton said. "But you're also infuriating, and I'd very much like to punch you in the mouth."

"Wanna punch me in the mouth with your mouth?"

Well *that's* not something Ashton was expecting. James stared at him expectantly, his stupid smirk still on his lips, awaiting an answer.

"Was that a pickup line?"

"That depends," James said. "It's only a pickup line if it works."

Needless to say, Ashton spent most of the night in a secluded corner of the nightclub punching James in the mouth with his own mouth, regretting it more and more as the night went on.

And maybe he had a few drinks, and maybe he took a puff of the cigarette that James had held out to him, and maybe he walked to CVS at 2:30 a.m. to buy a box of black hair dye.

But Ashton's life was just a jumbled cluster of *maybes*.

***

James was nice. Ashton would admit that to himself.
James was damaged. Ashton would admit that to himself.
James was a good kisser. Ashton would also admit *that* to himself.

His relationship with James—if it could even be considered a relationship—was nowhere near "healthy." They dyed their hair, got stoned together, and made out while they were drunk. It wasn't ideal, but it was something to numb the punches. Alana had alcohol and pot once in a while, and Ashton had James.

Damon did not like James, or the black hair for that matter. But for some reason, nights out in the nightclub were worth the abuse that came afterward. The drugs dulled the pain of the beatings, the alcohol made him forget about the constant thump of power that ran through his veins, and James made him forget about a certain someone whose name wasn't allowed to be spoken in their house.

His junior year was put into perspective after Ashton received one of his semester report cards, and the change in grades from sophomore to junior year was so drastic that he was called to the office for guidance. School had fallen off of Ashton's list of priorities after he had taken the first drag of a blunt. He didn't care if he made it to 25, so he didn't care about any life he would have after high school. As Alana hit rock bottom, so did he.

Ashton only realized that he had hit rock bottom after James had mentioned something to him while they were lounging around in Ashton's bedroom.

"Ash, I think someone's been lacing our shit with something trippy," James had said, leaning back against the headboard.

"What do you mean?" Ashton replied, mindlessly scrolling through YouTube on Alana's stolen computer.

"I mean—the stuff we were smoking on Sunday night, whatever it was. At one point, you were so high you were just rattling off orders, and everybody was laughing. But then, I swear people's eyes were changing colors, and I felt like I was having a bad acid trip."

Ashton froze instantly, looking up at James from behind the computer screen and trying to get his heart to leave his throat. He had controlled people without even knowing it, and he was so high when it happened that he didn't even remember it.

"What are you talking about?" Ashton choked out.

"I have no idea, man. It was so weird; I'd never seen anything like it," James said. "Not even when I tried LSD. This was some heavy duty stuff."

"And I was just controlling people?" Ashton choked out a laugh, trying to make it sound as if mental manipulation was the most unbelievable thing in the world.

"Crazy, right?" James laughed, pulling a crushed pack of cigarettes out of his back pocket along with a lighter. "You were like some crazy magical dictator. I'm gonna kill whoever spiked the stuff."

Ashton tried to push the thoughts and images out of his mind, but he could almost see himself in vivid pictures scattered throughout his brain: drunkenly forcing people to try drugs that they didn't want to and making people drop pipes and cigarettes onto wooden floors. The drugs that James had put into Ashton's system no doubt would affect the power and *its* affect on other people.

Quickly, Ashton asked James to leave. James never got offended. He just put out his cigarette on Ashton's bedside table, ruffled up Ashton's hair, and walked out the door. The minute that James was out the door, Ashton raced to the bathroom. He rested his head on the cool porcelain of the toilet bowl after every round of sickness.

If Alana asked, it was because he had drunk too much the previous day—because it wasn't *really* a lie—not really.

***

At the next party that Ashton attended, he was set on monitoring his alcohol intake. And that lasted for a good half hour.

He wasn't drunk—not yet. There was a pleasant buzz running through him, but his speech wasn't slurred, and he could still walk in a semi-straight line. It was just like any other random night at the nightclub: some creepy guy breathing down his neck, enough alcohol to keep him sated, and a joint if he needed one.

The only thing that was off was that he hadn't seen James all night—Alana was missing as well—and Ashton spent most of his evening nursing his beer in his favorite corner of the club. It wasn't until he heard Alana's squealing laugh that he got up off the couch.

Following the laughter, Ashton ended up in a room he had never seen before. Smoke hung thick in the air, and the stench of pot gave Ashton a pounding headache, even though he had only been in the room a few minutes. *This must be where James gets his drugs from*, Ashton thought.

In the corner of the room, Ashton spotted figures that seemed to be Alana and James, who were surrounded by a group of James's friends, all of whom seemed to be high.

"You've got to relax, Alana," James giggled, grabbing her arm. "If you don't stop fidgeting, the needle's gonna hurt."

Ashton pushed his way through the groups of stoners upon hearing *that*, dropped his beer on the floor, and fought his way into the corner of the room. When he finally saw Alana and James clearly, his stomach launched up into his throat.

James was holding Alana by the arm, a dark syringe shaking in his wobbly hand. His eyes were glazed and lidded. The people surrounding Ashton and James watched drunkenly as James attempted to inject the contents of the syringe into Alana's arm.

"What the hell is going on?" Ashton growled, pushing his way into the circle. James looked up blearily, but Alana kept her eyes glued to the syringe in James's hand.

"We're just havin' a little fun, babe. It's no big deal," James giggled, the needle dripping a bit onto his thigh.

"What's in the syringe?" Ashton said, not letting his eyes leave the needle.

"Just a bit of the good stuff."

"You're kidding me."

"The good stuff" was James's favorite out of all of the drugs he had tried. Ashton had tried to get him to stop using heroin after he had discovered the scars on James's arms, and as far as Ashton knew, James had stopped when he was told. Staring down at James holding the syringe made Ashton realize that James had only recently begun wearing long sleeves, despite temperatures in Lawndale approaching 90 degrees.

"James, what were you about to do?" Ashton asked slowly, looking toward his sister, sitting submissively on the ground.

"Alana'll like it," James slurred. "Promise."

"There's no way I'm letting you inject that stuff into my baby sister. Are you crazy?"

"Lighten up, Ash," James laughed, placing the syringe on the floor, which was no doubt a germ-infested wasteland. "I know you won't get high on this stuff with me, but Alana would be so down for it. Getting high alone is boring."

"James, I swear to God," Ashton said, stepping as close to the two of them as he could get. "If you bring that needle an inch closer to my sister, I will step on your hand and break your fingers."

James giggled at the threat, picking the syringe up off the floor again and wiggling it in the air. "Nah, you wouldn't."

Ashton took another step before he could stop himself and stomped down, hard, on the hand James had resting on the floor. James yelped but held onto the needle, almost breaking it in his hands. Ashton couldn't stop himself when he spoke next.

"Drop the syringe," he growled.

James's eyes faded to gray as the heroin dropped slowly from his hand. Once it hit the floor, the color began to return to his eyes, but Ashton wasn't going to stay and watch. He grabbed Alana's arm and lifted her up off of the floor. She didn't fight it or stand up on her own; she just sat there like a rag doll as Ashton heaved her up.

James was momentarily stunned by what had happened, just like people usually were after they had been under Ashton's control, but after he realized that Ashton was walking away with Alana's arm over his shoulder, he found his sea legs. James tried to chase after Ashton and Alana, but he didn't do a very good job of it.

"Get back here, Ashton!"

"Alana, I know you'll like it; just give it a chance!"

The Dwellers

"You're gonna regret this, Dweller!"

"I never gave a damn about you anyway!" James finally yelled, tripping over his own feet in his drug-induced haze. "I just used you so I could get closer to Alana!"

His words stung—badly. But Ashton refused to let James get to him because he needed to get Alana home. She was mumbling about something into Ashton's shoulder, but her words were too slurred for Ashton to understand. He finally decided on picking her up and carrying her out of the nightclub and into a taxi. James had driven them here anyway.

"Drive us to 560 Edwards Lane, now," Ashton said to the driver, turning his head away the minute he knew that the cabdriver's eyes had turned gray. When they pulled up in front of the house, Ashton turned to the driver and stared, as the brown color returned to the driver's eyes. Ashton didn't have any money.

"I'm going to get out of this car with my sister," Ashton said. "I'm not going to pay you for this ride. Drive away now."

The color left the cabbie's eyes again, and he put the key in the ignition the minute Ashton stepped out of the car, with Alana still in his arms. When the cab turned the corner, Ashton let out a sigh and carried Alana into the house.

Laying her down on her bed, Ashton left Alana in her room and walked toward his own. He was sick in the garbage pail before he fell onto his bed, regretting using his powers to his own advantage. He curled up into a ball and promptly passed out, praying that his uncle wouldn't make it home.

***

Ashton continued to dye his hair and Alana stopped drinking. Ashton continued to smoke, and Alana stopped using drugs. Uncle Damon continued to beat Ashton every time the kitchen wasn't clean, and Alana stopped trying to please the man altogether.

Maybe was never really an appropriate answer anyway.

4

September 15th rolled around, and it was just like any other day.

Damon went out to the bar at around ten o'clock in the morning, swearing that there'd be hell to pay if the house wasn't clean by the time he got back. Ashton waved him off with the flick of his hand, knowing that he wouldn't be back until at least one in the morning, when he would typically fall on the couch and drift off to sleep, mumbling about nothing.

In Ashton's experience, however, it was better to be safe than sorry when it came to his uncle. So he cleaned his room as much as he could and quietly removed some clothes from Alana's floor, being careful not to wake her up. She had worked hard at school through the first week and deserved the weekend to catch up on whatever sleep she could get.

The cleaning wasn't difficult and didn't require much manpower. He sprayed disinfectant on paper towels and washed away the grime stuck on the glass tables in the kitchen and basement. He used a dustpan to clean the dirt piled up under his uncle's bed and dressers and sprayed Febreze to rid the smell of whiskey and vomit from the air. To prevent getting sick himself, he didn't spend much time cleaning the room.

By 11:15 he was done, so he sat down on the couch and flipped through the channels aimlessly. A few minutes later, there were arms around his neck and a sloppy kiss being pressed to his cheek.

"Happy birthday, Ash," Alana fawned, while running a hand through his hair. "How does it feel to be 18?" She skipped into the kitchen and pulled out a bag half full of white powder.

"The same as it felt to be 17," Ashton replied in a monotone voice. "And 16, and 15. Honestly, it feels like I barely even age anymore. I guess I'm an 'official adult' or something now," he sighed.

Alana turned to him from the kitchen, frowning slightly. "Well," she started, "'official adult' or not, I'm still making you pancakes." The statement was blunt and matter-of-fact, and Ashton knew it would be pointless to try to coerce her out of cooking. He stayed seated on the couch and decided on watching Animal Planet after 10 minutes of channel surfing.

***

The pancakes were fantastic, and the siblings ate in calm silence until Alana picked her head up and stared Ashton right in the eye. "Doesn't it bother you that your siblings have never *once* picked up a phone or sent a card to wish you a 'Happy Birthday?'"

Ashton looked at her solemnly and said, "They're your siblings too."

Alana huffed out a laugh, looking back down at her dish. "Aren't siblings supposed to care about you? I'm sorry for the confusion, but the only sibling I'm sure I have, is you."

The fondness in Ashton's chest at his sister's words slowly faded as the words sunk in and he realized that Alana really felt that their older siblings had abandoned them. Ashton sighed and bit into his food once again, trying to ignore the dread in his stomach and putting on a fake smile. He was going to enjoy his birthday if it killed him.

***

A few hours later, Ashton and Alana were stretched across the couch in the living room, Ashton reading and Alana watching some documentary on the small television. A half an hour or so later, Alana excused herself to take a shower, so Ashton retreated to his room.

When there was a knock at the door a little while later, Alana was in her room changing and Ashton had returned to the couch with a bag of Funyuns. There was a prompt yell, sounding something like "Ash will you get the damn door?" A string of profanities followed, so naturally, he went to open the door.

The boy standing in the doorway was not much taller than him, standing a bit slouched and staring at the molding on the doorway. He jumped slightly as Ashton opened the door, almost falling into him. The boy gazed up at him with questioning brown eyes. Ashton stared at him for a few seconds before realizing who the boy was, the realization slapping him in the face.

His brother Chase had gotten older, his eyes had drooped lower, and the dark circles under his eyes were more prominent. But the mischievous smile still stood on his face as he smirked at the figures in the car that stood behind him. He looked at Ashton like he had two heads before taking a step back and coughing awkwardly.

"Um, Ash is . . . um . . . is Ashton home?"

"Yes, that would be me," Ashton said, scratching the back of his neck idly.

The boy laughed before shoving his hands into the pockets of his sweatshirt. "Nah, you can't be," he said with an astonished laugh. "My brother is this tiny little thing who doesn't talk. And I'm pretty sure he has blond hair."

It took a few seconds before Ashton realized he was joking and merely stared at him in disbelief. He let out a small breathy laugh as Chase pulled him into a hug, mumbling a 'Happy Birthday' into his shoulder. Ashton didn't hug back; he just stood there and accepted the hug, but didn't reciprocate. Chase realized this and pulled away quickly, coughing awkwardly and extending a hand behind him to motion at the silver car parked in front of the house. "Can we um . . . come in?"

***

    The Dwellers were worn out, obviously due to the long car trip to California. They all looked older somehow in Ashton's eyes, as if their parents' death had hit them all with a maturity stick, but he also hadn't seen them in years, so he couldn't really tell.
    Lucas looked the same apart from his eyes, which had dark circles under them as though he hadn't slept in weeks. He carried a small overnight bag over one of his shoulders and smiled at Ashton and Alana before setting the bag down on Damon's couch. Thomas's face held the same tiredness, but he seemed genuinely happy to have all of the Dweller children back together. Beth had her hair tied up in a sloppy bun, and she smiled so radiantly that Ashton had to fight himself to not smile back.
    The four eldest Dwellers stood awkwardly in a line after they had walked in and dropped their bags on the ground. Lucas was studying the small house in disgust, taking note of the mountain of empty beer bottles in the corner of the kitchen, awaiting disposal. The three others stared at their youngest brother, smiling, just as they had when he was young, mute, and trembling. Ashton felt his blood boil at the condescending looks and clenched his fists in anger.
    It had been *years* since the Dwellers had even sent a card to wish Ashton a "Happy Birthday," and his older siblings merely stared at him now in the same expectant manor as they had when he was 12. They were waiting for Alana to come booming down the stairs to read Ashton's expressions, translating what he was trying to express for them. If the black hair wasn't enough of an indi-

cation, Ashton was determined to show his older siblings how much he had *really* changed.

He turned his back to his siblings for a short moment, reaching over to the kitchen table to grab his pack of cigarettes. He reached into his pocket, pulled out his lighter, and lit a cigarette in front of his siblings, who stood like statues with their mouths hanging open. He took a drag of the cigarette before blowing out the smoke and yelling up the stairs, "Alana! We have guests."

Lucas stood still with his mouth hanging open, staring blatantly at the cigarette hanging from his brother's lips. Alana's footsteps could be heard running down the steps, and when she got to the bottom and looked into the living room, the color drained from her face. When her eyes landed on the cigarette that Ashton had in his mouth, she got even paler.

"What the hell are you doing here?" she asked her siblings—to no one in particular. "If you've driven over from Iowa to finally throw a 'Happy Birthday' in your brother's face, you can shove it up your ass."

Beth swallowed uneasily, and Thomas looked down at his feet, visibly embarrassed. Lucas opened his mouth to retaliate when Ashton decided that it was about time he stuck up for himself, instead of letting Alana verbalize his feelings.

"I don't want to hear your excuses, Lucas," Ashton said. It sounded weird coming from his own mouth, as he had never genuinely had a true conversation with his eldest brother. The true last words spoken between the two of them had been hurtful and angry, and Lucas had used Ashton's mutism as an insult. He sat down on the chair that sat in front of the large couch where his siblings were sitting, crossing his legs and glaring in their direction.

"Lucas, I'm giving you 30 seconds to explain why the hell you're here, and if you don't give me a good reason, I want you all out of this house." Ashton could feel his face heating up, and he could practically *hear* Alana smirking behind him as she placed a placating hand on his shoulder.

Lucas looked flustered and nervous, as he played with his hands and looked around at his siblings. When Alana smiled Cheshire cat-like and began to count down from 30, Lucas caved and blurted out, "I want to tell you all how our parents *really* died."

Alana's grin fell from her face, and Ashton suddenly felt like throwing up. The other Dwellers looked just as confused, judging by their facial expressions. Ashton could tell that whatever Lucas was about to confess would be news to his elder siblings as well.

"Lucas, what the hell are you talking about?" Thomas questioned, looking up at his brother, who was the only one still standing.

Lucas sat down on the arm of the couch and sighed, covering his face with his hands. "The night that Mom and Dad died, the police asked me to lie to all of you." He ran one hand over his mouth and continued shakily. "I didn't want to keep it from you, but the cops on the phone said that most of you were probably too young to handle the news. Mom and dad weren't actually hit by a drunk driver on Tanglewood that night."

Alana raised her eyebrows and looked down at Ashton questioningly. Ashton returned her confused stare and shrugged. He took another drag of his cigarette and tapped the end of it, watching the butt drop ashes onto the floor. "If they weren't hit by a drunk driver," Ashton said. "Then what happened to them?"

Lucas played nervously with his hands, making sure he didn't make eye contact with any of his siblings when he said, "The police said that it was a suicide."

Ashton dropped his lit cigarette on the floor.

"It was a *what?*" Beth said, jumping up from the couch to pick up the cigarette before it started a fire. She put it out in the ashtray on the table next to the couch before sitting down again. "Mom

The Dwellers

and Dad were hit by a drunk driver and crashed that night. That's all we know."

Lucas sighed again. "No," he said. "That's not all we know. When the police called, they told me the whole story. There was no other car that night that caused them to crash."

Ashton swallowed thickly. "Then why was the whole front of their car wrecked? If there wasn't a second driver, what caused the collision?"

Lucas stared at his brother sadly. "I was getting to that."

The Dwellers were all focused on Lucas, as he bit his lip and debated how to word his explanation.

"There's no proof that it *was* a suicide, guys," Lucas said uneasily after a few moments. "The police told me that with the evidence they had, it was *most likely* a suicide. But there were no notes left, no pills, no alcohol or drugs, no good-byes." He took a breath, trying to prevent himself from crying. "It doesn't make any sense."

Alana squeezed Ashton's shoulder, and he looked up at his sister and saw that she was teary eyed and confused. "What happened then?" she asked. "What's the real story?"

Lucas looked at her and tried to smile. Those were the first words she had spoken to him in years that weren't filled with hate. "There was a tree," he said. "That was all the evidence the police had. If you didn't know the story and just looked at the wreckage, you'd think that someone just collided with them head on. But the police officers at the scene said that the car had driven directly into a tree. It had destroyed the entire windshield. Dad died on impact, and Mom had lost too much blood by the time the cops had made it through the blizzard. It's the same story, except all signs point to suicide. The cops on the phone that night told me that it looked as though Mom and Dad crashed into the thing on purpose."

The siblings looked around, trying to read each other's expressions and to process the new information. Chase was the first one to speak.

"They weren't suicidal." His voice was so small and soft that Ashton could barely hear it. He had never heard Chase talk like that in his entire life.

"They obviously were if they drove headfirst into a damn tree," Alana snapped. Her voice was thick with tears but angry. Her hands were balled up into fists at her sides, and she looked as though the only thing she wanted to do was punch her eldest brother in the face.

"How could you keep this from us for so long?" she questioned, pointing a finger in Lucas' direction. "Or were you never going to tell us? How *old* do we have to be to find out how our parents really died? Don't you know that this changes *everything*?"

She moved out from behind Ashton to stand in front of him, throwing her hands up in defeat and staring Ashton in the eyes. "Suicide," she scoffed. "Our parents *killed themselves*, and Lucas waited until now to let us know! What a stand-up guy our Lucas always has been. The golden child of the damn family keeps the biggest secret that the Dwellers have ever known!"

Her voice was a scream by the time she was finished, her face beet red and distraught. Her facial expressions rapidly changed from pained to furious to pained again, and all Ashton wanted to do was wrap her up and protect her. She was 16 years old and way too young to be having a screaming match with their 28-year-old brother. Maybe "screaming match" wasn't the correct term for it though, considering that Lucas had barely made a sound since he had explained how Madeline and Nathan had died. Now the eldest Dweller just looked lost.

Ashton grabbed his sister's hand, running his thumb over her knuckles just like he did whenever she was scared as a kid. She looked down at their intertwined hands and sighed, the red color draining from her face. "Lucas, why are you really here?" she finally said, after regaining her composure. "I know you didn't take a 27-hour ride over here just to drop that bombshell."

Lucas smiled brightly for the first time since the eldest Dwellers had arrived. Reaching into his pocket, he pulled out an envelope and resituated himself on the arm of the couch. "We're here to give you this," Lucas said, handing the envelope to Ashton.

Alana stared at Ashton expectantly, begging him with her eyes to open the envelope. Ashton fiddled with the flap of the envelope, but kept it closed, keeping his gaze firm on Lucas.

"What is this?" he asked, waving the envelope above his head. "Is it another family secret that you're going to drop on me? Because I don't think I can take that."

Lucas shook his head slowly. "No, but it *is* another thing that I regret keeping from you. I should've told you years ago what you were entitled to, even though you couldn't claim it at the time."

Ashton tilted his head in confusion. "What the hell is that supposed to mean? What's in this envelope?"

Lucas stood up from where he was sitting on the arm of the couch to crouch down in front of the chair where Ashton was sitting. He placed a hand on his shoulder and smiled up at him. "Happy 18th birthday," he said.

Ashton shook his head. "I don't understand."

"Now that you're 18, you have complete access to what Mom and Dad left you in their will," Lucas explained. "What's in the envelope is the complete invoice of the money you receive now that you're legally an adult. You know that Mom and Dad were wealthy; dad was a state senator! They left me and Thomas and the others huge sums of money and small sentimental items, and that's why you'll see that your sum is a bit smaller than ours and Alana's when she turns 18."

Ashton was still confused. "Why though? I mean, I'm not

complaining. Mom and Dad could've left me nothing, and I wouldn't have cared. But what's so special about what I got?"

Thomas, Beth, and Chase smiled in his direction after he spoke the last few words, punching each other in the shoulders lightly and urging on Lucas. Lucas looked confused until Thomas whisper-screamed, "Give them to him!"

"Give me what?" Ashton said.

Lucas reached into his back pocket and pulled out a set of keys, placing them into Ashton's hand on top of the envelope. He smiled once and then stood up, returning to the arm of the couch.

"Are these the keys to a car?" Ashton asked. "I'm not that great of a driver, and I didn't even think that dad had any extra cars—"

"Ashton," Lucas cut him off. "Those are the keys to the house."

Ashton squeezed the keys in his hand so hard; he could have sworn one pierced his skin. "Keys to what house?" he squeaked. "The beach house in Florida?"

Lucas rolled his eyes, laughing a bit. "You know what house they're for," he smiled. "Mom knew how much you loved Iowa, and she knew that even when you graduated high school and college, you'd want to live there—maybe even raise a family there—so she and Dad left you the house to make sure you'd always have some place to come home to. That's what it said in the will anyway."

Ashton swallowed, trying to keep the tears in while he looked down at the keys in his hands. *So you'd always have some place to come home to.* His mother's voice rang in his head like a bell and he closed his eyes to keep the tears at bay, although they fell anyway. He felt Alana's arms around his neck, and he wiped his eyes and smiled. The envelope could wait until later. The money didn't matter in the slightest if he could finally get the chance to go home.

"The house has been uninhabited for a while," Lucas said. He took a look around the living room where they were sitting. "The whole house still looks the same, and I've been maintaining the interior. It's move-in ready."

Lucas took another look around the living room and gave his youngest siblings a hard look. "But listen to me, the two of you," he said.

Ashton and Alana turned their attention away from the keys in Ashton's hand and looked at their brother. "You need to get the hell out of this place," Lucas said, as Ashton drew shapes on his hand with the black house key. He looked up when Lucas mentioned leaving, and his eyes widened in understanding.

"That's why you gave me this," he said, quietly.

Lucas nodded and pointed to the keys and the envelope. "That's your one-way ticket out of skid row, kid," he said. "You're 18 now, and if you were in the foster care system, you would technically be allowed to run freely."

Ashton bit his lip. "Lucas, I'm not in the foster care system. And even if I were, I wouldn't leave Alana behind. I'd have to obtain legal custody of her. God damn it, there's gonna be a custody battle."

Lucas nodded solemnly. "Of course there's going to be a custody battle," he said. "But trust me, it's better that you're not in foster care. The foster care system can claim that they're better equipped and funded to keep Alana safe and healthy, as opposed to you, who has no job and looks like a smoking 'punk rebel.'"

Ashton huffed and debated whether to take another cigarette from the pack.

Lucas watched Ashton's movements with a judgmental eye but continued. "You can win this custody battle, easy as pie, as long as you can prove what I'm seeing right now."

Alana squinted at Lucas, trying to break down his thoughts.

"What exactly are you seeing right now," she asked, tracking the movement of his eyes.

"If you can prove that our uncle is an abusive alcoholic who needs psychiatric help, CPS will hand Alana over to you as quick as they possibly can," Lucas stated simply, shrugging in Ashton's direction.

"How do you know that?" Ashton snapped. "How can you tell he's an abusive alcoholic when most of this town can't tell?"

Lucas sighed. "I couldn't tell. Hell, I assumed most of the beer bottles in the kitchen were either yours or Alana's. You're both teenagers and Uncle Damon has always been a carefree guy. I had just assumed you had a party or something. Thomas told me after you went to call Alana down from upstairs, though. He's the psychologist."

Ashton stared at Thomas, waiting for some kind of response or explanation. His brother rolled his eyes and rolled up his sleeves, standing up from the couch to explain exactly why he hypothesized that Damon was an abusive alcoholic.

"The minute I saw Ashton's black eye, I knew Damon was abusive," he said, explaining himself to his siblings. "Ashton hates conflict, and although he's no longer selectively mute and he's trying desperately hard to prove to us that he's changed, he's still the last person to initiate or get caught in the middle of a fight. Also, it's not just the black eye but the three bruises under his arm that also indicate abuse."

Ashton rolled his eyes at his older brother's know-it-all attitude, which he had always had, and rubbed the bruises under his arm self-consciously. The bruises were old and didn't hurt much anymore. Plus, they were inflicted when he was too drunk and too high to even feel the punches. Despite Alana's wordless protests, Thomas continued.

"A year before Mom and Dad died, Damon went through a

divorce that practically none of us knew about, which is probably what first contributed to the drinking problem. He probably targeted Ashton first because of his mutism and then realized that he could let out his anger by using him as a punching bag, considering he was willing to stand in the line of fire to protect Alana, which is why—"

"Thomas, I think you can stop now," Lucas said, standing up as well and putting a hand on his brother's shoulder. Looking over at his youngest siblings, Thomas could see that Alana looked furious again and that Ashton had gone sickly pale. He sat down on the couch again, quietly apologizing, while Ashton fiddled with the keys again. Alana's heavy breathing slowly calmed down, as an awkward silence filled the living room.

Finally, Beth spoke again, with a teasing tone in her voice to lighten the mood. "Hey Thomas, if you know so much about all this, you should just testify."

All of the Dwellers turned to look at Beth and smiled. "That's genius," Lucas said. "Of course it'll be risky considering he's family, but he's a noted psychologist. If we can prove that Damon isn't fit to have custody of Ashton and Alana, they might consider giving Ashton custody, even as young as he is."

Thomas smiled at Ashton, hoping to ease the tension, and he apologized again for bringing up the abuse in detail. "Hypothetically, it should work," he said. "We just need to make sure Ashton looks nice and professional in court."

Ashton smirked, pulling his pack of cigarettes toward himself. "I guess I'll be throwing these out," he laughed uneasily. Smoking was the main way that Ashton was able to calm his nerves. When he felt himself craving something bad like alcohol or pot or *power*, smoking would calm the urge. Even though it definitely wasn't the best thing for him, and it was probably slowly deteriorating his lungs, it was something that could keep him stable and in control.

He wasn't sure how he was going to cope without it.

Before he could even think about smoking, however, he was hit with a scary realization. "Lucas," he said. "I don't think I can stay here for another day now that I have these keys in my possession. I want to go home now. I can't just stay here in California and wait two weeks for a custody trial."

Lucas and Thomas shared a knowing look and smiled. "We were kind of hoping you would say that," Lucas laughed. Thomas reached into the pocket of his hoodie and handed Alana an envelope this time. Alana, as opposed to her brother, ripped open the envelope the minute that it was in her hands, pulling out the two plane tickets and shoving them into Ashton's hands.

"What are these?" Ashton asked.

"They're plane tickets, you knucklehead," Chase teased. "Did you hit your head roof hopping or something, or did the pot fumes do something to that genius brain of yours?"

"CHASE!" the three eldest Dwellers scolded, while Ashton and Alana laughed until their stomachs hurt.

"The plane leaves in six hours for Iowa," Lucas said seriously, although he was smiling with his eyes. "You both need to write some crappy letter to Damon telling him where you've gone and what will be waiting for him in a week or so in Iowa. I'll be able to pull a few strings and arrange to have the custody case set in a Davenport courthouse because the two of you 'do not feel safe around your dangerous and abusive uncle.'"

Ashton and Alana looked at each other and laughed, Alana running into the kitchen to grab a notepad and a pen. Lucas, Thomas, Beth, and Chase heaved their small overnight bags over their shoulders and walked back toward the car. Beth and Chase climbed into the backseat. Thomas shoved the overnight bags near his feet on the passenger side and climbed in as well. Thomas returned to the house to help Ashton and Alana pack their bags, which were not very large, despite holding all of their possessions.

Lucas left once more to put the suitcases in the trunk of his car. When he returned to the house for the last time, Ashton was reading over the note he had written for Damon, and Alana was busy pouring a six-pack of beer down the kitchen sink. When Alana finished, she placed all the empty beer bottles back in the cardboard container and placed Ashton's letter on top of the case. They left the kitchen and walked back into the living room, where they saw Lucas.

"Everyone's waiting outside in the car," Lucas said. "Go hop in, although I think you may have to sit on Ashton's lap, Alana."

Alana laughed and followed Ashton outside, while Lucas walked into the kitchen to inspect the little present that his youngest siblings were leaving for their uncle. The letter atop the empty beer bottles read:

The next time you see me, we'll be in court, and you can't punch me there. And hopefully, the next time I see you after that, it'll be in Hell.

Also, I would advise you to learn how to clean your own room. I don't know if you were ever notified, but child labor laws exist, asshole.

-Ashton

P.S. Alana hopes you enjoy your beer. It's her own recipe called BudLight-Light. It's so light that it's not actually even beer anymore: it's just air.

Lucas laughed at the end of the letter, opening the fridge and realizing that there really was no beer left. Also, upon closer inspection, Alana had actually written an extra "light" on the empty Bud Light bottles in sharpie.

He left the kitchen for the last time, walked out the front door, and locked the door behind him. When he entered the car, sure enough, Alana was on Ashton's lap, and the two of them were laughing at themselves and the prank they had pulled on their uncle. The ride to the airport was filled with laughter and chatter, and the siblings shared stories and memories as though they had only been separated for a few weeks, as opposed to four years.

When Ashton and Alana boarded the plane, their older siblings insisted that they would be fine driving back to Iowa and that they would meet them at one of the Davenport courthouses in a few days time to discuss what the trial was going to entail.

When the plane took off, Ashton grabbed Alana's hand in the same way that he had four years ago. He listened to the roar of the engines as the machine flew high through the clouds. As much as he tried not to think about it, he worried about the trial for the entire flight and weighed the odds of winning legal custody of his sister.

When the plane landed, there was the predictable clapping and many groans from people who had finally returned home to Iowa after a vacation in Los Angeles or Santa Monica. But through the moans and groans of unhappy travelers, Ashton only heard the voice beside him—the voice of his little sister breaking out: "God, it's good to be home."

5

The black house looked almost identical to the way it was when he had left it. It still stood tall and almost menacing looking next to the small, light-painted Mitchell home. It still had the white shutters on the sides of each glass window, which made the house less dark, even though they were in need of repainting. The flowers that were placed in the white window boxes had been replaced long ago with fake ones that would not wilt under an unoccupied home. It felt familiar, like *home*.

Ashton all but ran through the door. He looked at his surroundings and realized that the interior had hardly changed at all from the way he had left it four years ago. The interior, like the exterior, had been well maintained by Lucas, as he had said. The mirrors weren't too covered in dust, and although the couches were covered in plastic, the home was almost exactly the same.

Ashton touched the walls lightly, and Alana trailed closely behind. He had a smile on his face as he dragged his bag behind him. He walked up the staircase with Alana, diverging from the hallway and into his childhood bedroom. The bed was just as he had left it on the night before he had been sent to live with his uncle. His high-marked report cards from eighth grade were still stuck to his mirror that extended from his desk; they had been placed there years ago by his mother. Old posters of obsolete bands and artists still hung on his periwinkle walls; he couldn't remember the names of any of the members in the groups.

On his desk, besides the report cards, sat two framed pictures: one of the Dwellers at Beth's graduation party and one of himself and Cayden at some summer barbeque. He picked them both up, examining the frames and photographs. The picture of his family was old and tattered around the edges, but the family members all looked so genuinely *happy* that Ashton almost cried.

Lucas had a huge smile on his face and crinkles by his eyes from laughing as the picture was being taken. Thomas smirked at the camera and made guns with his fingers. Beth, holding a diploma in her hand, stood between Madeline and Nathan in a purple graduation gown. The purple hat on her head dangled dangerously, but her father had a hand on her head to keep it from falling off. Madeline smiled fondly at her daughter, with an arm wrapped protectively around her shoulders. Chase pouted at the camera, trying to look sexy and mysterious and failing, causing Alana to look up from next to Ashton and laugh. Ashton wasn't looking at the camera, but at something to his right, and he was smiling nonetheless.

The picture of him and Cayden was different but similar; the two of them sat on the swing in the Mitchell's backyard. They had their arms wrapped around each other's shoulders as they smiled up at the camera. They couldn't have been more than nine years old at the time it was taken.

Ashton put the pictures back down, tears prickling at the backs of his eyes, as he thought about his parents and missed the past when everything was simpler. Who knew if Cayden even lived next door anymore? He certainly wasn't going to knock on the door and wait to see Sandra's bright smile, only to watch her eyes darken with recognition when she realized who was standing on her porch. God knows he had caused the family enough trauma.

There was a piece of him that wanted to knock on the door of the Mitchell home to feel Sandra's embrace and to hear Mason's soft voice. In Ashton's eyes, they had always been a second set of parents, and he knew for a fact that they would have adopted Ashton and Alana if they had been allowed to. Ashton wanted to be tackled by Alex and Noah again, like when they were kids, not caring that they were most likely just as tall as he was by now.

But more than anything, Ashton wanted to knock on the door to the house next door and see it open to reveal his best friend.

***

The courtroom was hot and sticky, and Ashton was all but sweating to death in his oversized suit. He knew it was only a matter of time until he had to go up and testify, and a small slip-up could result in Alana being sent back to California. And this time, she wouldn't have anyone to step in front of her to block the punches.

Damon sat at the table next to the Dwellers with his lawyer, nervously tapping on the wood and looking like he would rather be anywhere else. Damon's lawyer looked nervous as well. Thomas had blown the court away when he was called to the stand, shining a light on Damon's alcohol problem and anger management issues. On top of that, Lucas had asked one of Damon's neighbors in California to testify, and the old woman rambled on for 15 minutes about the yells that she sometimes heard coming from Damon's home, as well as seeing Ashton bleeding on more than one occasion.

Next to Ashton sat all of the Dweller children and their lawyer, a soft spoken, but passionate African American woman named Kayla, who had grilled Damon to death when he was on the stand. She had been a friend of Beth's in college and had jumped at the opportunity to help Ashton get custody of his sister. So far, she had been exceeding all of their expectations, and although Ashton was hot and stifled, he felt better and better about the trial as time went on.

"I would like to call Ashton Dweller to the stand," Kayla said finally, giving Ashton a reassuring smile as he walked up to the podium. Kayla held her folder close to her chest as she approached the podium, while Ashton sat down and tried to get comfortable.

"Mr. Dweller, would you say that your uncle has an alcohol problem?"

Ashton looked Kayla in the eyes so that she knew he was being legitimate. "Yes, definitely."

"And would you say that he has a different demeanor or acts differently while he is under the influence of alcohol?"

"You mean 'does it make him angry and delirious and ready to punch the closest person'?" Ashton looked at Lucas, who was making a cutthroat motion, and Thomas was shaking his head and mouthing "too sassy."

"Yes, he acts differently while under the influence."

Kayla nodded and uttered a noticeable *tsk*. She walked up to the podium and stood close to Ashton while pointing at his eye. "Was that bruise inflicted on you by your Uncle Damon?"

Ashton took a breath and nodded. "Like I said before, he acts differently under the influence. He was intoxicated, and my sister had come home five minutes past her curfew. He tried to go after her, but I wouldn't let him hit her. So, he took his anger out on me instead and gave me this black eye. I also have fading bruises on my body from different instances of abuse." Ashton clenched his fists, trying to calm his heartbeat. The abuse wasn't something he was very keen to talk about in a room full of complete strangers and a judge who didn't know him in the slightest. Plus, the "mature" vocabulary that Thomas wanted him to use in court was making him antsy.

"Do you have any evidence of these other instances of abuse?" the judge asked.

Ashton sighed and, with a serious expression, looked up at the judge. "Yes I do. Would you like to see the bruises, your honor?"

When the judge nodded, Ashton slipped out of his suit jacket and undid his tie. He popped the first four buttons of his white dress shirt and pulled the right side of the collar over his shoulder to expose his lightly purpled collarbone.

"The bruises are from weeks ago, so they're fading," Ashton explained. "But they're still there, and my uncle is the one who put them there." After pulling his shirt back into place and buttoning his shirt back up, he looked up to see the judge studying him closely. He squirmed under the intense gaze but let the judge analyze him for a few seconds. Finally, he stopped staring and turned to Kayla.

"Any further questions?" he asked.

Kayla turned to Ashton once more and smiled at him, looking down at her files one last time. "Ashton, why do you think you are the better candidate for custody of your sister? Why do you think that it is in her best interest to have you as her legal guardian?"

Ashton wrung his hands together. He knew this question was coming. He cleared his throat and scratched at his thigh to keep from biting his nails. "Alana would be safest with me," he started. "As I've already stated, my uncle was abusive toward both me and my sister, and I believe that he will continue to be abusive toward her if Damon is given custody of her again. In my parent's will, I was given the family home as well as a large sum of money. While I'm looking for a job, I will be able to provide for my younger sister until I can find one. Also, as Alana stated in her testimony, she would rather live with me than with our uncle, as we have always been close growing up, and she feels safest with me."

When Ashton finished, he let out a deep breath and relaxed his hands, laying them flat on his thighs. When Kayla rested her case, Ashton left the stand with a breath of relief and headed back toward the table where Alana was sitting and smiling up at him. She took his hand under the table and didn't let go until Ashton was officially Alana's legal guardian.

The end of the case was celebrated with a dinner date at one of their old favorite restaurants; Ashton ordered the same thing he had when he was 13. He smirked at Lucas as he slowly dipped his fries into the puddle of mayonnaise on his plate.

"Ashton Dweller, you disgust me," Lucas said, looking away from his brother and making a gagging noise.

Ashton smiled around the French fry and dipped another. It felt oddly normal—all of them being together for a family meal. It was almost like nothing had changed, and they were all still together again. Ashton half expected his father to come running to the table, apologizing about a senate meeting that had run late. He swallowed around the lump forming in his throat and smiled in Alana's direction, although she was too caught up in her nachos to pay any attention to her brother.

It wasn't going to be easy now, considering he had to keep his promise to the judge about finding a steady job once he was out of school. But he and Alana had made it through much worse, and Ashton was sure that spending his senior year in Davenport would be a million times better than spending it in Lawndale with James breathing down his neck.

***

Ashton had never taken a woodshop class in his life.

The minute the bell rang, the machines whirred to life as the students got to work, quickly cutting materials, not sparing the new kid a second glance.

The teacher, a small Hispanic woman with a tattoo hidden under her sleeve, pulled Ashton to the side and smiled. Before she could say anything, Ashton sheepishly smiled and blurted out, "I've never cut a piece of wood before."

The woman smiled wider, and Ashton blushed when she handed him a pile of papers and clapped him on the shoulder.

"I'm not going to throw you under the blade without preparation, hun," she laughed. Her accent wasn't heavy, but it was there, faintly. "These are a few safety exams," she said, referring to the papers. "You can start working on them now and finish them at home if you'd like."

Ashton graciously accepted the papers, nodded, and then headed over to a wooden table at the corner of the classroom.

He worked there for over half the period, defining the uses and precautions that went along with each of the tools in the classroom. He doodled a saw blade in the corner of his paper when he had finished. His peers, many attacking their wooden boxes furiously with sandpaper, looked at him occasionally. They squinted as though they recognized his face but didn't know where they had seen him before. Ashton recognized many of them from middle school, but he had changed considerably since then; he didn't blame them for being apprehensive about the "new kid."

When woodshop was over, he handed his completed exams back to the teacher and slung his backpack over his shoulder, bracing himself for the hell he'd have to endure in his first math class since coming back to Davenport.

***

Mr. Ostello paced up and down the aisles, eyeing everyone's papers and occasionally stopping to analyze Ashton's work.

The pressure and contemplating looks made Ashton uncomfortable, but he continued working on his final problem under Mr. O's watchful eye. When the bell rang, Ashton hopped from his seat. The day had gone on for too long, in his opinion, and he was ready to get home and go to sleep. Knowing Alana, she had already made a group of friends and had plans made for the evening.

He handed his test to Mr. Ostello, but as he was about to

leave, the small man grabbed his wrist.

"Ashton, do you mind staying after class for a second?"

Ashton nodded dumbly, making his way back over to his seat. What could he *possibly* have done in one day? He fiddled around with his thumbs anxiously and waited for the stampede of seniors to leave the classroom before he let his mind wander. He could always use *it*. He could make Mr. Ostello let him leave the room and go home—and while he was at it, he could make him draw a big fat 'A' on the top of Ashton's exam.

What was he *doing*? *This reckless use of power was going to wind up getting someone killed one day*, he thought. Memories of his childhood flooded back into his brain like waves on the shore. The fear of hurting someone he cared about had crawled back into his throat after it had lain dormant for years. The drugs and the alcohol and *James* had caused him to forget about this fear; he had bottled it up, popped another pill, and not cared in the slightest about who he might accidentally control in the next few hours while he was high off his rocker. *But not today—not now.* He was different, and he had changed. He was determined to stay clean no matter what it took—sober from the alcohol, clean from the drugs, and pure from his *curse*.

Mr. Ostello approached his desk after the last of the other pupils had left the room. The man looked nervous and hesitant to speak. Ashton looked up expectantly, trying to keep his nerves under control. "I was wondering if you would be able to do me a favor," the man finally said after a few short moments.

"What kind of favor?" Ashton asked.

Mr. O sighed. "Math is arguably the hardest subject a student has to take through their years of schooling, and a considerable percentage of your grade is currently failing this course. If a student completely flunks this class at the end of the year, they don't graduate."

The Dwellers

Ashton swallowed nervously. There was no way he was failing. The past few years in California had not exactly been easy on his average, but after he had cleaned himself up, he had compensated for the points he had lost taking tests while hungover. The practice exams he had taken before coming back to school had been easy in his opinion, and if he really hadn't done well on them, were they really not going to let him graduate?

"Mr. Ostello, I promise I'll clean up my act or do extra credit or—"

Mr. O cut him off with the wave of his hand and a quizzical look. "You think *you're* failing?" he asked.

"Why would I be here if I wasn't failing?" Ashton said hesitantly while Mr. O laughed.

"Ashton, you have a 100% average in this class. As I said before, a considerable percentage of your grade is failing this course, so we have a tutoring program twice a week after school for an hour. The AP level seniors who are excelling in this class are tutoring the ones who are struggling. However, I'm amazed you're not in the advanced placement class, and I was going to ask you to tutor one of my students."

Ashton stared up at his teacher, knowing his mouth was hanging open. However, he couldn't bring himself to close it. "I have a 100 average?" he asked.

Mr. Ostello laughed again. "Yes, you do. You aced every test I gave this marking period, even though you took them at home without any previous instruction in this class, and I sincerely doubt you didn't do well on the test I gave last period. I was looking through your records from when you went to school in California. You used to live here—didn't you?"

"Yes sir," Ashton said, trying to smile. "I went to middle school here, and when my parents passed away, I went to live with my uncle in Lawndale. I'm back now, though, for good."

Mr. Ostello nodded in understanding, and Ashton could almost *feel* his teacher's eyes analyzing the shiner he had covering his left eye. "You know, every teenager has that one year in high school where everything goes downhill. You're a smart kid, and I know last year must've been tough for you if your grades are any indication. But I think you've got a knack for math, and the program *really* needs you. We don't have an equal ratio anymore. One of our tutors moved to Ohio last week, and now we have one failing student without a tutor. Plus, K is my *worst* student. He won't listen to a damn thing I say."

Ashton nodded slowly. "'K' is his name?"

Mr. Ostello nodded. "That's what I call him, at least."

Ashton nodded again. "Mr. O, if you need my help, I'm willing to do it. Is there a meeting today? Is that why you're asking me?"

Mr. Ostello nodded again. "If you can stay after today for just a little while, it would be incredibly helpful." He looked toward the clock, which read 3:10. "They're going to be here soon, and if you wouldn't mind staying for a half hour or so, I would be extremely grateful."

Ashton smiled genuinely at his teacher, the relief washing over him in waves. "Yeah, of course I can stay," he said. "I just have to text my little sister and ask her to find a ride home."

Mr. O smiled, nodded, and turned toward the blackboard to erase the weekend's homework and to prepare for the tutoring session. Alana replied to Ashton's text in less than a minute, assuring him that she was going to hang out with some of her old friends after school and catch up. Ashton put his phone back into his pocket and walked over to Mr. O's desk. When the students arrived, Ashton stayed by the desk, trying to see if he could pinpoint who "K" was.

The AP level seniors lined up against the backboard, most of them standing in front of each other because the room wasn't wide enough for them all to line up straightly. The failing seniors filled all the desks in the room, some standing against the radiators when the last seats filled up. Ashton was shoved up next to Mr. Ostello's desk, where the petite man was trying to quiet down the class of rowdy teenagers. As soon as the students were quiet, Mr. Ostello began matching up the standing students with the sitting ones, reading their names off of a sheet in his hand and pointing to different corners of the room where they would be working for the next hour. Soon, there were no longer any students sitting, and Ashton was the only one left standing next to Mr. O.

"K always comes late for these meetings," Mr. Ostello sighed, attaching two exams together with a paper clip. "I told him at summer school that he was going to have to fix his tardiness problem if he wanted to graduate."

It didn't seem as if Mr. Ostello was talking to Ashton directly, but he processed the information anyway. He wondered if this infamous "K" was as bad as Mr. O was making him out to be.

The door swung open a second later, and a few of the students who were dispersed around the room began to snicker at the boy in the doorway.

"How nice of you to join us, K," Mr. Ostello sneered, with no fondness in his voice whatsoever. Then the boy in the doorway spoke, and Ashton all but broke his neck whipping his head around.

"You know I'd never miss a meeting of yours, Mr. O."

The boy's voice had barely changed at all since the last time Ashton had heard it. Standing in the doorway was Cayden Mitchell, taller and leaner than Ashton had ever seen him. His eyes still held the mischievous glint they always had, looking much greener than brown in the bright light of the math classroom. He sauntered toward Ashton and Mr. Ostello in the middle of the classroom, the same familiar swing in his step that had always been there.

Ashton looked from Cayden's face to Mr. Ostello's glare at his former best friend and wanted to slap a hand to his own forehead. "K" had never been a letter—"Cay" was short for *Cayden*. Mr. O kept his glare firm before turning to Ashton with the semblance of a smile on his face.

"This is Cayden Mitchell," Mr. Ostello said, gesturing his hand from Cayden to Ashton in introduction. He then turned to Cayden, crowding up in his personal space. Mr. O whispered, "No funny business—you hear me? This kid is nice enough to volunteer to be your saving grace so that you can graduate. Don't give him any trouble and pay attention to him, or else you can kiss your cap and gown good-bye."

Ashton swallowed nervously. How badly was Cayden doing? He had always known that his best friend never took a liking to school. He rarely studied and had never been the kid that got good marks on his exams, but he had never *failed*. Or maybe he had; Ashton hadn't seen him in four years.

Cayden didn't have the smirk on his face anymore when Mr. Ostello turned away from him and placed a hand on each boy's shoulder. Mr. O didn't even bother trying to smile when he said, "Cayden this is your tutor," gesturing his hands in Ashton's direction now.

Ashton glanced up through his lashes, expecting to see Cayden's mouth drop open in surprise or to see his eyes widen in recognition. But Cayden simply smiled and waved at Ashton before focusing on Mr. O again.

He doesn't recognize me. Ashton's stomach churned unpleasantly with the newfound realization, and he wondered whether this was a good thing or a bad thing. If Cayden didn't recognize him, Ashton could come up with some fake name for himself and save Cayden the burden of being stuck with him again. But as badly as he wanted to protect Cayden, his selfish side ached to have his best friend back.

Lost in his thoughts, it didn't register with Ashton that Mr. Ostello had finished their conversation and was sending Ashton and Cayden off to a location to start the tutoring session.

"Hey, you okay there buddy?" Cayden asked, placing a hand on Ashton's shoulder and breaking him out of his reverie. Ashton looked him in the eyes and nodded slowly.

"Yes, I'm fine."

"Mr. O wants us to go out and work in the hallway because there are 'too many distractions in the crowded classroom.'" Cayden put air quotes around Mr. Ostello's directions and imitated his low, gravelly voice, making Ashton laugh.

Ashton followed Cayden out into the hallway where they sat against the wall with their books, Ashton opening the textbook to the chapter they were currently on. He looked up at Cayden, who was flipping through his disorganized notes, trying to find the most recent ones. Suddenly, he looked up at Ashton and laughed comically.

"Shit, man I never even got your name! Mr. O was too busy grilling me on why I'm gonna fail. I'm Cayden, again, but who're you?" He extended a hand in Ashton's direction, and Ashton had to bite his tongue to stop himself from spewing out a fake name like 'Jerry' or something. The internal battle inside him kept raging on: protect Cayden from himself, or get his best friend back.

"I'm Ashton," he said, sincerely, gripping Cayden's hand tightly and shaking. "Ashton Dweller."

Cayden kept their hands clasped together, as his mouth fell open in shock before twisting into a smile. "No way in hell you're Ashton Dweller."

Ashton felt like he was floating. "You need me to prove it?" he teased.

"You look—" Cayden started. "You have the same eyes, but . . . the black hair and . . . the black eye . . ." His voice trailed off, and he finally pulled his hand out of the handshake.

"It's really me, Cayden," Ashton said. "I know I look different, and I'm talking without hesitation, but being away from home—it changed me. I'm not exactly mute anymore, and I rebelled a bit. And I'm sorry, okay. I know I promised you at the airport that we would stay in touch, but the minute I landed in California my uncle took my phone and most of the stuff in my bags and my life just-"

Ashton didn't get to finish his sentence before Cayden was jumping into his arms and hugging him to death, just like old times. Even though they had both grown considerably since they were 14, Cayden was still a bit shorter than Ashton, and he still hugged like a straightjacket. Ashton smiled into Cayden's shoulder and reciprocated the hug, fisting the back of Cayden's t-shirt. He smelled the same and felt the same, and Ashton was so relieved that he wanted to cry. They stayed in the embrace until Mr. Ostello came outside to ask what the *hell* they were doing.

After explaining the situation to a very disgruntled Mr. O, the teacher nodded in understanding and dismissed both the boys to go home and "catch up."

"I really hope I didn't make the wrong decision here," he said threateningly, as Ashton and Cayden rounded up their books from the floor.

"You didn't, Mr. O," Ashton said. "We'll get to work right after we catch up. Cayden *will* pass your class—I promise."

Cayden smiled at Ashton and turned the smile onto Mr. Ostello, who rolled his eyes and retreated back into the classroom. Ashton pulled his backpack over his shoulder and grabbed his phone from out of his pocket to send a text to Alana to see if she was still in the school and needed a ride home. She replied by saying that she was at a friend's house, and Ashton pocketed his phone again without a second thought. He and Cayden started toward the exit, and Ashton could feel Cayden's eyes on him.

"Do I really look all that different?" Ashton asked, locking eyes with Cayden, who quickly dropped his gaze and shoved his hands into his jean pockets, embarrassed.

"It's the black hair, man," Cayden said with a breathy laugh. "I mean it looks really . . . good, but it doesn't feel like you."

Ashton laughed, running a hand through his hair. "Yeah, you're right. It isn't me. I was kinda pressured into dying it, and then I never had the desire or the money to dye it back."

He pressed a button on his keys, unlocking the car that Lucas had given him when he got back to Davenport. He climbed into the driver's seat and waited expectantly for Cayden to open the passenger door. After Cayden slid into the seat, they sat for a moment in awkward silence before exploding into fits of laughter.

"Man, I'm not going to be able to do this if it's all awkward," Ashton laughed. "I know—I talk now, but I'm still the same person I used to be."

Cayden smiled and nodded as Ashton pushed the key into the ignition and turned it. "We've definitely got a lot to catch up on," he stated.

"Yeah," Ashton smiled. "We do."

6

Most people would assume that two friends being away from each other for four years would put a damper on the friendship, creating awkward silences and terse conversations. But Ashton and Cayden jumped back to being as close as they always were, almost like they had never been separated at all. Alex and Alana reconnected as well and planned on spending more time together than they had before Madeline and Nathan had died.

Cayden was more than surprised when Ashton took a pack of cigarettes out of his pocket after they pulled up in front of Cayden's house. He lit one quickly and took a puff, letting it hang between his lips as he put the car into park. Sensing Cayden's discomfort after a few seconds, Ashton pulled it out of his mouth and looked at his friend sympathetically.

"Sorry Cayden, does this bother you? I'll put it out if it does."

Cayden shook his head. "No, no, I'm fine. My dad took up smoking the year after your parents passed, so I'm used to it. I just didn't expect you to be a smoker."

Ashton scoffed. "It's a dirty, dirty habit, man. Don't ever start."

"How did you start?" Cayden asked almost hesitantly.

"I had a boyfriend in California who was a bad influence—not just on me but on Alana too," Ashton replied. "Smoking, drugs, drinking, the lot—he wasn't exactly the best guy." Ashton paused for a second to take another drag. "But hey, who am I to talk? We all have our demons."

Cayden wasn't sure what he wanted to address first. The drugs? The drinking? The demons? The fact that Ashton had had a *boyfriend* while he was in California?

The fact that this significant other also happened to be male didn't faze Cayden in the slightest. Cayden didn't consider *himself* to be exactly 100% straight, in reality. The fact that Ashton had been in a relationship at all was what had baffled him.

It wasn't as if Ashton was unattractive, or mean, or someone who wouldn't be a good partner. But he was timid, soft-spoken, and had so many issues; a psychologist would have a field day if they could get the chance to write a book about him. Relationships were never something he had pictured Ashton to be interested in, but times had changed.

Ashton sensed the questions running through Cayden's brain and looked at him hesitantly. "Are you still thinking about the cigarettes?" he asked, nervously. Cayden could feel his fearful gaze, and for a second, he looked like the old Ashton. Then it hit Cayden exactly why Ashton was nervous about his last confession, and he had to fight the urge not to laugh.

"No, I'm not thinking about the cigarettes anymore, actually," Cayden started. "I'm actually trying to figure out how to rate this ex-boyfriend of yours on my douche bag scale."

Ashton let out a sigh of relief and opened the car door, dropping the cigarette onto the street and stomping on it. Cayden followed him out and reached into his pocket for his house key. He unlocked the front door, and with Ashton in his wake, he yelled up the stairs: "Mom! We have a visitor!"

***

The stories flew out of Cayden and Ashton's mouths almost uncontrollably, as they laughed for hours as they sat in Cayden's bedroom. They kept telling tales, one after another, sometimes interrupting each other to ask pointless questions.

"You're *kidding*," Cayden laughed loudly, rolling on to his stomach on the bed.

"I promise I'm not," Ashton chuckled, leaning back against Cayden's dresser and extending his legs.

Cayden squinted his eyes in disbelief and scoffed: "Although I would *love* to know how Alana made it over the cliff without dying . . ." His voice trailed off as he rested his head on one of his hands. He pointed under his own eye and then gestured to Ashton's shiner and continued, "I would rather hear about how you got that."

Ashton got quiet very quickly, and Cayden took note of it, debating whether he should try to push the issue. He sat up on the bed and sat on the edge, facing the dresser that Ashton was leaning up against. Ashton stared at the ceiling and then slid over from the dresser to the bed. He sat in front of Cayden's knees, and with one swift tap, hit him right under the kneecap of his left leg.

Cayden's leg swung upwards pathetically, and he looked down at Ashton in confusion until his memory proved itself to be stronger than he had imagined. When they were young, during annual doctor's visits, Ashton's reflexes had never been very prominent or extreme, while Cayden's were more sensitive than most. Ashton would get a kick out of hitting Cayden slightly under his knee once in a while and watching his leg soar upwards, since Ashton's own leg didn't react as much.

Cayden smiled down at Ashton fondly, watching as his friend tried to recreate their memories as kids, but his smile faltered a bit when he realized that this was only Ashton stalling, so he could avoid talking about the black eye.

"I can kick my leg at you all you want, Ash," Cayden said, hesitantly. "But I want you to tell me about how you got the black eye first."

Ashton laughed bitterly, knowing that his plan of stalling wasn't going to work. "Well, you know my uncle who I went to live with in California?" Cayden nodded.

"Yeah, well he was an alcoholic. Even worse, he was an alcoholic with a temper, and I'm a stubborn little shit," he said with a cocky grin, trying to mask any other emotions and draw attention away from his face, which he knew was rapidly paling. Cayden's face fell, and the smile on his face turned from sadness to astonishment to anger.

"You just let him beat the crap out of you?"

"Well what did you expect? I couldn't sit there and watch him take it out on my kid sister."

Cayden recoiled at that. Ashton hadn't snapped at him—his voice was still calm and collected, but the words made something sour pile in Cayden's gut. "He went after Alana?"

Ashton tapped his fingers aimlessly on his knees and nodded. "Yeah, of course—it wasn't like she was scared or anything. She actually used to snap at me for taking the punches because she wanted an excuse to bash his head in. It was quite a life. It's part of the reason why I took up smoking. It calms the nerves."

He was definitely done talking. He snickered and picked up the last brownie from the plate on the floor, making exaggerated moans about the taste.

Cayden forced out a laugh, as Ashton's demeanor made him uneasy. Ashton was always someone who was sensitive and quiet, who disliked conflict and situations where voices got too loud. Brushing off abuse was something Cayden definitely wasn't expecting from his friend. But neither was the black hair, frequent swearing, smoking, or loud voice.

As Ashton called down the hall to beg Sandra to bring him another brownie, Cayden wondered if he even *really* knew Ashton at all, or if his best friend's personality was all a facade.

***

On Monday morning, Ashton walked into school happier than

he had been in a long time. He had spent the whole weekend with Cayden, Alex, and Noah, catching up on what he had missed while he was away in California. The minute that Alex had laid eyes on him, she had jumped into his arms and tried to squeeze him to death.

After seeing Ashton, her instant reaction was to ask whether Alana was back as well, and when Ashton answered positively, Alex all but ran out the door. Ashton felt that being with the Mitchells was akin to having his own family back together again. Sandra and Mason were the closest things to parents that Ashton had, and they were so happy to have him back that they threw a *party*.

It felt good to be reunited with the only people he had ever really seen as his family. Alana and Alex spent most of the party on the old swing set in the Mitchell's backyard, rocking absentmindedly and talking. Ashton tried to catch up with as many people as he could, but by the end of the night, he was getting a headache. Cayden could see Ashton's dilemma and pulled him up into the dilapidated tree house they had played in as kids.

"Are you sure this thing is going to be able to hold our weight?" Ashton said, hesitantly sitting down.

"Of course," Cayden laughed, despite the protesting creaks coming from the tree branch.

"This is so surreal," Ashton said, trying to get comfortable on a piece of wood that was sticking out of the bottom of the tree house. "It feels like it was just yesterday when we were sitting in here discussing high school, but it also feels like forever ago."

Cayden laughed again and slung an arm around Ashton's shoulders. "It *was* forever ago," he said, trying to situate himself as well. "I'm surprised we can both still fit in here together."

Ashton's eyes widened. "You just said that this thing could hold our weight."

"Yeah," Cayden said. "Probably."

Ashton glared and prayed that his father's old wood-chopping techniques would hold strong as he extended his legs onto a long wooden plank that might have been a bookshelf when they were kids.

"So what have I missed?" Ashton asked, placing his chin on his hands and smiling. "Did Iowa stop growing corn or has everything stayed somewhat the same?"

Cayden threw his head backwards and laughed. "Nah, we're still the corn capital," he sighed. "To be honest, not a lot has changed since you moved away. I imagine your California life was much more eventful than what happened here while you were gone."

They spent the night in the old tree house, reminiscing a bit more before promptly falling asleep on top of each other, just like old times. However, September in Iowa was not exactly warm, and they woke up an hour later shivering and laughing.

It felt like they were kids again, and even though Ashton was technically an adult now and the legal guardian of a minor, the first weekend back in Iowa felt more like childhood than his past four years in California had.

The first few weeks back at school weren't as difficult as Ashton had thought they would be. He wasn't exactly included by his peers, but he wasn't excluded either. His grades stayed on the higher side, and he was beginning to atone for the low GPA he had accumulated in California. He and Cayden were practically inseparable again, despite the fact that they only had one physics class together. For the first time since his parents had died, Ashton was enamored with learning.

The first quarter of the school year flew by, and Ashton couldn't remember ever being happier. Alana had made heaps of new friends, and people were drawn to her like moths to a light, just like they always had been. She spent a lot of time out of the house and with her friends, but after tagging along with her to one of her parties, Ashton realized that she would turn down every drink she was offered. Ashton had to excuse himself to try and compose himself in the bathroom after that one.

Ashton and Cayden spent most days after school together. Though a lot of the time was spent studying and trying to improve Cayden's average in Mr. O's class, they spent a considerable amount of time coming up with games, as they had done when they were younger.

Life was good, *really* good. Until Cayden missed a week of school.

***

Ashton walked from English class to the attendance office, deciding to skip woodshop. He walked into the office, put his hands on the desk, and smiled at one of the secretaries.

The secretary in front of Ashton, Ms. Patterson, looked up from her computer, and returned Ashton's smile. "You're the Dweller boy, yeah?"

Ashton nodded as the woman continued to speak. "How do you like the school so far? You and your sister doing okay?"

"Yeah, yeah we're fine. That's, uh, not the reason I'm here though."

"Well, what can I do for you, sweetie."

Ashton scratched the back of his neck absentmindedly. "Um, it's my friend. Cayden—Cayden Mitchell. He hasn't been in school all week, and I was wondering if he got called in or something."

Ms. Patterson gave him a once over and leaned closer. "I'm not supposed to give that kind of information to other students-"

Ashton's face fell, but he nodded to indicate his understanding and turned to walk away when Ms. Patterson grabbed his arm and spun him around.

"But, I'll check the records for you."

Ashton grinned and murmured a "thank you," as the secretary went through the school's recent records of absentees and tardiness. She scrolled down to "M" and clicked her tongue. She reached around the computer to the printer and pulled out the papers. She slid them across the desk to Ashton, pulled out a highlighter, and motioned him to pay attention.

"Your friend Mitchell has been out all week." She dabbed the highlighter over the check that was next to his name. "His siblings, Alexandra and Noah, have been present all week. The thing is, Cayden had not called in sick any of the days, which means that the absences were unexcused. After 10 unexcused absences, we're required to call Child Protective Services and investigate, but Cayden's only had eight so far this year. On top of that, Cayden is 18 now, and seniors have a pretty flexible schedule and can sign themselves out whenever they want. The most I can do for you right now is to fill out a Missing Persons Report," Ms. Patterson said.

The secretary slid the papers together and handed them over to Ashton, her eyebrows still raised. Ashton sighed, shaking his head. "That isn't necessary, Ms. Patterson. Thank you, though." He took the papers from her hands, smiled at her, and walked out of the Attendance Office.

The rest of the day's schedule was pretty empty, and Ashton didn't feel like showing up to woodshop 20 minutes late, as he would probably come up with a non-believable excuse. He pushed his way out the main exit and walked toward the parking lot. He pulled out his phone and quickly typed out a text to Alana, telling her that he was leaving early and that she was going to have to find a way home.

Cayden missed school frequently—that was true—but he was never dumb enough to leave a trail. He would sign himself in, attend the required amount of classes to be considered "present" for the day, and then cut the rest of them. He didn't get sick often, and even if he were, Mason would have called him in at least once so far.

Back in the day, Ashton could simply walk up to the Mitchell's door and knock and ask for Cayden or Alex. But after everything that had happened and everything that Sandra had done for him and Alana since they returned from California, Ashton didn't want to be a burden to them.

However, with Cayden possibly missing, he had a perfect excuse to knock on the Mitchell's door.

After only the second knock, the door opened to reveal Alex, who looked scared and flustered and incredibly relieved to see Ashton.

"Thank God you're here," she said, pulling on Ashton's arm to tug him into the house. "I don't know when they'll be back, and Noah is *freaking* out."

Ashton grabbed Alex's hands, trying to calm her down. "Stop pacing," he said. "Alex, I need you to explain to me what's going on because I have no idea. All I know is that Cayden hasn't been in school all week."

Alex sighed and shook her head. "My mom's missing."

Ashton stared at her in amazement. "Missing? What are you talking about?"

"After you left on Sunday, she went out to get *groceries* of all things and never came back. She's been gone for almost a whole week, and my dad and Cayden have gone crazy trying to look for her. Cayden's missed school all week; he's just been out searching and driving up and down the streets trying to find her. My dad filed a missing person's report but there's nothing. Her car's gone too." She played with her hands nervously. "My dad should be back in a little while because I've been home alone with Noah for a while now, but Cayden's been out all day, and I have no idea where he is."

Ashton ran a hand over his face, as he sighed and nervously chewed on his thumbnail. "I'll wait here with you and Noah until your dad comes home, and then I'll go out to find Cayden."

Alex rolled her eyes. "No," she said. "Go out looking for Cayden now, just in case he gets himself into trouble. My dad borrowed your older brother's car, and I've been watching Noah all week. We'll be fine. Just go find my brother."

Ashton huffed, knowing she was right. He placed a hand on her shoulder and squeezed reassuringly before leaving out the front door and walking to his car. He opened the door, climbed in, started the engine, and turned the car around to head in the direction of the grocery store.

***

It didn't take long to find Cayden. The boy was pulled over on the side of Rosen Street, which was directly across the street from the Whole Foods grocery store. He was pacing back and forth across the pavement. Ashton pulled his car over a few feet behind him and hopped out.

"Ah!" Cayden yelled, putting his hands up in self-defense, when he turned around to find Ashton in front of him.

"Hey, it's just me," Ashton said, grabbing Cayden's arm before he could actually hit him. "Why are you out here pacing?"

"My mom is missing," Cayden said, frantic. "She's been gone for a week, and I haven't been in school because I've been out looking for her every day, and I'm freaking out—"

"Cayden," Ashton said, trying to calm him. "I know your

mom's missing, Alex told me everything. I'm wondering why you're standing on the side of the road looking like you're going to rip out your hair."

Cayden sighed and rubbed his hand over his face. The bags under his eyes were deep and black, and Ashton knew he hadn't been sleeping. "I've looked literally everywhere," Cayden said. "I followed the route my mom takes to the grocery store, I've driven up and down Tanglewood Drive more times than I can count, and I've asked everyone who lives on the damn street if there have been any accidents lately or if they've seen anyone that matches my mom's description—but nothing—absolutely nothing. It's as if she just fell off the face of the Earth."

"She's gotta be somewhere," Ashton assured him. "And I know you'll find her. But you can't be driving in the condition you're in now. God knows I've lost enough people in car accidents."

Cayden paled at that and looked toward the ground finally, his shoulders slumping.

"How long has it been since you've slept?" Ashton asked.

"I don't know, maybe a day or two."

"I'm going to drive you back home, okay? And then you're going to sleep for 12 hours. Then tomorrow, your dad can call us both in sick to school so that CPS doesn't show up at your house and we can go looking for your mom together, okay?" Ashton ushered Cayden toward the passenger side of his car.

Cayden opened the door and hopped into the seat begrudgingly, putting his cheek on his hand as he gazed out the window. Ashton situated himself in the driver's seat and held out his hand expectantly in front of Cayden, waiting for him to drop the keys to the car into his hand.

Cayden reached into the pocket of his hoodie, pulled out the keys, and placed them in Ashton's outstretched hand. Ashton

The Dwellers

started the car and pulled off of Tanglewood, but before they moved even a half a mile, Cayden spoke up again.

"Ash, you kinda left your car back there."

"I'll come back for it; it's no big deal."

Cayden rolled his eyes. "You know I'm okay to drive, right?"

"Yeah, sure."

Cayden was quiet the rest of the ride home, and when they pulled up onto Woodland Drive, Ashton discovered why. Cayden was passed out against the passenger window, his shoulder leaning on the door and his breathing even. Ashton considered waking him, but decided instead on parking the car in front of their houses, so he could lean back in the driver's seat and take a nap of his own.

When he woke up again, the time on his watch had only changed an hour, but Cayden was still asleep in the seat beside him. Before Ashton had the chance to wake him, however, Cayden's eyes opened on their own and he looked around in confusion, wondering how he had gotten there.

"C'mon, your brother and sister are probably worrying their little heads off right now," Ashton said, opening his door and stepping out of the car. Cayden stumbled out after him, a little winded, asking about the time.

"It's about 6:30 p.m.," Ashton said, yawning.

"That's not possible. You picked me up on Rosen at 5 p.m. It doesn't take an hour and a half to get home from the freaking grocery store."

"We got back here at five thirty, and you were asleep. I didn't want to wake you up."

Cayden laughed for the first time in a week, and Ashton was glad to hear the sound.

"I'm going to turn in, Ash," Cayden said then, yawning. "Thanks for driving me home. See you tomorrow." He unlocked the front door and waved. Soon, Alex and Noah, who looked delighted to have their brother back home, were tackling him. Alex mouthed a "thank you" to Ashton, who waved to her before he decided to turn in as well.

Tomorrow was going to be a long day.

***

Ashton woke up earlier than usual and scribbled out a long note to Alana to explain what had happened the previous day and why he wasn't going to be in school. She was still snoring when Ashton left the note on her bedside table, so he closed her bedroom door softly on the way out and headed to the kitchen to make something to eat.

After swallowing down a pathetic excuse for a bagel, he headed out the door and walked next door. Cayden answered the door after one knock, still looking tired but looking much more alive than he had the previous day.

"You ready?" Ashton asked.

"You bet," Cayden said, stepping out onto the stoop. "I was thinking that it might take up a bit of our time, but we should drive back over to Rosen, so you can get your car back. Then we can look separately for a little bit and regroup back at my house. Then one of us can leave our cars home, and we can go looking together."

Ashton nodded. Although he would rather they spend most of their time looking together, he had forgotten that he had left his car on the side of Rosen the previous night. He hopped into the passenger seat of Cayden's car and leaned his head back as they drove down Tanglewood.

When they got to Rosen a little while later, Ashton hopped out of Cayden's car and walked over to his own car. Plugging the key into the ignition, he thanked his lucky stars that the old car started and gave a thumbs up to Cayden, who nodded and drove past Ashton, heading off of Rosen and back onto Tanglewood. As he drove past the grocery store, Ashton assumed that he was going to look farther down Tanglewood, leaving Ashton to retrace Sandra's steps backwards, back toward Davenport County.

They searched independently for about an hour and a half until Ashton's phone buzzed with a text from Cayden that said that he had found nothing once again and that they should regroup back home. Ashton, who had found jack squat as well, drove the small distance back to Woodland Drive and waited for Cayden to arrive.

When Cayden pulled up in front of Ashton and parked in front of his house, he got out of the car and opened the passenger door of Ashton's car.

"Tell me you found something," he said, running a hand over his face.

"Nope, nothing," Ashton said sadly. Cayden groaned.

"She had to have left something behind," he said shaking his head. "People don't just disappear without leaving anything behind."

"We can drive back toward the grocery store," Ashton proposed.

"How many more times are we going to drive up Tanglewood?" Cayden sighed. "There's absolutely nothing. The road is so damn long—I swear it goes on forever, and there's nothing at all to signify that anyone has crashed or gone missing along the strip."

Ashton nodded, understanding Cayden's frustration. Tanglewood Drive went on for miles, all the way from Davenport County and not ending until more than halfway through the entirety of Iowa. The scenery on the sides of the road stayed almost the same, with farms in every direction and an occasional city or grocery store. There were barely any trees at all along the sides of the road, and going only one lane in each direction could be dangerous. Ashton knew that all too well.

"Let's look one more time, okay?" Ashton said. "If we don't find anything, we'll go to the police again and tell them that we suspect that foul play is involved."

Cayden looked to his friend fearfully and asked, "Like murder?"

"More like serious kidnapping," Ashton said. "If we can't find *anything* at all to even suggest where she's been, then someone else is involved."

Cayden nodded solemnly as Ashton took off again. He turned onto Tanglewood and opened the windows. Cayden stared out the window with a determined look, and Ashton slowed the car down so that Cayden could get a good look at their surroundings. Tanglewood Drive was almost deserted, except for the few cars that passed in the other direction once in a while.

After 15 minutes of driving down the seemingly endless stretch of road, Cayden gasped loudly.

"Did you see that?" Cayden breathed, clutching the sides of the passenger seat.

"Did I see *what* Cayden? I'm looking at the road, dude."

"The rocks around the bottom of that tree just freaking *sparkled*."

Ashton pulled the car over, which on Tanglewood meant pulling up onto the grass past the curb. He parked the car on the grass, pulled the key out of the ignition, and turned to stare at Cayden.

"Are you insane?"

Cayden balked. "No!" he spluttered. "The rocks around the tree back there *glistened*; I swear to God. It was the weirdest thing. It could've just been the sunlight on raindrops or something, but no—no, the rocks around that tree are sparkling. They're still sparkling—look!"

For a second, Ashton almost rolled his eyes. Maybe Cayden was lying about actually sleeping last night and his sleep-deprived mind was playing tricks on him. But when he turned to look at the lone tree on the side of the road a small distance behind them, the rocks around its roots were indeed shining.

"What the hell," Ashton whispered, rubbing his eyes. The rocks were shimmering as if someone had poured glitter all over them. Some rocks were shining brighter than others. Although it looked more like glitter than anything, Ashton thought hard about what Cayden had said about the sunlight reflecting off water.

"Cayden, I don't want to freak you out, but I think we should go check out that tree. Sunlight reflecting off liquid could cause sparkling like that, and if it's not water it could be—"

"Blood," Cayden finished. "I know. We should drive by it again but on the other side of the road. We need to get closer, so I can see if it's blood or not."

Ashton nodded and took the car out of park, staring at the lane they had just come out of to make sure there weren't any cars before making a U-turn. As Ashton approached the tree and the glistening rocks, he took his foot off the gas pedal lightly, so they could get a good look at the tree while they were going slowly. But as Ashton lessened the pressure, the car did not slow.

"Cayden," Ashton said, in a panic. "The car's not slowing down."

"What are you talking about?" he asked, finally taking his eyes off of the tree to stare down at the pedals by Ashton's feet.

Ashton removed his foot from the gas pedal completely now, and the car still wasn't stopping. If anything, it was only speeding up.

"The brake, Ashton!" Cayden yelled.

Ashton stomped his foot down on the brake pedal, but the car wasn't stopping. The car swerved slightly to the right. If they kept accelerating in the direction they were going, they were about to smash right into the tree.

"Ash, look out!"

Ashton slammed on the brakes once again, closed his eyes, and braced himself for the impact that never came.

7

Ashton opened his eyes slowly, one hand white-knuckling the steering wheel, his other wrist in Cayden's grip. He looked down at his own body and then over at Cayden, whose eyes were squeezed shut. There was no blood, which surprised him. They had crashed into a giant tree at 60 miles an hour; Ashton assumed there would be some blood or broken bones. The realization hit him pretty quickly after that: they were dead.

Cayden let out a breath that he didn't know he was holding in, opened his eyes, and slowly extracted his hand from his friend's wrist.

"Are we dead?" he asked in a small voice.

Ashton didn't answer. He just stared out the flawless windshield. This wasn't possible. The car was in perfect shape, with no dents or scratches or expanded airbags. He listened to Cayden's question and looked out the driver's side window.

If they were dead, heaven (or hell—wherever they were) was nothing like he had assumed: beaches maybe for heaven, fire—naturally—for hell—a parking lot—not really what he was expecting. Except, it wasn't really a parking lot; there were no parking spaces, and none of the cars looked to be shifted into park. There were cars surrounding them from all angles, most of them older looking and run down. There were rows and rows of them, abandoned a long time ago. As far as he could see, there were only cars.

There were cars from old time periods—Ashton realized, mentally noting a '65 Malibu and a '68 Mustang—as well as more recent models. His eyes raked over a Honda from '06 and one of the newer sedans from Hyundai. He soon realized that none of the cars had license plates except for the one almost directly in front of him. The license plates all seemed to be deliberately removed, as if they were unscrewed one by one with a screwdriver.

Ashton realized that his eyes were lingering on the car in front of him for a little too long—staring at the Iowa license plate. Ashton did a double and looked at Cayden and then at the license plate. It was an *Iowa* license plate on a *silver Dodge Viper*. Ashton hit Cayden so hard in the arm that he knew it was going to leave a bruise.

"Cayden that's your *mom's car*," he hissed, hitting him in the arm again. Cayden stared at him, still dazed and concerned.

"So my mom's dead too?"

Ashton stared out the windshield at the cars again. Like the car he was currently sitting in, none of the cars around him looked wrecked in any way. Some of them had small keys and nicks, but nothing to indicate that they had crashed into a tree. Ashton reached for the button on his door to unlock the car. "Cayden, I don't think we're dead."

After he heard the click of the lock, he reached for the door handle, wrapped his hand around it, and started to push it. He only got the door open about an inch before there was a strong hand on his chest, pushing him back into the seat.

"Are you crazy?" Cayden said.

Ashton stared at him in confusion. "What?"

"You have no idea what's out there. We could get shot down by some mafia or . . . what if we *are* actually dead? What if this is a test or something or Judgment Day?"

Ashton had to fight the urge to bark out a laugh at his friend's concern. "Cayden," he started, laughing a bit under his breath. "We crashed into a *tree*."

Cayden scowled and kept his hand planted firmly on Ashton's chest. "Well, tree or not, you're not leaving. Your car just pulled a freaking *Christine* on us, man."

Ashton rolled his eyes. "Cayden, get your hand—" He stopped himself before the command could leave his mouth. He swallowed down his anger and put on the biggest fake smile he could muster.

"If you would be so kind, removing your hand from my sternum would be much appreciated."

Cayden looked at his friend quizzically before dropping his hand to a black button on the right side of the steering wheel, locking the doors once again.

"Ashton, we are not getting out of this car. We have no idea where we are, and we have no idea who else could be lurking around. One near-death experience per day is enough; thank you very much."

Ashton pressed the black button on his door in retaliation, unlocking the doors once again and smiling teasingly in Cayden's direction. He opened the door completely this time and hopped out of the car before Cayden could force him back inside.

Once outside the car, Ashton took a deep breath, breathing in the air and seeing if he could smell anything particularly unpleasant.

"Ash, what the *hell?*" Cayden was at his side all of a sudden. "The air here could be laced with freaking *formaldehyde* or *chloroform* or something."

Ashton turned around, placing a hand on Cayden's shoulder and staring him in the eyes. "Cayden, my friend, we are still on *Earth*—you know that right? The atmosphere is still the same. Taking a breath is not going to kill me—quite the contrary actually."

Cayden rolled his eyes as Ashton jogged away from their car. Cayden sighed loudly in disbelief but followed him nonetheless. When he got to the end of a row of cars, Ashton took a sharp left, starting to break into a run. Cayden groaned, but picked up his pace as well until, of course, Ashton stopped short, causing Cayden to crash right into him.

"Ash, seriously, what the f—"

"This parking lot is *gigantic*!"

Ashton's voice was downright *giddy*, as he looked around the parking lot, smiling. Cayden slapped a hand to his forehead and ran the hand over his face.

"Ashton, we are probably in serious danger right now, considering we have absolutely no idea where we are. Maybe we should stop ogling old cars and start figuring out how we're going to get out of here."

Cayden knew his speech was pointless the minute that Ashton ripped his gaze away from a run-down car from the '40s and was suddenly staring into the distance at a blinking blue light.

"Oh no," Cayden whispered at the same time as Ashton said, "Oh, yes."

With one last glance at the cars around him, Ashton sprinted toward the blinking light; Cayden following him reluctantly. He knew that if he left Ashton alone, he would end up doing something reckless and get himself hurt, so following him into the unknown was, regretfully, his only option.

When they arrived at the source of the blinking blue light, Cayden was panting, and Ashton was smirking. Cayden rested his hands on his knees, bent over, and tried to catch his breath.

"I told you that you should've joined track when we were in middle school," Ashton said with a giggle. "Maybe then you'd be able to keep up with me."

Cayden glared and stared up at the source of the blue light: a large welcoming sign introducing them to a place called "The Citee." Under the name of the town, an electronic counter read, "Population: 1,567"

Ashton wrinkled his nose as he studied the sign. "Seems like a small town," he said. "The Citee." He weighed the name on his tongue, as he walked around the sign a few times trying to analyze it. "I wonder if the people who founded this town took second grade spelling."

"Ash," Cayden groaned and pulled him away from the sign. "We should just go back to the car and forget all this. It's all way too weird. We have no idea what lies beyond that sign."

"What are we supposed to do?" Ashton asked. "Go back to the car? Sit there and wait to die of starvation? Well technically, we'd die of dehydration first. But the point is that if we go back to that parking lot and wait for someone to find us, we'll end up dying. Alternatively, if we walk past this sign and into the city, we might be able to pass as beggars on the street and get fed something."

Ashton patted his stomach with his hand and whined, looking from Cayden to the sign, a hopeful glint in his eyes. Cayden rolled his eyes and groaned.

"Once we walk over that hill, there's probably no turning back—you know that right?" Cayden said, analyzing the sign.

Ashton nodded enthusiastically and grinned. "Of course—that's why I'm gonna do it." Ashton took a step forward before jogging over the hill, leaving the sign in his wake.

Cayden groaned again but followed Ashton nonetheless, and when he reached the bottom of the hill, he swore he could hear a hitch in Ashton's breath.

"Cayden, what the hell is going on?" Ashton said. Panic was evident in his voice as he turned to look at his friend and then back at the sight in front of him. Cayden stared open-mouthed at the city laid out in front of him, his heart in his throat.

Cayden had been on airplanes before. He had been to Disneyland once in his life, and he had visited his great aunt in New York a few times. He knew what Davenport looked like from an aerial view, and he knew the basic outline of the city. The look on Ashton's face made Cayden think that Ashton knew those things too.

The city laid out in front of them was identical to Davenport in shape, size, and layout. The only difference was a gigantic estate placed strategically in the middle of the town, like a castle in the center of a medieval manor. The roads ran similarly to those in Davenport, and the buildings and homes seemed identical as well. Ashton's stomach clenched, and his heart was in his throat.

"Okay, Cayden, maybe you were right. Maybe we should, um, turn back," Ashton said, scared.

Cayden nodded in agreement. The layout of the town made him feel sicker than he had felt when they first crashed. He turned his head quickly and sprinted back up the hill toward the sign. When he reached the sign, he looked over the opposite end of the hill, and his heart launched back into his throat.

The parking lot that Ashton and Cayden had originally entered was gone, replaced by nothing more than a desolate wasteland, similar to a desert. Cayden whipped his head in all directions trying to find the parking lot, but it had completely disappeared.

Ashton joined Cayden on top of the hill, placing a hand on his friend's shoulder and shaking his head. "We're screwed," he said matter-of-factly.

***

After the initial shock of the "disappearing parking lot" wore off, Ashton and Cayden sat dolefully on the hill, with the sign lying below them. Cayden kept staring back at it, and Ashton was beginning to notice.

"I know, Cay," Ashton said, placing a hand on his friend's shoulder. "The spelling is still pissing me off too."

"That's not it," Cayden corrected. "I mean—that's part of it. But I could've sworn that the population counter said 1,567 when we first walked over the hill toward The Citee. Now it says 1,569."

Ashton looked down over the top of the hill and eyed the sign, realizing that Cayden was right. The sign that had first read 1,567 when they had arrived now read "Population: 1,569."

"Do you think it's counting us?" Ashton asked, working the numbers around in his head. "Maybe that's why it's an electronic counter instead of just part of the sign—because it counts you as a citizen the minute you step into The Citee's territory."

"And then once you're in their territory, you can't leave," Cayden said nervously.

"Hey, don't be a pessimist yet," Ashton said, punching Cayden's shoulder. "We don't know that. We've just got to find someone who knows their way around this place and ask for a little bit of a tour."

Cayden looked at Ashton like he was crazy. "A tour? Of course, Ashton, why didn't I think of that?" he asked sarcastically. "It'll be easy to just walk into this tiny deserted city, which looks exactly like home, and ask some stranger on the street for a tour of their magnificent county."

Ashton rolled his eyes. "Well we can't just sit here at the top of this hill just like we couldn't just sit in the car and wait for someone to rescue us. We've got to save ourselves."

Cayden gulped. "Who said we're in any danger?"

Ashton realized what he had said and sighed. "We're not in any immediate danger," he said. "But this place seems creepy. It's way too small to actually be a city, and the fact that it looks exactly like Davenport is just a tad unsettling."

"Just a tad."

"Yes, Cayden, a tad. It's not unsettling to the point where we should run in the opposite direction. You don't have to follow me if you don't want to, but I'm gonna go find someone who can help us navigate." Ashton stood up on top of the hill and walked down toward The Citee, sticking his hands out on both sides of himself and trying to keep his balance, so gravity didn't send him tumbling down toward the town.

Cayden glanced backwards at the sign and the vast desert where the parking lot had been and sighed. Picking up his pace, he jogged down the hill to meet Ashton at the base of it. The Citee looked bigger now that they were viewing it from level ground, and one look around indicated that it wasn't as similar to Davenport as they had originally thought.

Another incorrect assumption that Ashton and Cayden had made about The Citee was that it was deserted. While sparsely populated, people walked beside them occasionally as Ashton and Cayden made their way slowly through the town's streets. Now and again, a lone car would drive past, and the boys would stare in amazement as it turned a corner on the narrow streets. Most of the townspeople gave the boys weird looks but kept to themselves and never said a word.

Ashton and Cayden walked around aimlessly for a few hours, avoiding the mansion and its surrounding houses because of its intimidating stature. When Ashton finally worked up enough courage to grab Cayden by the arm and walk toward the mansion, two boys stopped them in their path.

"Where are you going?" one of them asked.

Ashton became defensive immediately; these two teenagers were the first people to pay any actual attention to them since they had landed themselves in The Citee. The boys looked nice enough, and about their age, but Ashton wasn't having any of it.

"Who's asking," Ashton asked slowly.

The boy who had asked the question laughed, and it made Ashton a bit calmer. It was a normal teenage boy laugh, nothing strange or suspicious about it. The boy was Ashton's height, but built a bit stockier. He had large brown eyes, blond hair, and much tanner skin than Ashton or Cayden had. Ashton thought that that was odd, particularly because The Citee didn't seem like it got a lot of sun, judging by the ever-present clouds above their heads.

"You two are new around here, aren't you?" he asked.

Ashton looked to Cayden for help, raising his eyebrows in a questioning way as if to ask Cayden whether they should reveal who they were to the two boys who had randomly approached them on the street. Cayden shrugged, and Ashton couldn't tell if the gesture meant that he didn't know or that he didn't care.

"Yeah, we are," Ashton said curtly.

The boy laughed again. "We could tell. You look it." He held out his hand in greeting and waited until Ashton grasped it. "I'm Carlton," he said, before gesturing to the boy to his left. "And this is Aidan."

Aidan was smaller than Carlton and bore brown hair and blue eyes. He wore a large smile on his face and nodded as Carlton introduced him, but he did not say a word. Ashton found it odd but didn't comment.

"I'm Ashton," Ashton said instead, putting his hand on his chest.

"And I'm Cayden," Cayden said, saluting them with one finger.

Carlton nodded and smiled. "Well it's nice to meet the two of you, then. Aidan and I have been living here for a while, so we can kind of tell when someone here is new. Sorry for kind of sneaking up on you like that. However, if you two would like, we could show you around The Citee? It really isn't that big of a town, and after you get settled, I know you'll like it here."

Carlton spoke as if Ashton and Cayden were going to be living here forever, and the thought made Cayden a bit queasy. Nevertheless, Cayden convinced Ashton to let Carlton and Aidan show them around The Citee and teach them what they knew. Cayden tried to speak to Aidan a few times, while Carlton explained various bridges and housing models, but the boy would listen intently and never speak. To answer Cayden's questions, he would nod, shake his head, or shrug, but Aidan didn't communicate beyond body movements and facial expressions.

In the middle of one of Carlton's rambles about a house that was currently up for sale, Ashton butted in to finally say what Cayden was thinking.

"Hey, Carlton, sorry to interrupt, but why doesn't Aidan talk? I mean, you've been explaining everything since we first met—does Aidan not know as much about The Citee?"

Carlton turned to Ashton and Cayden and laughed. "Oh, it probably would've been a good idea for me to explain that when we first met. That's my bad. I hope you guys don't think that Aidan's ignoring you or doesn't know the answer to your questions. Aidan is mute."

Ashton froze in place and locked eyes with Aidan. They were blue eyes. His stomach flipped weirdly, and he tried to mask any emotions that might be showing on his face.

"Are you selectively mute?" he asked Aidan with a smile.

The look Ashton got back from Aidan was one of pure confusion.

"What's that?" Carlton asked.

"Well there are different kinds of mutism," Ashton explained. "There's muteness, where someone physically cannot speak because there's something wrong with their vocal cords or they have a serious speech disability. And then there's selective mutism, which is usually a childhood thing. Sometimes it's brought on by trauma, or sometimes it's just because of general anxiety around people. I used to have it."

Hearing Ashton speak about his mutism was weird for Cayden, considering Ashton barely spoke at all when they were kids, and when he did, it was very little. To hear him full out explaining everything made him think about how many doctors he truly had been to when they were kids. The thought didn't make him feel very good.

Carlton looked to Aidan and expectantly waited for an answer, in any way that he could answer. "Do you think you're selectively mute?" Ashton asked. Aidan looked from Carlton to Ashton before nodding once and smiling.

Carlton and Ashton were smiling at Aidan, but Cayden felt anything but happy. Nerves were piling in his gut, and as he watched Carlton rest a hand on Ashton's shoulder, Cayden stepped closer to the three other boys.

"Can I just steal Ashton for a second?" Cayden asked, grabbing Ashton's arm and pulling him a few feet away from Carlton and Aidan, so they couldn't hear their conversation.

"Dude," Cayden said, eyes widening.

"What?"

"Am I the only one completely weirded out by this? By Aidan and Carlton?"

Ashton looked confused. "What do you mean? I mean, Carlton's a little bit too peppy for me, but he's nice. And Aidan doesn't even speak."

"That's the thing," Cayden said. "First we come here randomly by chance to a place that looks almost identical to the town we grew up in. Then, we meet two boys, our age, who even kind of look like us. And now one is mute. This isn't creeping you out even a little bit?"

Ashton glanced behind him at Carlton and Aidan, who were now engrossed in their own conversation, with only Carlton actually speaking of course. He would admit, the mutism thing kind of threw him for a loop, considering he had never met another mute in his life. And it *had* felt a little weird—locking blue eyes with a boy who looked a bit like him and was also a selective mute. Aidan had eyes and pale skin like him and hair like Cayden. Carlton had tanner skin and brown eyes like Cayden, but his blond hair was almost the same color that Ashton's had been before he had dyed it.

Ashton looked back to Cayden, who raised an eyebrow. "What are you trying to say?" Ashton asked. "You think Carlton and Aidan are actually us?"

"I have no idea," Cayden said. "All I know is that they're freaking me out and that they're too much like us for it to just be a coincidence—just like how The Citee looks way too much like Davenport for it to just be a coincidence."

Ashton nodded in agreement. "You're right," he said. "But we're also lost here. We have no idea what we're doing, and it seems as though Carlton knows *exactly* what he's doing. I just don't think we should drop them just yet, no matter how suspicious they may be."

Cayden agreed and they made their way back over to the boys, who were now simply standing there waiting for them to return.

"You two good?" Carlton asked.

"Yeah we're great," Ashton smiled, nodding in his direction. "We were wondering if you could tell us about that big house over there."

"The mansion?" Carlton asked. When Ashton nodded, Carlton smiled. "That's where the people who run the government here live. Usually, when newcomers enter The Citee in the parking lot, people from the government greet them there and take them to the mansion to help them get settled in. They want to make sure that every new citizen in The Citee has shelter and enough food to live nicely until they can get on their feet and find a job here. I'm surprised they didn't greet you two in the parking lot."

"And who runs the government here?" Cayden asked.

"We have a monarchy," Carlton said. Before Cayden and Ashton could ask any more questions about the mansion and the monarch, Carlton was pulling them past the mansion to another ring of The Citee, which was filled with specialty shops and small grocery stores.

Cayden thought it odd that Carlton was so quick to get off of the topic of the government in The Citee, but he pushed the thoughts out of his head the minute he smelled food. Carlton laughed when he saw Cayden eyeing the sandwiches being held up in front of one of the grocery markets and bought four of them, handing three of them out to Aidan, Ashton, and Cayden.

Ashton was a bit hesitant to eat anything that was being sold in this town, but after Cayden had taken a few bites and didn't die, he decided that it couldn't hurt to eat.

They spent a bit more time in the commercial district of The Citee before night fell, and Ashton assumed that Carlton and Aidan would be leaving them to go home and sleep. But to Ashton's surprise, they laid out a blanket that they took out of Carlton's backpack and sat down on it, staring up at the sky.

"Don't you guys need to get home?" Cayden asked them, watching them stargaze.

"We don't have a home," Carlton said. "We work occasionally and get enough money to buy food and clothes, and we live out of my backpack. The weather in The Citee is like this all year round, and if it gets a bit cold, we just buy sweatshirts. There's no harm in sleeping outside."

Ashton's eyes widened upon hearing that Carlton and Aidan were homeless. They seemed to know everything there was to know about The Citee and if the government cared about their citizens so much, why weren't Carlton and Aidan being taken care of. They *were* only kids.

"We have an extra blanket if you guys want to sleep on it," Carlton said, handing out a blue blanket to Ashton. "You guys are new, and if the government people didn't meet you in the parking lot, I assume that you don't have a home either."

Ashton shook his head and accepted the blanket graciously, laying it out on the ground next to Carlton's and Aidan's. They were right. The weather in The Citee was very nice, and there wasn't much wind to make them cold. Ashton plopped down on the blanket and waited for Cayden to join him. He stared up at the stars and watched the clouds move until he heard Cayden fall asleep. Ashton looked to his right, and he thought Carlton and Aidan weren't there for a second, but with a blink, they were back, fast asleep on their blanket.

Ashton yawned and rubbed his eyes. *Seeing things already.* It had been a long day, and he was exhausted. He fell asleep to the sound of Cayden's breathing and thoughts of home. All of this would be worth it if they could just find Sandra.

8

The four boys woke up early the next morning and fled from the place they had slept as quickly as they possibly could. Carlton and Aidan had assured Cayden and Ashton that people in The Citee usually paid no mind to people who had spent nights lying out on the grass, but Cayden didn't want to stick around to find out if that was true. The only thing on his mind was finding his mother.

Ashton was starting to agree with Cayden's concerns, and their comrades were actually starting to give him the creeps, so when Ashton let the fact slip that they were only in The Citee to find Cayden's mother, he cursed himself for never knowing when to just shove his foot in his mouth.

"You're looking for your mother?" Carlton asked Cayden. "Do you have any idea where she might be?"

Cayden threw an apprehensive glance at Ashton, but Ashton only shrugged. "No, we have no idea," he answered.

"Then we might as well look everywhere," Carlton laughed. "I know we kind of surveyed most of The Citee yesterday, but we can take a closer look at some of the sights and districts today. Maybe we can even ask some of the residents if they've seen anyone who looks like your mom?"

Cayden nodded—a fake smile was plastered on his face, but Carlton and Aidan didn't seem to notice. Ashton squeezed Cayden's shoulder and gave him a genuine smile, trying to cheer him up.

"We'll find her," he whispered. "I promise."

Carlton was set on going toward the business district again, and although Ashton was curious about the mansion, he knew that maybe some more food would cheer Cayden up. This time, instead of eating the random cart food that Carlton had found, they actually sat down at a small table in a tiny restaurant in the business district. Carlton assured Cayden and Ashton that he had enough money to pay for food again, which Ashton thought was bizarre.

They ate small sandwiches, and in his head, Ashton labeled the contents as mystery meat. The sandwiches tasted fine, but whatever kind of meat was inside of them was unrecognizable to Ashton's taste buds. Cayden didn't recognize the taste either, and Carlton and Aidan refused to reveal the secret of what was in their sandwiches.

When Carlton paid, Ashton finally got a better look at the currency of The Citee. They didn't use paper dollars, but coins in different sizes and colors. The ones that seemed to be worth the most looked like silver dollar coins, and the ones that were worth the least looked like pennies. Ashton thought it probably wouldn't be so hard to figure it out if he actually paid attention to how Carlton was paying.

They left the business district almost directly after they finished eating, only stopping to ask some local shop owners if they had seen anyone who matched Sandra's description lately. All of them replied "no," but wished the boys luck on finding whomever it was they were looking for.

Cayden was discouraged for the rest of the day, although he tried to smile at Carlton every time he stopped one of his stories to ask Cayden if he was all right. Cayden would nod and assure Carlton that he was fine, but the minute the boy resumed his story, Cayden would go back to sulking again. But, as much as Ashton wished he could focus his attention on trying to make Cayden feel better, a few hours into their second tour of The Citee, Ashton's concern was somewhere else entirely.

The first time it happened, Ashton thought he had just been

seeing things. But when it happened a second time, Ashton had to physically stop and stare. Aidan was twitching, not slightly, but fully snapping his head and neck to the right and winking his right eye tightly. It happened once every 10 minutes or so, and Ashton wasn't sure what was happening or what he should do.

Carlton figured it out an hour later after watching Aidan spasm once. "Are you okay?" he whispered to Aidan, but the mute boy only nodded, smiling in confusion as if he had no idea why Carlton would be asking him the question.

Cayden didn't notice the twitching much, but when he did catch Aidan's eye when the twitch happened, he just looked away. Carlton continued to babble away about The Citee's history, while Aidan occasionally twitched. Ashton kept his eyes locked on Aidan, and Cayden searched obsessively for his mother. The trip was slowly but surely going downhill.

When Cayden suggested that the group should stop looking in the foothills and actually get closer to the mansion, Carlton seemed hesitant, but Cayden pleaded enough that Carlton turned around so that they could walk toward the mansion.

Ashton, who was still staring at Aidan and mentally recording every twitch, realized that Aidan's twitching became less harsh but more frequent as they got closer to the mansion.

"What's up, Aidan?" Carlton finally asked, after a few minutes of walking toward the mansion. Aidan's twitching now way too frequent to brush off.

Cayden turned to look at Aidan, who was twitching slightly every few seconds now and looking frantically around as if he was seeing a ghost. Ashton and Cayden shared a nervous look, as Carlton approached Aidan more closely, trying to figure out why he was twitching.

"Aidan, seriously what's going on?" Carlton asked, more quietly this time, placing a hand on his friend's shoulder. "Why are you twitching like that?"

Aidan locked eyes with Carlton in a frantic manner, blinking rapidly and looking around with a terrified look on his face. He was breathing heavily, and his hands were shaking slightly as Aidan tried to calm him down. Ashton and Cayden tried to follow Aidan's frantic gaze, but it changed too quickly to pinpoint. After a minute or so of trying to calm his breathing, Aidan finally calmed down, and the twitching seemed to almost stop.

Ashton, Cayden, and Carlton decided to keep a watchful eye on Aidan but to keep moving. Carlton was set on showing Ashton and Cayden as much of The Citee as they could reach, and it seemed that the closer they got to the mansion, the more that there was to learn.

"The roads were repaved a long, long time ago, but the original road system is still buried underneath the new pavement. The original road system is ancient—probably thousands of years old. The government repaved it when they came to power, but the foundation of The Citee has been based off of these roads for as long as this place has existed."

Ashton learned as they walked, listening intently to Carlton's stories and experiences. As they would pass significantly older buildings or ruins, Carlton would explain the ins and outs of how it got there and what purpose it was serving now. Aidan would stand next to Carlton and nod and smile, never saying a word. He wasn't twitching as much as he was earlier in the day, but once in a while, he would blink tightly and would only calm down when Ashton stared at him long enough for him to notice.

When night fell again, this time, the boys took refuge under the dripping roof of an abandoned house close to the mansion. Cayden made a snarky comment about the roof falling in and killing them all, but Ashton slapped his arm and said that if they could spend a night in their old tree house, they could spend a night in the abandoned house. Carlton and Aidan fell asleep, almost instantly, and they breathed so quietly and evenly as they slept that Ashton and Cayden forgot that they were even there a few times.

Cayden couldn't sleep. His dreams were plagued with thoughts of his mother and what on earth she could be doing in a place like this. For a few seconds, he saw horrific images play through his brain of his mother being tortured and beaten. He sat up in a cold sweat. Ashton sat up on the blanket next to him, realizing that Cayden was awake.

"Hey, you okay?" Ashton whispered, trying not to wake Carlton and Aidan.

Cayden exhaled shakily and ran a hand over his sticky forehead. His hand was shaking slightly, and he felt like he was suffocating. He hadn't had a panic attack in years, but he remembered the feeling all too well. Trying to calm his breathing, he closed his eyes tightly and tried counting to 10.

He felt Ashton pull him back down onto the blanket on the floor of the abandoned house and tried to lull him back to sleep by telling another story about Alana's escapades in California. Cayden finally fell asleep an hour later with a smile on his face, as he thought about how maybe one day he'd get to punch Ashton's uncle in the face.

***

When the four boys awoke in the abandoned house, sunlight was streaming in through the thin openings in the boarded up window. Cayden wasn't used to seeing sun in The Citee and welcomed the rays on his face with open arms.

Ashton looked exhausted when he sat up from the blanket on the floor, rubbing at his eyes and looking around for the other boys. Carlton and Aidan looked amazingly well rested, and Cayden was starting to wonder how two homeless boys in a city like this one never seemed to look tired.

Carlton and Aidan packed up the two blankets back into Carlton's backpack, which he slung over his shoulder excitedly.

"There's a really awesome old ruin near the left side of the mansion that I want to show you guys today," Carlton smiled. "We should get going soon."

Ashton and Cayden stepped out of the abandoned house with Aidan and Carlton a few minutes later. They were tired from their few hours of sleep, but a bit excited to be finally seeing the mansion up close and personal. The excitement didn't last forever though because soon Aidan was twitching again.

The twitching was no longer a violent blink or a neck spasm, but it started as a small shaking of the hand, which is why Ashton wasn't able to detect it as quickly. Soon, Ashton saw Aidan's trembling hand, and when it didn't stop shaking after a few minutes, he leaned over and whispered to Carlton, "Aidan is twitching again."

"What's wrong, Aidan," Carlton said, finally, taking the backpack off of his shoulders and placing it on the ground. "I'm not walking another step until you show me what's going on. Why are you twitching?"

Aidan's head was starting to snap around frantically again, and Carlton grabbed Aidan's chin to stop his neck from jerking to the right.

"What's wrong?"

"She's . . . here," Aidan choked.

Ashton's eyes widened, and he turned to Cayden in amazement. Aidan had never spoken before. Carlton's mouth was open in surprise as well. He gaped at Aidan and let go of his chin, and the twitching resumed.

"What's here?" Carlton asked. "Who's 'she'? Who is here?"

"She . . . followed us," he hissed. "Danger."

Carlton looked terrified as he tried to figure out what Aidan meant, but he didn't have to think very hard because Aidan was soon pointing over Carlton's shoulder to a random speck in the distance.

All of a sudden, from the exact area that Aidan had been pointing, an arrow shot through the air, aimed right toward where the four of them were standing. Ashton and Cayden lunged to the left to avoid the arrow and rolled down a small hill until they were a jumbled pile of limbs at the bottom of it. Standing up at the bottom of the hill, Ashton looked over the hump and tried to watch the scene in front of him.

The arrow flying through the air hit its target, and the blade piercing through Aidan's chest made a horrific sound, like fingernails on a chalkboard. Ashton jumped in front of Cayden impulsively, and Carlton ran toward Aidan's body. Ashton and Cayden simultaneously yelled for Carlton to stop, but it was no use. A second arrow soared through the air, striking Carlton right below his ribcage. The arrow made the same shrieking sound, and Carlton collapsed next to Aidan on the ground. Ashton and Cayden ran up the hill to where the corpses lay.

Cayden tried to lunge past Ashton toward their attacker, but Ashton refused to let him move. He looked in the direction in which the arrow had come from and squinted into the distance, where a girl was running toward them. For a second, Ashton was almost relieved: *someone had seen the arrows and the murders and had come to help*. But the minute he saw the bow the girl had wrapped around her shoulders, he planted his feet more firmly on the ground and put up his fists.

When the girl arrived in front of the corpses, she studied them intently before gripping the arrow lodged in Carlton's stomach and tugging it out. Cayden closed his eyes behind Ashton, but Ashton studied the blade of the arrow, his mouth dropping open when he saw that there was no blood. As the girl removed the arrow from Aidan's chest, and it came out clean as well, Ashton walked toward the girl, his hands still in fists.

"Who the hell are you?" Ashton questioned.

The girl returned the arrows to the container attached to her belt, looked up at the sound of Ashton's voice, and smiled.

"Ashton," she said happily. "I'm glad I was finally able to find you."

Confused, Ashton stared at the girl. She was pretty, in a weird sort of way. Her hair was long and blond, and she looked as if a professional makeup artist had done her makeup. The appearance of her face was in sharp contrast to the rest of her. She wore black dress pants and ballet flats, which looked a bit dirtied, as if she had fallen into the dirt on the way. She wore a black blazer over a white dress shirt, which was partly tucked into her pants. Embroidered into the side of her blazer was a white symbol that Ashton didn't recognize. In the outfit she was wearing, with her shirt half untucked, dirt all over her pants, and a bow strung across her shoulders, she looked like a real estate agent who had gotten stuck in the middle of a zombie apocalypse movie.

"Who are you?" Ashton asked again.

"That's not important," the girl laughed. "The only important thing is that I've finally found you. The government requests your appearance at once."

Ashton raised his eyebrows in Cayden's direction, and Cayden shrugged, not knowing what they were supposed to do. Aidan and Carlton had said that people who usually came to The Citee were greeted by people who work for the government in the parking lot, which made Cayden feel as if that may just be standard protocol. However, they were far away from the parking lot now, and the parking lot had disappeared just as fast as it had appeared. Also, this girl was not a "group of people from the government." She looked more like a homeless teenager, as Carlton and Aidan had been.

"What does the government want with us?" Ashton asked.

"Ashton, you're very important."

Ashton raised his eyebrows in confusion. "I don't know exactly *how* I'm important, but I'm 99% sure I don't want to help the government here. Do you work for the government?"

The girl nodded, adjusting her bow across her back. "I guess you could say that, yeah."

"Well now I'm 100% sure I don't want to help the government here."

"Well why not?"

"Because you just killed my friends!" Ashton exclaimed, gesturing to the ground to the right of him.

"What friends?" the girl asked.

"The ones that are right—" Ashton stopped speaking instantly when he looked over to where the bodies of Carlton and Aidan had once been. Now, there was nothing there but a patch of grass and Carlton's backpack—not one drop of blood or string of fabric from one of their clothes.

"They were right there!" Ashton yelled, terrified. "You shot them with your freaking bow and arrow! Their bodies were right there two seconds ago, and when I find out what you did with them—"

"Ashton, calm down," the girl laughed. "Everything is going to be okay. Just come with me, please."

Ashton turned to Cayden, who was staring at him fearfully. The girl had not said a word to Cayden or even acknowledged his presence. If he didn't know any better, he would've thought that she couldn't even see him.

"We're not going anywhere with you until you explain what the hell is going on," Ashton said. "Tell me who you are, tell me where we are, and tell me what you did with Carlton and Aidan and why you killed them."

The girl smiled and sighed. "Well my name is Ali, I'll tell you that much. But I can't spoil most of these surprises for you. I promise you that when you get to the mansion, everything will be explained. You're confused now, which I completely understand, but it is not my duty to explain it to you. You will learn everything in due time."

Ashton rolled his eyes. "Can you at least tell me what the government wants with me? Why am I so important?"

"You just are," Ali said, like it was the simplest thing in the world. "You will learn soon enough."

Ashton ran a hand over his face in frustration, once again looking over to the patch of grass where Carlton and Aidan's corpses had once been. Cayden still stood behind him silently, waiting for instructions.

"Fine, we'll go with you," Ashton said. "But if you try anything funny with that bow and arrow, I will not hesitate to kill you. Understand?"

Ali smirked and nodded, turning back in the direction she had come and waving her hand to gesture Ashton to follow her. When she heard two sets of footsteps following her, she turned around and stared at Cayden, a hint of confusion in her eyes.

"What?" Ashton asked, catching up with her, while Cayden stayed a bit behind.

"Who is he?" she asked, pointing behind them at Cayden.

"My friend," Ashton said dangerously. "He's coming whether you like it or not."

Ali held up her hands in surrender. "Of course he's coming," she said. "My orders were to retrieve you and anyone else that you wanted to join us. If he's your friend, then he's coming with us."

"Aidan and Carlton were my friends, and you killed them.

What if I wanted them to join us?"

"You will learn in due time."

Ashton rolled his eyes again and held back, letting Ali lead the way again. He joined Cayden a few steps behind, where he was grabbing Carlton's backpack off of the floor. Cayden looked nervously at the girl in front of them every few minutes, but Ashton stood straight ahead, as the mansion got larger and larger in their field of view.

Ali finally stopped when they were in front of the mansion doors and wiped the dirt off of her pants, as if she were trying to make herself look more presentable. Ashton fixed his hair self-consciously, as she unstrapped the bow from her back and shoulders and held it in her hand. She also unhooked the arrow container from her belt and handed both the bow and arrows to one of the guards standing upright in front of the mansion.

The guard that Ali had handed the bow and arrows to stared Ashton and Cayden down, trying to figure out who they were and why they were being permitted to enter the mansion. But Ali leaned toward the guard's ear and whispered in it, and the guard's expression soon turned from an angry one to one of amazement. Bowing slightly in Ashton's direction, the guard reached for the ornate knob of the door closest to him, gesturing for the other guard to do the same with his door.

Ashton bowed uncomfortably back to the guard, unsure of whether that was a customary greeting for people in the mansion, and followed Ali through the doors, Cayden in tow. Ashton was completely baffled the minute he walked through the doors.

9

The mansion was huge. Stone columns hugged every doorway, and the hallways looked like they extended forever. Ali led them through the main hallway, which broke in places and exposed gigantic rooms either piled high with items or completely empty.

There were glass cases that lined the main hallway, revealing small tidbits about The Citee's past. Cayden glanced into the glass cases, trying to figure out the seemingly unknown language scribbled onto the sides of some of the relics. Ashton was less concerned with the glass cases, and he stared upwards to admire the intricate carvings in the crown molding and stone ceiling.

Ali simply continued walking onward, ignoring the two boys behind her every time they would stop and stare. As Ashton followed closely behind Ali most of the time, Cayden stopped frequently. As they neared their destination, Cayden became fascinated with a glass case holding a small black dress.

The dress was sewn by hand, Cayden noted, as he admired the white lining across the bottom and the white symbol sewn onto the breast. It was a symbol he had seen sewn or carved into a lot of things around the mansion. It also happened to be the symbol that was embroidered into the side of Ali's blazer.

Flags hung draped over some of the walls, all of them sporting the crest. Some looked torn and tattered in places, but most were in pristine condition, and all of them were clean as they could be.

As they followed Ali, Cayden admired more of the artifacts placed in the glass cases and occasionally stopped to get a closer look. Many items in the glass cases looked to be hundreds of years old, and many were covered in cryptic messages written in a language that Cayden didn't understand. One particular artifact was a large slab of stone with the cryptic language carved into it, likely by hand. The only English letters on the stone spelled the signature in the corner, which read "Bel."

Tempted to ask Ali about who "Bel" was, Cayden looked up from the stone only to find that Ashton and Ali were paces ahead of him, and he jogged to catch up. The walk through the hallways seemed endless, and Cayden wondered what their destination was.

Ali approached several groups of what seemed to be elite officials, and they parted to let her, Ashton, and Cayden through. Cayden hesitated or walked through some of the groups slowly, anxious to eavesdrop and hear what the people in the mansion were talking about. The men in suits chatted somewhat loudly, laughing every so often and talking in hushed whispers while spewing secrets. Cayden heard multiple conversations about potential wars, an army, and something called "Sanrid."

Cayden didn't have time to question what in the world "Sanrid" could be, as he was pulled into a dark room. When his eyes adjusted to the light, he could see that it was Ashton who had pulled him into the room, his hand still on Cayden's sleeve.

"Why weren't you following me and Ali?" Ashton pestered, slapping Cayden's arm. "She almost freaked out because she thought she had lost you. But you were just standing and staring at those weird guys in the suits."

"Those weird guys in suits were up to something," Cayden said. "They were talking about some pretty weird stuff. I wasn't able to catch a lot of their conversations, but they said something about—"

"Don't you think we have bigger problems?" Ashton said, raising an eyebrow at Cayden and pointing behind him. Looking over Ashton's shoulder, Cayden could see that Ali was no longer next to them, but standing on the far side of the room, looking at them curiously. Another woman, draped in black clothing, stood by the opposite wall. There was a white symbol embroidered onto the bottom of her floor-length dress, and Cayden was willing to bet a million dollars that it was the same crest that seemed to be embroidered into everything that stood in the mansion.

Directly behind Ashton and Cayden, who were standing in the middle of the room, sat a man in a large throne-like chair. He had gray-blond hair, styled to the side with gel as if he was trying to immortalize his youth, which seemed to be long gone. The man was incredibly old and looked so frail that it was as if a gust of wind could have knocked him off his chair. He was dressed in black robes that went all the way down to the ground, even when he was sitting. He had a pendant on a chain around his neck, and stamped onto the pendant was that crest again, shining faintly in the light above the man's head. The light seemed to be the only light in the room; the rest of the room basked in an eerie dim lighting.

Cayden kept an eye on Ashton, who was nervously clenching and relaxing his fists. Ashton stepped in front of Cayden, blocking him from the sitting man's view.

"Who are you?" Ashton said, trying to keep his voice from wavering.

The man in the chair sighed, as if Ashton's question was not the acceptable greeting that he was looking for. He eyed the two boys in front of him curiously and with confusion, keeping his eyes locked on Cayden.

"Ashton—" the man started, but Ashton cut him off.

"How do you know who I am? And you didn't answer my question—who are you?" Ashton clenched his fists, looking around him slowly. Every exit was blocked by two or three guards, both men and women, in black outfits with white crests sewn onto their breasts. The guards were not all that large, but they all had black belts around their waists and a pistol on their hip. Ashton wasn't sure he wanted to take a chance on whether or not the pistols were loaded.

The old man sighed again, fiddling with the pendant around his neck. "Grandfather," he answered, matter-of-factly.

Ashton scoffed and Cayden laughed softly behind him.

"Grandfather?" Ashton said, although it was more of a laugh. "Did your parents hate you or something?"

Grandfather smiled, which was a scary thing that made Ashton's stomach flip. "Everyone in The Citee calls me 'Grandfather.' And I know your name because you are one of my descendants."

Ashton took a small step backward, with Cayden following his movement.

"So I'm related to you?" he asked.

"Yes."

"But you said that you're 'Grandfather' to everyone in The Citee," Ashton said. "Does that mean every citizen here is related to you—and related to me?"

"No."

Ashton narrowed his eyes and sighed, finally pointing to Ali. "Who's she?"

"Alison Dweller."

Cayden's eyes widened, and Ashton let out another breathy laugh. "Dweller? So she's related to me too?"

Grandfather nodded and beckoned for Ali to walk over to him. She kneeled in front of him, bowing, before approaching the chair up close, where Grandfather rested one of his hands on her shoulder. "She is your sister," he said.

Ashton actually laughed at that one, bringing a hand up to cover his mouth. "No, no, no, no," he said, shaking his head. "You see, I know a thing or two about siblings. I'm one of six; I have three older brothers and only *two* sisters. That's it."

"Crossing many, many, *many* bloodlines, Alison is your sister—

long-lost sister one might say." Grandfather gestured in front of him in Ali's direction again, and the girl smiled innocently, in a way that made Ashton feel less threatened.

However, Ashton still felt uneasy. He paced back and forth while looking from Grandfather to Ali. Cayden stood behind him still, biting his bottom lip and studying the intricacies of the flags that hung over Grandfather's head.

"So if I'm a Dweller, and you two are Dwellers, are there any other Dwellers I should know about?" Ashton finally asked.

"Most people who reside in this mansion are Dwellers," Grandfather said, calmly. "They're all your ancestors in some way, shape, or form, from many years ago. Some are related to you through marriage, and some are related to you directly, but if they live here, it is likely that Dweller blood runs through their veins."

Ashton swallowed nervously before asking, "How many Dwellers are there, exactly?"

"Many."

Ashton put his face in his hands and inhaled sharply. Grandfather's answers were all terse and to the point, and he knew there had to be something that was being kept hidden. The guards who blocked the visible exits were threatening and looked like they could snap him in half without a second thought. They all wore the same blank expression and barely looked like they were breathing.

"Where are we?" Ashton said, gesturing to himself and Cayden. If this all went downhill, Ashton really wanted to know where he was going to die.

"The Citee," Grandfather answered.

Ashton scoffed again. "Yeah, I figured that from the huge glowing sign outside. Seriously, that thing is huge. Where are we, really?"

"A world not unlike the one you have become accustomed to—a reflection of your world." Grandfather seemed pleased with his answer, sitting back in his chair again.

"Are you just going to keep talking in riddles?" Ashton said, frustrated. He tried to ponder Grandfather's words, but none of it made sense. The guy was a nutcase. "Just tell me where we are."

"A reflection of your world—one not unlike your own," he repeated.

Ashton sat down in defeat. The movement caused the guards at the doors to stiffen. He gave a dirty look to the tall man blocking the nearest exit and put his hands up in mock surrender. "I'm not going anywhere," he said. "I'm just trying to understand all this."

Cayden knelt down next to him suddenly, his eyes widening as he whispered, "Ash, it's a parallel universe." It was too quiet for anyone but Ashton to hear, and he whipped his head around toward Cayden.

"A *what?*"

"A parallel universe."

Ashton sighed. "Cayden, you've been watching way too many sci-fi movies."

"No, it makes sense," Cayden urged. "The tree and all the cars in the parking lot—the fact that The Citee looks *way* too much like Davenport for it to be a coincidence—a 'reflection' of a line would be *parallel*, Ashton. Grandfather just spelled it out for you."

Ashton laughed in disbelief. "Look at that; maybe you won't fail Mr. Ostello's class after all."

A blush rose up on Cayden's cheeks, and Ashton stood up finally, causing the guards to stiffen again. "Is Cayden right?" he asked Grandfather. "Is this a . . . parallel universe?" And then he said, "God, I sound like an idiot asking that."

Grandfather tapped a finger to his chin, contemplating the question. "You could say that," he said gruffly.

Suddenly, the realization hit Ashton like a truck. "Aidan and

Carlton," he breathed, blood boiling. "Were they parallel versions of Cayden and me?"

"You could say that," he repeated.

"Were they or were they not?" Ashton said angrily. "Because they just *disappeared* into thin air, and if that's some kind of indication about what's going to eventually happen to us—"

"Ashton," Grandfather interrupted.

Ashton stopped after he heard his name; he crossed his arms and waited for an explanation.

"Everyone in your world, your universe, does not have a parallel copy in this one," Grandfather explained. "However, we needed to coerce you out of that car of yours and into The Citee, so you could find the mansion and find me. We created parallel versions of you and your friend. We figured that if you were going to trust anyone, it was going to be someone who reminded you of yourself. We got you to trust Aidan and Carlton, and once you did, Ali disposed of them and you had no choice but to follow her here."

"Disposed of them?" Ashton asked incredulously. "Ali *killed* them. Are you a monster? Aidan and Carlton were human beings, not dead animal carcasses."

"Ali did not kill anyone," Grandfather said. "And Aidan and Carlton were not human beings. I told you; we *created* them. We have very advanced technology in this mansion, but we sadly cannot create human beings. They were merely holograms."

"There's no way in hell that they were holograms," Ashton argued. "I touched Carlton with my own hands. There was skin and bone and a *person* there."

"Maybe you did," Grandfather said. "But just think for a moment. Did you ever have to turn around because you felt like one of them wasn't following you? Did you ever see one of them out of the corner of your eye, and maybe for a second they looked like someone else? When Ali killed them, was there any blood? You just told me that they disappeared into thin air. Do you know of any people who can do that?"

Ashton stood in a shocked silence and stared at Grandfather. There *were* instances when he had felt like Aidan hadn't actually been there. There had been times when he had seen Carlton whispering to Aidan, and for a second, he just saw two random children whispering. He was starting to get a headache.

"They weren't real," Grandfather said, simply.

"What else isn't real then?" Ashton said. "Are you real? Is Ali real? Are any of the Dwellers real? Is this place real? Is *any* of this actually real, or am I just having a really, really bad dream?"

Grandfather tried to speak again, but Ashton cut him off. "Or maybe Cayden and I just crashed into a tree and we're dead. Maybe this is hell. Who knows?"

Grandfather laughed for the first time, and instead of putting Ashton at ease, it made him even more anxious. "You're not dead, and you're not in hell," he said. "You are very much alive; trust me."

"Trust you," Ashton scoffed under his breath. "Yeah, sure."

Grandfather smiled demonically again, and Ashton tried not to look him in the eye. He sighed, keeping his eyes off of Grandfather and staring at the floor. "Let's say, by some off chance, that everything you've just told me is true. I'm one of your long-lost descendants, this is a parallel universe, Aidan and Carlton were holograms, and I can trust you. That means that you wanted me and Cayden here," Ashton said. "Why?"

Grandfather folded his hands in his lap and stared out the small window next to him. "Ashton, a long, long time ago my wife Malia, my daughter Alison, and I came to this land, and we've been stuck here ever since. We know about your power."

Ashton's stomach rolled unpleasantly, and he felt like vomiting and fainting at the same time. Determined to keep Cayden from finding out, he tried for nonchalance. "What power?" he choked out.

"Your raw, unadulterated power," Grandfather said. "Your *gift*—and if you use that gift in the right way, you can save us. You can bring us home."

"Bring you home?" Ashton asked. "You mean, to my universe?"

"It's not just *your* universe," Grandfather said. "It was ours once, too. The portal sucked us in as it did you."

"What portal?" Ashton asked.

"Do you not remember how you got here?" Grandfather said. "The tree you crashed into was not an ordinary tree, Ashton, by any means. It is an old tear in space that has existed since long before you and me."

"The glistening rocks," Cayden said in bewilderment.

"Yes," Grandfather said, smiling. "I'm glad you noticed. The glistening rocks are a—" He hummed and stared at the ceiling, trying to find the right words to use. "They're a *side effect* of the tear. Think of it as the stars infused into the earth."

Ashton couldn't believe what he was hearing. Maybe he could believe that his friends were holograms, and maybe he could even believe that they were in some kind of parallel universe—but a tear in space and a portal? All of it was becoming too unbelievable, even for a person who could telepathically control people.

"I understand now, I think," Ashton said. "But I still don't know why you need me."

"We need you to break us out," Grandfather said. "If you can use your gift to break open the portal and break down the wall, we can go back home."

"I don't want this," Ashton sighed. "How do I even know you're telling the truth about where you came from—or about who you are?"

"You don't," Grandfather said. "You have to trust me—remember?"

"I don't know if I can do that."

"We'll give you some time for you to make up your mind about whether you would like to help us. But, as for your friend-"

"No!" Ashton all but screamed, pushing Cayden behind him. "No, no, no. If . . . if you don't hurt Cayden, I'll do whatever you want. I'll help you."

"We weren't going to hurt him," Grandfather said. Ashton shook his head; he didn't want to hear it. "Cayden leaves here *alive*. Understand?"

"We have no intention of hurting or killing either one of you," Grandfather assured him. "You need to let it sink in that Aidan and Carlton were not real, and their fates have no correlation to what will happen to the two of you."

"Fine," Ashton nodded. "They weren't real."

Grandfather nodded with satisfaction. "The Citee can be a very dangerous place, and we do not want Cayden getting hurt. We will keep you both here, where you will be safe." He motioned for two guards to move away from the exits and to lead Ashton and Cayden to their respective rooms.

Cayden was led away first, and Ashton's stomach clenched at the thought of Cayden being beaten to a pulp by the emotionless guards. He tried to shake the thoughts away while he was led in the opposite direction to his room. Before walking out the now unguarded exit, he was stopped directly in front of Grandfather.

The man stood up from his throne and walked down the few steps to greet Ashton face to face. The man was taller than he looked sitting down, and when Ashton locked eyes with him, he saw that they shared the same sharp blue eyes.

"You are stronger than you think, Ashton Dweller," Grandfather said, quietly. "You are very important. And you *will* save us."

Ashton nodded dumbly, not wanting to anger the man who had probably just spared his life. He looked to the guns on the belts of the guards and swallowed, allowing himself to be led away to his room.

He was led by the guards down another long hallway, where more people in suits chatted away as if there was a dinner party being held in the mansion. The guards kept a firm grip on his arm and ushered him away from the prying eyes of the men in suits, who tried to study him more than once. Ashton made sure not to reciprocate their eye contact and stared straight ahead. Finally, the guards stopped him in front of a stone wall.

Slowly, the stone parted at the middle, revealing a glass interior. After Ashton was led into the wall and the stone "doors" closed again, the whole thing started to move.

There was a short trip down a small shaft, which proved the whole device was probably an elevator of some sort, because when the stone doors opened again, they were in the basement of the mansion. The basement, however, looked more like a dungeon as Ashton walked down hallways lined with bars. Occasionally, a finger or hand would reach through the bars, and Ashton would jump back in fear, while the guards held their guns toward the cells. The hands would retract automatically the minute they saw the guns, the prisoners shrinking away in fear.

Ashton tried to peek into some of the cells, anxious to see what some of the prisoners looked like, but he was constantly pulled away by the two guards, who still hadn't uttered a word to him.

"Where are you taking me?" Ashton asked.

The guards didn't answer. They only gripped his arm tighter and forced him along. When Ashton tried to pull his arm out of their grip, one of the guards reached for his gun, and Ashton froze. The guard still holding onto Ashton's arm whipped his head toward the armed one, shaking his head quickly.

"We can't kill this one," the guard said. "No matter how much he struggles, we're not allowed to damage him."

Ashton watched as the other guard returned his gun to his belt, nodding in agreement and grabbing Ashton's arm again. The guards were silent the rest of the way, and when they arrived at their destination, Ashton was baffled.

"A cell?" he questioned. "He's throwing me in a cell? I thought I was *important?*" He put finger air quotes around the word "important" and smiled at the guards sarcastically. He tried to look through the bars of his cell from the outside, but the guards pushed him inside the door and closed it.

"Ali will meet with you soon to discuss whether you would like to help us or not," one of the guards said. "Depending on your answer, Grandfather will give you further instructions."

"What about Cayden?" Ashton said. "Where are you keeping him?"

The guards paid Ashton no notice, turned their backs to him, and started their journey back from where they had come from.

"Tell me what's going on!" Ashton said, raising his voice. He began to pound on the bars with his fist, but the guards still didn't turn around. Once they had rounded the corner, Ashton stopped yelling and slid down the wall, putting his head in his hands.

"I'm an idiot," he said to nobody, still looking at the floor from between his hands. "What the hell have I done?"

***

The cell Ashton was being kept in was akin to a jail cell, but a bit more comforting, if that word can even be used to describe a cell. There was a cot-like bed, which had a thick blanket draped over it, unlike the thin sheet that covered the cots in a prison cell.

There was also a restroom with a door, which Ashton was grateful for, along with a small shower nestled in the corner of the small bathroom. As one unit, it was probably the size of his Uncle Damon's living room.

Ashton spent most of the first day in his cell thinking. Grandfather's words had confused him to no end, and the aching question of where Cayden was being held crept back into his brain every few minutes. As it always did when Ashton was nervous, the power was a throbbing drum, thumping in time with his heartbeat.

Ashton had no idea how Grandfather and the other Ancestors knew about his power. No one knew. He hadn't told a soul about it since it had surfaced. He hadn't even told James when the boy had become skeptical about whether the gray-eyes thing was his drugged-out brain or something that was actually happening. His parents had never found out, and neither had any of his siblings. He hadn't even told Cayden, who knew practically everything about him at that point in his life.

Another troubling thought was the ever-present idea in Grandfather's head that Ashton would be their saving grace and their way out of The Citee. Ashton knew he was powerful; he had figured that out at three years old, but he wasn't sure that he was powerful enough to break down a wall between two universes—if Grandfather's whole story was even true in the first place. The parallel universe theory that Cayden had come up with seemed plausible and made sense, but Ashton was having a hard time wrapping his head around it.

As far as Ashton knew, he was just a kid who had been cursed since birth with a weird kind of sixth sense. He wasn't some superhero or magician who was going to be able to save an entire universe. Grandfather made him uneasy, and Ali had made him defensive since she had murdered—or *disposed of*—Aidan and Carlton. He didn't know when he was going to see Cayden again or *if* he would ever see him again, and every hour spent in his cell was another hour wasted.

Once again, Ashton's thoughts drifted to Cayden. If anything happened to Cayden, it would be his fault. He had pulled Cayden into all of this. Carlton, Aidan, Ali, and Grandfather - they had all spelled it out for him. He was the only one who Grandfather needed to break out of The Citee. Aidan and Carlton had been set on showing *Ashton* the entirety of their town. Ali's job was to bring *Ashton* back to the mansion and to Grandfather. And Grandfather needed *Ashton* to break down the wall between The Citee and Davenport. If anything went wrong, Cayden would be nothing but collateral damage.

Collateral damage. There was a lump in Ashton's throat that was too quick for him to catch, and he sat up on the cot trying to slow his breathing. He'd never be able to forgive himself if something were to happen to Cayden. Breaking through the wall seemed dangerous enough for him, and he was apparently powerful enough that the ruler of an entire universe had personally requested his help. If *he* was in danger, how much danger was Cayden in?

***

Cayden stared at the ceiling from his cot, one hand on his stomach and the other hand mindlessly tapping on the edge of the small bed. The room was more like a jail cell than what he had been expecting. The place was a mansion, after all, and he expected to possibly be treated like a guest, not a prisoner.

He thought about how Ashton was doing and if he was in a cell as well. *Probably not*, he thought to himself. *Grandfather talked to Ashton like he was royalty.* Thinking back, the conversation in the meeting room made Cayden feel sick. What kind of gift could Grandfather have been talking about? Ashton was the best friend

Cayden had ever had, but there wasn't anything out of the ordinary about him. And there definitely wasn't anything so out of the ordinary that could result in Ashton saving an entire civilization, let alone an entire *universe*.

He ran a hand through his hair in frustration, worrying as he held his bottom lip between his teeth and letting his thoughts go to Aidan and Carlton. Sure, they had been a little weird. And maybe sometimes they seemed more like apparitions than actual people. Plus, the not-bleeding-after-getting-brutally stabbed thing, but nobody's perfect, right?

The theory that Aidan and Carlton hadn't been real people made Cayden's head swim. He had *seen* them and *touched* them. They had feelings and expressive faces and seemed too real to be imitations. If they truly hadn't been real, he was going to have to congratulate Grandfather on his work the next time he saw him.

No—he definitely would not be congratulating Grandfather because he hoped he would never have to see the man again in his life. Thinking about Grandfather made a shiver run down his spine and made his hands unconsciously tighten into fists. The man didn't seem exceptionally threatening, but his voice seemed almost too calm and too quiet. He was calm to the point that he was intimidating and way too calm for a man who had been stuck in a parallel universe for years.

He was vague in his speech, almost as if he was speaking in riddles. However, when Grandfather had spoken about Ashton's power or his *gift*, it was as if Ashton had completely understood what the man was talking about. The thought made Cayden a bit nauseous, as he thought about what Ashton's *gift* could possibly be.

He and Ashton had always had secrets. Ashton had never been a big talker, naturally, so he wasn't one to spew out his deepest darkest fears to Cayden. And while Cayden trusted Ashton more than he trusted anyone in the world, there were just some things that would always stay secret.

Cayden had already made peace with the fact that he would probably never actually find out everything that had happened to Ashton while he was in California. Alana seemed as haunted by the whole experience as Ashton did, and it was fruitless trying to get information out of her. Most of Ashton's bruises had faded, he had stopped drinking alcohol, and he had given up drugs as well as talking about James, but whenever Ashton pulled out a cigarette, Cayden knew there had to be countless stories that he hadn't heard and probably would never hear.

Cayden's secrets probably weren't as groundbreaking as Ashton's were. Cayden had a few dull scars up the sides of his arms from one night when he was 15 and did something stupid. It hadn't actually gotten him what he wanted: peace. But it got him a long stay in the hospital and routine psychotherapist visits. When he was finally free from that hellhole, he had returned to school and pretended as if nothing was wrong. The kids gave him weird looks most of the time, but he integrated back into the school almost seamlessly, despite missing a large chunk of the year. No one ever asked him where he had been, and sometimes he was glad. He'd never have to explain himself to anyone. But there was a small part of him that partly wished that someone cared, even a little bit—just enough to wonder where he had been when he missed three months of school.

Cayden's thoughts were interrupted by the clattering of metal, as a woman rolling a cart stopped outside of his cell. It was too dark to make out the woman's face as she unlocked his cell and opened the door. She wordlessly rolled the cart in. Cayden smelled food, sat up from the bed, and stared over at the woman and her loud metal cart. She was the reason that prisoners didn't starve to death.

The woman leaned under the cart and pulled plates full of food from under it. Cayden watched her curiously as she inspected each metal tin for kinks in the material or any sign that they had been tampered with. Then, she removed the tops of the tins, revealing a meal akin to a high school lunch. Cayden's stomach turned at the idea of food and turned his head away from the food cart woman.

For a second, Cayden contemplated making a run for it. The woman had left his cell door open, and she didn't look too large or strong to knock down from behind. Cayden sat up slowly and tried to step off the bed, but the minute his foot met the ground, a large threatening guard passed by the cell. Cayden's eyes met the dead, gray eyes of the man. It was a warning look. Cayden shrunk back onto his cot and, for a few seconds, even considered hiding under the covers.

The woman looked up at him, and although they could not see each other in the darkness of the cell, Cayden could tell that she was looking into his eyes.

"I know how scary those guards can be," she said. "They used to follow me around when I started doing my rounds here to make sure I was doing my job correctly. You can come get your food, sweetheart. It'll be all right."

Cayden's heart jumped up into his throat after the woman uttered the nickname "sweetheart," and Cayden had to stop himself from launching himself at her. He needed to make sure he wasn't going crazy.

"Mom?" he whispered into the darkness.

10

Cayden's hands were shaking as he fumbled with the lamp on the bedside table next to his cot. Finally being able to click it on and blow some dust off the top of the shade, he could see clearly across the room to the food cart woman, who was also very clearly his mother.

"Cayden, is that you?" she asked quietly, still not looking in his direction, too afraid of what it would reveal.

"Yeah it's me," Cayden laughed. But before he could ask her about what she was doing in The Citee or how she had gotten there, she was running toward him.

"Cayden," Sandra breathed, pulling her son into her chest and resting a hand on the back of his head. Cayden hugged back tightly, letting his body be held. They pulled away the moment they heard footsteps down the corridor, and Sandra resumed her duty of giving Cayden his dinner. But once the monitoring guard had passed, Sandra let out a sigh of relief and dropped the dinner plate on Cayden's cot.

Cayden smiled up at his mother, pushing the food away and hugging her again. When he pulled away for the second time, the first thing he said was, "Ashton was right. It was your car in front of us in the parking lot."

Sandra looked at him quizzically until she understood. "Yes," she said. "I was so close to crashing—this huge truck just came out of nowhere. But the minute I thought I was going to die crashing into this tree, I opened my eyes and I was in a parking lot."

"Me and Ash went out looking for you," Cayden said. "You've been gone about a week now. We went out looking and got sucked in too."

"Sucked into what?"

"What happened after you realized you were in a parking lot?" Cayden asked.

"I thought I was dead at first," Sandra explained. "But I got out of the car to try and look around, and all I saw were cars—for at least a mile."

"Did you follow the blue light?" Cayden asked.

"The blue light?" Sandra asked. "What blue light?"

"The blinking blue light on the top of the sign."

Sandra looked confused for a moment before Cayden's message made sense. "The welcome sign, you mean?" she asked. "I didn't follow it. I was met in the parking lot by a group of people who claimed to work for the government here. They escorted me back to this mansion. The people here said that they'd give me shelter and food as long as I agreed to do some work around here. I had no idea where I was—I still have no idea—so I agreed. They brought me here, and I met 'Grandfather,' whoever the hell he is, and they gave me the job of bringing the prisoners their daily meals."

"They just found you in the parking lot? So you never saw it disappear?"

Sandra raised her eyebrows. "The parking lot disappears?"

Cayden laughed and realized that his mother had definitely not had an experience here like the one that he and Ashton had.

"Yeah, it does," he said. "But that's really not that important anymore, I'm assuming."

"You said that you and Ashton went out looking for me. Is he here? Do you have any idea where he is?"

Cayden sighed. "I think Grandfather might be keeping him in a different section of the mansion because apparently he needs him."

"What do you mean?"

"When Ashton and I first got here, no one came to retrieve us in the parking lot," Cayden started. "We left the parking lot on our own and followed the light at the top of the welcome sign. We walked around for a little while, trying to find our way around this place until we met two boys who agreed to show us around.

"We were led around by Carlton and Aidan for a while until Aidan started acting weird. Apparently, he was acting weird because he sensed that we were being followed. Soon, the girl that was following us—Ali, who's apparently Grandfather's daughter—shot Carlton and Aidan with a freaking bow and arrow and led us back to the mansion. When we got here, Ali brought us to Grandfather, who went on and on about how Ashton was going to save this entire universe."

Sandra stared at her son open-mouthed. "Are you feeling all right?" she asked him.

Cayden nodded. "Mom, I'm fine. This is what's happening. Grandfather needs Ashton for some big mission to free him from this world. Apparently, Ashton's related to them through tons of bloodlines or something. But I don't trust Grandfather, and I don't know what he's done with Ashton or where he's keeping him."

"I don't trust Grandfather either," Sandra said. "But I also don't know what kind of story you're telling. I've been in this mansion for a little while now, and I know that there is no other place that has any kind of cells or sleeping quarters where they could be keeping Ashton. Even the women who work the food carts and the maids sleep in these chambers. The only other rooms with beds are the ones that Grandfather, his wife, and his daughter sleep in."

"What about the men in suits?"

"Men in suits?"

"Yeah," Cayden said. "When Ashton and I were first brought to Grandfather by his daughter, the main hallway was filled to the brim with these men in suits. I assumed they lived here too. Grandfather might be keeping Ashton in one of their bedrooms."

"Those men are government officials," Sandra nodded. "They aren't related to Grandfather and his family—or Ashton either, I guess—if Grandfather's telling the truth. They help Grandfather run The Citee because he's too old and fragile to run everything on his own. They're the ones who came to greet me in the parking lot and brought me here."

'They're the ones who greet everyone in the parking lot, according to Carlton and Aidan," Cayden said.

"Whatever they actually do, they don't live here in the mansion," Sandra said. "They have their own homes located in close vicinity to the mansion, but they don't occupy any rooms here. If they did, they'd probably be sleeping down here with the other prisoners, because like I said before, there aren't any other rooms."

"Then where the hell are they keeping Ashton?"

"They've gotta be keeping him down here somewhere," Sandra said. "They have to be. There are *no* other rooms. Even if Ashton is Grandfather's family and he's telling the truth, if Ashton is so important to Grandfather, he's not going to be treating him like a guest. He's going to be treating him like a prisoner and putting him under lockdown."

"So he'll be down here?" Cayden asked. Sandra responded with a nod.

"Why is Ashton so important to Grandfather?" Sandra asked her son. "I understand that if Ashton truly is Grandfather's family, he would want to connect with him. But why is he so important?"

"He said that Ashton is incredibly powerful and that he has a gift that can save him and his family from this universe. He said that the universe we're in right now is one that's parallel to Davenport. He told us that his entire family is stuck here and that they need to get out. He says that Ashton is the only person powerful enough to save them."

"You know I love Ashton like he's my own son, but Grandfather thinks he's powerful?" Sandra asked.

"That's what I don't get," Cayden said. "Ashton isn't exactly super strong. He's a genius, but he's not exactly built. I have no idea what kind of 'power' Grandfather could be referring to, but it's apparently really important."

Sandra nodded. "So you want to find his cell, which makes sense," she said. "But what are you going to do after that? The guards will find out sooner or later that you're in Ashton's cell with him and either send you back to your own cell or worse."

"I was thinking that if the three of us put our heads together, we could find a way out of here."

"I know a way out," Sandra smiled. "It might not be foolproof, but there's an employee exit door that the food cart women are allowed to leave through to dump out the scraps from the meals that the prisoners don't finish. They don't lock the door because most of the food cart women are happy with their jobs and lives here and don't want to run away. However, there's a guard that blocks the door, and you would have to get permission to leave through it."

"Then all we have to do is find Ashton," Cayden said, happily.

"It might not be that easy," Sandra said.

"Why not?"

"Because we can't just walk around outside together—you're a prisoner, and if they find you outside of your cell, you're toast. You'll have to hide."

"Hide where?"

Sandra smirked and Cayden gulped. His mother smirking was never a good thing.

***

"This is probably the dumbest idea I've ever heard," Cayden groaned, ducking his head under the food cart. "It works all the time in the movies, but there's no *way* we'll get to Ashton's cell and successfully make it out of here with me hiding under this—"

"Will you stop being so negative?" Sandra said, lightly pushing the rest of her son's body under the plastic table of the food cart. "No one checks under these food carts. They take the food off of the top, and then I move on to the next cell. You'll be fine under there as long as you don't make noise."

Cayden shifted under the cart, trying to get comfortable in any way possible. His movement caused the food cart to lurch a few times, but Sandra merely tilted it back into place to keep it from toppling over. Cayden clung to the edges of the cart when Sandra picked up the pace, hoping that Ashton's cell wasn't too far away. Whenever Cayden could hear the footsteps of guards next to the cart, he held his breath, praying they wouldn't want to do a random check on Sandra's cart to make sure everything was in order.

Suddenly, Cayden felt the cart being turned sharply to the left and held on for dear life until its wheels stopped. His mother came around the side of the cart and picked up the tablecloth, putting a finger to her lips to make sure he remained quiet. One look around and Cayden could tell that she had pulled the cart into a deserted corner of the hallway to talk to him without it being suspicious.

"I just heard one of the guards talking about Ashton and they're on their way to his cell right now," she said. "He's being kept down here, but he's definitely being kept separate from the other prisoners, so our best bet is to follow them to his cell."

"Isn't that risky?" he whispered.

"If they ask what I'm doing, I'll just tell them that his cell is the next one listed on my schedule."

"And if they don't believe you?"

'Then I'll quickly write Ashton's cell number onto my schedule to prove it to them," she said. "This might be the only way we'll be able to find Ashton's cell, so I think we should just take this idea and run with it."

"Maybe we shouldn't actually run, though," Cayden clarified. "I swear, I'm going to get car sick because of how fast you push this food cart."

Sandra laughed and pulled the tablecloth down over Cayden's face, trying to flatten it out before she pulled the cart out of the corner of the hallway. She started down the corridor that the guards had gone down. Despite her son's previous protests, she picked up the pace, trying to catch up with the guards without seeming suspicious. Cayden had to close his eyes to stop his head from spinning.

When Sandra slowed down the cart's wheels, Cayden could only assume that they were getting closer and closer to Ashton's cell. Soon, they were close enough to the guards that Cayden could hear their muffled conversations. He held his breath again. They mentioned the cell number 209, and Sandra started moving the cart more slowly, so she could scratch the number onto her schedule to make it seem like Ashton was due for dinner. Suddenly, the cart stopped moving completely.

"What are you doing in this corridor, woman?" one of the guards asked harshly.

"This cell is the next one on my schedule," Sandra replied, not an ounce of fear in her voice. "This prisoner requires dinner."

"Are you sure about that?"

"Would you like to check my schedule?"

The guards shared a look, and the larger one nodded, holding out his hand so Sandra could hand him her clipboard. When he had the clipboard in his hand, he read down the schedule in confusion.

"Woman, your schedule is based around the cells numbered 139 through 167. It makes no sense for you to be serving dinner to cells 165, 166, 167, and then 209. Take your food elsewhere."

Cayden gulped, praying that the guards couldn't tell that 209 had been written in just minutes earlier.

"What kind of food are you bringing the prisoners anyway?"

Cayden froze. He looked around him and stared at the food tins surrounding him under the food cart. He held his breath and waited for the inevitable.

"They're mostly cheap sandwiches from the western business district," Sandra chirped. "Every prisoner gets basically the same food."

"Well this one's a special prisoner, Grandfather says." One of the guards laughed, pointing to cell 209. "I think he should be getting more gourmet food than the shit they're sellin' in the western business district."

"I'm pretty sure I've got something a little more gourmet in this cart if this prisoner is really as special as Grandfather says he is."

"Mind if we take a look under that cart of yours then?"

Cayden froze again, trying to make himself as small as possible and trying to calm his breathing. If the guards caught him under the food cart, he didn't know what would happen to him and his mother. He could imagine Grandfather killing or torturing them. He bit his tongue to keep as quiet as possible. He crossed his fingers and toes and eyes and prayed to every god he could name that the guards would only reach under the cart and not pick up the tablecloth completely.

When Sandra replied "yes," giving the guards approval to check under her cart, Cayden rolled over so that he could see the tablecloth that was being lifted up. He almost sighed in relief when he could see only the hairy hand of one of the guards. He grabbed the closest tin to his hand, took it out from under the cart, and then his hand was gone.

Cayden could hear him opening the tin, inspecting the food, making "hmmm" sounds, and picking it up off the platter.

"This actually doesn't look half bad," the guard said.

A second later, the tablecloth was lifted again and the same hand was back, now reaching a little farther forward to grab a different tin. For a second, the guard's hand almost grabbed Cayden's ankle, but he yanked his foot away at the last second. Cayden had to struggle to keep his balance as the hand retreated again.

This time, when the top of the tin was removed, the guard made a noise of contentment. "This actually looks delicious. If anything, this is the food that Grandfather would want this prisoner eating. Give him this, you hear?"

Sandra nodded in agreement, taking the tin back from the guard and placing it on top of the food cart. The guards let her pass finally and walked away from the corridor, only stopping once to peek through the bars of Ashton's cell to get a look at him.

Arriving in front of cell 209, Sandra took her key ring out of her pocket and unlocked the cell door. She walked into the cell with the foot cart and called Ashton quietly by name.

Ashton picked his head off of the pillow of his cot at the sound of Sandra's voice and ran to the cell door.

"Sandra!" he almost screamed, hugging her. Sandra laughed and hugged him back, trying not to topple over with the intensity of the hug.

"It's good to see you," she smiled. "I have your dinner, as well as a surprise." She handed Ashton the food tin that the guard had opened and then picked up the tablecloth from the food cart.

"Cayden?" Ashton asked, looking under the cart.

Cayden rolled out from inside the cart, falling onto the cold floor of Ashton's cell while breathing a sigh of relief. "The guard almost grabbed my leg when he tried to grab your food tin, Ash," Cayden breathed. "Jesus Christ."

Ashton laughed, setting the food tin down on his cot and picking Cayden up off the floor.

"What are you two doing here?" he asked. "Cayden, how'd you find Sandra? Sandra, how'd you go from driving through a tree to working for Grandfather?"

"She brought me food," Cayden laughed. "Do you remember when Aidan and Carlton told us about the people from the government that greet new citizens in the parking lot? They found my mom and brought her here to give her a job."

Ashton's eyes widened. "Wow."

"And now we came to get you, so we can escape."

Ashton's wide-eyed, surprised expression soon changed to one of confusion and hesitance. "I'm not leaving," he said, confused.

"My mom knows a way out. We can get out of here," Cayden protested, pulling on Ashton's arm and trying to get him to follow him toward the cell door. "The two of us hiding under the food cart might get a little cramped, but we can get out."

"Cayden, I can't leave. They're desperate for a way out, and I need to help them." Ashton, who looked genuinely sad, stared wide-eyed at his friend.

Cayden laughed bitterly at Ashton's comment. "They locked you in a cell."

"They're my ancestors and my family, Cayden. Hell, they're probably the only family I have left. I can help them get out of here, and we can go back home. They can help me and Alana and support us for a little while—maybe she'll finally get a chance to actually be a kid," Ashton pleaded sadly.

"Ash, you can't be sure of that. You can't assume they'll be able to support you when you're not even sure they're your blood. They could be some crazy people that control this parallel world.

Ash, man, we don't even know where we are. You don't even know if they're actually related to you."

"They knew about my powers."

The last line was whispered in a small voice that Cayden hadn't heard Ashton use since they were kids. He looked frightened to even hear the words come out of his mouth. He touched his lips hesitantly, seemingly trying to force the words back in.

"What?" Cayden asked slowly, trying hard not to scare Ashton. "What powers? What do you mean?"

"It started before I could talk," Ashton said. There was a note of panic in his voice, but he was no longer whispering. "When I was a baby, I mean. If I wanted something, if I was tired or hungry, I could almost, like, telepathically tell people what I wanted. And if that wasn't enough, they actually *did* what I told them to do. It never worked on my parents, or my older siblings, but other people would always follow my commands. And then all of a sudden, it wasn't just telepathic commands anymore. All of a sudden, I could control people by just telling them to do something or say something. I did it to Mrs. Robertson when we were in kindergarten: she didn't ask me any questions or call on me once for a whole month. It scared the shit out of me, man. It's why I was mute for so long. I thought that if I just didn't speak at all, I wouldn't hurt anyone."

Feeling confused, Cayden squinted and said, "You always talked to me."

Ashton sighed. "That's because I made myself a promise to never use it on you, no matter what. The *thing*. The *power*. I never gave it a name over the years, and it still doesn't make sense to me. I've never even told anyone about it; that's why I think that if Grandfather understands it, he *must* be important to me."

Cayden stared at Ashton in disbelief. He sat down next to his friend on the small cot and put his head in his hands. "Ashton, I really wish I could believe you—I truly do. But *mind manipulation*? That sounds like something straight out of a movie. And if you made yourself a promise to never use it on me—"

Ashton sighed and chewed on his lip. "You want me to show you?"

Cayden looked at Ashton like he had just asked the stupidest question in the world. "Of course I want you to show me. This thing can literally make or break the lives of everyone who lives in this mansion. It must be pretty astounding."

Ashton felt his face heat up. "It's not. It's more like a curse, actually."

"Show me," Cayden said again.

Ashton sighed and walked over to the food cart where Sandra stood, who was trying to give Cayden and Ashton some privacy so that they could talk. He took Sandra's hand and led her over to the cot where Cayden was still sitting.

"Sandra, do you trust me?" Ashton said.

"Of course I do, sweetie," she replied, holding Ashton's hand. "You're like a son to me."

Ashton smiled at her and nodded. "Okay then. I need you to trust me for a second." He took a deep breath, trying to reawaken the power and light behind his eyelids and quietly whispered, "Bring me that plate," as he pointed to the food cart sitting in the corner of his cell.

Sandra's eyes changed first, her brown irises dissipating into a sea of gray. Then she walked robotically over to the food cart, picked up the plate, and walked it back to Ashton. Cayden watched in terror, his mouth dropping open and his eyes widening, as he watched his mother place the plate in Ashton's hands. The minute the ceramic touched Ashton's waiting hands, Sandra's eyes turned back to normal. She looked a little delirious for a few seconds, but the color returned to her face quickly. It was like nothing out of the ordinary had happened at all.

"What was that?" Cayden said, sounding terrified.

"I can do it telepathically too," Ashton said, taking a shaky breath and staring at Sandra again until her eyes shifted to gray. She took the plate from Ashton's hands and walked over to the food cart again, placing the plate back where she had taken it from. When she returned, her eyes were already starting to change back to normal.

Cayden couldn't stop staring, and Ashton scratched the back of his neck nervously, trying to decide if the face Cayden was making was one of shock or terror.

"You're like some kind of superhero," Cayden said incredulously.

That was definitely not something Ashton was expecting. He walked in front of the cot where Cayden was sitting and stared at him hard in the eyes. "No, I'm not," he said. "I'm a monster."

Cayden stared up at him with sad eyes. "No you're not," he said. "Just because you can do . . ." His voice trailed off as he tried to find the words that could describe what he had just seen.

"Just because you can do *that thing*," he said, tapping Ashton's temple. "Doesn't make you a monster."

Ashton let out a sigh, dropped his gaze away from Cayden, and sat down on the floor in front of the cot. "But the *thing* is almost impossible to control, Cayden," he said, pinching the bridge of his nose. "It's so hard to explain. It's like my head is on fire sometimes. But it also feels like I'm drowning."

Cayden didn't know how to react. He still sat on the cot trying to process everything he had seen. In front of him on the floor, Ashton raised his hand up and Cayden flinched, moving backwards slightly.

Ashton's face fell and he dropped his hand, sensing Cayden's fear. His stomach twisted, and a lump formed in his throat that he couldn't swallow down. Cayden was *afraid* of him—afraid that Ashton was going to control him with the flick of his hand—afraid that Ashton wouldn't be able to control himself now that he had let a little bit of his power fly free. The thought made Ashton want to dig a hole, crawl in, and never come out of it.

Cayden could sense Ashton's sadness and immediately felt horrible. He didn't know exactly why he was so afraid; this was his best friend—the same best friend who had promised to *never* use his power on Cayden, *ever*. Thinking back on their childhood, Cayden realized there had been many times when Ashton could've used his power on Cayden to make his life a hell of a lot easier. But he hadn't.

"Hey, hey," Cayden said, tapping his finger under Ashton's chin and coaxing him to look back up. His gaze was hesitant and cold, and Cayden felt like a complete jerk. "What were you going to do, just now with your hand," he asked.

Ashton looked hesitant and scared, as if raising his hand again would scare Cayden away completely. But eventually, he raised his hand again and tapped Cayden once under the knee, watching his foot kick upwards before returning his hand to his lap.

Cayden had no idea why, but all of a sudden, he was laughing. He was laughing so hard that there were tears rolling down his cheeks, and he was sliding off the edge of the cot to meet Ashton on the floor. Sandra tried to shush him at one point, pointing outside of the cell to indicate that there were people outside, but Cayden merely slapped a hand over his own mouth as he continued to laugh.

When the coast was clear again, Cayden leaned his head on Ashton's shoulder as he tried to calm down, willing himself to stop laughing. Ashton looked confused and concerned for Cayden's well-being. He placed a hand on his shoulder and narrowed his eyes.

"Are you okay? Why are you laughing?" Ashton asked anxiously, worried that Cayden's laughter was somehow a bad sign.

"Because after all of that," Cayden choked out while laughing. "After the mind manipulation and the monster conversation and the fact we're in a parallel universe and everything screwed up in our lives right now, you're still infatuated with my freaking knee-jerk reflex."

Ashton flushed and tried to laugh, but it came out as more of a pathetic sigh of relief. Cayden wasn't scared of him, just confused by the whole situation, like any sane person would be. The realization made Ashton feel a lot better.

"I can't go with you, Cayden," Ashton said, finally. "I wish I could, but if they need my help, I can't just abandon them here. Even though I'd love to get out of this cell, I don't know what will happen if I leave."

"Isn't that reason enough to get out of here?" Cayden asked. "You're afraid of what will happen to you if leave, which means that deep down, you're afraid of Grandfather and what he might be able to do to you."

"I'm not afraid of Grandfather," Ashton laughed. "He's just an old man. He probably has a hard time opening up a new bottle of ketchup. I'm afraid that if I leave with you and we do end up finding a way out of here, Grandfather and the rest of my family will be stuck here forever."

Cayden desperately wanted to roll his eyes and try to explain to Ashton again that the people living here might not actually be his family, but one look at Ashton proved to him that any attempt to sway him from his decision would be fruitless. Ashton was going to be staying in the mansion whether Cayden liked it or not, and he was going to have to come to terms with it sooner or later.

"You're really staying here," Cayden sighed.

"I'm really staying here."

Another guard walked past the cell, and Cayden had to hide behind Ashton's bedside table, holding his breath until the guard greeted Sandra with a grunt and walked away.

"The encounters are getting too frequent now," Ashton observed. "That's two guards passing in front of this cell in less than 10 minutes. They're starting to suspect that something weird is going on. Prisoners usually just take their food and go, and it's suspicious for a food cart woman to stay outside of a prisoner's cell for too long. That's what I've seen at least. If you two want to get out of here, I'd suggest that you start moving now."

Cayden sighed, reluctant to leave without convincing Ashton that fleeing was the right thing to do, but when Ashton reached up to get his food tin off of the bed, Cayden sighed and stood up.

"Are you sure you're not coming?" Cayden asked for the last time.

Ashton smiled sadly up at him from the floor before jumping to his feet and wrapping his arms around Cayden's middle.

"No, I'm not coming," he said, muffled, into Cayden's shoulder.

Cayden hugged back with a sigh, and looked back toward his mother and the food cart. "I promise I'm gonna keep you safe," he mumbled into Ashton's neck.

Ashton pulled away and laughed. "Keep me safe from what?"

"I'm not sure yet, actually," Cayden said, scratching the back of his neck. "All I know is that I don't have a good feeling about this place, Grandfather, or any of your ancestors. So if I have to save you from them, I will."

Ashton shook his head and laughed, pushing Cayden toward his mother. "Get out of here," he said. "Another guard will be coming soon, and this time, they're probably going to come into the cell to check on me. Text me if anything huge happens."

Cayden nodded, hugging Ashton again before returning to his

place under the food cart, pulling the tablecloth down in front of his face. Ashton hugged Sandra once before she turned the cart out of Ashton's cell, locking it before walking away.

Ashton finally sat on his bed and opened up the tin that held his food. It actually looked appetizing and was miraculously still pretty warm, despite how long it had been sitting on his bed while he and Cayden talked. After finishing the meal, he left the tin on his bedside table, put his hands under his head on his pillow, and stared up at the ceiling.

The text came 30 minutes after the Mitchells had left for town.

Come back in one piece, please. Don't let them dwell on you too much.

Ashton rolled his eyes at the phone.

Ha, see what I did there?

Ashton tucked the phone on the bedside table near his boots and empty food tin, turning it on silent. If he was going to be training in the morning, he needed to get at least four or five hours of shuteye. He curled into himself on the cot, closing his eyes and trying to imagine nicer surroundings to fall asleep to.

Whatever, I'm terrible at jokes anyway.

Please stay safe.

Love you.

When Ashton woke up in the morning, his phone was gone.

11

Leaving the mansion proved to be more difficult than Cayden and Sandra had anticipated. The employee exit was guarded during the daytime, which meant that Cayden would have to stay hidden under the food cart for more than three hours. By the time dusk fell, and the exit was no longer guarded, Sandra and Cayden had to sneak past the night guards to get to the door safely.

While the night guards were more heavily armed, and though they surveyed most of the premises, they were more lenient when it came to the employee exits. Sandra kept a watchful eye on the door, while Cayden tried to comfortably shift his body on the food rack that hung under the main table of the food cart.

"I've been under here for *hours*, Mom," Cayden groaned when the last of the night guards had left the employee exit.

"I'll get us out of here as quickly as possible," Sandra assured him. She started to roll the cart toward another cell. She reached under the cart to grab another prisoner's food, accidentally grabbing her son's nose at first. When the last prisoner on Sandra's list had eaten their food, Sandra moved stealthily toward the employee exit, pushing the cart in front of her.

Right as they were approaching freedom, a night guard appeared, dressed in all black. He blocked Sandra's food cart from the door. Cayden held his breath as he listened to the guard ask his mother questions, silently praying that the guard didn't pick up the tablecloth.

"What are you doing over here?" the guard asked in a monotone voice.

"I got word from Grandfather that he wants the leftovers from prisoners' meals to be disposed of outside," Sandra replied without missing a beat.

The guard contemplated her words for a few seconds with a disbelieving look on his face before rolling his eyes and moving out of her way.

"If that's what Grandfather wants," he said as he opened the employee door for her. "You know where the mansion dumpster is?"

When Sandra nodded, the guard shrugged and walked away from the cart. He headed in the direction of the main room and left the employee exit completely deserted. Sandra rushed through the door, pushed the cart as fast as she could, and rounded the side of the mansion to move toward the dumpster.

Cayden jumped out from underneath the cart and looked around frantically to make sure no one had followed them out the door. Sandra quickly opened the dumpster and looked to her son,

"Help me pick this up," she whispered, gesturing to the cart.

"What?"

"If the night guards do any rounds outside and see the food cart just sitting here, they're going to know that we ran for the hills. If we hide the cart in the dumpster, they might not find the cart for a few days."

Cayden nodded and helped his mother lift the heavy food cart into the dumpster. Once the wheels of the cart touched the metal bottom of the dumpster, Cayden let go, and Sandra stepped away. She held up her hands in surrender, willing the food cart not to move, roll, or make any noise. They closed the plastic top and waited.

"What do we do now?" Cayden asked his mother.

"I have no idea," she replied. "I didn't think we would make it this far, to be perfectly honest."

Cayden wanted to laugh or crack a joke, anything really, but his insides felt sour, and his brain felt like putty. He didn't know what they were supposed to do now that they were free of the mansion. He had promised Ashton that he would keep him safe, but he wasn't very sure of what that was going to entail.

"We need to find out more about Grandfather and the people who live here," Cayden said, speaking his thoughts out loud. "The more we can find out about these people, the more we know about what Ash is in for while he stays there."

Sandra nodded in agreement, but didn't follow her son, as Cayden walked away from the mansion. Cayden stopped and turned around when he realized she wasn't following. He shrugged his shoulders as a form of inquiry. He felt too tired to even open his mouth to vocalize his question.

Sandra seemed to be on the same page, as she silently held up one finger to say "wait" before she walked toward the dumpster again. She raised the plastic top once again before placing her foot on one of the ridges of its base and jumping into it.

Cayden ran toward the dumpster, peeked into it, and tried to figure out why his mother was currently sifting through a pile of garbage in a dumpster outside of a mansion—in a parallel universe that was almost identical to his hometown. What the hell had happened to his life?

It was too dark to see inside the dumpster, so Cayden leaned back against it while his mother looked for whatever the hell it was she was looking for. He silently prayed that no one would walk by and find him there. He wondered what he would do if he was caught by one of the night guards. Panic rising within him, he banged slightly on the side of the metal dumpster, trying to get his mother's attention.

"Mom, come on," he said.

Sandra emerged from the dumpster a second later, smiling in victory as she held up what she was holding in her hands. Clasped in her fist was a pearl necklace, a small pad of paper, a pen, and a tube of lipstick.

She jumped out of the dumpster quickly, grabbing Cayden's arm and pulling him away from the mansion. Cayden followed her until they got far away from the mansion and reached a small section of houses that were all painted bright colors and more or less separated from society. They were basically as far away from the mansion and from Grandfather as they could get, and Sandra finally plopped down on the ground and let out a long sigh of relief.

Cayden was so tired that he felt as if he was going to pass out right there, standing up. But he was too curious about the dumpster dive to sleep just yet, so he sat next to his mother on the ground as she placed her treasures on the ground.

"Not that I don't want to go to sleep," Cayden said, "but are you going to explain to me what those are for?"

Sandra laughed quietly. "These are going to help us with the next phase of our lives as refugees."

Cayden tapped his chin with his index finger. "Y'know, technically we aren't actually refugees right now, more like internally displaced people because we never formally crossed the boundary line of—"

Cayden stopped speaking when he saw that his mother was staring at him with wonder in her eyes. He shut his mouth quickly. "That's like the one lesson I ever actually listened to in history, okay?" he mumbled.

Sandra just nodded and laughed and took the cap off the tube of lipstick in her hand. The pad of paper and pen still lay in her lap, and Cayden was starting to get antsy.

"Seriously, Mom—how are a pad and paper, lipstick, and pearls, which are probably fake by the way, supposed to help us here?"

"You said that we needed to find out more information on Grandfather and the people living here if we wanted to be able to protect Ashton," she said. Cayden nodded. "Well, I thought, who could give us more accurate information about the people who live here than the people who live here?"

"The people who live here aren't going to just open up about their entire lives and tell us every secret they know about Grandfather," Cayden scoffed.

"I know they won't," Sandra said. "Or, maybe, they *wouldn't*, not originally. " Sandra stopped speaking to clip the pearl necklace around her neck and apply the lipstick to her lips. "But if someone who works for Grandfather comes to the door and starts to ask people questions, they might actually talk."

Cayden had a million reasons jumbled in his head about why that was a bad idea, but he was too tired to vocalize them. He merely nodded and lay down on the ground, desperate for sleep.

"We should probably find somewhere more inconspicuous to sleep, Cayden," Sandra said, tapping her son's arm and standing up. "If we fall asleep out in the open like this, we're begging to get caught."

Cayden groaned—though he knew she was right—and stood up. They walked for a little while longer until they found the abandoned house that Cayden and Ashton had slept in after they had met Carlton and Aidan. The roof still looked as if it were about to collapse, but it was a good, dark hiding space. Sandra leaned up against one of the splintered walls, and Cayden curled up on the floor next to her, willing himself to fall asleep.

When day broke, Cayden forced himself awake, stood up, and stretched. Walking over to the broken vanity table in the corner of the room, he looked at himself in the broken mirror. If they were going to be trying to convince people that they worked for the government, he needed to try and not look like a homeless person. Grandfather had given him a few pairs of clothes in his cell to change into when he was first forced into it, and he still had a pair or two stuffed into Carlton's backpack. He walked over to his mother, who was in the process of waking up, and he reached into the backpack and pulled out a pair of jeans and a wrinkled sweater. That was nice enough.

He pulled the clothes into the one secluded room of the abandoned house and shoved his pile of dirty clothes back into Carlton's backpack. Pulling the backpack over his shoulder, Sandra rubbed the sleep out of her eyes and walked over to the broken mirror as well. Instead of sitting on the three-legged chair in front of the vanity, which was only standing because of balance and luck, she kneeled in front of the mirror while she fixed her hair, tied the pearls around her neck, and applied the tube of lipstick.

"How do I look?" Sandra laughed, posing stupidly in the doorway of the living room of the abandoned house.

"Like a typical government douche bag," Cayden said, smirking.

Normally, Sandra would be scolding Cayden for swearing, but all she could do was laugh. Making sure they had everything with them that they had brought into the house, they walked outside toward a group of houses far enough away from the mansion that they weren't in any danger of being caught or recognized.

Walking up to a small, white house, Cayden became nervous. "Are you sure this is going to work?" he asked. "The people who live here seem either secretive or oblivious."

"Won't know unless we try," she answered, flattening down her dress and making sure that the Dweller crest was visible on her chest. She rang the doorbell and waited with her hands clasped behind her back and gestured for Cayden to do the same.

The door opened, and a short red-haired woman stood in the doorway. "What can I do for you?" she said, all smiles.

"Hello ma'am," Sandra started, trying to sound legitimate. "I work for Grandfather in the mansion, and I was wondering if you would be willing to take a survey on behalf of The Citee."

The woman seemed hesitant at first, but after her eyes landed on the crest sewn onto Sandra's dress, she let the Mitchells in without a second thought. "What will the survey entail?" she asked, leading Sandra and Cayden over to her kitchen table, which was patterned with leaves.

"I'm just going to ask you a few questions about your life here," Sandra said. "Grandfather wants to make sure all of his citizens are living happy and healthy lives."

Cayden had to dig his fingernails into his thigh to keep from rolling his eyes as he looked over at his mother, who was holding her dirty pad of paper and pen in her hands. The woman nodded in Sandra's direction and sat across from the Mitchells at her table.

"What's your name?" Sandra asked. The woman replied, "Amanda Regal," and folded her hands on the table.

"How long have you been living here?"

"I came here years and years ago. I was very young when I first passed through the tree; I was probably only about 16."

"How old are you now?" Sandra asked, writing down what Amanda said on her pad of paper.

"I'm 47," she answered. "I've been living here ever since then."

Sandra nodded. "Would you mind telling me about your experience when you first passed through the tree and how you were treated?"

Amanda looked suspicious about the question at first, and Cayden held his breath hoping that the question hadn't been too forward or personal.

"Well, I was treated just fine," she answered. "When I first passed through the tree, I was nervous and lost. I was found in the parking lot by a group of men in nice suits who told me that they would be able to help me get settled in here. I was a young girl who had just gotten my permit and who had narrowly escaped death by crashing into a tree, so I was up for anything. They told me that they worked for the government here and took me to Grandfather, who told me where I was."

"And where did he tell you that you were, exactly?"

"The Citee," she answered simply. "He was very vague, but very nice, and told me that he always had new residents brought straight to him because he personally wanted to know everyone who was living in his city. He told me that The Citee was a place where I could live peacefully and happily. I was afraid and asked him if I was ever going to see my family or friends again, considering I was only 16 at the time. He replied that I wouldn't be able to because the tree only chose very special people to let pass through. He said that I was chosen."

Cayden's stomach turned. Those were the lies that Grandfather was pumping into these people—that they were chosen by some higher power to be let through the tree and would able to live out the rest of their days in peace?

Sandra wrote down what Amanda was saying quickly, as she went hastily through pieces of paper. "Chosen for what?" she asked.

"Hell if I know," Amanda laughed. "All I knew was that I was safe and that the government was going to keep me safe until I died. They set me up with this beautiful house and gave me enough food so that I was able to get on my feet the first few months that I lived here. After that, I got a job in the commercial district working at a cute little specialty shop. There I met my husband, Max, and we were married and had our daughter. Everyone I've ever talked to who lives here has had a similar experience. I'm very happy to live here."

Sandra wrote down the last of Amanda's thoughts and smiled at her, thanking her for her time. Cayden shook her hand and then followed his mother out of Amanda's house. When the front door was closed, Sandra let out a sigh of relief, and Cayden wanted to vomit.

"Can you believe that?" he asked his mother. "Grandfather tells them that the tree chose them and then treats them with houses and food until they get a job, get married, and have kids here."

Sandra nodded. "I know. And she was only 16. How did she not lose it when Grandfather told her that she was never going to see her parents again?"

Cayden shook his head, pinched the bridge of his nose, and walked a few houses down from where Amanda lived. He knocked on the door of a large gray house and put his hands behind his back, letting his mother step in front of him when he heard a voice from inside call, "one minute!"

Sandra played with her hair a bit and fixed her necklace before turning back around to Cayden. "I guess we'll see what this person has to say."

The person living in this house was named Molly, a young woman with black hair and a large smile. She let the Mitchells in without a second thought after Sandra had said her opener. Molly was a single mother of a young son—she bounced him on her hip in her large kitchen while she answered Sandra's questions. She had lived a similar life to Amanda and had passed through the tree at 20, being brought to Grandfather in the mansion a few hours later. Grandfather had offered her a job in the mansion, which she had declined in favor of working in the commercial district just like Amanda had. She then bought her own house along with her own shop. After working in the specialty shop for a few years and making quite a lot of money, she sold it when she found out that she was pregnant. Her son was three now, and Molly was living in a large house with enough money to keep her and her son fed. She loved her life.

After thanking Molly for her time and leaving the large gray house, Cayden sat on the ground opposite Amanda and Molly's homes, defeated. Sandra picked him up by the arm and dragged him to another street adjacent to the one they had just been on, set on questioning at least a few more residents before nightfall.

From almost everyone, they got the same story. Regardless of gender, age, race, sexuality, relationship status, or parental status, almost every person they interviewed gave the same story. They had arrived in The Citee a few years ago, got brought to the mansion by Grandfather's posse of government men in suits, Grandfather had either given them a house or a job, and they had made a nice life here. Not one person had complained about anything. Cayden was completely and utterly lost.

"I just feel like we should give up, Mom," Cayden said finally, sitting down on the ground and sighing. "We haven't gotten any useful information from the residents here, and it's only a matter of time before someone from the mansion realizes that I'm gone and you haven't reported for work." He rested his chin on his hand and looked down at the ground. "They'll find your abandoned food cart sooner or later, and then we're screwed."

Sandra sat down on the ground next to Cayden and put an arm around him. "We can't give up now, okay?" she said. "We made it out of the mansion alive, which was a huge feat. Plus, you made Ashton a promise. You can't keep him safe if you're dead now, can you?"

The words should've made Cayden miserable, but instead they motivated him to start moving again. He stood up from the ground and held out a hand to help his mother up.

"You're right," he said. "The least we can do is to try. We'll talk to a few more citizens before it gets dark, and then we can have a stakeout or something. Take shifts sleeping, maybe?"

Sandra laughed and nodded. "Let's not get ahead of ourselves. But that sounds like a good plan."

They were able to talk to two more people before darkness fell. The first person was a young man named Henry who had a similar story to Molly's. He too was a single parent who had recently divorced from his wife, but he was doing pretty well for himself. He owned a shop in the commercial district for specialty clothing and thanked Grandfather for everything he had.

The last person they talked to was a woman named Brooke. Although every person they had talked to previously was a bust, Brooke actually gave them some information that they could work with. Brooke loved her life in The Citee. She had arrived there as a teenager as Amanda had, and she had been given a home and some money until she could get on her feet. Currently, she and her wife owned a significant amount of property in the dining area of the commercial district and were already landlords, despite both of them only being in their mid-20s. Brooke was very grateful for what Grandfather had given her, but unlike all of the other citizens that Cayden and Sandra had talked to, Brooke actually had a complaint about The Citee.

"It's rare to see homeless people in The Citee," Brooke said as she was cooking dinner. "Grandfather makes sure that none of his citizens are homeless and makes sure that everyone at least has the materials to be able to find a job and buy a small home. If they can't afford it, he lets them live in one for free until they can get a job. Homelessness is so rare, which is why I don't understand why I see this one figure so often. He's usually sneaking around at night trying to find somewhere to sleep or sneaking around during the day trying to find something to eat. That's really my only complaint."

Thanking Brooke for her answers, Cayden and Sandra left Brooke's house at around 8 p.m., just as dusk was hitting.

"That's something," Cayden said as he looked at what Sandra had written down on her pad. "Maybe it's nothing big, but we can create another question for the survey now. Maybe instead of asking them about their complaints or how they're feeling about living here, we can ask them if they've ever seen any dark figures sneaking around or if they ever see homeless citizens."

Sandra nodded and clicked her pen closed. She slipped it into the pocket of her black dress. "We can discuss it more in the morning, Cayden," she said. "I'm exhausted."

Cayden agreed and asked his mother whether she thought that they should try and trek back to the abandoned house and sleep in it again. Sandra shrugged and agreed, as it would be safe and inconspicuous in the abandoned house, and they wouldn't have to take shifts sleeping.

On their way back to the abandoned house, Cayden saw a dark figure run across the bushes in front of him. Rubbing his eyes, he wondered if his tiredness was making him see things that weren't really there. However, even after rubbing his eyes, he could still clearly make out a human-sized shadow trying to hide among the bushes. The dark figure saw Cayden staring and sprinted toward a large dumpster a few yards away and squatted down behind it. "Did you see that?" he whispered to his mother. "I think that was a *person* moving behind the dumpster."

Sandra replied that she hadn't seen the figure, but agreed to follow Cayden behind the dumpster. She thought that if what Cayden saw was the dark figure Brooke had been talking about, she could crack the case once and for all. Cayden and Sandra made their way over to the dumpster quietly, sneaking behind trees and other shrubbery to keep themselves hidden from the person—definitely a person—who was hiding behind the dumpster.

When they finally got close enough, Cayden turned to his mother and put a finger over his lips to urge silence. He crept toward the dumpster, making sure the figure didn't move as he got closer and, finally, pushed the dumpster to the side by its wheels.

The girl didn't move when she was suddenly in plain view. She kept her head in her hands and refused to look up at whoever had exposed her. When Cayden tried to take a step toward her, she pulled one hand from her face and held it out in front of her defensively.

"What color are your eyes?"

12

"Hazel—my eyes are hazel. Well, sometimes they're green . . . and sometimes they're brown but, no they're . . . why are you asking?" Cayden's voice shook slightly as he spoke, more frightened of the girl then he had anticipated. Despite not seeing the girl's face at all, as her head was still tucked into her hands, she intimidated him. Sandra and Cayden stood in front of the girl for a short while, waiting for her to move or say something.

After a few moments, the girl raised her head from out of her palms slowly and cautiously, and Cayden tried his best not to stare when she was facing him completely and staring him straight in the eyes.

She was tragically beautiful, her blond hair hanging over her face in choppy bangs, as though she had cut the ends with a razor blade. Her hair was a pretty shade, although the dirt and dust covering most of her head blocked the blond strands from seeing daylight. Instead of looking apprehensive, like Cayden had assumed, her facial expressions were hard and defensive.

Before even looking at the girl's face, however, her physical appearance immediately drew Cayden in. First of all, she was barefoot, which Cayden thought was extremely odd in a city where broken glass lined all of the streets. The fact that she was barefoot didn't seem to bother the girl though; she stood tall and proud, and her gaze did not stray from Cayden's face. Her tights were ripped and tattered in most places, with numerous holes and a dash of blood on her right calf. Cayden wasn't sure if the blood was hers or not, and he wasn't sure he wanted to find out. The girl's dress was in the same condition: tattered and torn in most places, especially near the ribs and bottom. Something about the dress was eerily familiar, and Cayden knew that he had seen it somewhere before; the black intricate lining of the design, although ripped and destroyed, gave him a nagging sense of déjà vu.

If the girl's clothes weren't enough, her face was testimony to why the girl was hiding and sheltered in a corner of The Citee. The burn was not new—the scar had darkened with age. It covered the entire right side of her face, even overlapping one of her nostrils. Cayden winced internally, thinking about the pain the girl must have endured when the wound was fresh and what possibly could have happened to cause a scar of that magnitude.

The weirdest thing of all to Cayden was her eyes. He had learned about heterochromia in school, and he thought the whole idea of having two different colored eyes was pretty amazing. But here, with the girl staring intensely at him, he wasn't sure that he still believed that. Her one blue eye, so similar to Ashton's that it made Cayden's heart sink with familiarity, stood out against the aged burn, as if it was trying to bring attention to it. Her other eye was a dull gray, a sad color that reminded him of a rainy sky or cloudy day in April. She kept the stare hard and firm, and Cayden stared right back almost unwillingly.

Soon, the mask broke and the girl let out an honest-to-god laugh. "You're staring," she stated nonchalantly.

Cayden retracted, taking a step backwards and scratching the back of his neck. "Sorry," he mumbled. "It's just that you—you remind me of someone."

They stood there in silence for a few more moments, the girl's hand placed firmly on her hip until she smiled a bit mischievously. "Listen, kid, you're a newbie around here, right?" Her voice rang in Cayden's ears until he processed the words and nodded slowly.

The girl sighed. "Well I'm going to give you three tips for staying alive here. Number 1, there is no way out. Don't bother asking old residents or driving cars into trees. You'll get yourself killed, for one thing, and you'll just draw attention to yourself. Number 2, stay away from anyone who might want to kill you. It seems simple, but The Citee is unpredictable, and there are a lot of desperate people here. And number 3, stay away from anyone and everyone with blue eyes."

"You have . . . blue eyes."

"Exactly. Run."

She turned on her heel quickly to run in the opposite direction, but Cayden grabbed her arm before she could get away. "Wait! Wait . . . wait . . . please. I need your help."

The girl turned once again, now squinting in disbelief at Cayden's request. "You think I can help you?"

"Yes . . . you . . . why are you in hiding?"

The girl pulled her arm out of Cayden's grasp, but did not try to run again. She straightened out her back, trying to look taller, although Cayden towered over her. "What makes you think I'm in hiding?"

Cayden laughed sarcastically, the girl's sassy demeanor making her a lot less threatening. "You were curled up behind a dumpster before I found you, for one thing. And the minute I got within a foot of you, you freaked out about what color my eyes are."

The girl put her hands on her hips defensively. "I don't see what me being in hiding has to do with helping you."

Cayden smirked. "People in hiding usually have something to hide—some type of secret. And I need answers."

"I just told you everything you need to know about The Citee. What kind of questions could you possibly have? You probably haven't even been here a week!"

"What's Sanrid?" Cayden asked calmly.

The girl paled dramatically, blinking rapidly with her mouth open in shock. "Where did you hear that?"

"In the mansion," Cayden said. "When Ali took us to meet

Grandfather, we had to walk through a hallway with all these men in suits. I didn't hear a lot of their conversations, but one of them was talking about something called 'Sanrid.' Is it, like, an acronym or something—some kind of agency?"

The girl just stood there for a few moments, her mouth hanging open and a look of pure shock and terror in her features. She opened and closed her mouth a few times, as if she was contemplating her words carefully. "How did you get into the mansion?" she finally said.

"Ali took us after she found us with Aidan and Carlton," he said.

The girl gaped at Cayden before backing away from him so quickly that she almost fell over her own feet. "Who the hell are you?" she said.

"My name is Cayden Mitchell, and that's my mother Sandra," Cayden replied, gesturing behind himself. He took a better look at the girl now, her hands trembling and her feet positioned so that she could run away at any moment. She didn't look defensive anymore, he realized. She just looked scared.

"You don't have to be afraid of me," Cayden assured her, trying his luck by taking another step toward her. She mirrored his step forward with a step backward, trying to keep the same distance between them. He continued anyway, despite her frigidness. "I still need your help. My best friend is still in the mansion, and he might be in danger. You have to trust me."

She scoffed and locked eyes with Cayden again. "You want me to *trust* you— when you've been in the mansion? You could be one of their spies, for all I know!"

Cayden sighed and turned behind him to glance at his mother, who looked just as confused as he felt. He turned back toward the girl in front of him—she was still staring at him with her arms up in a fighting position.

"My name is Cayden Mitchell. I am 18 years old, and I was born and raised in Davenport, Iowa. My mother's name is Sandra, my father's name is Mason, and I have two younger siblings named—"

"What are you doing?" the girl cut him off, with a confused look on her face. Cayden took another step toward her, and this time she didn't retaliate with a step back.

"You don't trust me," Cayden stated simply. "So I'm going to tell you everything that's happened since a week before I got here. Then, you can decide whether or not you want to help me. Deal?"

He extended his hand in the girl's direction, and she shook it feebly.

"Okay then. A week before I got here my mother went missing. She had been driving to the grocery store when a truck had come out of nowhere and caused her to swerve into a tree, which I now know, is actually a one-way portal. I went crazy with grief, searching for a week straight, driving up and down Tanglewood Drive trying to find any indication that she might have been there. You following me?"

The girl nodded her head slowly, processing the information. Cayden continued.

"I searched constantly, and I had no luck," he said. "I was starting to give up. My friend Ashton realized that I hadn't been in school for days and got worried. When he found out about what had happened, he offered to help me look for my mom. Then about two weeks ago, while we were driving up and down Tanglewood again, we saw the rocks around the tree start to glisten. At first, I thought that it might have been blood, so I approached the tree slowly. But before we knew it, the tree was basically pulling us into the portal, without Ashton's foot even being on the gas pedal. After trying to find our way around this place, we finally met two boys, Aidan and Carlton, who were willing to help us understand this place better. However, we only spent two days with them before they were both killed by Alison Dweller."

The girl backed up considerably again at the mention of Ali, holding her hands up defensively. "Ali killed?" she questioned in a quiet voice.

"Yes . . . but no," Cayden said. "I still don't know whether Aidan and Carlton were real or not. After Ali took us to the mansion, Grandfather told us that they were just holograms that were used to lead us in the direction of the mansion, and Ali was only terminating them because they had completed their job."

The girl shook her head in disgust. "So they're using holograms now?" she questioned, mostly to herself. "That's just great," she said, sarcastically.

"That's what Grandfather said, at least. I don't trust him as far I can throw him, but he seemed right about this one. When Ali shot them, there wasn't any blood or anything. They just dissipated into thin air."

The girl nodded and took a step closer to Cayden now. "What happened after you got to the mansion?"

"Ali took us right to Grandfather," Cayden said. "And Grandfather told my friend that he was one of his descendants or something and that he needed to use his gift to break them out of this universe."

If there was any color left in the girl's face, it was gone after Cayden had uttered his last sentence. "Didn't you say your friend's name was Ashton?" she said.

She tried to run again the minute Cayden said "yes."

Cayden grabbed her arm to prevent her from running, and she stared back with hatred in her eyes. "Let me go, or I'll kill you," she spat.

"No way," Cayden said. "Not after that. Why do they want Ashton so badly? What the hell is going on?"

The girl kept struggling until she realized it was no use. Cayden was much bigger than her, and he could take her down without a second thought. She sighed and relaxed, facing Cayden again.

"If I've put all the puzzle pieces together correctly," the girl said, "your friend is Ashton Dweller. *The* Ashton Dweller."

Cayden, confused, stared at her. "Yes."

"And now Grandfather has him. He's in the mansion right now."

"I told him that I didn't trust Grandfather and the other Dwellers. But he felt bad for them and didn't want to abandon them if they really needed him. So yes, he's still in the mansion right now." Cayden swallowed nervously, debating whether he should tell this girl about Ashton's powers. She seemed trustworthy, but she also seemed like she had a lot to hide, and he wasn't sure if it would be wise to tell her a secret so big that it could make or break Grandfather and the other Dwellers.

The girl groaned and shook her head in disbelief. "I can't believe they've finally got him." She finally was able to pull her arm out of Cayden's relaxed grasp, but she didn't try to run this time. She sat down against the brick wall behind them and put her head in her hands. "We're doomed."

Cayden could almost feel the wheels turning in his brain, trying to make sense of what the girl was saying. Why would they be doomed? What did this girl know about Grandfather and the mansion that he didn't? Cayden slid down against the brick wall and sat next to the girl, considering it a success when the girl didn't flinch or try to move away.

"Listen," Cayden said. "I know you may not trust me, but Ashton is my best friend, and I don't know what I'd do if something were to happen to him. Why are we doomed now that Grandfather has Ashton? What's happening? You said it yourself: I'm a newbie here."

When the girl looked at him again, there was no longer anger or fear in her eyes, only pity. "You're not going to like it," she said quietly.

"I need to know what's going on," Cayden urged. "I promised Ashton that I'd keep him safe, but I can't protect him if I don't know what I'm protecting him from."

The girl sighed. "Well the first thing you need to know is that Grandfather is not who he says he is. And Sanrid isn't an agency of any kind, it's just Grandfather's real name. No one knows it except the people who are close to him."

"Well, I kind of assumed his name wasn't actually Grandfather," Cayden said with a small laugh. "But keeping your real name a secret isn't that big of a deal. What do you mean by saying he's not who he says he is?"

"It's a long story," the girl said.

"I have all the time in the world," Cayden replied, crossing his legs where he sat against the wall. Sandra was next to the two of them now, keen on hearing what the truth was about the man who used to be her boss.

"A long time ago, there was a civilization that controlled this universe. They had a strong army and a strong leader who wrote countless books on how to control the portal. You know about the portal?"

"Yeah, like I said, it's the tree," Cayden said, "the link between The Citee and Davenport."

The girl nodded. "Well when The Primaries got here, they destroyed the entirety of the first civilization," the girl said.

"Primaries?" Cayden asked.

"Sanrid, Malia, Ali, and Bella. That's what they used to be called."

Cayden raised his eyebrows. "There are four of them? I've met Grandfather and Malia, and Ali took me to the mansion, but who's

Bella?"

The girl said, "I'll get to her later," before continuing.

"The first civilization that controlled this universe was powerful—way more powerful than Sanrid. They knew everything there was to know about how this place and the portal ran. We don't know much about them, though. When Sanrid conquered them centuries ago and named this place 'The Citee,' he burned any record of them that didn't have to do with controlling the portal."

"Four people took out an entire super-advanced civilization?" Cayden asked. "Sorry, I find that a little hard to believe."

The girl nodded again. "Exactly. It's impossible. But that's where Bella comes in. I'm assuming you know why Ashton is important to Sanrid. You know about his gift, right?"

Cayden swallowed nervously. "How do *you* know about it?"

"Isabella Dweller had the same gift," the girl explained. "She was Sanrid's eldest daughter, a few years older than Ali. She had these powers of mind manipulation that Sanrid didn't understand, but wanted to use. He knew that if he could harness Bella's power into the pure, unadulterated thing that it was, he would be able to take out the first civilization.

"But Bella had a different idea. She was completely against what her father was doing. She knew that she and her family had come to this universe on accident and wanted to talk to the people of the first civilization to see if they knew of a way to reverse the portal. Maybe if she had gotten the chance to ask them the questions that she wanted to, we'd know of a way to reverse the portal, and Sanrid wouldn't need Ashton at all. But instead of avoiding war, Sanrid created a process called "draining" and then drained his own daughter."

"What's *draining*?" Cayden asked horrified, as his stomach dropped.

"It's an extremely brutal and painful process, with many needles and screws involved" the girl said, choosing her words so carefully that it was as if she was speaking from experience. "It's called draining because it does just that; it drains your brain of everything that makes you human. You lose your memories first and then your emotions, and soon, nothing is left in your brain except what the person draining you wants there to be. Sanrid drained his own daughter into a mindless killing machine, using her power to kill every last person who lived here during the first civilization's reign."

"What about after Bella killed all of the people living here? Did Sanrid turn around and kill his own daughter afterwards?" Cayden was mortified, his heart beating fast, trying to imagine the quiet Sanrid shoving needles into his daughter's head and consequently shooting her.

"No," the girl said. "Sanrid killed Bella, but not after she murdered all of the people of the first civilization. Bella killed many people under her father's control, but eventually she broke away from her father and regained control of her own mind."

"How did she do that?"

"There are tons of theories," the girl said, now playing with a leaf in her lap. "There's only one that truly makes sense, though. Like I told you before, Sanrid didn't really understand the power that his daughter had; he had only seen it in action once or twice. If you've seen it in action, you know what it's like."

Cayden nodded. "Ashton showed it to me a few days ago. Once people are under his control, their eyes lose their color, and they move like robots."

"That's all that Sanrid understood," the girl said. "He thought that since people's eyes were drained of color when they were under Bella's control, perhaps he could drain someone in a similar way, but physically. That's how he came up with the entire draining process. The point is that Bella broke away at some point, and while some thought it was because of her powers, it was actually the opposite."

"What do you mean?"

"Draining strips away your humanity. People believed that since Bella had been given her power naturally, she was less human than them. The truth was that Bella had more humanity than her family and felt terrible about what her father had done to the first civilization. As Sanrid used his daughter to kill more and more people, Bella slowly fought the draining process and tried to regain control over her own body, so she would be able to fight her family alongside the first civilization."

The girl seemed visibly upset at this point, as if she had known Isabella Dweller personally. "Why would she want to help the people?" Cayden asked. "I understand why she would want to fight her family, after what they had done to her, but why help the first civilization?"

"I had a feeling you would ask that," the girl said. "You've been in the mansion. Sanrid acts like he single-handedly took over this land because he got stuck here. He acts like the people of the first civilization tried to have him murdered, and when he took over this place, he changed it for the better. He tries to manipulate the real story so that he looks like a *hero*. The truth is that the people of the first civilization were happy to welcome the Dwellers and let them live peacefully here. They were willing to provide housing for them as well as food and clothing until they could get on their feet. But Sanrid only wanted domination."

"Bella understood that the people of the first civilization just wanted to help them, and she wanted to help them beat her father in the end. Even though there weren't many civilians left alive by the time Bella regained control of her brain, she worked until her dying breath to try and save the first civilization. When Sanrid stabbed her, she was in the process of carving something into a clay tablet in the first civilization's language. According to legend, she was carving the instructions on how people could take back control of their minds and bodies after being drained. It's never been proven though because no one can translate the language."

"Clay tablet . . . clay tablet . . ." Cayden said, tapping his chin and trying to think about why the girl's story was evoking some kind of déjà vu. "Yes!" Cayden suddenly blurted out loud, remembering the tablet encased in glass when Ali had led him and Ashton down the grand hallway to Sanrid. "Did Bella finish signing her name on the tablet?"

The girl looked at Cayden in a confused way until the realization sunk in. "You've seen it," she said. "Sanrid stabbed Bella while she was carving into it, so she only ended up signing half her name."

"Bel," Cayden murmured. "That's who Bel is."

The girl nodded, smiling now. "How much have you actually seen in the mansion?"

"Quite a lot—Ashton kept getting pissed at me because I started to fall behind. I got a pretty good look at the clay tablet, but it looked too much like hieroglyphics to decipher. Plus, it's sloppy and messy and half covered in blood. Besides the tablet though, I saw a dress that looks similar to the one you're wearing right now. And it's kind of hard to miss that stupid symbol that's embroidered into everything in the mansion."

"The crest?" the girl asked.

"*That's* what that is?" Cayden said. "I thought it was a symbol of some sort, but it's a *crest*?"

"Yes," she said simply. "It's the Dweller family crest. After they took over this place, they carved and embroidered it onto everything here. They wanted to symbolize their possession over this land and make sure that any surviving citizens knew that this universe was *theirs* now."

Because Cayden still looked confused, the girl reached behind her, and pulled a dagger from the right side of her waist. Cayden almost fell over his own feet trying to escape, but she only laughed and shook her head.

"I'm not going to kill you, you know? After what you've told me, I trust you. I just want to show you something."

Cayden let out a sigh of relief and watched the girl, as she carved symbols into the dirt with the knife. After she drew the crest on the ground, she returned the dagger to her dress, which Cayden could now see was modified to let the girl's dagger hang against her waist.

"You see the 'D' in the middle of the crest there?" the girl said, pointing to the symbol she had drawn. "The 'D' stands for Dweller." She then gestured with her finger to the swirls emanating from the central letter.

"Notice how there's four of them," she explained, "just like there's four more lines extending from the star in the middle of the 'D.'"

"Just like there are four Primaries," Cayden tested.

The girl beamed up at him and nodded. "Exactly—I'm not sure why they still keep the crest, after all this time, especially because Bella's long gone now."

"About her, what happened after she died? Cayden asked. That was centuries ago, wasn't it?"

The girl nodded. "After Bella died, Sanrid, Malia, and Ali knew that they had won the war. Anyone who had lived through the war was allowed to either live peacefully under the Dwellers' rule or was sentenced to death. It was during this time that Sanrid read up on all of the old records of how to control the portal and manipulated it for his own use and his new city's benefit."

"What do you mean?"

"The portal can work through bloodlines, which basically

means that it can read your DNA and determine whether to allow you to pass through safely or to cause you to crash into the tree, which is its physical manifestation. When Sanrid first became supreme ruler, or dictator—whatever you want to call it—he closed the portal to anyone who wasn't a Dweller so that he could build his army, which would later become the Army of Descendants."

The girl shivered when she spoke of the army, absentmindedly scratching at the scar on her face. Cayden wished he could pretend that there wasn't an elephant in the room, but the girl's movement made him almost certain that this Army of Descendants and her scar had some kind of connection.

"There were enough Dwellers to create an entire army?" Cayden asked.

"You need to realize the time period, Cayden," the girl said, using Cayden's name for the first time. "This is a time when dynasties ruled and men had thirty plus wives and tons of children. On top of that, it's not like incest was a taboo. Dwellers in the Army of Descendants centuries ago made more Dweller babies with other Dwellers, creating an unstoppable family army that was known as the Secondaries."

"But what's the point in having an enormous, unstoppable army when you're governing a city of only a hundred war-torn people?" Cayden asked. "That makes no sense."

"Trust me; Sanrid wasn't planning on governing a city full of war-torn rebels," the girl laughed. "After building up his army, he manipulated the portal again to allow anyone to pass through the break so that he could build up his population. Most of the residents who live here now are grandchildren of those first people. Back then, when Sanrid opened the portal to all, most people assumed it would stay that way, especially because that was a time of peace and stability within The Citee."

"What happened then? What screwed everything up?" Cayden

was completely lost. The story about the first civilization had taken him for a spin, and he was now completely convinced that Grandfather was *not* a good guy, but he still failed to see what any of this had to do with Ashton and why any of it equaled the fact that they were doomed.

"Sanrid's lust for power and fear of death destroyed everything," the girl said simply. "He didn't want to die—that's what it comes down to in the end. He searched his whole life to find immortality. And all of the potions and concoctions that he tried ended up going to his head and driving him mad. It took him years to come up with the right immortality potion, but he did it eventually, which is why he's still kicking today. By the time he had administered the correct potion to Malia and Ali, the incorrect mixtures had already gotten to his head. That was when he started draining again, and he drained the entire army so that they would only follow his commands. This time, he also grew interested in complete domination over both universes, and the Prophets only made it worse."

"The Prophets?"

"They were a group of scholars who had a pretty prestigious rank in society. They got the name 'Prophets' because sometimes they had visions, and sometimes those visions would come true. Most of them hated Sanrid, and Sanrid was wary of them because he believed that they were secretly conspiring to assassinate him. But Sanrid was also just a paranoid bastard and thought everyone was out to assassinate him."

Cayden laughed at that, trying to imagine a calm, serene Grandfather, frantically pacing the mansion and murmuring about conspirators.

"The Prophets came up with a prophecy and presented it to Sanrid years ago," the girl continued. "They called it the Ashton Dweller prophecy."

Cayden stopped laughing immediately. He whipped his head in the girl's direction, with his breath hitching in his throat. "The *what?*"

"The Prophets told a story to Sanrid about a boy named Ashton Dweller, who had a power similar to Bella's. This boy would come to The Citee eventually and be the key to Sanrid's plan for complete domination. The Prophets made it clear to Sanrid that if he wanted control of both universes, he needed control of Ashton first. Most of the people in The Citee assumed that Sanrid would take the prophecy with a grain of salt, considering that Sanrid was apprehensive about the Prophets, but in actuality, Sanrid took all the necessary precautions to prepare The Citee for Ashton's entrance. He closed the portal to all Dwellers except Ashton and merely sat and waited for his arrival—for *years.*"

Cayden had stopped breathing at this point; his stomach was in his throat, and he could tell that his face was losing color by the second. The constant manipulation of the portal explained everything. Sandra's entrance, Ashton's parent's death, and the way the tree had seemingly pulled he and Ashton through the portal. His head was swimming. "What are they going to do to him in there?" he choked out, turning his head in the direction of the mansion.

"At best?" the girl contemplated. "They will manipulate him into leading an army."

"And at worst?" Cayden breathed, even though he didn't want to know the answer.

"Drain him."

Cayden let out a pained noise and put his head in his hands. "I'm a complete moron," he groaned. "How could I let him stay there?"

The girl placed a comforting hand on Cayden's shoulder, trying to placate him. "You didn't know," she said. "That's the problem with everyone who goes into the mansion. They have no idea about the story behind this town, and they allow themselves to get tricked by the bread and circuses. I did too once."

Cayden looked up at her and tried to smile, knowing she meant well. But if Ashton really was in danger in the mansion, Cayden needed to break him out before Sanrid could stick needles into his brain.

"Thank you for telling me all that," Cayden said, trying to calm his breathing. "But I've got to be honest. This all sounds too big for me to accomplish on my own, or for just my mom and me, especially because we have barely any knowledge of this place at all. I feel that the mission of saving two parallel universes from a crazy dictator is more of a three-person job."

"Is that your way of asking me to join you on your crazy suicide mission to rescue your boyfriend—the same boyfriend who just happens to be a telekinetic, mind manipulating powerhouse?" The girl's smirk did nothing to lessen the blush creeping up Cayden's neck.

"He's not my boyfriend," Cayden protested, and the girl laughed.

"I love how that's all you comprehended from that statement."

Cayden crossed his arms, frustrated. "Is that a yes or a no?"

The girl smirked again and stood up from the ground, extending a hand down to Cayden. She helped Cayden up and waited for him to steady himself before offering a hand out in greeting.

"What are you doing?" Cayden asked.

"You still don't know my name," she said, grabbing his hand and shaking it once. Cayden looked down at her and smiled, suddenly realizing the obvious.

"Well I'm Cayden Mitchell, as you know. It's very nice to meet you . . ." Cayden's voice trailed off, as he waited for the girl to complete his sentence.

The Dwellers

"Sasha Dweller," she girl said with a curt nod. "My name is Sasha Dweller."

13

"Sasha Dweller?"

"Yeah, that's my name," she smirked. "Don't wear it out."

Cayden stared at her dumbly for a few seconds, taking in her face. He now realized from looking a little closer that she looked a bit similar to Ashton, with her small nose, dirty blond hair, and blue eye.

"You're staring again, pretty boy," she said, with a hint of annoyance in her voice.

"You're a *Dweller*," Cayden said again, the panic more evident in his voice.

Sasha paled again, as if she didn't like being reminded of her surname. She puffed up her chest again. "I thought that was obvious."

Cayden scoffed and stared at Sasha, throwing his hands in the air in frustration. "Of course it wasn't obvious! How was I supposed to know that? You didn't exactly tell me a lot about yourself!"

"I look like all of them!" she protested. "And what, did you think I was born with this scar or something? Why do you think I'm in hiding? I've pissed some people off."

Cayden ran a hand over his mouth in frustration, trying to decide whether or not he should follow through with his original idea of having Sasha as an ally. She seemed nice enough, and she trusted him, but if she was a Dweller who had angered people to the point of making them burn her, she could be dangerous to associate with.

"Tell me about yourself," he said.

"What?"

"I just told you my entire story, since the moment I got here. You told me about the history of The Citee, but I've only just learned your name. What's your story?"

Sasha looked hesitant, as if telling Cayden her name was all he was allowed to know about her. But soon, his expectant gaze got to her, and she huffed angrily.

"You're not going to like it," she said. "It's not a fairy tale, and there is no happy ending. It's not going to give you more hope for Ashton- in fact, it's going to lessen any hope you have that he'll make it out of all of this alive."

Cayden swallowed nervously but stood his ground. He wasn't going to let Sasha scare him away from finding out the story behind her scar and her tattered dress. When Sasha realized that her threats were fruitless, she caved.

"I came to The Citee years ago, a little while before Sanrid closed the portal to all Dwellers except Ashton," she began. "I was pretty young and totally scared of my own shadow, so this place threw me for a loop. I didn't get any holograms as you did, but Ali found me eventually and took me to the mansion. Remember, this was a time when Sanrid was frantic and foaming-at-the-mouth crazy, not like he is now.

"He asked me tons of questions about me and my parents. I don't remember most of my past, but I'm pretty sure my last name wasn't Dweller. I have Dweller blood in me because my mother was of Dweller descent, but I don't think it was my last name before I came here."

"What did Sanrid do after he found out that you were a Dweller?" Cayden said.

"He offered to let me stay in the mansion," she said. "I had nowhere to go, and I figured that living in a mansion was better than living out on the streets of The Citee. He kept me in this basement dungeon thing, and I basically felt like I was in jail. But I got food and water and clothing, so I didn't complain."

Cayden nodded. "I know what you're talking about. It's where Sanrid kept Ashton and me before my mom broke me out."

Sasha nodded. "I stayed in my cell chamber for about a week, and then Sanrid wanted to talk to me. I got sent to sit with him in his office, where he explained that he wanted me to be part of something *bigger*. He wouldn't answer any of my questions, and when I started getting scared and antsy, he took it as a cue to hold me down and drag me to draining. Apparently, 'being part of a bigger picture' actually meant nothing more than being a brainwashed soldier in the Army of Descendants."

"He drained you?" Cayden asked, terrified.

"Sort of."

"What do you mean sort of?"

"I broke away from the draining process. It was incredibly painful and left me with scars I'd rather not show you, but essentially, I had to pull needles out of my forehead and nails out of my arms. The draining process was only halfway completed when I broke away, which is why I was left with one blue and one gray eye. Only half of my brain was drained, so only one of my eyes lost its color. See, they drain you of your memories first, followed by your emotions, which is why I'm merely an amnesiac instead of a robot."

Cayden stared in amazement, wishing he could say something that could make it better. "They burn you during the draining process?" he asked, the only question he could think of.

Sasha looked at Cayden in a confused way for a second before touching a hand to her burned cheek and shaking her head. "No, the burning came afterward," she said dryly. When Cayden didn't speak again, she continued.

"It took them a few minutes to realize that I had broken away from the operation. Draining used to be performed in a section of the mansion that was warded off against anyone who wasn't going in for an operation or performing one. That all changed after me, though. When they realized that I had broken away, they evacuated everyone from the draining section of the mansion and set it on fire. They couldn't risk that I would run away and tell people about the things the Ancestors did while people were locked away in the mansion."

"They burned an entire section of the mansion to the ground just to try and kill you?" Cayden said.

"The section of the mansion dedicated to draining wasn't very big," she explained. "It was more like a small extension than anything. But yes, they burned it all down just to kill me. And they didn't even succeed. The fire burned the entire right side of my body, but by some miracle, I got away. The first few months away from the mansion were hard. Not only was I in hiding, but I had third degree burns that needed to be tended to every single day. That's why I was so glad when I found the Rebels."

"The Rebels?" Cayden asked. "That's not another damn social class like the Prophets, is it?"

Sasha laughed bitterly. "Not exactly—they were more like the Untouchables actually. It was a group of people who hated the Ancestors and were either the descendants of citizens who had lived during the first civilization's reign, or they were Dwellers who had broken away from the army and from Sanrid."

"Where are they all now?" Cayden asked hopefully. "If there are enough people like you, we can all band together and get Ashton back from Sanrid before he can drain him and use him to break through the portal."

Sasha looked upset for a quick second before masking her emotions again. "A week ago, my best friend Taylor was killed by soldiers in the Army of Descendants."

Cayden wasn't sure what Sasha's friend had to do with his

question, but he let Sasha continue.

"There used to be so many of us," Sasha said. "There had to be at least a hundred rebels. We didn't all travel in one big pack together because we'd look too suspicious, so we broke up into smaller groups. We worked to keep each other alive. We were pretty good at keeping each other safe until Sanrid started sending out his soldiers to hunt us, as if we were animals. The groups starting dying one by one."

Cayden stood awkwardly, not knowing what he was supposed to say. Sasha continued sadly, after it became obvious that Cayden was not getting the message.

"Taylor died in battle last week," she said slowly. "She was killed by a soldier in the army, and luckily, I got away. Cayden, I'm the only one left."

Cayden's heart lurched, and for some reason, he wanted to cry. He hadn't known Taylor or any of the Rebels for that matter, but the circumstances were making him feel dizzy. If all the Rebels were dead with the exception of Sasha, it was going to be him, Sasha, and his mother up against Sanrid, Ashton, and his enormous brainwashed army of super great grandchildren. If Cayden had had any hope left, it was gone now.

Sasha could feel Cayden's disappointment, and for a few seconds, she pitied him. He wasn't supposed to be involved in this, and she knew it. The Ashton Dweller Prophecy stated that he was to enter The Citee alone, not accompanied by anyone. Cayden had merely been pulled into this mess against his will. Fighting in this war may have been part of Ashton's destiny, but it wasn't a part of Cayden's.

"Hey," Sasha said, stepping closer and placing a hand on his shoulder. She wasn't very good at comforting people, and sometimes she wondered if maybe the draining process *did* actually end up encroaching on the emotions in her brain and destroying them.

"Listen, we're down but we're not out, not yet," she said. "We may not have an army to go up against Ashton and Sanrid, but we've got us. I assumed your mother would be terrified here, but she seems like she's actually doing pretty well. You seem like you'll do anything if it means saving Ashton. And I know The Citee better than anyone else. We may be small in number, but we might actually have enough power to cut the head off the snake."

Cayden looked at her with a confused look on his face, trying to figure out what she meant. "I don't understand," he vocalized, thinking she couldn't read the emotions off his face.

"The three of us might not be enough to take down the entire army and Sanrid, but if we can save Ashton before Sanrid drains him, we can have the most powerful weapon on Earth in our hands."

"Ashton's more than a weapon," Cayden said angrily.

"Yeah, yeah," Sasha said. "Cool your jets. I get it, okay. I've lost a best friend too, and you're scared as hell to lose him. Hell, technically he's my brother. The point is that right now all he is to Sanrid is a weapon. And if Ashton has any loyalty to Sanrid and the Ancestors at all, Sanrid's got him, and there's no way we'll win this war."

"If Ashton knew everything that you've just told me about The Citee and Sanrid and you, he'd lose all loyalty to them in a minute," Cayden said. "And who says this is a war, anyway?"

Sasha rolled her eyes. "This has been a war since the minute the Prophets came up with Ashton's prophecy. Sanrid has always known that this was going to be a war, whether we're part of the prophecy or not. He assumed that there'd always be people who would band together to fight against the Army of Descendants when he passed through the portal, so that's what he's prepared for."

"I don't know what it's like to fight in a war," Cayden said, in a panicky voice. "This isn't what I signed up for."

Sasha barked out a laugh. "You didn't sign up for anything. I didn't sign up for anything, either—same thing with Ashton. We all got pulled into this, and now we have to figure out how to deal with what we've got and survive. It's our destiny."

"I don't believe in destiny," Cayden said.

"Well you should start believing in it because it's destroyed my life and Ashton's life, and soon enough, it's going to destroy yours. You can't change it, but you can sure as hell try to slow it down, at least a little bit."

Cayden rubbed a tired hand over his face. "So we're allies now?"

Sasha laughed again, placing a hand onto Cayden's shoulder. "Yeah, I guess we are, pretty boy."

"Stop calling me that."

"Make me."

Cayden rolled his eyes, and Sasha waggled her eyebrows. She reached around her back for something. When Sasha's hand emerged with a dagger, Cayden fell over his own feet trying to get away from her again.

"Jesus, you can call me anything you want- just don't kill me," Cayden spluttered, backing away from Sasha on the ground with his hands held high in surrender. Sasha doubled over with laughter before Cayden could compose himself.

"I'm not gonna kill you," Sasha laughed. "Weren't you trying to convince me that *you* weren't gonna kill me, like a few minutes ago?"

Cayden shook his head in disgust and stood up, wiping off his pants. "What's the damn dagger for then?"

"Protection," Sasha assured. "When you're the only Rebel left, you need to be able to defend yourself. Plus, sometimes when no one will throw you scraps and you can't steal anything, you have to kill if you want to eat."

"Like killing people?"

"Yes, Cayden I'm actually a cannibal," she said, sarcastically, before rolling her eyes. "Animals you moron."

"Well what do you need the dagger for right now?" Cayden asked.

"Nothing," she smirked. "I just wanted to scare you—kinda wanted to see your reaction when I pulled out a knife."

Cayden scoffed as Sasha returned the knife to her belt, spinning it once between her fingers for good measure. Cayden looked to Sandra who was smiling at Sasha with amusement in her eyes. Cayden groaned.

"Okay, well if we're going to get anything done, we're not going to be stabbing each other with anything," Cayden said. "If we're gonna get anything done, actually, we should be heading toward the mansion now so we can get there before nightfall."

Sasha paled. "What are you talking about?" she asked.

"You just said that if we can save Ashton before Sanrid drains him, then we have a chance at stopping him," Cayden said, slowly. "That means we have to start moving now."

"I'm not going over there."

"What do you mean you're not going over there?" Cayden exclaimed. "It was your idea."

"If Sanrid, Malia, one of the guards, or *anyone* sees me over there, you could stick a fork in me because I'll be done. I literally just told you why I look the way I do, and you think I can actually just skip into the mansion like, 'hey! How ya doin' Sanrid? Yeah, can I borrow Ashton for a sec, he's mine now! Peace, homie.'"

Cayden rolled his eyes. "Of course I don't think you could actually do that. I'm not saying we barge into the mansion guns blazing by walking through the front door. I'm talking about sneaking around for a while and figuring out what Sanrid is up to. And then, when we know what his plan is, we create our own plan to stop him before he drains Ashton."

"You say that like it's the easiest thing in the world," Sasha groaned. "You've met Sanrid how many times? Oh yeah, once. And during that one time you actually met him, he was putting on a show to make sure you and Ashton felt at home. Also, that whole time that you were talking to him, he was probably on a whole bunch of meds just to make sure he didn't snap at the two of you and blurt out his entire plan. You have no idea who Sanrid really is."

"I'm not saying that it's going to be easy," Cayden retorted. "I'm just saying that I don't wanna sit here with my thumbs up my ass waiting for Ashton to walk out of that mansion with gray eyes!"

He didn't know precisely when the conversation with Sasha had turned into a screaming match, but after Cayden's last comment, the birds in the nearest tree fled. Sandra stepped between the two of them, putting her arms out on each side.

"Listen," she said to the two of them, using her mom voice. "Sasha, you need to understand that Cayden is desperate right now. He'll do anything to save Ashton from Sanrid and just wants to stop him as soon as he possibly can."

Cayden smiled, but Sandra turned to him next. "Cayden, you need to realize that Sasha is terrified to go back to the mansion and to Sanrid, even if she refuses to say it. On top of that, this is going to be a war, and it's a war that she knows we're not prepared for. We need to be trained in some way and have the right weapons and knowledge before the three of us can go smash through the front doors of the mansion."

Sasha and Cayden looked to Sandra in silent thanks, but she only laughed and shook her head. "If it truly is only the three of us up against Sanrid, Ashton, and the entire Army of Descendants, the three of us can't be fighting each other. You two are gonna have to work out your differences like human beings and, unless you want to get caught or murdered, not have screaming matches."

Sasha and Cayden nodded. Cayden stuck out his hand for Sasha to shake.

"No more screaming matches. Deal?"

"Deal."

"What do we do now, oh mighty captain?" Cayden asked his mother.

Sandra was about to protest when Sasha took off her invisible cap and bowed to Sandra, laughing.

"Yes," she said. "What do you suppose we do, great captain?"

Sandra shook her head and laughed. "Well, Sasha is right in the fact that we need more materials and weapons before we can go straight to the mansion. But Cayden is right in the fact that we can't wait forever if the key to winning the war is getting to Ashton before he's drained. I think we should wait to head in the direction of the mansion, but not wait too long."

Sasha and Cayden shared a look and nodded in agreement—a compromise.

"Question," Cayden said, raising his hand. "Where are we going to get these weapons and materials etcetera, etcetera?"

"I know where," Sasha said.

"Where?"

"Were you a bad kid?" Sasha asked.

"What are you talking about?" Cayden said, confused.

"I mean, in your early teen days? Did you ever, like—shoplift?"

Cayden had never been the rebellious type. When they were kids, Alex did all the rebelling, and Cayden had watched from the sidelines. Once Ashton had left for California, Cayden had tried a few things, but he had never gotten into the drug scene or had a group of would-be alcoholics as friends. He had joined the football team and a gym and had taken his anger out on punching bags. He had never been good at school. He didn't care much about his reputation, but all in all, shoplifting seemed petty.

"Nah," Cayden answered. "The whole thing seems kind of dumb and pointless to me—why steal a pack of gum or lip gloss and possibly get probation over two bucks."

Sasha barked out a laugh and shook her head. She pointed to Sandra and cocked her head questioningly. "Did you ever shoplift?"

Sandra shrugged. "I probably stole a few little things off of cashier counters in my teen years, yeah."

Cayden's eyes widened in his mother's direction, and Sandra only shrugged again. "I was young and stupid," she said.

Sasha smirked and began to tap her fingers on the concrete. "Basically I'm getting the gist that neither of you have ever stolen anything large nor anything someone would actually *miss*."

Cayden and Sandra shared a look with raised eyebrows and replied "no" in unison.

"Well then you need to learn how," Sasha said. "You think I'm able to survive out here because people throw me scraps on the street?"

Cayden gave Sasha a look, but she only smirked again.

"I'm going to teach you two how to be criminals. You need to learn the art of raiding if you're going to become a true Rebel."

"But I don't want to become a true Rebel," Cayden said, taking a step away from her. "I just want to get Ashton out of the mansion before he's drained and make sure the people I love don't die—remember?"

"If you want to make sure the people you love don't die, you have to become a Rebel," Sasha said, patting Cayden on the shoulder. Before Cayden could fumble out another complaint or excuse, Sasha removed her dagger from her belt again.

Cayden sighed, knowing that Sasha wasn't going to take "no" for an answer. He gazed at the knife. "We're not going to kill anyone, are we?" he asked.

"Not if we don't have to."

Cayden and Sandra shared another look but knew it would be fruitless to ask any more questions. They followed Sasha, who was now sneaking in between houses, trying to blend into her surroundings. "Where are we going?" Cayden asked after a few minutes.

"I just told you," Sasha said. "You two need to learn the art of raiding. So I'm taking you on a raid."

Cayden gulped. "What exactly does a raid entail? And what are we raiding."

"A lot of stealing," she said. "And a department store."

Cayden nodded but turned to his mother and raised an eyebrow. Of course there was the commercial district, but he hadn't seen anything that looked like a department store since he and Ashton had arrived, and he wondered if Sasha was lying. The commercial district was filled to the brim with specialty shops and grocers, but a department store seemed out of character for The Citee.

"This way," Sasha said, leading them through more shrubbery and past the mansion.

"I thought you said we weren't going near the mansion," Cayden said.

"We're not," Sasha huffed. "Come on."

She grabbed his hand and pulled him through the bushes, with Sandra following close behind. Once out of sight of anyone who might be circling the mansion's premises, Sasha stood up taller again and led the way to the department store.

Cayden hadn't explored the area behind the mansion since he and Ashton had arrived in The Citee. The abandoned house, which was starting to feel more like home to Cayden than anything, was on the front side of the mansion. The commercial district, the places they had traveled with Carlton and Aidan, and the people that Sandra had interviewed were all on the front side of the mansion. A whole other world opened up behind the mansion.

The commercial district behind the mansion, as opposed to the main district that held mostly specialty shops, had more department stores.

"Whoa," Cayden said, looking around.

"I know right," Sasha laughed. "Everyone spends so much time staring at what's in front of the mansion. No one takes the time to look behind the curtain."

Sasha seemed more at ease in the commercial district behind the mansion, and Cayden assumed that the people who lived behind the mansion were more cut off from the news and gossip that surrounded the people who lived in front of it.

Nearing a particularly large, mall-looking building, Sasha placed her hand over her dagger and signed for Cayden and Sandra to follow her up the fire escape attached to the side of the building. Climbing up the ladder, Cayden and Sandra followed Sasha up to the top of the building, where Sasha reached over the ladder and fiddled with her dagger under a loose window, popping it open with ease. She hopped through the window. Cayden and Sandra followed suit, and soon, the three of them were in a large storage room.

"This is where I get mostly all of my stuff," Sasha said, admiring the tall stacks of boxes. "This place is chock-full of weapons, clothes, food products, and basically everything else. This room stocks most of the stores in this entire mall, and there are lots of different stores. I always steal new tights, but they rip so quickly, I don't even know why I bother anymore. Food products that aren't raw are stored up here, and they are actually usually pretty tasty.

The weapons aren't always in good working condition, especially because Sanrid has pretty strict gun laws here, but there's always a lot of ammunition. To get a gun, you have to steal it from the mansion. I found my trusty dagger here though—that's probably my biggest accomplishment."

"There's so much stuff in here," Cayden said, looking around in awe. "If it's so easy for you to get in here, why are you still wearing the same dress that you were wearing when you were drained?"

Sasha laughed loudly before covering her mouth, worried someone might hear her. "This isn't the dress I was wearing when I was drained," she giggled. "The dress I wore when I was drained was mostly destroyed in the fire. In the back of this storage room, there are always tons of boxes of dresses that Sanrid has rejected—y'know, ones that didn't fit the girl they were meant for or ones that were manufactured the wrong way or asymmetrically or something. They're only here so the guy who runs the incinerator in the basement can burn them. Although it could make me stick out here, there aren't any clothes that I can find that are as comfortable as the army's dresses. To make myself a little bit more inconspicuous, I cut off the Dweller's crest with my dagger before I steal a new dress."

Cayden nodded before heading over to a particularly large box that was labeled "weapons." Inside, he found a weaponry belt and a knife similar to Sasha's. He slipped the knife into the hole made for knives in the belt and tightened it around his waist.

"This good?" Cayden asked Sasha.

"Perfect!" Sasha exclaimed. "That's a really awesome weaponry belt. I've been looking for one of those to replace mine for ages."

Cayden reached into the box again, pulled out another one, and held it out to her. She laughed and ripped the plastic off, smiling at the belt like a kid opening a gift on Christmas morning. "This one holds guns too," she said, smiling and feeling the leather. "That'll come in handy when I finally get to steal one."

Cayden looked around the weapon box some more, finding another belt to hand to Sandra, as well as a smaller, sharper knife that he found in the bottom of the box. Closing the box back up, he pushed it to the back of the storage room, so no one would see that it had been opened.

Sasha looked through a box of clothes; she was disgusted with some of the clothes, which were obviously made for high-fashion department stores. She headed to the back of the storage room to look through the box of reject army dresses and found three in her size.

Walking over to Cayden, who was hovering over a clothes box of his own, she unzipped his backpack and threw the dresses inside of it. She then zipped it back up and patted the front of it.

"That thing is sure gonna come in handy," Sasha laughed. "I should probably get myself one of those one day."

Cayden grabbed a few more pairs of jeans and comfortable shirts and threw them in the backpack as well. After going through one more weapons box and helping his mother through her clothes box, Cayden looked around the room. Open boxes lay everywhere, and some were closed back up and hidden behind mountains of other boxes.

"How does no one realize that these boxes have been broken into?" Cayden wondered out loud.

"Oh, they do," Sasha replied. "But people from the stores come up here so rarely that by the time they get up here, they just assume that the rats got to the boxes and ripped them open."

Cayden opened up a food box quickly, shoving a few cold loaves of bread into the backpack along with a few bananas and other fruits that didn't look *too* spoiled. However, as he was closing up the box and kicking it into a corner, they heard someone unlocking the door to the storage room.

Sasha squeaked "hide," and Sandra and Cayden hid behind the closest box and tried to make themselves as small as possible. Thank the Lord that Sasha had closed up the window after they had jumped through it, or whoever was walking into the storage room would know that there was someone else in there.

The person walked into the room whistling, and suddenly the room smelled like smoke—not cigarette smoke, but fire smoke, the kind that someone would be covered in if they spent the entire day next to an . . . incinerator.

Cayden moved as quickly as he could away from the box of reject dresses that Sasha had opened up. Diving behind a different mountain of boxes, Cayden covered himself with boxes until he couldn't see anything but cardboard in front of his eyes.

The man tilted over the box of reject dresses and when he saw that they had been broken into, he didn't look around the room, but mumbled "friggin' rats" under his breath.

Picking up the opened box and three other boxes, the man carried them out of the room, locking the door as he left. Cayden could hear Sandra and Sasha simultaneously sigh in relief, so he sat up, letting the boxes tumble off of him.

"I guess that's a sign that we should be getting out of here," Sasha laughed.

Cayden nodded weakly and tightened his backpack on his shoulder, while Sasha made work of opening the loose window again. Sandra and Cayden jumped down from the window to the fire escape and waited for Sasha to close the window again before she joined them on the ladder.

Laughing the whole way down, Sasha slid down the side of the stairs instead of walking down them, and when she reached the bottom, she giggled as she tumbled onto the ground. The minute they passed the mansion again on the way back toward the abandoned house, Sasha's grin left her face. They were in front of the mansion again, which for Sasha meant business.

When they entered the abandoned house, Sasha opened Cayden's backpack, grabbed one of the dresses she had stolen, and excused herself to go change. Cayden sighed as he changed into a new pair of jeans and then fastened the weaponry belt around his waist. Sandra changed after Sasha, blissful to finally be rid of the food cart woman getup.

Lying down on one of the blankets from Carlton's backpack, Cayden fell asleep thinking that if he had to live in The Citee, maybe living behind the mansion wouldn't be all that bad.

14

After telling Grandfather he would stay on the morning following Cayden's departure, Ashton was handed a schedule of training. Apparently, in order to break through the wall, he needed to train his brain to be stronger and awaken the "gift" that he had kept dormant for so many years.

Ali would be his trainer for a week to see how well he progressed. There would be three sessions, each spanning two and a half days, and each session would focus on a different skill that Ashton needed to be trained in if he wanted to take down the wall. Ashton didn't see why so much rigorous training was required just to break down a dumb wall, but he decided it would be better to just keep those thoughts in his head.

That morning, he followed Ali down to the basement of the mansion silently to begin his first session. The basement was a gigantic room, which was almost completely empty except for the tables that lined the left wall. Behind the stairs, which led back up into the main area of the mansion, there were showers lined up against the wall that Ashton could use as he pleased during training. In the right corner of the basement, there was an opening that led behind the right wall of the basement and into another room that Ashton was prohibited from entering. Ali told Ashton to stay put in the middle of the room, while she went behind the wall to retrieve something for the start of training.

"Let's see what you've got," Ali said with a smirk. She emerged from behind the wall with a teenage boy in tow. The boy seemed to be only a bit younger than Ashton himself, and Ashton was confused as to what he was supposed to do. He stood quietly and waited for his sister to instruct him to do something, but she only introduced the boy as "Jack" and waited expectantly for Ashton to make a move.

"What do I do?" Ashton asked quietly after a moment of awkward silence.

"Control him," Ali said simply. "I want to see how strong your mind is—how strong the power is."

Ashton felt uncomfortable and shifted slightly from one foot to the other while the boy stared back at him with a completely trusting look. Ashton didn't even want to know where the boy had come from or how many people Grandfather had stocked away in the mansion—only to be used as test subjects.

Ali sighed at Ashton's discomfort and retreated back behind the wall, emerging a few minutes later with multiple sticks in her hand. Moving toward the table in the corner of the room, she placed the sticks on the table and then returned to Ashton's side.

"Tell him to bring a stick to you," Ali said into his ear.

Ashton rolled his eyes and asked, "Like a dog?"

Ali smiled widely and nodded. "Now you're getting it!"

Ashton stared at her open-mouthed before laughing bitterly. "He's a person—like a human being with emotions and feelings. I'm not going to play *fetch* with him."

Ali's smile fell off her face, and she rolled her eyes. "Turn off your moral compass, and control him already. We don't have all day."

Ashton gritted his teeth and stared at the boy sympathetically before saying, "bring me one of those sticks."

The brown quickly faded from the boy's eyes as they turned to gray, and he turned and walked slowly toward the table, and then picked up a twig. He then walked to Ashton and placed the stick in his hand, his eyes slowly regaining their brown color after the branch touched Ashton's palm.

The boy walked back to where Ali had originally placed him

and stood silently, waiting for his next command.

"Now do it telepathically," Ali urged, tapping Ashton's shoulder. Ashton sighed but complied, bringing two fingers to each of his temples and commanding Jack to bring him another stick. His eyes were closed as he forced the power through his head, and for a few seconds, Ashton thought that it hadn't worked. But soon, he felt breathing on his neck and opened his eyes to see a gray-eyed, expressionless Jack holding one of the sticks out in front of him patiently.

Ashton took the stick and watched as Ali led the disoriented boy out of the room and back behind the wall.

"Is that it?" Ashton asked with a sigh of relief.

"Of course not," Ali laughed. "That was just practice, silly. You know how to do that already."

Ashton scratched the back of his neck nervously. "Are you going to bring out someone else then? What do you want me to do?"

"Stand in front of the table with the sticks on it," Ali instructed. Ashton did as he was told. "Now make the stick come to you."

"Are you crazy?" Ashton said. "That's . . . that's—"

"Telekinesis," Ali finished.

"Yes, exactly," Ashton urged. "I'm not a telekinetic. I'm a mind controller, as crazy as that sounds, but I'm not *telekinetic*."

"Of course you are," Ali said with a smile. "You just don't know it yet."

Ashton sighed and rolled his eyes in disbelief.

"Ashton, do you know how your mind manipulation works?"

Ashton froze. If he was being honest with himself, he had absolutely no idea. Controlling people had been as easy and natural as breathing when he was a kid, and he had never given an actual thought to how the powers worked or where they had come from. He was born with them, and they hadn't developed much over time. The power had always just been there, like a piece of his personality.

"No," Ashton said. "I don't know how it works."

Ali smiled and rested a hand on Ashton's shoulder, squeezing encouragingly. "Basically, although you think you're a mind manipulator, you merely control cells, and on a smaller scale, atoms."

"I don't understand," Ashton said, rubbing his temple. He really wasn't in the mood to get a lesson in physics from his long-lost sister, who reminded him more and more of Beth as the day progressed.

"You've always thought that you've controlled people's minds, and that's true to an extent. But really, you're controlling the atoms that make up the cells in the mind—mainly the cells in the cerebellum and motor cortex, since your commands usually involve getting someone to do something for you."

"So I'm just controlling atoms?" Ashton asked.

"Exactly," Ali said. "You take control of these atoms and these brain cells and then are able to manipulate their atomic makeup or neurological transmissions for your own benefit. However, you have no idea what you're doing on an atomic level because your gift works so rapidly, and the minute you command someone to do something, they do it."

"I don't understand what this has to do with me being telekinetic."

"You're still thinking like you're a mind controller. Only living things have cells; that's true, but everything is made of atoms, even air. The stick that I'm asking you to pick up is made of atoms, and so are Jack's brain cells, and so is the wall we need to break down to break out of The Citee. It'll take practice, but telekinesis is going to be the key to breaking us out."

Ali was standing close to him now, and Ashton was getting anxious. The table, stacked high with twigs, was giving Ashton a headache, and the power seemed to be fighting to pump right out of his veins. He felt like he was drowning again.

"So you want me to tell the stick to come to me?"

"Verbally commanding something that's nonliving may feel weird, I know," Ali said. "But it'll be too hard for you to just jump into controlling nonliving things telepathically, especially when you're only used to controlling people."

Ashton stared uneasily at the table of twigs as if one was going to hop off the table and attack him. He took a deep breath and approached the table again. He held out his hand hesitantly while staring hard at the pile of sticks.

"Come to me," Ashton said, staring down the stick that was closest to him. He cringed at how idiotic he probably looked, talking to a stick, and he immediately closed his eyes. When he didn't feel the stick in his hand, he repeated himself—a third time and a fourth time.

Finally, after the fifth time, he felt a light weight in his right hand and let out a sigh of relief. He heard Ali let out a whoop of excitement and opened his eyes to see one of the sticks clasped tightly in his fist, raised high toward the ceiling. His head swam a bit, but there was no pain or migraine, as he would've expected from such a rigorous use of his suppressed powers.

Ali was beside him quickly. She placed a hand on his shoulder and smiled. "That's only the start of what your gift can do if you let it," she said. "You can move much bigger objects and control more complicated things. If you try hard enough, you can even begin to break down the neurons of humans to begin mind reading to a certain extent, as opposed to just mind controlling."

Ashton met her eyes with a sigh. "Ali, this is nuts."

Ali laughed loudly, giving him a few slaps on the back and backing away from him once again. "It's really not that hard," she said in a singsong voice. "That's what father says, at least."

Ashton shook his head. "Before we try anything harder than

mind manipulation, maybe we should see if I can move something bigger than a stick."

Ali nodded in agreement and, with a small smile, walked toward the table and pushed the pile of sticks to the side of it. She retreated behind the wall again, and the nerves piled up in Ashton's gut again with the thought of Ali bringing out another person. But she didn't. She only reemerged from behind the wall with an armful of random objects.

She emptied the objects from her arms out onto the table next to the sticks: a few toy cars of varying sizes as well as a few dumbbells that looked as if they had come from a weight room. As she spread the items out on the table, Ashton started to understand the thought process behind the training.

"What's going to be hard about breaking down the wall is not going to be its size," Ali explained. "Technically, it's going to be its location in space and its relative mass and density and a lot of boring science stuff. So for now, we're just going to call it weight. Let's say, for argument's sake, the wall weighs thousands of pounds. I've got to train you in working your brain telekinetically to be able to move tons of objects of different weights. You following?"

Ashton nodded and stepped toward the table again.

"Let's get started then," Ali said with a smirk.

***

By the end of the first session of training, Ashton was able to pick up a 250-pound dumbbell with his brain and make it land in his hand, which although couldn't support the weight normally, was able to hold the dumbbell perfectly just by using his mind. Dropping the weight back onto the table, he brought a hand up to rub his temple. Assuming there would be some tension there, Ashton was amazed when his head didn't hurt at all.

"Am I supposed to be in pain?" he asked Ali.

"I don't know; you tell me?" she replied with a wink before leaving Ashton in the training room to take a shower.

***

During the second session of training, Ashton successfully picked up and moved every item that Ali had behind her "wall of things," as Ashton was starting to call it in his head. Ali was beside herself with excitement, set on the fact that even though they had only started training a few days ago, Ashton was almost ready. She decided it was finally time to teach Ashton what came after mind manipulation.

"So, first mind manipulation, then telekinesis, and now *mind reading*?"

Ali nodded happily, retreating behind the wall of things to return with a young girl, probably no more than eight years old. Unlike Jack, the girl didn't look indifferent to the situation. Jack had been expressionless and up for anything, while this girl looked terrified and fought slightly against Ali's grip on her arm. Ashton immediately wanted out. He didn't want to do anything that could possibly hurt a little kid. No way.

When he voiced his concerns to Ali, she laughed. "You won't hurt her," she assured him. "All you're going to be doing is reading her mind."

"How am I supposed to do that?"

"Just do what you would normally do when you're controlling someone or controlling an object," she said. "Tap into its atoms and, instead of taking control of the atoms, simply read into them."

Ashton looked to the girl hesitantly before closing his eyes.

"Tell me the girl's name," Ali said, as she backed away from him.

Ashton could feel his head starting to burn. Lifting weights with his brain didn't bring him any pain, but this definitely did. He brought his fingers to his temples, as he tried to break into the girl's neurons. "Name, name, name, name," he whispered to himself as the burning in his head turned from an inferno to a candle.

"Clara Foster," Ashton said, opening his eyes.

The girl stared at him in amazement, and Ali clapped.

"Sex . . . Female. Age . . . seven. Status . . . living."

"You're ahead of the game," Ali laughed, staring down at her watch. "And you did all of that in only nine minutes. I've gotta say that I'm impressed."

"Nine minutes passed?" Ashton asked. It sure hadn't felt like nine minutes to him.

"Yes," she answered. "But although that might seem like a long time to you, it can take people with your gift up to an hour to mind read for the first time."

A part of Ashton wanted to ask Ali how she knew that, but he decided it would be better for him to just keep his mouth shut.

"I honestly think that one is enough for today, but tomorrow I'll bring someone else out," she said. "And you'll learn that if you're this good, you'll be able to find out a person's family tree and everything."

Ashton felt a bit lightheaded but smiled as Ali walked with Clara out of the room. He felt accomplished. Maybe he was better at all of this than he had thought.

***

Ashton was very, very wrong.

Ashton's gift allowed him to be very skilled when it came to mind manipulation and telekinesis, but no amount of talent that he possessed could prepare him for the worst training of all: physical training.

His core was burning, and his legs were shaking by the end of the third session. His arms were going into lactic acid fits, and he felt like he was going to pass out. He had done a few sports in middle school, the occasional basketball or track season, but vigorous exercise was new to him.

Ali heard his grunting, and she walked in suddenly, leaning down to his level on the floor. "Do 20 more sit ups and a 30-second plank. Then, after your shower, meet me in the main room." Her voice was calm, but she sounded like she was in a hurry, so Ashton skipped the plank and jogged to the showers.

The shower was quick and rushed a bit, but Ashton was anxious about what Ali had seemed so impatient to show him. He ran a towel and his fingers through his wet hair, which turned black. It had been a while since he had dyed his hair. He wondered if it would eventually start fading back to blond. He walked toward the main room after haphazardly throwing on a t-shirt and jeans, still mussing his hair with the (now black-stained) white towel. He found Ali sitting on one of the monstrous couches clutching a plastic bag. "What did you want to show me?" Ashton called out, as he walked into the dimly lit room.

Ali's head perked up at the sound, and she moved over to make room for Ashton, although the size of the couch made her movement unnecessary. "I have something for you," she said, handing him the bag. "If you want me to leave while you change, just say the word."

Ashton opened the bag and looked inside to find clothing covered in a thin layer of dust. It looked as though they hadn't been worn in a century. He took each article of clothing out of the bag, brushed the dust off it, and laid them flat on the table in front of him.

"What do I do with them?" Ashton asked.

"Put them on," she replied.

"Yes, obviously. But what are they?" Ashton proposed.

"Clothes."

Ashton rolled his eyes at Ali's sudden secretiveness but couldn't help the knot in his stomach that was tugging at his brain and telling him that Ali wasn't secretive about anything. He nodded anyway, turned to look at her, and then looked in the direction of the door. She took that as her cue to get up and leave, so she walked toward the open door. "Yell if you need me," she called out before closing the door quietly and stepping into the hallway.

Ashton decided to ignore his thoughts, as he pulled off his t-shirt and unbuckled his jeans and eyed the clothes in front of him. They were a bit old-fashioned, but not in a bad way. He slipped out of his jeans and into the black dress pants. They were a bit snug around the waist, but comfortable, compared to the other business attire he had been forced to wear in the past. He put on the white dress shirt next. He tucked it into the pants and slowly realized that the outfit was fancier than he anticipated.

The next item on the table that caught his attention was the tie. He hadn't worn a tie since his parent's funeral, but he was pretty sure that ties didn't change colors. When he had first looked straight down on it, he had assumed the tie was black. But now, looking at it from a sideways angle, it was a bright shade of blue. He stood ramrod straight again, looking down at the black tie before tilting his head and watching it change. Either trying to summon his dormant powers was becoming too much for his brain, or the tie was actually changing colors in front of him. Now that he thought about it, it was probably a little bit of both. With a shrug, he wrapped the tie around his neck under the collar of the white shirt and let it hang down his chest.

The waistcoat caught his eye, so Ashton brought it closer to inspect it. Now *this* was old fashioned, but not unwelcome. He undid the buttons, slipped his arm through each of the holes, and pulled the coat tightly onto his body. He made sure the tie was tucked into the waistcoat before he buttoned it and then reached for the black jacket.

It was simple, just a black suit jacket that came down to about his waist. He put it on and rolled the cuffs of the sleeves, realizing that the fabric on the inside of the cuffs were blue—the same shade as the tie when observed from an angle. Ashton decided that the coat looked better with the sleeves rolled, so he left the blue peeking out from the bottom.

He walked over to the mirror by the entrance and pulled the jacket into place. The entire outfit was a bit tight fitting, and it showed—the pants hugging his hips and the waistcoat shaping his chest—but he looked *good*. At least, he looked better than he did in regular casual clothes. He turned away from the mirror to call Ali back in when something on the jacket caught his eye.

He turned toward the mirror again, running his fingers over the embroidery on his breast. The symbol was not new; Ashton had seen it almost everywhere since he had decided to stay in the mansion. It had been embroidered onto the black dress that he and Cayden had first seen when they walked in. The symbol had been sewn onto the flags he had seen in Grandfather's study and stitched onto the scarf around his neck. The pendant Grandfather wore around his neck also bore the same symbol, and Ashton sensed that it was important. The swirls taunted Ashton as he ran his fingers over the patch. "You can come in now, Ali," he said.

Ali stumbled into the room, looking a bit delirious and dizzy, like someone had pushed her into the room. Her eyes fell on Ashton, and she smiled. "It looks good! Father is going to be happy that it fits."

Ashton looked away from the symbol and up at Ali, pulling at the collar that was chafing his neck. "What is this?" Ashton said, gesturing to his outfit.

The secretiveness that Ali had seemed to possess before was now gone. "It's your uniform, Captain."

"Captain? Captain of what? What am I supposed to do with these clothes?"

"You're going to lead the army."

Ashton tried to ignore the bluntness in Ali's voice, but he couldn't ignore her facial expressions. Only a few minutes ago, his sister had been wide-eyed and secretive, her blue eyes constantly shifting and looking around as she fiddled with the plastic bag in her hands. Now, she was blunt and authoritative, her eyes hard-set. If Ashton didn't know any better, he'd think her eyes were gray.

"What army?" Ashton asked, growing more anxious by the second.

Ali only tilted her head a bit in confusion; she seemed surprised that Ashton had no idea what she was talking about.

"The Army of Descendants."

***

"What's the Army of Descendants?"

Ashton had managed to be let into Grandfather's study, having to ask only once before they ushered him in. Apparently, he had been promoted from "powerhouse to be left in his cell" to "give him whatever he needs, whenever he asks." He had gone directly to Grandfather's desk, needing answers, because Ali was ceasing to make much sense.

Grandfather looked up at him when he asked the question and raised an eyebrow as though the answer was obvious.

"Did you think you could just break down a multidimensional wall by yourself?"

"Well you sure made it seem like I could when you talked to me and Cayden the first day you brought us here."

"Well you can't," Grandfather said. "Ashton, you are probably the most powerful living being in all the universe at the current moment, with the small exception of the tree you passed through. But even you, as powerful as you are, cannot achieve what I desire on your own."

"What is it exactly that you desire?" Ashton asked. "When Cayden and I were with you in the main room, you told us that you want a way out—that you're stuck here and you want to go home."

"That is what we want."

"Then I can do that," Ashton said. "I've been training with Ali for a week now, and she thinks that I'm ready. I can control people much better telepathically than I could before, I can lift about three thousand pounds with my mind, and I can find out people's identities by reading their minds, to an extent. I'm ready."

Grandfather raised his eyebrows. "Well I'm very glad to hear that. And I trust Ali's judgment, so if she says that you're ready, then you're ready."

"But what's the Army of Descendants?"

"They're a group of your brothers and sisters who will obey your commands. They're simply there for backup," Grandfather said.

"Backup for what?" Ashton asked. "You're being vague again."

Grandfather laughed. "For what I desire."

And they were back to square one. Ashton brought his fingers to the bridge of his nose and squeezed. Grandfather could truly be infuriating.

"Do you desire more than just getting out of here?" Ashton asked.

"I want to control."

"To control what?"

"I want control," Grandfather said simply. He toyed with the pendant around his neck. "Do you know what this is, Ashton?" he asked, holding up the crest on the bottom of the chain.

"I've seen the symbol all over the place here," Ashton said. "I'm not very sure what it is though."

"The symbol is the Dweller family crest," Grandfather said. "But that's not what this is. The symbol on the pendant may be our crest, but the metal that the pendant is made from is even older than me. And I am extremely old."

Ashton wasn't sure why Grandfather was telling him this or why it mattered.

"This pendant is called the Ianti Pendant, and it will help me gain control. You may be able to control people, but I control you, and I control the army. I have control!"

The last sentence was screamed, as Grandfather let go of the Ianti Pendant and slammed his fist down on his table. Ashton gulped. One of the food cart women walked into Grandfather's study quickly with a small green tablet between her fingers and a cup of water in her hand. She handed the pill to Grandfather and whispered something in his ear, as well as a cup of water. Grandfather swallowed it.

Ashton stared, dumbstruck and completely confused. He took a step away from Grandfather's desk and put his hands up in front of his face. "You're crazy. You must be. You're . . . you're a psychopath."

Grandfather didn't flinch at the comment; he merely threaded his hands together and looked up at Ashton. He narrowed his eyes and let out a patient breath.

"Psychiatry involves observance; it is not a ruler to measure an amount of crazy."

Ashton sighed, turned his back, and rolled his eyes at the statement. He was sick of the riddles. "What is that even supposed to mean?"

The response came too quickly.

"Craziness cannot be measured by the amount of pills you take or where that mental instability is stored. It is not a measurement at all. *It's who you are.*"

***

Ashton had never been an exceptionally religious person. Despite being Christian, the Dwellers had rarely gone to church when Madeline and Nathan were alive; they had always been too busy with work. And in the rare instances when they were able to attend a sermon or Sunday mass, Ashton had never exactly felt comfortable. The priests always knew about Chase's antics and would give him sideways glances throughout the hour, much to Lucas's dismay. On top of the embarrassment felt because of being "Chase Dweller's brother," Ashton wasn't an idiot.

Their church's views on homosexuality were not exactly well masked. The priests made frequent digs, referring to other types of "lifestyles" that would not be accepted in *their* church. Pamphlets were distributed every once in a while, and Ashton would gaze over at them with a knot in his stomach, but his father would only shake his head in disgust and rip them up. That fact had always made Ashton feel a bit better.

The church that the Dwellers had attended was very big on hell. If you sinned, you were going to hell, and that's the way they saw it. Everything was in black and white—people were either bad or they were good, and shades of gray did not exist. Ashton was never a very big believer, but there was always the small thought in his innocent brain as a child, that he might be going to hell.

If there was a hell, this was it.

Every morning during the second week in the mansion, a food cart woman, dressed in the attire that Sandra had been wearing, would come into his cell to bring him breakfast and a pill that he was supposed to take, which he was told was developed by Grandfather to strengthen his brain and help him with the pain that followed the training sessions. He was hesitant about taking the pill after the encounter with Grandfather in his study, but he swallowed it without a fight after one of the guards peeked into his cell with a stern look on his face.

The second week of training sessions was more painful than the first, and he worked his brain and body until he could barely walk. Ali would have to yell sometimes because Ashton would blank out and forget the instructions for what Ali wanted him to do. The training was working him to death. After the second week was over, Ashton was called into the main room to talk to Grandfather, this time at Grandfather's request.

Ashton walked into the room hesitantly, wondering what Grandfather wanted from him now, but the man sat quietly in his chair with a smile on his face.

"The Army of Descendants is finally complete," Grandfather said happily. "And now it is time for the second phase of my plan."

"And what's that?" Ashton asked.

"To reveal my plan to you."

Ashton looked at Grandfather nervously, balling his hands up into fists on impulse. "I thought I already knew the plan. You take me to where the portal is, and I use my mind to break it down. Then you're finally free, and you can go home."

"That's not my plan," Grandfather laughed. "I've been stuck here for so long, and I've studied the portal for so long, don't you think I know how to break it down? It would take a lot of work and blood and sweat, but I could break it down if I wanted to. But if I get you to do it, then I don't have to risk my life doing so. And if I have you under my control, I have the most powerful weapon in the world—which means I have control."

Ashton's eyes widened, and he took a step backwards, trying to get away from Grandfather. The man was crazy. He had to be.

"You can't control me," Ashton said, trying to find his courage.

"Oh, but I can," Grandfather laughed. "Do you think that the Army of Descendants does what I tell them to do because they like me? No, it's because I'm the only thing they know. They're mindless, emotionless soldiers who would blow their own brains out if I asked them to. Their eyes are gray, because what you can do so well because of your *gift* and your *talent*, I can do with needles and pokers."

"What do you want?" Ashton said, his voice wavering.

"Respect," he answered. "The citizens of The Citee do not respect me; they *fear* me. It's like all of those religions—they claim to respect their God, but there is no respect there at all—only fear of His wrath."

Ashton backed up farther. He had tried to ignore the way that the Dwellers had trapped him from all angles and closed any open door out of the main room. "You—you're *insane*. All of you! I want *out* of this. Cayden was right—" His mind flashed with horrific images: Cayden tied to a chair by his wrists and ankles, needles digging into his head—the brown slowly fading out of his eyes.

Grandfather's face had not changed throughout the entire conversation. He was still stone cold, with his blue eyes focused on Ashton's face.

"Take him to be drained," he ordered to the Dwellers that were standing behind Ashton.

Ashton whipped his head around and stared at the group of

Dwellers behind him. Some of them wore jackets with the crest embroidered into them, and some wore the black dress he had seen on the first day. One look into their gray eyes, and he knew that they were part of the army.

"*Drained?* What the hell do you mean *drained?* I knew . . . I knew I shouldn't have trusted you. Who . . . who even *are* you?"

Grandfather smiled for the first time since Ashton had met him. It was not a warm smile like Ali's or a hesitant smile like Malia's, but deranged. He smiled wide and crazily like a serial killer or a monster out of Ashton's worst nightmare. "Most of them call me Grandfather. But my name is Sanrid Dweller. Who are you?"

Ashton stared blankly at him. "I . . . I'm . . . who am I?" He ran a hand over his face, stopping to pinch his fingers on the bridge of his nose. *Who was he?* He thought back to the events of the past week, only now realizing the slow deterioration of his memory. He had been forgetting the answers to Ali's questions, such as how heavy certain dumbbells were after he picked them up, simple facts about his past, and how long his powers had been dormant. The pills had been messing with him the whole time, tearing away at his memory until he couldn't remember basic facts.

He took another step backwards from Sanrid, momentarily cursing himself at how close he was getting to the soldiers behind him. "What have you been doing to me? What is going on?" He tried to keep his voice straight, but it wavered as his hands started to shake. He had been working on hand-to-hand combat with Ali the past few days, but he was outnumbered. His powers were the only thing he could use to protect himself now.

He turned toward the soldiers that were behind him and extended his hand out in front of him, as Ali had told him to do. He closed his eyes and concentrated on them, repeating the command *Move out of the way* in his head over and over. The soldiers merely looked at each other, shrugged, and grabbed Ashton's arms to pull him out of the room.

Ashton howled and tried to pull his arms out of their grip, but there were four soldiers holding each of his arms. He wasn't strong enough to break out of their hold. And he was clearly not strong enough to telepathically control the soldiers—he yelled commands at them, screaming at the top of his lungs. He yelled commands at Sanrid as well, screeching until his throat was hoarse and he realized why nothing was working. The Dwellers were his *family*, and his powers didn't work on other Dwellers.

"You've been using me and my powers—this whole time. You had this planned from the start! What do you even want?" Ashton screamed and kicked, trying to break free from the hold to lunge at Sanrid and kick him, punch him, or bite him—*anything*. But the grip was too tight.

"Take him to draining. *Now*." The calm facade that Sanrid had put on was slowly falling apart as he started to lose his cool. Ashton didn't stop screaming until the soldiers had brought him to the door and they were ready to take him away. There were tears running down his cheeks, and he couldn't yell anymore. His head was hanging low between his shoulders until he looked up at Sanrid and yelled as loud as he could, "WHO AM I?"

Sanrid stared at him for a few seconds before turning his head away and staring at the ground. He wrapped his fingers around the pendant hanging from his neck and squeezed it.

"You are Ashton Dweller. And you are going to save us."

15

Sasha put her cheek in her hand and stared out at the mansion, sighing at the sight. She looked over at Cayden, who was staring at the view with the same strange intensity. She wondered if he felt the same way about it as she did.

"It's beautiful, isn't it?" he said, seemingly out of nowhere.

Sasha turned her head to look at him, smiling slightly and sighing. "Yes, The Citee is a beautiful place. I just wish—" She didn't finish her sentence, and Cayden didn't need her to. He understood her feelings, especially after learning the true secrets buried deep beneath The Citee's bright shell.

Cayden wanted to say something philosophical, something about true evil being hidden behind a shield of beauty, but Sasha cut off his train of thought.

"The light of this place is the first thing I remember. That's as far back as my memory goes."

Cayden stood silently beside her, fiddling with his hands and not wanting to say anything else. Sasha didn't like to talk about herself or her past. She had told Cayden what he needed to know about the Ancestors, and that was it. She had told him about the draining operation and its effects but had ceased conversation when the topic changed to *her* eye colors.

"Sasha . . . you don't have to— Sasha cut him off.

"No. It's only right. You told me everything about you and your mom and Ashton. It's not fair that you know nothing about me besides the scar that takes up my face."

Cayden swallowed. Everything she had said was right, and he *was* curious. But he wasn't sure he wanted to know the whole story. He had heard the story behind the scar, and he knew that images of Sasha burning alive would haunt his dreams for enough nights to come.

"Well, first things first," she said. "I'm older than I look."

Cayden laughed. "You can't be much older than me."

"You're 18," she said. Cayden nodded, although it wasn't a question.

"Well, I'm 26."

Cayden gaped at her. "But you're like six inches shorter than me."

She laughed at that, resting a hand on his shoulder. "My height is a curse."

Cayden thought something along the lines of *your height isn't your only curse*, but the look Sasha gave him told him that she already knew that.

"You know I had a life before all of this—the army—the Dwellers? I had a life. I just don't . . . I don't remember it." Sasha's voice fell and she looked at the ground below, resting her head on her hand again. Cayden looked at her sadly, trying to sympathize, but failing to. He couldn't imagine how terrible it would be to forget so much of his life. He put a hand on Sasha's shoulder in an attempt to console her, and she smiled at him, which was a refreshing sight for Cayden to see.

"I don't remember much of my life, only bits and pieces," Sasha continued, exhaling sharply and trying to keep her composure. "I remember that I had a single father, but I don't remember what had happened to my mom to cause that. And I remember that I had a boyfriend and that he had this—amazing red hair." She laughed once, although there was no humor behind it. "He had red hair, but if you were to ask me his name, I don't remember that either."

Cayden's face fell, and he fiddled with his hands, silently hoping that Sasha would stop talking. He didn't know how much of

Sasha's life story he could handle. The story about her draining process made Cayden's stomach flip sickly, and thinking about her and her father or her and her boyfriend made his heart twist painfully.

"The one person I remember more than anyone is my little sister," Sasha said slowly, as if she were afraid to admit the words to herself. "Her name was Rosie and . . . she was everything to me. She was only six when I left for college, and I just remember promising her that I would send her some dumb souvenir home from Iowa." She swallowed slowly, although the tears were already burning in her eyes.

"That is the only promise I've ever broken."

Cayden didn't know what possessed him to hug her, but he did. The minute he did, he regretted it, knowing that Sasha had trust issues and had lost way too many people. He tensed, expecting her to push him away and punch him in the face.

Sasha froze at first, unsure of what to do, but after a few seconds, she reciprocated, wrapping her arms around Cayden's waist. Cayden rested his chin on her head and let the hug go on for a minute before pulling away.

"Thanks," Sasha said quietly after disentangling herself from the hug. "I needed that."

"You've lost so much," Cayden said, in almost a whisper. "How the hell are you still standing?"

Sasha smiled genuinely now, turning her eyes away from Cayden and looking out at The Citee again. "I love this place more than I hate Sanrid and what he's done to my life," she said. "I lost all of my memories, so in my mind, this is the only home I've ever had. I guess the need to protect it is what's kept me going."

"The people here, do they know about you and your story?" Cayden asked.

Sasha sighed. "The Rebels knew everything about me. But

now, since they're all gone, the citizens of The Citee know me as nothing more than the 'refugee girl they see on the street sometimes.' That might change soon, though. I've seen a few signs recently in the less dense sections of The Citee with my face on them. I'm the last Rebel left, and Sanrid probably wants to tie up his loose ends before he sets Ashton loose."

"Will he send out more bands of soldiers to try and kill you?" Cayden asked.

Sasha smirked. "Hey, it's not just me. It'll be you and your mom too, once they find out the two of you have disappeared—if they haven't already."

Cayden exhaled shakily. "We should really start moving now; shouldn't we? We only have so much time before everything falls apart."

Sasha stared at Cayden uneasily. "We're not going over there. I told you that already, Cayden. I can't go back there, especially now. They know who I am, and if they saw me, it could ruin everything—not just for me, but for you and Ashton too. It's better to just wait it out here."

"We can't just wait it out," Cayden said. "If we're lucky, Ashton's still got control of his own mind. But I know that's not very likely, and so do you. We've got to get to them and stop them before they can break down the wall."

"We can't," Sasha sighed. "We're not strong enough."

"Who says we're not?" Cayden questioned. "I won't go down without a fight if I can save Ashton, and you're one of the strongest people I've ever met."

Sasha scoffed.

"You're kidding me," Cayden said, raising his eyebrows. "You don't think you're strong? Hell, anyone I know would never be able to go through what you've endured and still come out on top."

"Do I look like I'm on top?" Sasha asked seriously, gesturing to the scar on her face and her ripped tights. "The only thing 'top' about me is that I'm not buried six feet under."

"Don't you want to kill Sanrid? Isn't that what your whole life has been leading up to since you were drained?"

"Of course I do!" she exclaimed. "The sooner he's dead, the sooner I can dance on his grave. I've told you already, there's nothing I want more than for him to be wiped from existence."

"Then that means we have to get moving," Cayden said. "The quicker we get to the mansion, the sooner you kill Sanrid."

Sasha paled, and she turned away from Cayden. She tucked her short hair behind her ear and chewed on her lip.

"What?" Cayden said, exasperated.

Sasha shook her head. "I'm not me," she mumbled.

"What?"

"I'm not me. I'm not who you think I am."

Cayden huffed. "Don't tell me that you're keeping secrets from me now too. Cut me some slack. A few weeks ago, I found out my best friend of 18 years is actually a mind controller, and now you're not who I think you are either?"

Sasha rolled her eyes. "That's not what I mean. I don't have any big bombshell to drop on you. All I'm saying is that you put me up on too high of a pedestal. You keep making me out to be this big, strong hero, when that's all a facade. You see this hard exterior—this shell I put around myself so I don't get hurt? The truth is . . . I don't think I'd ever really be able to kill Sanrid. I seem all intimidating but I'm . . . that's not me." She looked dejected and almost angry with herself, and Cayden had to fight himself to keep from hugging her again.

"Well you can drop the shell around me," he said, trying to seem nonchalant. "You know damn well that I'm terrified, and I can see right through you. It's extremely likely that neither of us will make it through this war, and I know that. You don't have to pretend to be strong and brave if you don't feel that way—I'm scared shitless. But we've got to get to the mansion before Ashton is drained, or we stand no chance against the Ancestors."

Sasha stared at Cayden and then sighed loudly. She rested her cheek on her hand again. "I hate it when you're right," she groaned.

Cayden looked to her sympathetically. "I know you don't want to go back to the mansion. If I were you, I wouldn't want to even look at it ever again. But if that's where they're keeping Ashton, we've got to get there before he's brainwashed. And if he's brainwashed already, then we'll improvise, just like we've been doing since we met. We're surprisingly good at improvising."

Sasha smiled at him—a real *genuine* smile with teeth and everything—and Cayden could have thrown a party. She nodded, looked out once again at the mansion, and sighed. Then she flipped up her middle finger toward the mansion and walked away from the wall and back toward the bottom of the hill and The Citee. "Pretty boy—you comin' or what?" she said.

Proud, strong, sassy, pig-headed Sasha was back. Cayden smiled up at his mother, who just winked. That was the Sasha they loved anyway.

***

Moving toward the mansion at night was a piece of cake, but moving toward the mansion during the daytime was equivalent to hell on earth. Sasha was constantly paranoid of them being recognized or noticed and made sure to pull Cayden down onto the ground to hide every time she heard or saw anything out of the ordinary. They hid behind modestly painted houses and inside random garages before reaching the main mansion area by noon. The air was crisp, and the sun was actually out, which instead of making Cayden feel reassured, only made him all the more nervous.

When they reached the mansion property, they could tell something was off. The normal day guards, who were required to survey the premises all through the day, were absent, leaving the mansion completely unguarded.

"They've started," Sasha whispered, as she pulled Cayden into a chunk of shrubbery that decorated the left side of the mansion.

"Started what?"

"Cayden I'm so sorry."

Cayden was confused. What was Sasha apologizing for? As Cayden tried to ask Sasha what was wrong, she clapped a hand over his mouth and pointed in the direction of the front doors of the mansion.

The doors were currently slowly opening, and once they were open completely, Ashton walked out. Before Cayden could say or do anything, Sanrid, Malia, and Ali were walking behind and to the sides of Ashton, each resting a hand on his shoulder. Cayden watched as Sanrid whispered something in Ashton's ear, and Ashton nodded wordlessly.

Ashton then turned back toward the opened doors of the mansion and stood, putting his hands behind his back. With Ashton facing the mansion, Cayden could finally see him up close. His hair was actually *styled*, and his face was expressionless as he stared into the open doors of the mansion. He was dressed in a suit and waistcoat, and the jacket of the suit had the Dweller crest sewn into the front of it. Cayden barely had to look into Ashton's eyes once to know they were gray.

Ashton opened his mouth to speak, and although Sasha and Cayden couldn't hear him very well, they knew that whatever he had said had an effect on the army. Suddenly, there was a wave of people flooding out the front doors of the mansion, all dressed in black, most with blond hair, and all with gray eyes and emotionless faces. They stopped when they approached Ashton, all in their orderly lines, waiting for their next command. Ashton turned around and walked forward, past Sanrid, Malia, and Ali, and toward the houses in front of the mansion.

Most people were standing outside of their houses; many of them hadn't seen Grandfather since the first day they had landed in The Citee, and there was never this much commotion going on near the mansion. Children stared as Ashton climbed to a bit higher elevation to shout to the army, "You will follow me!"

Ashton continued to walk forward, with the Ancestors following close behind him and the army in their immaculate lines behind them. Sasha, Cayden, and Sandra ran behind the army, knowing that it was too late to stop Ashton from breaking through the portal—but it was not too late to fight. Pushing through the thousands of soldiers in the army would have been impossible, but jumping through the portal after them wouldn't be too hard.

Ashton walked toward the welcome sign and eventually passed it. The electronic counter dropped from 1,569 to 1,568 as Ashton walked past it and then dropped to 1,565 after the Ancestors had followed. The electronic counter exploded off the welcome sign after half of the army had left the sign in its wake. Sasha, Cayden, and Sandra knew that that couldn't be a good sign.

Once they were over the hill where the welcome sign was, Cayden gasped as the parking lot came into view, showing off its thousands of cars in all its glory. Cayden didn't know how it had returned, but he ran to the bottom of the hill and tried to catch up with the army. The soldiers were speed walking as they tried to keep up with Ashton.

Walking through the parking lot, Ashton surveyed his surroundings. He stared at some cars longer than others and analyzed the placement of each one. Sasha and Cayden tried to figure out what he was doing, but they couldn't get a good enough look with the army in their way.

Sanrid approached Ashton slowly after Ashton had stopped. Sanrid then placed a hand on Ashton's shoulder and leaned close to his ear. "You know where it is, Ashton," he said slowly. "I know you can feel it. Follow your gut."

Ashton closed his eyes, and instead of watching where he was walking, he let his feet guide him. Starting up again, the Ancestors and the army followed, as Ashton twisted and turned through the parking lot, looking for the location of the portal. Of course, no one could see it, but Ashton could feel it. As he got closer and closer, his head burned, so he followed the pain until his nose began to bleed.

Opening his eyes and bringing a finger to his nose, he blinked. When he pulled his finger away, it was covered in crimson. "This is the place," Ashton said in a monotone voice, and he pointed east—exactly in the direction of his car, the only car in the parking lot, with the exception of Sandra's, that still had a license plate.

"It's time, Ashton," Sanrid said, as he smiled and tightened the Ianti Pendant in his grasp. "Break through."

Ashton looked toward his car and stared. Bringing his palm to his temple, he squeezed his eyes shut tightly, and commanded the atoms of the portal to rip themselves in two. He ignored his nose as it began to bleed again and focused on ripping the portal in two.

The bonds between the elements making up the portal were tight, and Ashton had to break them one by one, some of them snapping through vocal commands. Ashton's nose kept bleeding as he extended a hand and made a fist, forcing the portal to snap. Pieces of metal slowly began to break off of Ashton's car, disintegrating into nothing as they hit the ground. As the car broke into pieces, all that was left was complete darkness in its wake.

When the car was nothing more than a few chunks of rubber

and colorless metal, a huge, gaping hole opened up. Upon first glance, it looked like a black hole—complete nothingness. But every few seconds, the darkness would shimmer like the rocks that surrounded the roots of the tree, and one could tell that whatever lay beyond the portal was real.

The portal grew and shrunk a few times, as if it were stretching and trying to get used to existing. The ground of The Citee shook as if there had been an earthquake, and there were a few screams from the children, who had never felt anything like this before.

Cayden and Sasha stared at it from behind the army.

"What do we do?" Cayden yelled to her over the roar of the portal.

"We wait," she said simply. "There's no use in trying to stop him now; we don't stand a chance. Now all we can do is to try and stop Ashton before Sanrid makes him kill every living person in Davenport."

Ashton walked through the portal as if it were nothing, with the Ancestors following him through the dark circle standing where Ashton's car had been. The army then began to walk through the portal, and after most of the soldiers had made their way through, Sasha, Cayden, and Sandra pushed their way through the last few stragglers and jumped through.

Cayden closed his eyes tightly, as he felt as if he were in a plane that was taking off, minus the plane. On the way to The Citee, he and Ashton had been in a car, and his eyes had been clenched so tightly shut that he had barely felt any movement at all when they had arrived. But now, on the way back, he felt as if he were being spun at a million miles a minute, his body on a completely separate plane than his mind was on. He reached out for Sasha but felt nothing but cold wind, as he was finally spit out into another dimension, his home.

Cayden didn't think he'd ever be so happy to see Tanglewood

Drive again in his life. Lying on the ground for a second, staring up at the cloudless sky, and trying his hardest not to be sick, he breathed in fresh air and smiled. Whatever was going to happen next, at least it was going to happen at home.

Looking around for Sasha and Sandra, he saw his mother running toward him, and he smiled. Sasha was only a few steps away as well. Although Cayden felt nauseated, and his mother looked pale as well, he knew that however the Mitchells felt was nothing compared to how Sasha had to be feeling. She looked positively green but shook off any comment Cayden tried to make about her resting for a few seconds. She pointed in the direction that the army was moving and broke into a jog.

Cayden rolled his eyes but ran after her, sliding up alongside her, reaching for the knife in his belt, and pulling it from its sheath. "What are we going to do now?" he asked her.

"Sanrid is going to want to move Ashton toward the river," Sasha explained. "Once he can cross over through Davenport and be confident enough that he can take down a major city, he'll cross the river with Ashton and start his reign of terror."

Someone screamed in the distance, and Sasha picked up her pace, trying to catch up with the army.

"Are you sure the reign of terror hasn't already started?" Cayden said sarcastically, running behind her.

Ashton, the Ancestors, and the army were not moving fast. On the contrary, they were actually moving quite slowly, as if they were admiring a paved road for the first time. To be exact, they *were* technically admiring a paved road for the first time, at least the first time in a few thousand years.

The large mob walking down Tanglewood had initially only caused a few lone drivers to do double takes, but soon, people were emerging from their houses to figure out what was going on. A few terrified-looking teenagers emerging from one of the houses had phones glued to their ears, and Cayden could only assume they were on the phone with the Iowa state police department. Cayden prayed in part that the police department wouldn't show up; they'd be no match for the army.

As the army and Ashton gravitated toward the more suburban part of Davenport, with Cayden, Sasha, and Sandra following closely behind, the masses waiting outside of their houses became more prevalent, and the sound of police sirens could be heard in the distance. Cayden held his breath.

Cayden had always been good at history. Math had never been his thing, and he had failed almost every math class he was put into. But history, he could deal with, pass, and maybe even get a higher-than-average grade once in a while. Wars had always interested him, and conflicts came up more often in history than not, whether they were over religion, resources, or culture. Cayden didn't understand how to write most kinds of equations, but he understood the Domino Effect.

The only phrase that Cayden could use to describe the scene in front of him when Ashton entered suburban Davenport was *Domino Effect*.

Ashton looked to a member of the army closest to him and nodded swiftly in her direction. The girl walked toward a terrified mother, standing protectively in front of her two children, and kicked her in the shin. When the woman doubled over in pain, the soldier ripped a knife from her belt and shoved it into the woman's abdomen. The sound of the woman's children screaming seemed to set off an alarm that sent the entire Army of Descendants into what could only be described as *murder mode*.

The lone mother being stabbed on the side of the road turned into innocent civilians being murdered by the hundreds, in mere minutes. Ashton barely moved a muscle, just stared into the eyes of soldiers in the army, telepathically giving them commands on what to do and whom to kill. Sanrid, Malia, and Ali stayed back, avoiding conflict in the same way that Ashton did: only killing if a civilian attacked them first.

And boy, did the civilians attack. The people of Davenport soon realized the difference between the army soldiers and The Ancestors, and ran toward the Ancestors with weapons that ranged from legitimate guns to gardening tools. They never made it very far; the minute they actually got close enough to Sanrid to inflict pain, an army soldier would appear behind them and stick a knife into their spine. Or on the contrary, Sanrid would pull out a weapon of his own, usually a large spear sharp enough to decapitate in one swipe.

Ashton's method of defending himself was a bit different. Most civilians assumed that Ashton was just another member of the army, but the ones that singled him out, ran at him for all that it was worth. Instead of pulling out any weapon of his own, which Cayden soon realized that Ashton did not possess, he held out a hand in front of him, and as quickly as the townspeople would run at him, he would stop them in their tracks. Then, with a quick swipe of Ashton's index finger, their heads would almost completely turn around, their necks snapping as they collapsed in front of him.

Cayden and Sasha tried to alert the civilians who were trying to fight back that any attempt to stop them would only end in death. Some people that they ran to were apprehensive of Sasha because of how similar her dress looked to the army soldiers, and they refused to trust Sasha and Cayden. But most took their advice, grabbing their families and fleeing from suburban Davenport.

As Cayden stared at a frantic woman trying to buckle her crying baby into a car seat, he gulped. The woman, with fear in her eyes, slid the door of the minivan closed and hopped into the passenger seat, and Cayden watched as her husband shoved the key into the ignition of their car and sped away.

Cayden prayed that the civilians he had told to flee knew the meaning of *flee* and would eventually pass over the bridge into Illinois and keep driving. Because the minute everyone in suburban Davenport was either dead or gone, Sanrid would consider it conquered, and he would be heading for urban Davenport next.

16

After a short half hour had passed, the suburbs of Davenport were silent. Most people were dead, lying across the landscape with knife wounds and bullet holes decorating them. Cayden could see that a few members of the army were dead too, usually leaning up against a tree, decapitated.

Cayden knew that he and Sasha had not participated much in this battle because this was only the start. As Ashton and the army walked toward the urban centers of Davenport, Cayden knew that more and more people would be dying—and stepping into the fight would be vital at that point. They couldn't just get people to flee anymore.

Following behind Sasha, Cayden ran with his mother to the end of Tanglewood Drive, where it finally ended and broke into more urbanized streets. Staring out past the army, Cayden could see red and blue lights, and his heart sank.

The Iowa police had lines of squad cars essentially forming a blockade so that Ashton, the army, and the Ancestors could not get any closer to the city.

The police officers standing in front of their cars looked terrified. They had never seen anything remotely like this before in their lives, and Ashton and the army's expressionless faces were not making it any better. One chief stood on top of his car with a megaphone and stared out at the lines of army soldiers.

"Soldiers, drop your weapons!" he yelled. "If you do not disarm yourselves or if you try to attack us or any civilians in any way, we are going to take you all down!"

Ashton stared up at the police chief on top of his car, and Cayden, Sasha, and Sandra ran down the line of army soldiers so that they could get closer to Ashton. The army soldiers did not make any movements to grab their weapons from their belts, and neither did any of the Ancestors. Hiding behind a bush, Cayden, Sasha, and Sandra watched for Ashton's next movement.

Without moving a limb, Ashton looked up at the police chief and said, "boom."

The megaphone exploded in the chief's face, and with a scream, the officer fell off of his car, clutching his burned face as blood dripped down the sides of it. In seconds, the man was dead, and the officers ran at the army, ready to kill.

Ashton faced little resistance after that. The "magic act" he had performed with the exploding megaphone was enough to scare any officer that approached him. If any of them were brave enough to raise a gun or weapon in Ashton's direction, Ashton would murder them quickly, snapping their necks just as he had with the people in suburban Davenport.

Some of the officers were smart enough to flee, running to tell people in the center of the city to run for their lives and flee as well before Ashton could reach them. Others stayed and fought, but it only took an hour or so for all of them to be defeated.

Cayden stopped one of the fleeing officers in his tracks, desperate to make sure that no more people would get hurt.

"Hey!" he yelled. "Stop, officer, please!"

The officer stared at him, terrified. "Get out of here, boy! Go home! You're going to get hurt here! These people—they're monsters. They aren't human."

Cayden thought back to the conversation that he and Ashton had in Ashton's cell the night before he and his mother had fled the mansion. Ashton had told Cayden that he was a monster, and Cayden had refused to hear it. But now, he wasn't so sure.

"You need to do something for me," Cayden said to the officer. "Make sure that no one calls in any other police departments from other cities or other states. Do you want something like this to happen again? This army is unstoppable, and they're going to kill anyone who gets in their way. Do not let any other officers die at their hands."

The officer stared, dumbstruck, but nodded before hopping into one of the only police cars that were left and speeding away quickly.

Staring at Ashton now, Cayden watched as he continued to move closer and closer to their homes, with the army following. Most innocent people were hiding inside of their houses, and instead of pulling them out by force, as Cayden had assumed Sanrid would do, Sanrid decided that if they were too scared to face him and his army, they were considered conquered and dominated already, so the army kept moving.

The portal still roared and seemed to be moving, following Ashton and the army as they moved. However, it was beginning to shrink in size slightly, and it was starting to close. Cayden felt hopeless and looked toward his mother, who was talking quietly with Sasha and trying to figure out good strategic moves to help people avoid the army and save their families. Cayden walked over to join them.

"We're screwed," Cayden said. "Nothing has stopped Ashton so far or even slowed him down. We can't just tell people to flee forever. What happens if we tell all of Iowa to flee, and then he moves into the rest of the United States? What then? We tell everyone in the United States to flee to another country? That would just make Sanrid feel like he's won and give him the confidence to keep conquering until he's got the whole world."

Sasha nodded. "Cayden's right. As much as I don't want to say it, we have to stop thinking about ways we can save small groups of people and start thinking about ways that we can stop Ashton and the army. People are going to have to die if we want to save seven billion people from Sanrid's reign."

Sandra sighed. "But there's no way to stop Ashton. Haven't we established this already?"

"There's no way that we know of."

Sasha and Sandra turned to stare at Cayden.

"Cayden, there *is* no way," Sasha said.

"But what if there is?" he exclaimed. "No evil mastermind ever sets up a master plan without thinking about ways that it could be foiled. And no one creates a machine without giving it an off switch. There's gotta be a way to stop him. And I think I know how we're going to do it."

"How?" Sasha asked. "I've known about this prophecy, Sanrid, and Ashton for years, and there's nothing that I know of that can stop him."

"That's because Sanrid's got it all under wraps—probably in the mansion somewhere, in his study. Sasha, you know the mansion best, don't you?"

Sasha nodded hesitantly. "I haven't been inside in years, but I could probably find my way around. Why?"

"Because," Cayden said, "right now no one is inside the mansion, and no one is protecting the secrets that Sanrid probably has locked up inside his study. If you run through the portal and into the mansion, you can grab Sanrid's secrets from his study and bring them back here."

Sasha stared wide-eyed at Cayden. "You're crazy," she said. "I can't do that." "Sasha you're a genius, you can do it," Cayden urged, pushing her toward the depleting hole. "The whole place is unguarded! Just run in, break into the study, and grab them."

"Cayden, if the portal closes and I get stuck, I'll cease to exist," Sasha cried.

"If there's something written in Sanrid's records that we can decipher, we can stop this," Cayden said, grabbing her hand. "We can save everyone."

Sasha took a deep breath and nodded, whispering, "You're right." She looked toward the portal once before placing a light kiss on Cayden's forehead and running full force at the portal.

***

Sasha had never seen The Citee in a time of chaos before.

When Sanrid and the Primaries had first come to the universe and attempted to steal the land from the first civilization, it had been horrible, as Sasha had been told. Sanrid would command Bella to murder thousands, and she would do so quickly and brutally, bodies falling around her in heaps. As the people of the first civilization tried to revolt and fight against Bella, she would murder even more efficiently, finding new methods of killing that went further than just controlling people's minds and weapons. The methods were unstoppable, and she could kill tens of thousands in mere seconds. The Rebels had never let Sasha in on how exactly she was able to do it, but she had the feeling that Sanrid had probably written it down somewhere.

The people in The Citee, Sasha knew, had never dealt with any kind of disorder or change. Sanrid kept them all comfy and sedated, fed and clothed, housed and content. Now, with the portal split open and threatening to wipe their whole town off the map, they were in a panic. People littered the once-empty streets, trying to find a means of escape. The portal was large, but far away from most of the settlements in The Citee, and most of the citizens were oblivious to its power. Of the few that figured out its purpose, some jumped through but many refused, fearful of what was on the other side.

For a second, Sasha almost stopped to explain to a few innocent civilians what the portal was doing in The Citee, but she

The Dwellers

turned back toward the mansion when she remembered that the portal would be closing in mere minutes, and she had work to do. Picking up her pace, she turned back toward the townspeople and wished she could pity them, but deep in her heart, she knew that she couldn't. They had done too much wrong to her for the years she was damaged and starving on the streets for her to help them now.

Sprinting the last few steps toward the mansion, she ripped open one of the large front doors and ran through the dimly lit hallway. The mansion was completely deserted—not even one guard was left. Sasha gazed around the main room for a few seconds, momentarily struck by how much bigger the room was than in her memory. Trying to rack her brain for memories of the mansion, she dashed out of the main room in an attempt to find Sanrid's study.

It didn't take her long to find it, and while she ran into the room assuming that the records and secrets of draining would be hidden behind a barricade of some sort, it took her all but seconds to break into the small padlock wrapped around Sanrid's desk drawer. She found the records stuffed in the bottom of it. Resisting the urge to scream in victory in fear that there were in fact guards left in the mansion, she spread the papers across Sanrid's desk, analyzing them. Most were written in English, modern English no less, and showed surgeons performing draining operations and the instructions on how to properly drain.

While the instructions were written clearly enough, along the margins of the papers were symbols in the hieroglyphic language of the first civilization. Sasha panicked momentarily until she realized that the records spread across Sanrid's desk were merely translations of what was coded into the margins of the papers. Sanrid had done most of Sasha's work for her.

Sasha indulged in this realization a little more, allowing herself a squeak of excitement. She bundled the papers together in a pile and threw a rubber band around them. Reaching back into the drawer, she found a revolver under some more papers. She held the weapon in her hands, which she had never done before, and dropped it into a gun holster on her belt. Slipping the papers through her belt and tightening it so they wouldn't fly free, she smiled and ran out of Sanrid's office back into the main room toward the main hallway.

She could see the portal getting smaller through the windows of the mansion, and she was ready to sprint out the door when something caught her eye. Enclosed in a glass case along the side of the main hallway was a red, clay tablet. Approaching it a bit closer, Sasha's mouth dropped open.

Bella's tablet was sitting right in front of her, enclosed in the glass and in almost impeccable condition, even with the blood splattered across the left side. Somewhere in Sanrid's records had to be a translation method of some sort or some way to translate the first civilization's writing into English, and somewhere on Bella's clay tablet could be the answer of how to reverse the draining process. In a burst of adrenaline, Sasha punched right through the protective glass case, grabbing the clay tablet the minute she felt the glass shatter around her knuckles. Maybe she'd regret doing that later, but for now, she was riding the wave of victory.

Running out of the mansion and slipping the thin tablet into her belt along with the parchment, she sprinted toward the portal, which was closing more rapidly than before. Jumping through it in the opposite direction didn't give Sasha as much of a head rush as it had the first time, but she still needed to stop and stand still for a few seconds after she landed, trying to calm the spinning of her head and the space in her ears.

Looking around for any sign of Cayden, she saw an abandoned car tilted to the side and two people huddled behind it. A woman was helping a boy clean the blood off of his knife. When Sasha saw that the woman was Sandra, she let out a happy sigh. Cayden looked up from where he was wiping off the blade of the dagger, and when he saw Sasha, he waved her over.

Sasha ran behind the car as quickly as she could, ducking her head down so none of the Ancestors could recognize her. When she finally reached Cayden, he wrapped her up in his arms.

"I thought you were gonna die, I thought the portal was just gonna swallow you up," Cayden laughed into her shoulder. He was laughing, but his voice was strained, and his breath was coming in sharp bursts. He felt like he was going to laugh and cry all at the same time. Sasha was alive. Sasha had successfully made it in and out of the portal alive. The fact that she had retrieved the records was just a bonus at this point.

Cayden looked to her expectantly, and she reached around her back, pulling a chunk of clay out of her belt along with a stack of what seemed to be papyrus or parchment paper of some sort. Placing it into Cayden's hands with a shy smile, she watched as he turned the parchment over in his hands.

"This is written in English," Cayden said in amazement.

"We lucked out," Sasha laughed. "On the margins of the records, there's the same language that the first civilization wrote in, which makes me think that Sanrid might have translated everything already—at least what's written in the margins. But I brought Bella's tablet too, because there could always be something that he missed or skipped translating on purpose. I don't know if there are any records that are exact decoders, but we can use the relationship between the margin symbols and the English words on the parchment to maybe help us translate. I was going to try to decipher some of it while I was at Sanrid's desk, but I needed to get out of there as fast as possible. The portal is about to close."

Cayden turned his head slowly from around the car to take a

look at the portal. It was nothing more than a speck in the distance now, even though it really wasn't too far away. A minute passed, and soon Cayden couldn't see the portal at all. When the ground shook slightly, and even Ashton stopped moving, Cayden knew that the portal was closed.

"We've got to figure something out," Cayden said, looking to Ashton. "Soon."

"You've got that right," Sasha agreed. "He's killing more and more by the second. It's just how the Rebels described Bella."

Cayden shook his head, trying to get the images out of his head as he looked through the pieces of parchment paper in his hands. There were numerous diagrams of tools and medical equipment. Cayden could only assume they were used while trying to break into someone's brain. Instructions on how to use them were clearly listed in a step-by-step process. There were a few pages on what the draining process entailed; the memories would go first, followed by the emotions. The color should leave their eyes completely before they're released from the draining room, and a test should be administered to make sure that they are mindless and cannot remember their identity. There was a small addition by Sanrid at the bottom of the page, mentioning that the subject, prior to being drained, was to be given a pill once a day to jump-start the memory loss. An asterisk under the note mentioned that Sanrid did not want another repeat of the "Sasha Incident," and Sasha smiled in victory.

A few pages later, the writings in the margins got longer, and Sanrid's handwriting on the parchment got sloppier as he translated. These pages went into detail about how the draining process affected people's minds. Sasha looked on as Cayden neared the last few pages.

Holding the last two pages in his hands, Cayden realized that there wasn't much written in the records that he and Sasha didn't already know. However, the last two pages included many drawings of the symbol—the crest that was carved and embroidered into everything that the Ancestors owned.

"Oh my god, Cayden," Sasha said, suddenly.

"What?"

"Look at what's written on these pages," Sasha said, grabbing the pages out of Cayden's hand and laying them down on the ground.

"This first page talks about condensing the power and control that a mind manipulator has into one object. It means that even if you don't have the powers of mind manipulation that Ashton and Bella do, you can still control people the same way, as long as that person is drained."

"So even if you're not a mind controller, you can control drained people?" Cayden asked.

"Yes," Sasha said, amazed. "Anyone can—as long as they follow the rules listed here and have the ingredients, they can turn any object into a device that can control numerous people, as long as they're all drained."

"So—like an army?" Cayden said, smiling.

"Exactly like an army," Sasha laughed. "And that's all this page talks about, and then the next page is covered in pictures of the crest."

"What does that mean, though?" Cayden asked. "The crest was embroidered and carved onto everything in the mansion. This object could be anything!"

"No, it couldn't," Sasha smiled. "What do you know of that has the crest carved into it? What does Sanrid never let out of his sight?"

"The pendant!" Cayden yelled. "Sasha, you're a genius!"

Sasha blushed and grabbed the papers out of Cayden's hands. "The realization does nothing for us unless we have it in our possession," Sasha said. "And right now, it's still around Sanrid's neck, so it's no help to us."

"We can get it from him," Cayden said. "I know we can. The chain doesn't look too strong, and we might actually be able to snap it off his neck when he isn't paying attention. There's a war going on, and he's going to be paying more attention to it."

Sasha shook her head. "The chain is stronger than we think it is," she explained. "If this thing is truly as powerful as the records say it is, Sanrid is going to be keeping a close eye on it and probably will be more focused on protecting the pendant than he is on protecting Ashton. We'll never be able to get it off of him."

"We will if we kill him."

He had said it so quietly that he didn't even think Sasha had heard him at first, but soon a grin formed on her lips, and she turned to him slowly.

"You've got a point there," she smirked.

Cayden's eyes widened as he nodded, knowing that even though Sasha preached about not being strong enough to kill Sanrid, she wouldn't hesitate if that were what it came down to.

"How are we supposed to be able to kill him?" Cayden said. "Sanrid will make Ashton tell the army to kill us if we got close enough to kill him, and we don't have any long range weapons."

"Yes we do," Sasha smiled, pulling the revolver out of its holster on her belt. "I found this puppy when I was looking through the records in Sanrid's desk."

Cayden laughed happily, grabbing the tablet and papers back out of Sasha's hands. "You try and get a good enough shot at Sanrid to kill him," he said. "And I'm going to look through the translation codes and see if I can find anything else on the stone or in his records."

Sasha nodded and smiled, ruffling up Cayden's hair and running toward Sandra, who was hiding behind an overturned car and staring at the army as they attacked more innocents. Sandra had a gun in her hand when Sasha reached her.

"Where the hell did you get that?" Sasha said, admiring the weapon in Sandra's hands.

"I stole it from a dead officer's belt."

Sasha nodded in amazement. "Wow."

A few yards away, Cayden hid himself behind a small house and laid out the records in front of him. He took a closer look at the pages that Sasha had initially skimmed over, the ones going into detail about draining and people like Bella and Ashton. He read quickly, trying to decode Sanrid's sloppy handwriting, which was, at times, harder to decipher than the hieroglyphics.

The talent that Isabella possessed was unprecedented. No Dweller I had ever known had possessed a power like hers. The Dweller prophecy that the Prophets have fabricated suggests the existence of a person like Isabella, with powers similar to hers. If this person truly does exist and I am able to train him in the right way, he will be unstoppable.

Cayden skimmed over the parts where Sanrid went into detail about what he thought Ashton was going to be like until he got to a part in the records that made his head spin.

Isabella had accomplished much with her power. Not only had she been able to mentally manipulate and murder, but she had been able to perform telekinetic acts and read into the cells of the human brain once she had been Drained and taught. The mind reading aspect came as a shock to me, but it was welcomed. Ali will do a good job of teaching Ashton in the ways that I taught Isabella, and he might be talented to the point where I might not even have to Drain him.

Cayden knew about Ashton's mental manipulation, and the way that he blew up the megaphone proved to Cayden that telekinesis probably was not very far out of Ashton's range—but mind reading? This was a new discovery that could help them or hurt them.

A sudden scream, which sounded distinctly like Sasha's voice, tore Cayden away from his thoughts. He shoved the records into his belt and ran toward the sound. He looked across the road and saw Sasha, who was lying in front of Sanrid on her back, blood dripping from her cheekbone.

Cayden ran closer to her and Sanrid, who was hiding behind a car parked on the side of the road. Sasha met his eyes and winked, as she made an exaggerated groan of pain.

Sasha was faking being hurt to make Sanrid feel like he was winning. The blood trickling down Sasha's face was definitely real, but her scream hadn't been, and neither were the moans she was making now.

Trying to distract Sanrid, Sasha slid her revolver across the road to Cayden. But Sanrid wasn't stupid. He saw Sasha slide the gun to Cayden, and for a second, Cayden was sure that Sanrid was going to charge at him, but he picked Sasha up by the throat instead and held her out in front of him, bringing his other hand around to tighten the hold.

Cayden, too shocked to do anything but stare, tried to hold the gun at Sanrid but realized that he had never shot a gun in his life. And Sanrid and Sasha were way too close. If Cayden missed, he could kill Sasha. Placing the gun back onto the ground, he screamed for Sasha to fight back.

Sanrid had Sasha tightly by the throat, and though she attempted to kick him, her legs were too short to reach his frame. She gasped for air, struggling to free her neck from Sanrid's grasp, but her eyes were slowly closing, and she was having a hard time moving any of her limbs. She wasn't faking anymore. If she didn't free herself soon, she was a goner.

Before her eyes could close completely, there was a bang of a gunshot, and Sanrid fell to the ground. Sasha fell as well, coughing and spluttering, trying to get her breathing back in order. When

The Dwellers

Sanrid was on the ground, Cayden could see completely behind him and locked eyes with his mother, who wielded a 45 in her hands.

17

Sandra stood in shock, her finger still on the trigger. The world seemed to stop for a few moments. No one moved or said anything. Ashton stood and stared, his gray eyes dead and focused. For a second, Sandra had a flicker of hope that since Sanrid was gone, Ashton's control would return. But they all knew that Davenport wouldn't be that lucky.

Everyone moved so quickly that it was almost a blur in Sandra's vision. One minute, Sasha was smirking at her and throwing a thumb up from the ground, and the next, there were hands at her throat. Sandra looked up to find Ali's eyes staring down at her, as the girl's lanky fingers tightened around her trachea and her gray eyes locked with Sandra's. There were dark circles spotting Sandra's vision, and she couldn't breathe.

"You just killed my father," she spoke in an even voice. "You are going to pay."

Sandra flinched when the hands tightened again, but suddenly there was another loud bang, and the pressure on Sandra's throat ceased. Ali collapsed in front of her, blood trickling from the side of her mouth. Cayden stood behind her with his arm still raised, smoke rising from the top of Sasha's revolver. His face was not hard-set or determined, but scared, his mouth gaping open like he couldn't understand what he had just done.

Ashton, however, seemed unfazed by the brutal murder of his sister, turning on his heel and walking on like nothing had even happened. Sandra regained her breathing slowly and looked toward the Ancestors once again. Sanrid's body lay bloodied on the grass—the Ianti pendant still wrapped around his neck.

Sandra retreated back to Cayden, pulling him in the opposite direction of Ashton and the Ancestors, when the army formed a circle around Sanrid's and Ali's bodies.

Malia, who had stayed quiet at the mansion and during most of the fighting, walked toward Sandra and Cayden slowly. For a few seconds, Sandra was sure that Malia was going to pull one of the knives from her belt, but when she got close enough to kill them, she turned and walked toward Sanrid's body. For a moment, Sandra assumed there was some kind of Dweller ritual happening, but Malia proved her wrong when she leaned over the body of her husband and simply ripped the Ianti pendant from his neck, momentarily causing some blood to rush to the surface of Sanrid's throat. The pendant was strong enough to have cut through his skin.

A unanimous gasp was heard throughout the group, some covering their mouths with their hands in disbelief. Malia stood proud and tall as she clasped the chain around her neck, letting the pendant fall to her chest. She turned to face The Dwellers and said loudly, in a voice no one had heard her use before, "I now declare myself the righteous owner of the Ianti pendant. Sanrid Dweller is dead. You will bow before me."

The army did what they were told, falling to their knees and laying their palms flat on the dirt. Ashton stared at them from yards away with a blank expression, unmoving. It was obvious that he wasn't going to bow to Malia, and Malia looked in his direction and nodded, understanding the situation. Ashton wasn't going to bow to anyone; his mind was only programmed to know murder and domination.

Malia's demeanor had changed the instant the pendant was around her neck. While she initially had been the quiet, obedient wife of the great Sanrid, she was in charge now. She continued on in the direction that Ashton was walking, following him and motioning for the army to follow.

Ashton's attitude did not change now that Malia was in charge. He still commanded the army to kill and pillage, murdering mindlessly as he walked down endless streets. The more officers that arrived, the more angry and violent the army became, while Ashton's face still remained stone cold. He rarely spoke, making most of his commands telepathically. He stared down everyone he killed with emotionless eyes.

Every new squad of Iowa police officers that appeared was murdered quickly and systematically. Ashton didn't have one ounce of mercy, but he seemed to realize that police officers were a force to be reckoned with. One sound of a siren or flash of a blue and red light, and Ashton was back into murder mode. The officers never stood a chance.

Whenever Cayden could find an officer fleeing, he tried to tell them what he had told the first officer he had met: do not call in any other police departments.

Malia decided that Sanrid's plan of action was not for her halfway through urban Davenport. People who stayed in their houses were cowards and deserved to be dragged from their houses by the army and murdered in the streets. Families dragged from their homes would have the father killed last, so he could watch the murders of his partner and/or children first. Malia sent a group of army soldiers back to the outskirts of urban Davenport to tie up loose ends and to make sure that no one who was alive stayed that way. Cayden wanted to be sick.

Sasha had felt defeated since her run-in with Sanrid. She touched the bruises on her throat self-consciously every few minutes. Malia still had the pendant and was still in control of Ashton and the army, so they were no closer to stopping the Dwellers.

Cayden tried to cheer Sasha up, but in the middle of a war, there was nothing cheery to put a smile on her face. He put a hand on her shoulder and squeezed it reassuringly, as they followed the army again and tried to block out the pained screams of fathers watching their families being killed before their eyes.

Ashton was close to their family homes now, with the army trailing along to the center of urban Davenport. It was quieter than the other battles had been, which was not a good sign. Looking over to the side of one of the houses, Cayden's heart leaped into his throat.

Sandra saw the sight almost immediately, at the same time that Cayden saw it, and the sound that his mother made was a sound he swore he would never forget as long as he lived. Leaning up against the side of a foreign house were Mason and Alex, with both their throats slit and still bleeding.

Sasha inhaled sharply when she saw Sandra and Cayden's faces, as the tears starting to fall from Sandra's eyes.

"Is that your family?" she whispered to Cayden.

Cayden couldn't reply.

Sandra held Mason's head in her hands and touched her fingers lightly to his bleeding neck. Her only daughter sat beside him, eyes and mouth open, blood turning the collar of her white shirt a deep red.

Cayden cried silently, watching his mother sob over the bodies of her husband and daughter. He was at a loss for words. Sasha was crying as well, because although she didn't know the Mitchells save for Cayden and Sandra, she knew that Cayden's father had probably had to watch as his daughter was murdered in front of him.

"Noah is probably okay," Cayden said thickly, placing a hand on his mother's shoulder. "He's not here, so he's probably okay."

Sandra nodded and tried to calm her breathing, as she wiped the tears off of her face. She knew that she couldn't spend her time mourning—more and more people were going to have their families taken away from them because of Ashton and the army. This needed to end now.

The quiet was finally starting to get to Cayden, and he looked around to see nothing but Ashton standing still, with the army and Malia unmoving behind him as well. Most of the people in urban Davenport were either dead or had fled, and the first significant sound that Cayden heard was a siren.

Cayden groaned when he heard the siren, knowing that another police department coming just meant more death. But when the cars and officers came into view, Cayden was shocked into silence.

Approaching them now was not a squad of police officers, but a small group of police officers being followed by trucks holding United States Army soldiers. Their guns and weapons were bigger than anything Cayden had ever seen, and he was half expecting a tank to roll past the bridge. He smiled for the first time in days.

The U.S. Armed Forces seemed to give Sasha hope too, and she smiled as well, telling Cayden that it was her time to shine. When Cayden asked what she meant, she pointed to Malia, who was frozen behind Ashton and the army, the pendant dangling off of her neck. She ran.

"You can do it! I believe in you!" Cayden yelled, trying to be heard over the roar of the police sirens and army trucks. As more and more cars and trucks pulled up to the scene, Cayden turned to look at Ashton, expecting to see his face twist into one of terror.

But Ashton's face was unchanging. He stepped up to one of the cars, and without even giving the American soldiers inside time to react, he flipped the car over with the twist of his wrist.

Cayden gasped as the metal from another car slowly started to retract into itself. Cayden stared paralyzed as he watched Ashton tighten the car into nothing more than a compact ball of metal, by doing nothing but tightening his hand into a fist. Blood oozed out of the openings, which had once been car doors, and Cayden had to fight the urge to vomit. Ashton's face had shown no signs of disgust or regret as he crushed the car into nothing, along with the officers inside of it.

As unharmed soldiers began to exit their cars, Ashton turned his head at them, cocked it, and smiled. As they began to shoot at him, Cayden closed his eyes because he wasn't prepared to watch Ashton die. But Ashton merely picked up two of his fingers and stopped the bullets in mid-air. As his smile grew wider, the bullets changed directions and shot forward toward the soldiers, with the blink of Ashton's eyes. He had killed seven without moving his feet.

The soldiers were terrified, some fleeing to find a safer area. One policeman ran at Ashton with a Taser, but Ashton turned in his direction and simply raised his eyebrows.

"Stop," he said calmly, and the officer's eyes faded to gray as he did what he was told. Ashton tapped a finger on his chin before smiling again.

"Turn the Taser around and use it on yourself," Ashton said. He watched as the officer followed the instruction, sticking the end of the Taser into his chest and holding it there until he collapsed onto the ground.

The smell of burning flesh finally broke Cayden, as he turned toward the nearest tree to be sick. Wiping his mouth, he ran from the scene trying to get Ashton's face out of his mind. He ran behind the car that he and Sasha had originally hid behind and pressed his back up against the cool metal. He tried desperately to catch his breath. Sasha walked up in front of Malia, raised her revolver, and pointed it at Malia's head.

"I haven't seen you in a long, long time," Malia sneered, staring down the barrel of the gun.

"Shut your mouth," Sasha snapped, waving the gun in front of Malia's face. "I'm in charge now; can't you see? If you keep your trap shut and do everything I tell you to do, I'll spare your life. But if you make one wrong move, I'm going to put a bullet in your head."

"I'm not afraid of you, girl," Malia laughed, staring down at Sasha condescendingly. "I have more power around my neck than you have in your entire body. I'm ashamed that you would attempt to kill me with such a human weapon. You could've become such a skilled warrior." Malia laughed and put her hands on her hips.

"I'm an amazing warrior on my own because I've lived for years in fear of you, your husband, and your pathetic army," Sasha snarled.

"Pathetic?" Malia laughed. "The Army of Descendants is currently being led by the most powerful weapon in the universe and has almost killed the entire population of Davenport. How pathetic do you think they are?"

"Pathetic enough that if I destroyed the stupid pendant around your neck, they'd all fall down." She sang the last few words to the tune of "Ring Around the Rosy," and when the words sunk in, Malia downright growled.

Lunging for the gun pointed at her head, Malia was thwarted by Sasha, who simply brought the gun down from Malia's forehead and smacked her across the face with it. Malia, momentarily stunned, reached for the gun again, but Sasha wasn't going to take another chance. Even if Malia survived this, she wasn't going to cooperate, and Sasha knew it. With almost impeccable aim, she put a bullet in the middle of Malia's forehead.

Malia stumbled backwards, not expecting the shot, and landed on the ground, stunned. Blood trickled from the wound in the middle of her forehead, and she gazed at Sasha in amazement. Spluttering, she tried to formulate words as the bullet lodged itself into her brain. Before she could utter a peep, her heart stopped.

Sasha stared down the barrel of the gun in her hand, her face not terrified like Sandra's, but determined and angry. Without a tremor of fear, she walked over to Malia's body and stared down at it. Then, she picked up her foot from the ground and stomped down on Malia's face.

Cayden could hear Malia's nose crack from yards away. He winced and ignored the other cracking noises coming from Malia's body as he turned away. Cayden knew that Sasha was going to beat and kick Malia's corpse until it was nothing more than a bloody pulp, and although he wanted to run to stop her and calm her down, he knew that she needed closure. And apparently, the only way to get that closure would be to mutilate Malia until she was unrecognizable.

When Sasha's grunts and kicks finally stopped, Cayden turned back toward Sasha and her bloody, bare feet, as well as the bloody mess on the ground that must have been Malia. Sasha reached down to Malia's neck and yanked the bloody pendant off of her throat, cutting the side of her neck just as Malia had done to Sanrid's body. Staring down at the Ianti Pendant, Cayden knew that Sasha was contemplating how she was going to destroy it.

It seemed as if Ashton was connected to the pendant, and in a way, he was. When Malia had ripped the pendant from her husband's neck, Ashton had turned to stare, but had not made a move when Malia declared herself the owner of the crest. Now, however, with Sasha "claiming" the crest, Ashton turned to stare and narrowed his eyes. He knew that she wasn't an Ancestor, and because of that, she wasn't fit to be claiming the pendant. She had to die.

By simply holding his finger up in the air, every soldier in the Army of Descendants stopped what they were doing to stare at Ashton and wait for further instructions. When Ashton pointed in Sasha's direction, the army took their knives out of their belts and approached her slowly from every angle, closing in around her.

"Destroy it, Sasha!" Cayden screamed.

Sasha held the Ianti pendant frantically and squeezed it as hard as she could, trying to snap it in half. Ashton only seemed to be getting closer, and the army looked not one bit less menacing as they advanced toward her.

She threw the pendant on the ground, stomping on it, hard. She tried crushing it under the heel of her foot, and for the first time in her life, she regretted not wearing shoes. The Ianti pendant was unharmed, only a bit dirty, when Sasha picked it up from the ground. She was completely lost.

She looked to Cayden, who was looking around frantically trying to figure out a way to destroy the pendant or slow down Ashton and the army to keep them from reaching Sasha. Staring at Sasha, he watched as she moved her hip, trying again to crush the Ianti Pendant under her heel. Cayden saw something shimmer on Sasha's hip, and he all but screamed.

"Sasha, the dagger! Use your dagger!"

Sasha turned to Cayden, and her mouth dropped open as she understood. She pulled her knife from her belt and picked her heel up off the Ianti Pendant on the ground. She got down on her knees, brought the blade down on the Ianti Pendant, and stabbed it.

The minute that the blade hit the pendant, it was as if a car exploded. The soldiers of the army closest to Sasha at the time were torn to pieces by the blast wave that emanated from the broken pendant. It was like a spark of electricity that ripped through Davenport. Almost everyone momentarily stopped moving to watch. When the light faded from around the pendant and became a light glow, the dust and blood faded around Sasha where she was still kneeling. She was completely unharmed.

The Ianti Pendant was in four pieces; Sasha had struck it directly in the middle. For a second, Cayden was afraid that it hadn't had any effect on anyone. But suddenly, the members of the army who were still alive all fell at once.

Everyone was quiet for a few moments, and for a second, Cayden wanted to cry. Sasha was right. They had won. They had won. He and Sasha and Sandra had successfully killed Sanrid, Malia, and Ali, and now the army was gone.

Slowly, the soldiers stood up from the ground, looking around aimlessly, trying to figure out where they were. Cayden stared at the soldier closest to him, locked eyes with her, and smiled. The girl's eyes were a beautiful shade of green, bright and expressive. All signs of gray were absent, and she looked to Cayden for help.

"What's your name?" he asked her, while trying to watch Sasha out of the corner of his eye.

"I think it's Olivia," she said uncertainly.

"Okay, Olivia," Cayden said. "I'm Cayden. You've been a bit, um, distracted recently, but that's all over now." From a few feet away, Cayden could see his mother waving him over, trying to get his attention. She was surrounded by a group of confused looking former soldiers. Cayden acknowledged her, and Sandra smiled.

"Do you see that woman over there?" Cayden asked Olivia, pointing in his mother's direction. When the girl nodded, Cayden gave her a little push and said, "She's going to take you somewhere safe. I want you to follow her to wherever she takes you, okay?"

Olivia smiled and nodded slowly, thanking Cayden and making her way over toward Sandra. Following Olivia, but keeping his eyes on Sasha, Cayden made his way over to his mother.

"What are you doing with all of them?" Cayden asked.

"I think I'm going to take them down to the river," she said. "They don't know who they are, but they're not stupid. I think they're going to be okay. I'm going to let them go their separate ways or travel in groups if they feel safer like that. They don't need to know that any of this happened. They can live normal lives."

Cayden wasn't sure if any soldier in the army would ever be able to live a "normal" life, but he nodded to his mother and watched as she rounded up more soldiers and told them to follow her. The soldiers were confused, and the younger ones looked scared, but Sandra's voice was calming. They followed her because they didn't know if there was anywhere else that they could go. The Citee was the only thing that they had ever known.

Staring toward Sasha and Ashton, Cayden walked to them. Ashton hadn't fallen with the rest of the army after the pendant had been destroyed, and that couldn't be a good thing.

Cayden rushed behind another car and stared at Ashton from Sasha's point of view. He saw that his face was still expressionless, and his eyes were still gray.

"Ashton, you should be free of this," Sasha said sadly.

Ashton didn't answer. He only stared Sasha down. He looked around again, as if he were trying to find the army. When he saw no one other than the bodies of the dead soldiers, he looked as confused as an expressionless person could look.

"Where is my army?" he said in a monotone voice.

"The army is gone. They're safe now," Sasha explained. "They're free, and you should be too. I don't know why you're not—"

But Sasha didn't get to finish her sentence. Before Sasha could even open her mouth again, Ashton had flicked his index and middle fingers to his right, snapping Sasha's neck.

18

Davenport was deserted when Sandra returned from the river. Most of the townspeople were dead, and the rest were long gone. Sandra wiped her hands on her tattered pants and looked around for any sign of Ashton or her son.

She spotted Cayden, bloodied and battered, sitting next to a burned bush with his head in his hands. It wasn't a very inconspicuous hiding place, but there were no signs of Ashton or any leftover soldiers. Cayden was as safe as he could possibly be, and that was all Sandra cared about.

Sandra walked over to him and tried to make her presence known, so she didn't startle him. Cayden turned his head slowly and jumped slightly as he saw Sandra. But his face slowly turned from terror to relief when he realized who she was.

"Hey," she said soothingly. She sat down next to him and ran a hand through his blood-caked hair. Cayden looked up at her, and suddenly Sandra didn't see an 18-year-old war-torn man, but a six-year old boy who fell off his bike. The right side of his face had a cut running from his temple to his cheek, and one of his eyes was black. He had his knees pulled close to his chest and his head in his hands, and if Sandra didn't know differently, she would have thought he was crying.

He looked up again and sighed. "Noah is okay," he said quietly.

Sandra's head snapped up, and she looked at him with panic in her eyes. "Where is he?"

Cayden sighed again and looked at his mother sadly. "A couple was evacuating and running from town during Ashton's l-last wave of killing. They h-had a daughter and saw how bad I looked, a-and they said they'd keep him safe. He's getting closer and closer to home."

Sandra's worries were lessened, as relief washed over her. "Did you get their names?"

Cayden sighed sadly again. "No, but I remember what they looked like. H-he's safe with them. That's all that matters."

Sandra nodded in agreement. That was all that mattered now, and she knew it's what Mason and Alex would have wanted. She took a seat next to Cayden on the grass and looked into his watery eyes.

"Illinois," Cayden whispered, his tears threatening to spill out.

"What about Illinois?" Sandra soothed, rubbing his back.

"Ashton is moving," he said in a braver voice, trying to wipe his eyes and stand up. Sandra held his arm down to prevent him from standing.

"What do you mean he's moving?"

Cayden stared at her, hard. "Do you really think the Ancestors are going to stop with Davenport? With Iowa? Sanrid said that he wanted world domination, and that's what he's going to get, whether he's alive to see it or not. Ashton is heading toward Illinois now, and after he takes control of it, he's going to take Indiana and Ohio. While Ashton is under the Ancestor's control, he isn't going to stop at the United States either." Cayden took in a harsh breath and shakily exhaled. "He's unstoppable Mom, he's just—too powerful." With the last sentence, the tears finally spilled out of Cayden's eyes, and he quickly put his fingers under his eyelids to try and stop the flow of water.

"Sasha's dead," he choked out, pointing out in front of him as he sobbed. Sandra turned around to look in the direction her son was pointing. Sasha's body was lying on the ground, her head turned at almost a 180-degree angle.

"What happened?" she asked, quietly.

"After you went to take the surviving soldiers back to the river, we realized that the destruction of the pendant didn't break Ashton out of Sanrid's control. His eyes were still gray, and he still had no emotions. Ashton realized that the army was gone and that he no longer had anyone to fight for him, and he realized that it was Sasha's fault. He snapped her neck the minute she tried to talk to him."

Sandra bit her bottom lip, as she continued rubbing Cayden's back to try to calm him down and quiet his cries. Sasha's body was laying a few feet from where they were sitting, and it made her sick to even look at it. The girl had given so much to try to protect Davenport and to get revenge on the people who had destroyed her life. And now she was nothing more than another body among the thousands of people lying dead across Davenport's landscape. Noah would be safe for a short while, but Mason and Alex were gone, and Sandra had a sinking feeling in her stomach that she and her eldest son would be next.

She watched as Ashton continued to walk toward the edge of town. Even without a large intimidating army following behind him, people were still terrified. Word had spread quickly that Ashton had taken down numerous police departments and even the Unites States Army, and almost everyone had fled from Davenport. There was no one left to stop Ashton from crossing over the bridge into Illinois and start his next wave of killing in another state—except Cayden.

Cayden stood up and ran toward Ashton, his mother following behind. When Ashton saw Cayden and Sandra, he almost looked surprised. He had been sure that Davenport was completely deserted.

Cayden kept walking toward Ashton, stopping the boy in his tracks. Sandra stayed to Cayden's right, but made the mistake of keeping her knife in her hand. Ashton saw it as a threat and commanded her to shove the knife into her leg.

Cayden screamed, but Sandra's eyes faded to gray anyway, and she stabbed herself in the calf. She didn't pull the bloody knife out until her eyes regained their color. Groaning in pain, she fell over against the nearest tree, dizzy from the amount of blood pouring out of her leg. "Ashton you need to stop," Cayden cried. "Please stop."

Sandra watched, terrified. Blood was draining quickly out of her calf and onto the grass, blurring her sight. She quickly ripped the bottom hem of her shirt off, along with a strip of the fabric, tied the cloth tightly around her wound, and applied pressure to stop the bleeding. Cayden wouldn't stop walking toward Ashton, and she was prepared to look away in fear. But Ashton had not said a word. He hadn't even advanced toward Cayden one step. He was frozen in place.

Cayden moved slower and more hesitantly as he got closer and closer to Ashton, but Ashton still did not move a muscle. Finally, when Cayden was almost directly in front of Ashton, Ashton locked eyes with Cayden and then grinned, in the same way that Grandfather had grinned at them when they had first entered the mansion.

The grin was twisted and almost pained, and Cayden wanted to be sick again. Ashton didn't look like himself. There was blood splattered up his neck, and his jacket was torn in more than one place. His face was covered in dirt, and he had what Cayden believed to be a fingernail lodged in his hair. Grandfather's smile was painted on his lips, which made Ashton look even more foreign. The entire Army of Descendants was either dead or had changed back to their normal selves, but Cayden was right: that wasn't going to stop Ashton. Ashton himself was more powerful than the pendant, and the destruction of it wasn't going to stop him.

When Cayden finally stopped in front of Ashton, he balled his hands up into fists, assuming that Ashton was going to try and kill him to make sure nothing was in his way. But Ashton did nothing. He just stared at Cayden and waited for him to make a move.

Cayden wracked his brain, trying to figure out something—anything—that he could say to get Ashton to talk to him or to remember who he was. If breaking the pendant wasn't going to free him from Sanrid's hold, then Cayden was going to.

He thought hard about the records that Sasha had pulled from Sanrid's study and that he had read while hiding behind the house in suburban Davenport—the records about Isabella and Ashton and the things that Sanrid wanted to teach Ashton before he was drained—tougher mind manipulation, telekinesis, and *mind reading*.

"Who am I?" Cayden asked, his voice wavering.

Ashton looked him over once and then spaced out, staring straight ahead at an abandoned car. He looked as if he were wracking his brain for information that he couldn't find. Finally, after a minute or two, he locked eyes with Cayden again.

"Cayden Mitchell," Ashton said. His voice was robotic.

Cayden let out a sigh of relief and waited for Ashton to continue.

"Sex . . . male. Age . . . 18. Status . . . living."

Cayden breathed hesitantly but did not take one step closer or farther away from Ashton. Ashton knew who he was at least—that was a plus.

"You got any familial records in that big file cabinet brain of yours?" Cayden asked. He intended a teasing tone, but it came out forced and pained more than anything. Ashton spaced out again for a second before short-circuiting back.

"Cayden Mitchell," he said, again. "Son of Mason and Sandra Mitchell—brother of Alexandra Mitchell and Noah Mitchell."

Cayden swallowed nervously. "And who's my best friend."

Ashton locked eyes with Cayden and blinked once.

"Ashton Dweller."

Cayden smiled. "Exactly! Ashton Dweller is my best friend."

Ashton stared at Cayden in confusion for a second before pushing him onto the ground and beginning to walk in the direction of the river again. Cayden landed on the ground hard, groaning as his left arm snapped under his own weight. He stood up again, however, and ran to Ashton again, putting himself in front of Ashton and the road to the bridge.

"Who are you?" he asked Ashton.

Ashton spaced out a bit longer than usual trying to find the answer to this one, his right eye twitching slightly every few seconds. But before long, he was locking eyes with Cayden again and answering. "I am nothing."

"No, you're someone," Cayden said, his voice breaking. "Look Ashton Dweller up in your records! Tell me who he is."

"Ashton Dweller," Ashton said, as his hand twitched. "Son of Nathan and Madeline Dweller—brother of Lucas Dweller, Thomas Dweller, Elizabeth Dweller, Chase Dweller, and Alana Dweller. Sex . . . male. Age . . . 18. Status . . . deceased."

"Ashton Dweller isn't dead!" Cayden yelled in Ashton's face. "You're Ashton Dweller!"

"I am nothing."

Another push and Cayden was on the ground again. He was so close. If Ashton could just remember who he used to be, he could break himself out of Sanrid's hold. Sanrid was dead, and the Ianti Pendant was in pieces. The only reason Ashton was still brainwashed was because his powers were overpowering the destruction of the pendant, leaving his eyes gray and his head still on the mission.

Cayden stood up again and refused to let Ashton keep him down for a second time. If anyone was going to break Ashton from this state, it was Cayden. Still clutching his broken arm, he ran and tried to catch up with Ashton, who was again killing anyone who came too close to him. He was heading toward the bridge to cross the river into Illinois, and Cayden knew that if he didn't stop him now, he was going to destroy Rock Island or Moline and eventually all of Illinois.

"Ashton, please stop—this needs to end now," Cayden cried, jumping in front of him again and blocking his path to the bridge.

Ashton's hand twitched again along with his right eye, and for a second, Cayden thought that he was going to get pushed down onto the ground again. But Ashton halted when Cayden stood in front of him. Ashton just stared.

When Cayden did not move out of his way again, Ashton growled. He was more determined this time. He was obviously getting fed up with people being in his way. His still dull face held a hint of annoyance, as he stared over Cayden's shoulder at the short road that led to the bridge to Illinois.

"Ashton, you have to listen to me," Cayden pleaded. "You're not dead. You're not just a person that doesn't count because Sanrid has you in his stupid database as a dead man. Ashton Dweller is not dead! You are Ashton Dweller."

It suddenly occurred to Cayden how easy it would be for Ashton to just tell him in his most commanding voice to "move out of the way." Cayden's eyes would fade to gray, he would leave Ashton alone, and he wouldn't be able to break out of Ashton's control until he had successfully crossed the bridge. Apparently, Ashton had other plans.

"Take the gun out of the pocket of your belt," Ashton said with no hesitation.

Cayden reached to the left of his belt and pulled out Sasha's revolver. He held it out in front of him. Sandra wanted to run from where she was, but her leg was still bleeding profusely. She knew that if she tried to walk, she wouldn't be able to get to her son without losing consciousness. So she sat by the tree and waited for the inevitable, tears rolling down her cheeks.

"Put the barrel of the gun to your temple," Ashton said, tilting his head.

Cayden did as he was told slowly. His gray eyes were unreadable, and all previous fear was gone from his features. Ashton stared at Cayden still, and Sandra could see now that the tilt of Ashton's head was not just an indication of where he wanted Cayden to put the gun, but a gesture of curiosity.

Cayden's hand was shaking as he held the barrel to his temple, and although his eyes were gray, they were blinking and starting to show signs of genuine feelings, which was not something that should've been happening now that he was under Ashton's control.

"Ashton, don't do this," Cayden cried behind clenched teeth.

Ashton looked confused now—actually confused. His face wasn't completely expressionless anymore, and confusion was etched into his eyes and mouth. Cayden should not be able to speak under Ashton's control. He shouldn't be able to do anything under Ashton's control that wasn't something Ashton told him to do. Ashton's head was starting to hurt, and for some reason, he felt as if he shouldn't be doing this—*this person was someone who was not supposed to be under his control—ever.*

"Stop talking," Ashton said, trying to get Cayden's words out of his head. But the command did not work either. Soon, Cayden was pleading again.

"Ash, please don't," Cayden groaned, as if speaking was physically hurting him. His nose was bleeding, even though Ashton had not hit him. Ashton was becoming more and more confused by the second.

Ashton twitched, and Cayden had a moment of déjà vu. He remembered Aidan and how worried Carlton and Ashton had been about him and his twitching problem. Ashton was twitching in the same way now. His head was snapping to the right, and he was violently blinking one of his eyes.

"Ashton, don't."

Ashton's head was burning. The name *Ashton* felt familiar in his ears, but he wasn't anyone. He didn't count in the database in his head because he wasn't anyone or anything. He was a machine—a tool. He didn't have emotions or feelings or memories or an identity. This boy with the shaking gun held to his head should not have meant anything to him, and he should have killed him ages ago—he and his mother and the other girl were nothing more than other casualties in this war. He was a machine, and that was his job. Kill.

"Pull the trigger."

***

Sandra's scream ripped through the tree that she was leaning against, causing the birds that were left to flee, just as the people had from Davenport. She was crying again and trying to breathe. But she was not able to, as she stared at her son on the ground, the revolver dangling limply in his hand.

Ashton reached up to his face and wiped a tear off of his cheek. He stared at his fingers when he brought them away from his face. He was crying, which was something he shouldn't have been able to do. He wasn't sad. He didn't have any emotions. He needed to compose himself, kill the boy's mother, and cross the bridge. His job wasn't done yet. He stared down at the corpse in front of him, trying to read through the boy's unmoving brain cells.

"Cayden Mitchell," he identified once again. "Sex . . . male. Age . . . 18. Status . . . deceased."

19

Ashton turned toward the woman lying against the tree. She got up quickly, ignoring the blood pouring from her leg, and hobbled toward her son's body. She cradled her son in her arms, crying, as the light fabric wrapped around her wound did nothing to stop the bleeding. He almost pitied her—almost. But pity was an emotion, and he didn't feel emotions.

He considered killing her for a second but then decided that it would be even better to let her suffer—to let her hold her dead son's body while she was bleeding out from her calf. That's what Sanrid would have wanted.

The bridge was so close that he could taste it, and he stared toward the Iowa border. He was ready for the next phase of domination and conquering. However, before he could reach the bridge and cross it, he needed to make sure there were no civilians left besides the bleeding woman. He looked down a street called Woodland Drive and found it deserted. However, before he could look down the adjacent street, two houses caught his eye.

The monstrous black house still towered over the small lightly painted one, just as it always had. A dilapidated tree house could be seen from where Ashton was standing. It was falling apart, and the branches of the tree were growing into the windows and the openings in the wood.

Ashton saw a young boy sitting on the curb in front of the black house and stopped to stare at him. He was sitting peacefully, as if war hadn't raged on around him. He had a sad look in his eyes, however, and the boy's head was in his hands with a blink of Ashton's eyes. Another boy came over and sat next to him, punching the sad boy's shoulders and trying to get him to laugh.

Ashton blinked again, and the boys were gone, but with another blink, they were back. Upon closer inspection, Ashton could see the sad boy's face.

"That's me . . . no that's not . . . I am me . . . who is me," Ashton said in a monotone voice, stumbling over his words and pointing toward the curb. Sandra looked over at Ashton, and tears were still running down her cheeks as she followed his gaze. With a defeated sigh, Sandra realized that Ashton was short-circuiting and seeing things that weren't really there. She supposed it could be an effect of the destruction of the Ianti Pendant. However, it was hard for her to think about much of anything—as her son lay dead in her arms.

Ashton had stopped moving. He was staring at his house, with confusion in his eyes. It was the only emotion that Sandra had seen out of him since he had been drained, and Ashton looked uncomfortable with the emotions crossing his face. He was completely and utterly lost.

Rapidly blinking his eyes, Ashton could see the boys on the curb disappearing and reappearing faster than he could comprehend. He shut his eyes tightly and took a deep breath before opening his eyes again. The boys were present when he opened his eyes, but they were no longer sitting on the curb in front of the black house. Now they were in the sad little tree house, huddled up close together as if it were cold. The sad boy didn't look very sad anymore, but was laughing now at something the other boy was saying.

Ashton's head was on fire. The two boys looked so familiar to Ashton, but as hard as he thought, he couldn't figure out who they were. The pounding in his head only got worse as he repeatedly closed and opened his eyes. He was trying to get the boys to just *go away*. A tiny voice in his head kept yelling the name *Ashton*, but he didn't know who Ashton was, and he was pretty sure he didn't want to know.

His gray eyes closed, and he heard more laughter. Ashton covered his ears with his hands as though the laughter was a high-pitched whine. When the laughter stopped and his gray eyes opened once again, all they saw in front of them was white.

The snow didn't look real, and Ashton knew that it wasn't. It covered the cars parked in front of the two houses and came down from the sky in clumps. As Ashton prepared to close his eyes again, the door to the black house opened wide, and a blond boy ran out the door. He was barefoot and still dressed in his pajamas. From the doorway, two 20-something blond men called out to the boy to come back inside.

The young men looked familiar, and their names were on the tip of Ashton's tongue. But he couldn't remember them for the life of him. The barefoot boy running through the snow turned to stare out at the snow-covered yard, and Ashton realized that it was the same sad boy who had been sitting on the curb previously, though now he was a bit older.

The boy raised a trembling fist to his next-door neighbor's door and knocked. He was shaking from the cold as he stood on the front steps of the small, lightly painted house. Then the other boy from the curb opened the door and pulled the blond boy inside.

Ashton turned away, put his hands on his knees, and doubled over. As opposed to the fire that had just been in his head, now Ashton was drowning. His vision was spotty, and his thoughts were clouded. He was surrounded only by the faces of the two boys from the tree house.

When Ashton finally looked back at the houses, they had disappeared, and he was even more lost than he had been a few minutes ago. Now he was staring at the inside of a doctor's office. The blond boy from the snowstorm was his younger counterpart again—the boy he had been while he was sitting on the curb. He sat quietly on a comfortable-looking chair, and two adults sat in the two chairs on each side of him. They appeared to be his parents. When the doctor sitting across from them opened his mouth, Ashton could hear words being spoken for the first time.

"Ashton's mutism is selective," the doctor said, shaking his head.

"It can't be," the father replied. "He hasn't said a word to me or my wife in years. And it's the same for all of our other children. They can't get a syllable out of him."

"He talks to Cayden."

The boy's father balked at the doctor and then turned to look down at the center chair where his son was sitting. Sighing, he asked the doctor if they could bring Cayden back into the room.

The other boy from the curb walked in the door then, and the blond boy—Ashton—moved over on the large center chair to make room for Cayden, who plopped down next to him.

"You told me that Ashton talks to you—is that correct, Cayden?" the doctor asked.

The small dark-haired boy nodded enthusiastically. "He doesn't talk a lot, but that's okay. He's really, really smart and usually only talks when he's trying to help explain a math problem when we have homework that I don't get. He talks about other things sometimes too though—like colors and nature and rocks and weird stuff. But I like him." Cayden smiled a big toothless grin, and the doctor smiled back.

"Is that true, Ash?" the doctor asked. "Do you talk to Cayden?"

Ashton nodded and smiled, and with that, the doctor told the two young boys that they could leave the office while the grown-ups talked. Ashton and Cayden left to join Cayden's parents outside the room. Once the door was closed, the doctor threaded his hands together on his desk.

"Cayden is what you'd call a security blanket," the doctor explained to Ashton's parents. "It's very common among selectively mute children, although their security blanket is more commonly one of their siblings rather than a friend because they feel like they can trust them more. However, if Cayden is the only one that Ashton is comfortable to talk around, Cayden is his security blanket."

Ashton's parents nodded their heads. "But what do we do now?" Ashton's mother asked.

"I want you to keep him on the medication he's on now to reduce his anxiety levels," the doctor said, pulling his pad of prescriptions out of his desk. "But I'd like you to ask Cayden as well as Cayden's parents if it would be okay if Cayden joined Ashton in some of his pathology sessions. If Cayden is enough of a security blanket for Ashton that he feels comfortable speaking, maybe Ashton would speak to me. Maybe he would tell me about how he feels if Cayden is in the room with him. Or if not, he could simply tell Cayden how he's feeling, and Cayden could tell me. It's obviously up to him; he's just a child, but it could help me with Ashton's diagnosis and treatment."

The "real" Ashton blinked, and the doctor's office was gone, replaced now with what seemed like the inside of an airport. A mass of people swarmed near the gate of a flight to California, and Ashton blinked a few times again. When he opened his eyes, the people were crying, and the image that he saw seemed to be a zoomed-in version of what he had been seeing before. He could see the faces of the people crying, and he recognized the sad boy from the curb again and the mute one whose name was *Ashton*. The dark-haired one from the doctor's office—Cayden—sat next to Ashton on one of the pale blue chairs in front of the gate, and his head was in his hands.

The two boys were talking about something, and then they

were hugging. More of the people surrounding them were crying, and soon the Ashton boy was holding a little girl's hand and walking her toward the entrance to the plane.

Blinking again, Ashton did not see an airport, but the inside of the black house. The boy who had once been a small blond thing sitting on the side of the road was now a tall black-haired teenager with a cigarette hanging out of the side of his mouth. He was admiring old pictures on the desk of his bedroom. The boy picked up one of the pictures, and with a blink of Ashton's eyes, he could see the picture up close. It was a picture of the boys sitting on swings in the backyard of a house, with their arms wrapped around each other's shoulders. The black-haired boy in the apparition put out his cigarette, and Ashton's vision went black.

Ashton pointed again at the houses, although he could not see in front of him. "Me," he said firmly. "Ashton is me."

From feet away, Sandra turned to him and stared. To her, Ashton looked as if he were having an episode. The short-circuiting she had believed to be happening was actually happening. Ashton's shoulders were twitching as he blinked rapidly and looked around himself fearfully, as if serial killers were approaching him from every angle.

He seemed to be terrified of the realization that he was Ashton, and the twitching got violent to the point that he fell onto the ground. He was still staring at the two houses as he shook and curled up into a ball. Closing his eyes, the ringing in his ears escalated in pitch again until his eardrums felt as if they were going to burst. The high-pitch whining was accompanied by flashing images in his vision of the past—his past—*Ashton's* past.

He squeezed his eyes shut and screamed.

***

The police sirens were loud in Ashton's ears, and he was suddenly completely aware of his surroundings. His head was pounding as he looked around at the bodies scattered around him. Sandra was staring at him, frozen with fear, waiting for him to make his next move.

Ashton's vision was blurry to an extent, but when it cleared, the only thing he could see in front of him was Cayden's body. There was blood pouring from a hole in his head, and the gun he had used to inflict the wound was still hanging limply in his hand. Ashton stood up on shaking legs, only to collapse again after he got a step closer to Cayden's body. Then Ashton started crawling.

The police officers from Illinois had begun to get out of their cars when Ashton had finally reached Cayden's body.

"What have I done?" Ashton whispered, touching his fingers lightly to the bleeding hole in Cayden's temple. Cayden's eyes were open, which somehow made everything worse. His eyes were dark and expressionless, and Ashton's hands were shaking as he placed a palm on Cayden's cold cheek. Ashton tried to shake the boy awake.

"No, no, no," he repeated until his throat was tight with tears. He pulled Cayden's corpse into his lap, squeezing him tightly. He tried to will him to wake up.

"Cayden, please," Ashton cried, shaking him.

Sandra was dumbstruck. She had no idea what had happened other than that Ashton was no longer a mindless killing machine. She tried to calm herself down and listen to his voice. The tears coming out of his eyes were real, and the pain in his voice was real. Suddenly, Ashton and Cayden were 14 again. Ashton's sobs were because he had lost his parents, and Cayden was only silent because he didn't know what he was supposed to say. For a fraction of a second, Sandra felt as if she was in Ashton's place, right after she was told that Madeline was dead. She knew what it was like to lose a best friend.

She tried to crawl closer to Cayden's body, but Ashton's head whipped around so quickly that she fell backwards in fear. There were tears running down Ashton's face, and as they locked eyes, Sandra could tell that Ashton's eyes were blue. All signs of gray were gone, and Sandra was momentarily shocked into complete silence.

"Sandra," Ashton said, choking as he clung to Cayden's body and gestured for Sandra to come closer.

"Ashton, what happened?"

"I just remembered," Ashton cried, shaking. "I remembered everything."

The police officers approached Ashton and Sandra. She tried to hold them back.

"It's not his fault!" she fought. "He's innocent!"

The officers tried to grab at his arms, but Ashton shook them off. He tightened his fists in Cayden's shirt, trying to pull him closer.

"It wasn't me!" he screamed. The officers' touched him, and it burned like fire. "It was them; it was them!" He tried to point in the direction of Sanrid and Malia's bodies, but that would mean letting go of Cayden.

Finally, an officer grabbed him by the waist and physically ripped Ashton away from Cayden's corpse. When Ashton looked down at his hands, they were covered in Cayden's blood. His head was on fire, and he couldn't stop crying. If he was going to save Cayden, Ashton knew he needed to get the officer to let go of him. As far as Ashton knew, Cayden could still be saved.

"Let go of me," Ashton shouted. He tried to make his voice as commanding as possible. He waited for the officers' eyes to fade to gray, but nothing happened. "Let go!"

He screamed and kicked and commanded, both verbally and telepathically, but nothing worked. One of the officers freed his

Taser from his belt. Ashton's eyes widened as he tried to work up all the power he could muster. He stared down the Taser, trying to will it to change course and send its shock waves through the officer who wielded it.

"Cayden!" he screamed, but one of the officers dug his fingernails into Ashton's arm so hard that he drew blood, and his scream was cut off by a yelp of pain. His powers weren't working, and he wasn't strong enough to force the officers off of him.

"Sandra!" he yelled in her direction. "You've got to tell them it wasn't me! It wasn't me, I swear! The Ancestors!"

Ashton was frantic, kicking harder now and trying anything he could to get the officers to free him, but it was no use. Even more officers were circling him now, grabbing every limb or article of clothing that they could reach.

Sandra tried to reach for Ashton as well, but officers were surrounding her too. They directed the paramedics to hover over her. The closest doctor ripped the fabric off of the wound on Sandra's leg and called for the officers to bring an ambulance over, so they could get Sandra on a gurney. Once she was loaded into the ambulance, she called for Ashton again as one of the doctor's stuck an IV into her arm.

"You're going to be okay," the doctor said soothingly as he ran a hand through her hair. "He's not going to be able to hurt you anymore."

"He didn't hurt me," Sandra tried to say, but all that came out were a few splutters. They had put her to sleep.

Ashton was still fighting the officers, trying to command them to let go of him and reaching for Cayden again. The officers finally got him into one of the police cars, held him against the car, handcuffed him, and then shoved him into the back seat.

"You have to listen to me," Ashton cried to the officers driving the car. "It wasn't me. I didn't do this. You have to believe me!"

One of the officers turned around and punched Ashton square in the nose, knocking him out. When Ashton woke up, he was in an Illinois police station holding cell. He could hear the officers outside the cell talking about his crimes and how the hell he could've possibly done it.

"He's only 18," one of the officers said. "He's just a kid. He's barely strong enough to hurt someone with a punch. How did he murder an entire city?"

"I didn't," Ashton coughed. He felt like he was swallowing razor blades every time he swallowed, and coughing was agonizing. "I didn't do this."

One of the officers spit on him, and the one who had punched him in the backseat of the car punched him again. He didn't wake up again until he was being dragged to federal prison.

***

Sandra woke up in a hospital bed.

A doctor's white lab coat was turned away from her. As he looked at the records of her blood samples, he made a disapproving sound. When he turned around, he had Sanrid's face.

Sandra shrieked and held up her hands in self-defense. When the doctor got close enough to touch her, she punched him across the face. Nurses and doctors from other units in the hospital had to be called in to hold her down from the episode. After the doctor's nose stopped bleeding, he requested that she be moved into a psychiatric unit.

***

Ashton's court case was a joke. He was sentenced to life without parole and shoved into a cell similar to the one he had spent weeks in when he was in the mansion. People avoided him like the plague and rarely even met his eyes. He was the "crazy" one who had murdered so many people that they had lost count.

He screamed names such as "Cayden" and "Sanrid" in his sleep, and people would scream back at him and tell him to shut up, so he stopped sleeping entirely. He was the youngest prisoner in the federal penitentiary, and he avoided everyone's eyes—just as they avoided his.

One night, he stole a camera with the help of a friend and recorded a video about his life. He told his story word for word, as much as he could remember. Some names sounded foreign even on his own tongue, but when he finished recording, he turned the camera off and left it on his bed.

He just wanted someone to know the truth.

He just wanted someone to know his story.

Epilogue

Name: Ashton Dweller
Sex: Male
Age: 22
Convicted for: Mass Murder
Status: Deceased

This is what Simon Hall will read as he walks out of his cell on September the 16th. Terror will pile up in his gut, momentarily, before he brushes it off—because there is no screaming or crying, just the silent moving of a body to the grounds in the back of the penitentiary.

Ashton Dweller will not be buried, but burned for the sins he has committed in the eyes of the town and the eyes of the people. The only person willing to vouch for him is Sandra Mitchell, long since gone bat-shit crazy. The people ignore every word she spews from her mouth.

Ashton Dweller's flesh and bones will be burned to ashes and sprinkled as far away from the town as humanly possible. They don't want any memory of him to live on. They do not want any recollection that he was ever even a citizen of Davenport—not after what he had done.

Years will pass, and Sandra Mitchell will die, alone, locked up in an institution with a new name—locked up with people just like her who claimed to be there, fighting the monsters. The monsters looked like people, blond-haired and blue-eyed people, who never ceased—never stopped clawing and ripping their way through thousands of lives, trying to reclaim land that had belonged to them centuries ago.

Years will pass, and Simon Hall, who was thrown into a penitentiary at the age of 16 for drug possession in the first degree, will be released from prison at the age of 30. He will get off on good behavior, which would seem ironic to anyone that had known him during his time at the penitentiary. The only thing was that he hadn't started a fight since Ashton Dweller had died.

Simon Hall will grow old, the oldest man in the town. At 97 years old, he will be sitting on a bench telling stories to wide-eyed children—stories of friends and unlikely friendships made through stealing and mutual agreements. He will assure the children and their parents that he doesn't condone stealing, but he will make sure that the kids know one thing: if a nutty guy with huge blue eyes asks you to steal a camera in exchange for a few packs of cigs, don't turn him down.

On Simon Hall's dying day, he will swear that Ashton Dweller did not commit suicide, but was murdered inside of his cell, his locked cell, on the night of September 15th, which was later discovered to be his birthday. The authorities had planned to put Simon in a mental institution—the same one that Sandra Mitchell had died in years previously. He died before they were able to.

Simon Hall will die at the age of 101.

Years and years will pass, and no one will mention Ashton Dweller.

The other Dweller children, and their children's children, the children of Chase and Beth and Lucas—they will grow. They will grow and have their own children, and never speak of their little ancestor and everything that happened because of him. Soon, it will be impossible to trace any of the Mitchell children or any of the Dweller children back to Cayden or Ashton and the story that took their lives.

Soon, the children that sat around Simon Hall—the old man of the town telling stories of trees that sent you to unimaginable dimensions and monsters that looked like people—would tell their children of it. And the stories would carry on because the kids that sat around Simon grew up and had children, and their children had children. They grew up as well, and the cycle continued, and Davenport stayed the same.

But it never would be the same because what Ashton did left a permanent reminder. The story was always just a story, and Ashton Dweller was a good kid from Davenport who went off the deep end and murdered a quarter of the town he grew up in, including his best friend.

Soon, Ashton Dweller's real story became just a story, a fairy tale or prophecy, just like it had been in The Citee before Cayden had told Sasha about her real half brother.

Ashton Dweller's story was never resolved because he never came back from the dead, as the townspeople expected him to. They spoke about the folktale that "The Mythical Ancestors" were buried under the old tree and would rise again to start another revolution. It never happened, of course, the story being *just a fairy tale*—something similar to Nessie or Bigfoot. If you really believed, you were naïve.

But nevertheless, the story still spread, and maybe people didn't want to forget. The people in the town would rather talk and spread the mythical story of Ashton Dweller and The Ancestors than face up to what they believed really happened: a boy went mad and destroyed a town.

Their descendants never would know the truth about their ancestors, which is how our story first started. They will believe what is told to them. They will believe what is *fiction* and what is *reality*, even though, in the real world, all they would have to do is switch the two around.

And this is why, when people pass by the old tree standing

The Dwellers

proud in all its glory on the side of Tanglewood—and maybe when they see the rocks glisten, just a little—they'll pass it off as the sunlight and just walk on by.